The First Leonaur Book
of Supernatural Detectives

The First Leonaur Book of Supernatural Detectives

Investigations of Ghosts and Strange Occurrences Including 'The Pot of Tulips', 'The Ghost Detective', 'The Gateway of the Monster', 'The Spectre in the Cart,' 'The House Surgeon', 'Green Tea' and Ten Other Short Stories

Morgan Tyler

LEONAUR

The First Leonaur Book of Supernatural Detectives
Investigations of Ghosts and Strange Occurrences Including 'The Pot of Tulips', 'The Ghost Detective', 'The Gateway of the Monster', 'The Spectre in the Cart,' 'The House Surgeon', 'Green Tea' and Ten Other Short Stories
By Morgan Tyler

FIRST EDITION

Leonaur is an imprint
of Oakpast Ltd

ISBN: 978-1-78282-439-8 (hardcover)
ISBN: 978-1-78282-440-4 (softcover)

http://www.leonaur.com

Publisher's Notes

Contents

The Pot of Tulips
Fitz-James O'Brien   7

Aylmer Vance and the Vampire
Alice and Claude Askew   23

Carnacki, the Ghost Finder: The Gateway of the Monster
William Hope Hodgson   41

Flaxman Low: The Story of Baelbrow
E. & H. Heron   59

The Levitant
Enoch F. Gerrish   71

The Ghost Detective
Mark Lemon   80

Selecting a Ghost
Sir Arthur Conan Doyle   83

Green Tea
Sheridan Le Fanu   99

The Wood Devil Thing
Gordon McCreagh   129

Carnacki, the Ghost Finder: The House Among the Laurels
William Hope Hodgson   147

Flaxman Low: The Story of Konnor Old House
E. & H. Heron   164

The Robbery on the "Stormy Petrel"
Richard Marsh   177

The House Surgeon
Rudyard Kipling   187

The Open Door
Mrs Riddell   209

The Spectre in the Cart
Thomas Nelson Page   238

The Deserted House
E. T. A. Hoffman   255

The Pot of Tulips

Fitz-James O'Brien

Twenty-Eight years ago I went to spend the summer at an old Dutch villa which then lifted its head from the wild country that, in present days, has been tamed down into a site for a Crystal Palace. Madison Square was then a wilderness of fields and scrub oak, here and there diversified with some tall and stately elm. Worthy citizens who could afford two establishments rusticated in the groves that then flourished where ranks of brown-stone porticoes now form the landscape; and the locality of Fortieth Street, where my summer palace stood, was justly looked upon as at an enterprising distance from the city.

I had an imperious desire to live in this house ever since I can remember. I had often seen it when a boy, and its cool verandas and quaint garden seemed, whenever I passed, to attract me irresistibly. In after years, when I grew up to man's estate, I was not sorry, therefore, when one summer, fatigued with the labours of my business, I beheld a notice in the papers intimating that it was to be let furnished. I hastened to my dear friend, Jasper Joye, painted the delights of this rural retreat in the most glowing colours, easily obtained his assent to share the enjoyments and the expense with me, and in a month afterward we were taking our ease in this new paradise.

Independent of early associations other interests attached me to this house. It was somewhat historical, and had given shelter to George Washington on the occasion of one of his visits to the city. Furthermore, I knew the descendants of the family to whom it had originally belonged. Their history was strange and mournful, and it seemed to me as if their individuality was somehow shared by the edifice. It had been built by a Mr. Van Koeren, a gentleman of Holland, the younger son of a rich mercantile firm in the Hague, who had emigrated to this country in order to establish a branch of his father's business in New York, which even then gave indications of the prosperity it has since reached with such marvellous rapidity. He had brought with him a fair young Belgian wife; a loving girl—if I may believe her portrait—with soft brown eyes, chestnut hair, and a deep, placid contentment spreading over her fresh and innocent features.

Her son, Alain Van Koeren, had her picture—an old miniature in a red gold frame—as well as that of his father; and in truth, when looking on the two, one could not conceive a greater contrast than must have existed between husband and wife. Mr. Van Koeren must have been a man of terrible will and gloomy temperament. His face—in the picture—is dark and austere, his eyes deep-sunken, and burning as if with a slow, inward fire. The lips are thin and compressed, with much determination of purpose; and his chin, boldly salient, is brimful of power and resolution. When first I saw those two pictures I sighed inwardly, and thought, "Poor child! you must often have sighed for the sunny meadows of Brussels, in the long gloomy nights spent in the company of that terrible man!"

I was not far wrong, as I afterward discovered. Mr. and Mrs. Van Koeren were very unhappy. Jealousy was his monomania, and he had scarcely been married before his girl-wife began to feel the oppression of a gloomy and ceaseless tyranny. Every man under fifty, whose hair was not white and whose form was erect, was an object of suspicion to this Dutch Bluebeard. Not that he was vulgarly jealous. He did not frown at his wife before strangers, or attack her with reproaches in the midst of her festivities. He was too well-bred a man to bare his private woes to the world.

But at night, when the guests had departed and the dull light of the quaint old Flemish lamps but half-illuminated the nuptial chamber, then it was that with monotonous invective Mr. Van Koeren crushed his wife. And Marie, weeping and silent, would sit on the edge of the bed listening to the cold trenchant irony of her husband, who, pacing up and down the room, would now and then stop in his walk to gaze with his burning eyes upon the pallid face of his victim. Even the evidences that Marie gave of becoming a mother did not check him. He saw in that coming event that most husbands anticipate with mingled joy and fear, only an approaching incarnation of his dishonour. He watched with a horrible refinement of suspicion for the arrival of that being in whose features he madly believed he would but too surely trace the evidences of his wife's crime.

Whether it was that these ceaseless attacks wore out her strength, or that Providence wished to add another chastening misery to her burden of woe, I dare not speculate; but it is .certain that one luckless night Mr. Van Koeren learned with fury that he had become a father two months before the allotted time. During his first paroxysm of rage on the receipt of intelligence which seemed to confirm all his previous suspicions, it was, I believe, with difficulty that he was prevented from slaying both the innocent causes of his resentment. The caution of his race and the presence of the physicians induced him, however, to put a curb upon his furious will until reflection suggested quite as criminal, if not as dangerous a vengeance.

As soon as his poor wife had recovered from her illness, unnaturally prolonged by the delicacy of constitution induced by previous mental suffering, she was astonished to find, instead of increasing his persecutions, that her husband had changed his tactics and treated her with studied neglect. He rarely spoke to her except on occasions when the decencies of society demanded that he should address her. He avoided her presence, and no longer inhabited the same apartment. He seemed, in short, to strive as much as possible to forget her existence. But if she did not suffer from personal ill-treatment it was because a punishment more acute was in store for her. If Mr. Van Koeren had chosen to affect to consider her beneath his vengeance, it was because his hate had taken another direction, and seemed to have derived increased intensity from the alteration. It was upon the unhappy boy, the cause of all this misery, that the father lavished a terrible hatred. Mr. Van Koeren seemed determined, that if this child sprang from other loins than his, that the mournful destiny which he forced upon him would amply avenge his own existence and the infidelity of his mother.

While the child was an infant his plan seemed to have been formed. Ignorance and neglect were the two deadly influences with which he sought to assassinate the moral nature of this boy; and his terrible campaign against the virtue of his own son, was, as he grew up, carried into execution with the most consummate generalship. He gave him money, but debarred him from education. He allowed him liberty of action but withheld advice. It was in vain that his mother, who foresaw the frightful consequences of such a training, sought in secret by every means in her power to nullify her husband's attempts. She strove in vain to seduce her son into an ambition to be educated. She beheld with horror all her agonised efforts frustrated, and saw her son, and only child, becoming, even in his youth, a drunkard and a libertine.

In the end it proved too much for her strength; she sickened, and went home to her sunny Belgian plains. There she lingered for a few months in a calm but rapid decay, whose calmness was broken but by the one grief; until one autumn day, when the leaves were falling from the limes, she made a little prayer for her son to the Good God, and died. Vain orison! Spendthrift, gamester, libertine, and drunkard by turns, Alain Van Koeren's earthly destiny was unchangeable, The father, who should have been his guide, looked on each fresh depravity of his son's with a species of grim delight. Even the death of his wronged wife had no effect upon his fatal purpose. He still permitted the young man to run blindly to destruction by the course into which he himself had led him.

As years rolled by, and Mr. Van Koeren himself approached to that time of life when he might soon expect to follow his persecuted wife, he relieved himself of the hateful presence of his son altogether. Even the link of a systematic vengeance, which had hitherto united them, was severed, and Alain was cast adrift without either money or principle. The occasion of this final separation between father and son was the marriage of the latter with a girl of humble, though honest extraction. This was a good excuse for the remorseless Van Koeren, so he availed himself of it by turning his son out of doors. From that time forth they never met. Alain lived a life of meagre dissipation, and soon died, leaving behind him one child, a daughter. By a coincidence natural enough, Mr. Van Koeren's death followed his son's almost immediately. He died as he had lived, sternly. But those who were around his couch in his last moments, mentioned some singular facts connected with the manner of his death.

A few moments before he expired he raised himself in the bed, and seemed as if conversing with some person invisible to the spectators. His lips moved as if in speech, and immediately afterward he sank back, bathed in a flood of tears. "Wrong! wrong!" he was heard to mutter, feebly; then he implored passionately the forgiveness of someone who he said was present. The death struggle ensued almost immediately, and in the midst of his agony he seemed wrestling for speech. All that could be heard, however, were a few broken words. "I was wrong. My—unfounded—For God's sake look in—You will find—" Having uttered these fragmentary sentences, he seemed to feel that the power of speech had passed away forever. He fixed his eyes piteously on those around him, and, with a great sigh of grief, expired. I gathered these facts from his granddaughter, and Alain's daughter, Alice Van Koeren, who had been summoned by some friend to her grandfather's dying couch when it was too late. It was the first time she had seen him, and then she saw him die.

The results of Mr. Van Koeren's death were nine days wonder to all the merchants in New York. Beyond a small sum in the bank, and the house in which he lived, which was mortgaged for its full value, Mr. Van Koeren had died a pauper! To those who knew him, and knew his affairs, this seemed inexplicable. Five or six years before his death he had retired from business with a fortune of over a hundred thousand dollars. He had lived quietly since then; was known not to have speculated, and could not have gambled. The question then was, where had his wealth vanished to? Search was made in every secretary, in every bureau, for some document which might throw a light on the mysterious distribution that he had made of his property.

None were found. Neither will, nor certificates of stock, nor title deeds, nor bank accounts, were any where discernible. Inquiries were made at the offices of companies in which Mr. Van Koeren was known to be largely interested; he had sold out his stock years ago. Real estate that had been believed to be his, was found, on investigation, to have passed into other hands. There could be no doubt but that for some years past Mr. Van Koeren had been steadily converting all his immense property into money, and what he had done with that money no one knew.

Alice Van Koeren and her mother, who at the old gentleman's death were at first looked on as millionaires, discovered, when all was over, that they were no better off than before. It was evident that the old man, determined that one who, though bearing his name, he believed not to be of his blood, should never inherit his wealth, or any share of it, had made away with his fortune before his death—a posthumous vengeance, which was the only one by which the laws of the State of New York, relative to inheritance, could be successfully evaded.

I took a peculiar interest in the case, and even helped to make some researches after the lost property, not so much, I confess, from a spirit of general philanthropy, as from certain feelings which I experienced toward Alice Van Koeren, the heir to this invisible estate. I had long known both her and her mother when they were living in an honest poverty, and earning a scanty subsistence by their own labour; Mrs. Van Koeren working as an embroideress, and Alice turning to account, as a preparatory governess, the education which her good mother, spite of her limited means, had bestowed on her.

In a few words, then, I loved Alice Van Koeren, and was determined to make her my wife, as soon as my means would allow me to support a fitting establishment. My passion had never been declared. I was content for the time with the secret consciousness of my own love, and the no less grateful certainty that Alice returned it, all unuttered as it was. I had, therefore, a double interest in passing the summer at the old Dutch villa, for I felt it to be connected somehow with Alice, and I could not forget the singular desire to inhabit it which I had so often experienced as a boy.

It was a lovely day in June when Jasper Joye and myself took up our abode in our new residence, and as we smoked our cigars on the *piazza* in the evening, we felt, for the first time, the unalloyed pleasure with which a townsman breathes the pure air of the country.

The house and grounds had a quaint sort of beauty that to me were eminently pleasing. Landscape gardening, in the modern acceptation of the term, was then almost unknown in this country, and the "laying out" of the garden that surrounded our new home would doubtless have shocked Mr. Loudon, the late Mr. Downing, or Sir Thomas Dick Lauder. It was formal and artificial to the last degree. The beds were cut into long parallelograms, rigid and severe of aspect, and edged with prim rows of stiff, dwarf box. The walks, of course, crossed always at right angles, and the laurel and cypress trees that grew here and there were clipped into cones, and spheres, and rhomboids.

It is true, that at the time my friend and I hired the house some years of neglect had restored to this formal garden somewhat of the raggedness of nature. The box edgings were rank and wild. The clipped trees, forgetful of geometric propriety, flourished off into unauthorized boughs and rebel offshoots. The walks were green with moss, and the beds of Dutch tulips, which had been planted in the shape of certain gorgeous birds, whose colours were represented by masses of blossoms, each of a single hue, had transgressed their limits, and the purple of a parrot's wings might have been seen running recklessly into the crimson of his head; while as bulbs, however well-bred, *will* create other bulbs, the flower-birds of this queer old Dutch garden became in time abominably distorted in shape. Flamingos with humps; golden pheasants with legs preternaturally elongated; macaws afflicted with an attack of hydrocephalus, each species of deformity being proportioned to the rapidity with which the roots had spread in some particular direction. Still, this strange mixture of raggedness and formality—this conglomerate of nature and art, had its charms. It was pleasant to watch the struggle, as it were, between the opposing elements, and to see nature triumphing by degrees in every direction.

Then the house itself was pleasant and commodious. Rooms that, though not lofty, were spacious. Wide windows and cool *piazzas* extending over the four sides of the building; and a collection of quaint old carved furniture, some of which, from its elaborateness, might well have come from the chisel of Master Grinling Gibbons. There was a mantle-piece in the dining-room with which I remember being very much struck when first I came to take possession. It was a most singular and fantastical piece of carving. It was a perfect tropical garden, menagerie, and aviary in one. Birds, beasts, and flowers were sculptured on the wood with exquisite correctness of detail, and painted with the hues of nature. The Dutch taste for colour was here fully gratified. Parrots, love-birds, scarlet lorys, blue-faced baboons, crocodiles, passion-flowers, tigers, Egyptian lilies, and Brazilian butterflies, were all mixed up in the most gorgeous confusion. The artist, whoever he was, must have been an admirable naturalist, for the ease and freedom of his carving was only equalled by the wonderful accuracy with which the different animals were represented. Altogether it was one of those oddities of Dutch conception whose strangeness was, in this instance, redeemed by the excellence of the execution.

Such was the establishment that Jasper Joye and myself were to inhabit for the summer months.

"What a strange thing it was," said Jasper, as we lounged on the *piazza* together the night of our arrival, "that old Van Koeren's property should never have turned up!"

"It is a question with some people whether he had any at his death," I answered.

"Pshaw! everyone knows that he did not or could not have lost that with which he retired from business."

"It is strange," said I thoughtfully; "yet every possible search has been made for any documents that might throw some light on the mystery. I have myself sought in every quarter for the traces of this lost wealth, but in vain."

"Perhaps he buried it?" suggested Jasper, laughing; "if so, we may find it here in some hole one fine morning."

"I think it much more likely that he destroyed it," I replied. "You know he never could be got to believe that Alain Van Koeren was his son, and I believe him quite capable of having flung all his money into the sea, in order to prevent those whom he considered not of his blood inheriting it, which they must have done under our laws."

"I am sorry that Alice did not become an heiress, both for your sake and hers. She is a charming girl."

Jasper, from whom I concealed nothing, knew of my love.

"As to that," I answered, "it is little matter. I shall in a year or two be independent enough to marry, and can afford to let Mr. Van Koeren's cherished gold sleep wherever he has concealed it."

"Well, I'm off to bed," said Jasper, yawning. "This country air makes one sleepy early. Be on the look-out for trapdoors and all that sort of thing, old fellow. Who knows but the old chap's dollars will turn up. Goodnight!"

"Goodnight, Jasper !"

So we parted for the night. He to his room, which lay on the west side of the building, I to mine on the east, situated at the end of a long corridor, and exactly opposite to Jasper's.

The night was very still and warm. The clearness with which I heard the song of the katydid, and the croak of the bull-frog, seemed to make the silence more distinct. The air was dense and breathless, and although longing to throw wide my windows, I dared not, for without the ominous trumpetings of a whole army of mosquitoes sounded threateningly.

I tossed on my bed oppressed with the heat; kicked the blankets into every spot where they ought not to be; gradually got the sheets twisted into a rope; turned my pillow every two minutes in the hope of finding a cool side; in short, did everything that a man does when he lies awake on a very hot night, and can not open his window.

Suddenly, in the midst of my miseries, and when I had made up my mind to fling open the casement in spite of the legion of mosquitoes that I knew were hungrily waiting outside, suddenly I felt a continuous stream of cold air blowing upon my face. Luxurious as the sensation was, I could not help starting as I felt it. Where could this draught come from? The door was closed—so were the windows. It did not come from the direction of the fire-place; and even if it did, the air without was too still to produce so strong a current. I got up in my bed and gazed round the room, the whole of which, though only lit by a dim twilight, was still sufficiently visible.

I thought at first it was a trick of Jasper's, who might have provided himself with a bellows or a long tube; but a careful investigation of the apartment convinced me that no one was there. Besides, I had locked the door, and it was not likely that anyone had been concealed in the room before I entered it. It was exceedingly strange; but still the draught of cool wind blew on my face and chest, every now and then changing its direction—sometimes on one side, sometimes on the other. I am not constitutionally nervous, and had been too long accustomed to reflect on philosophical subjects to become the prey of fear in the presence of mysterious phenomena.

I had devoted much of my leisure time to the investigation of what are popularly called supernatural matters by those who have not reflected or examined sufficiently to discover that none of these apparent miracles are supernatural, but all, however singular, directly dependent on certain natural laws. I became speedily convinced therefore, as I sat up in my bed peering into the dim recesses of my chamber, that this mysterious wind was the effect or forerunner of a supernatural visitation, and I mentally determined to investigate it as it developed itself with a philosophical calmness.

"Is anyone in this room?" I asked, as distinctly as I could. No reply; while the cool wind still swept over my cheek. I knew, in the case of Elizabeth Eslinger, who was visited by an apparition while in the Weinsberg jail, and whose singular and apparently authentic experiences were made the subject of a book by Dr. Kerner, that the manifestation of the spirit was invariably accompanied by such a breezy sensation as I now experienced. I therefore gathered my will, as it were, into a focus, and endeavoured, as much as lay in my power, to put myself *en rapport* with the disembodied spirit, if such there was, knowing that on such conditions alone would it be enabled to manifest itself to me.

Presently it seemed to me as if a luminous cloud was gathering in one corner of the room—a sort of dim phosphoric vapour, shadowy and ill-defined. It changed its position frequently, sometimes coming nearer, and at others retreating to the farthest end of the room. As it grew intenser and more radiant, I observed a sickening and corpse-like odour diffuse itself through the chamber, and despite my anxiety to witness this phenomenon undisturbed, I could with, difficulty conquer the feeling of faintness which oppressed me.

The luminous cloud now began to grow brighter and brighter as I gazed. The horrible odour of which I have spoken did not cease to oppress me, and gradually I could discover certain lines making themselves visible in the midst of this lambent radiance. These lines took the form of a human figure—a tall man, dressed in a long dressing-robe, with a pale countenance, burning eyes, and a very bold and prominent chin. At a glance I recognised the original of the picture of old Van Koeren that I had seen with Alice. My interest was now aroused to the highest point; I felt that I stood face to face with a spirit, and doubted not that I should learn the fate of the old man's mysteriously-concealed wealth.

The spirit presented a very strange appearance. He himself was not luminous, except some tongues of fire that seemed to proceed from the tips of his fingers, but was completely surrounded by a thin gauze of light, so to speak, through which his outlines were visible. His head was bare, and his white hair fell in huge masses around his stern, saturnine face. As he moved on the floor, I distinctly heard a strange crackling sound, such as one hears when a substance has been overcharged with electricity. But the circumstance that seemed to me most incomprehensible connected with the apparition, was that Mr. Van Koeren held in both hands a curiously-painted flower-pot, out of which sprang a number of the most beautiful tulips in full blossom. He seemed very uneasy and agitated, and moved about the room as if in pain, frequently bending over the pot of tulips as if to inhale their odour, then holding it out to me, seemingly in the hope of attracting my attention to it.

I was, I confess, very much puzzled. I knew that Mr. Van Koeren had in his lifetime devoted much of his leisure to the cultivation of flowers, importing from Holland the most expensive and rarest bulbs; but how this innocent fancy could trouble him after death, I could not imagine. I felt assured, however, that some important reason lay at the bottom of this spectral eccentricity, and determined to fathom it if I could.

"What brings you here?" I asked audibly; directing mentally, however, at the same time, the question to the spirit with all the power of my will. He did not seem to hear me, but still kept moving uneasily about, with the crackling noise I mentioned, and holding the pot of tulips toward me.

"It is evident," I said to myself, "that I am not sufficiently *en rapport* with this spirit in order for him to make himself understood by speech. He has, therefore, recourse to symbols. The pot of tulips is a symbol. But of what?"

While reflecting on these things, I continued to gaze upon the spirit. While observing him attentively, he approached my bedside by a rapid movement, and laid one hand on my arm. The touch was icy cold, and pained me at the moment. Next morning my arm was swollen, and marked with a round blue spot. Then passing to my bedroom-door, the spirit opened it noisily and went out, shutting it behind him. Catching for a moment at the idea that I was the dupe of a trick, I jumped out of bed and ran to the door. It was locked, with the key on the inside, and a brass safety-bolt, which lay above the lock, shot safely home. All was as I had left it on going to bed. Yet I declare most solemnly, that as the ghost made his exit, I not alone saw the door open, but *I saw the corridor outside, and distinctly observed a large picture of William of Orange that hung just opposite to my room.*

This to me was the most curious portion of the phenomena I had witnessed. Either the door had been opened by the ghost, and the resistance of physical obstacles overcome in some amazing manner—because in this case the bolts must have been replaced when the ghost was outside the door—or he must have had a sufficient magnetic *rapport* with my mind to impress upon it the belief that the door was opened, and also to conjure up in my brain the vision of the corridor and the picture, features that I would have seen if the door had been opened by any ordinary physical agency.

The next morning at breakfast I suppose my manner must have betrayed me, for Jasper said to me, after staring at me for some time,

"Why, Harry Escott, what's the matter with you? You look as if you had seen a ghost!"

"So I have, Jasper."

Jasper, of course, burst into a loud fit of laughter, and said he'd shave my head and give me a shower-bath.

"Well, you may laugh," I answered; "but you shall see it tonight, Jasper."

He became serious in a moment—I suppose there was something earnest in my manner that convinced him that my words were not idle—and asked me to explain. I described my interview as accurately as I could.

"How did you know that it was old Van Koeren?" he asked.

"Because I have seen his picture a hundred times with Alice," I answered, "and this apparition was as like it as it was possible for a ghost to be like a miniature."

"You must not think I'm laughing at you, Harry," he continued, "but I wish you would answer this. We have all heard of ghosts—ghosts of men, women, children, dogs, horses, in fact every living animal; but hang me of ever I heard of the ghost of a flower-pot before.

"My dear Jasper, you would have heard of such things if you had studied such branches of learning. All the phenomena I witnessed last night are supportable by well-authenticated facts. The cool wind has attended the appearance of more than one ghost, and Baron Reichenbach asserts that his patients, who you know are for the most part sensitive to apparitions, invariably feel this wind when a magnet is brought close to their bodies. With regard to the flower-pot about which you make so merry, it is to me the least wonderful portion of the apparitions. When a ghost is unable to find a person of sufficient receptivity, in order to communicate with him by speech, he is obliged to have recourse to symbols to express his wishes. These he either creates by some mysterious power out of the surrounding atmosphere, or he impresses, by magnetic force on the mind of the person he visits, the form of the symbol he is anxious to have represented.

"There is an instance mentioned by Jung Stilling of a student at Brunswick, who appeared to a professor of his college with a picture in his hands, which picture had a hole in it that the ghost thrust his head through. For a long time this symbol was a mystery; but the student was persevering, and appeared every night with his head through the picture, until at last it was discovered that, before he died, he had gotten some painted slides for a magic lantern from a shop-keeper in the town, which had not been paid for at his death; and when the debt had been discharged, he and his picture vanished forevermore. Now here was a symbol distinctly bearing on the question at issue. This poor student could find no better way of expressing his uneasiness at the debt for the painted slides than by thrusting his head through a picture. How he conjured up the picture I can not pretend to explain, but that it was used as a symbol is evident."

"Then you think the flower-pot of old Van Koeren is a symbol?"

"Most assuredly, the pot of tulips he held was intended to express that which he could not speak. I think it must have had some reference to his missing property, and it is our business to discover in what manner."

"Let us go and dig up all the tulip beds," said Jasper, "who knows but he may have buried his money in one of them?"

I grieve to say that I assented to Jasper's proposition, and on that eventful day every tulip in that quaint old garden was ruthlessly uprooted. The gorgeous macaws, and ragged parrots, and long-legged pheasants so cunningly formed by those brilliant flowers, were that day exterminated. Jasper and I had a regular *battue* amidst this floral preserve, and many a splendid bird fell before our unerring spades.

We, however, dug in vain. No secret coffer turned up out of the deep mould of the flower-beds. We evidently were not on the right scent. Our researches for that day terminated, and Jasper and myself waited impatiently for the night.

It was arranged that Jasper should sleep in my room. I had a small bed rigged up for him near my own, and I was to have the additional assistance of his senses in the investigation of the strange phenomena that we so confidently expected to appear.

The night came. We retired to our respective couches, after carefully bolting the doors, and subjecting the entire apartment to the strictest scrutiny, rendering it totally impossible that a secret entrance should exist unknown to us. We then put out the lights and awaited the apparition.

We did not remain in suspense long. About twenty minutes after we retired to bed Jasper called out,

"Harry," said he, "I feel the cool wind!"

"So do I," I answered, for at that moment a light breeze seemed to play across my temples.

"Look, look, Harry!" continued Jasper in a tone of painful eagerness, "I see a light—there in the corner!"

It was the phantom. As before, the luminous cloud appeared to gather in the room, growing more and more intense each minute. Presently the dark lines mapped themselves out, as it were, in the midst of this pale, radiant vapour, and there stood Mr. Van Koeren, ghastly and mournful as ever, with the pot of tulips in his hands.

"Do you see it?" I asked Jasper.

"My God! yes," said Jasper, in a low voice. "How terrible he looks!"

"Can you speak to me, tonight?" I said, addressing the apparition, and again concentrating my will upon my question. "If so, unburden yourself. We will assist you, if we can."

There was no reply. The ghost preserved the same sad, impassive countenance; he had heard me not. He seemed in great distress on this occasion, moving up and down, and holding out the pot of tulips imploringly toward me, each motion of his being accompanied by the crackling noise and the corpse-like odour. I felt sorely troubled myself to see this poor spirit torn by an endless grief; so anxious to communicate to me what lay on his soul, and yet debarred by some occult power from the privilege.

"Why, Harry," cried Jasper after a silence, during which we both watched the motions of the ghost intently, "why, Harry, my boy, there are *two* of them!"

Astonished by his words I looked around, and became immediately aware of the presence of a second luminous cloud, in the midst of which I could distinctly trace the figure of a pale but lovely woman. I needed no second glance to assure me that it was the unfortunate wife of Mr. Van Koeren.

"It is his wife, Jasper," I replied; "I recognise her, as I have recognised her husband, by the portrait."

"How sad she looks!" exclaimed Jasper in a low voice.

She did indeed look sad. Her face, pale and mournful in its cast, did not, however, seem convulsed with sorrow, as was her husband's. She seemed to be oppressed with a calm grief, and gazed with a look of interest that was painful in its intensity, on Mr. Van Koeren. It struck me, from his air, that though she saw him, he did not see her. His whole attention was concentrated on the pot of tulips, while Mrs. Van Koeren, who floated at an elevation of about three feet from the floor, and thus overtopped her husband, seemed equally absorbed in the contemplation of his slightest movement. Occasionally she would turn her eyes on me, as if to call my attention to her companion, and then returning, gaze on him with a sad womanly, half-eager smile, that to me was inexpressibly mournful.

There was something exceedingly touching in this strange sight. These two spirits so near, yet so distant. The sinful husband torn with grief and weighed down with some terrible secret, and so blinded by the grossness of his being as to be unable to see the wife-angel who was watching over him; while she, forgetting all her wrongs, and attracted to earth by perhaps the same human sympathies, watched from a greater spiritual height, and with a tender interest, the struggles of her suffering spouse.

"By Jove!" exclaimed Jasper, jumping from his bed, "I know what it means now."

"What does it mean?" I asked, as eager to know as he was to communicate.

"Well, that flower-pot that the old chap is holding—"Jasper, I grieve to say, was rather profane.

"Well! what of that flower-pot?"

"Observe the pattern. It has two handles made of red snakes, whose tails twist round the top and form a rim. It contains tulips of three colours, yellow, red, and purple."

"I see all that as well as you do. Let us have the solution."

"Well, Harry, my boy! don't you remember that there is just such a flower-pot, tulips, snakes and all, carved on the queer old painted mantle-piece in the dining-room."

"So there is!" and a gleam of hope shot across my brain, and my heart beat quicker.

"Now, as sure as you are alive, Harry, the old fellow has concealed something important behind that mantle-piece."

"Jasper, if ever I am Emperor of France, I will make you chief of police; your inductive reasoning is magnificent."

Actuated by the same impulse, and without another word, we both sprang out of bed and lit a candle. The apparitions, if they remained, were no longer visible in the strong light. Hastily throwing on some clothes, we rushed down stairs to the dining-room, determined to have the old mantle-piece down, without loss of time. We had scarce entered the room when we felt the cool wind blowing on our faces. "Jasper," said I, "they are here!"

"Well," answered Jasper, "that only confirms my suspicions that we are on the right track this time. Let us go to work. See! here's the pot of tulips."

This pot of tulips occupied the centre of the mantle-piece, and served as a nucleus round which all the fantastic animals sculptured elsewhere might be said to gather. It was carved on a species of raised shield, or boss, of wood, that projected some inches beyond the plane of the remainder of the mantle-piece. The pot itself was painted a brick-colour. The snakes were of bronze colour, gilt, and the tulips— yellow, red, and purple—were painted after nature with the most exquisite accuracy.

For some time Jasper and myself tugged away at this projection without any avail. We were convinced that it was a movable panel of some kind, but yet were totally unable to move it. Suddenly it struck me that we had not yet twisted it. I immediately proceeded to apply all my strength, and after a few seconds of vigorous exertion, I had the satisfaction of finding it move slowly round. After giving it half a dozen turns, to my astonishment the long upper panel of the mantle-piece fell out toward us, apparently on concealed hinges, after the manner of the portion of escritoires that is used for writing upon. Within were several square cavities sunk in the wall, and lined with wood, like the pigeon-holes of a desk. In one of these was a bundle of papers.

We seized these papers with avidity, and hastily glanced over them. They proved to be documents vouching for property to the amount of nearly two hundred thousand dollars, invested in the name of Mr. Van Koeren in a certain firm at Bremen, who, no doubt, thought by this time that the money would remain unclaimed forever. The desires of these poor troubled spirits were accomplished. Justice to the child had been given through the instrumentality of the erring father.

The formulas necessary to prove Alice and her mother sole heirs to Mr. Van Koeren's estate were briefly gone through, and the poor governess leaped suddenly from the task of teaching stupid children to the envied position of a great heiress. I had ample reason afterward for thinking that her heart did not change with her position.

That Mr. Van Koeren became aware of his wife's innocence, just before he died, I have no doubt. How this was manifested, I can not of course say, but I think it highly probable that his poor wife herself was enabled at the critical moment of dissolution, when the link that binds body and soul together is attenuated to the last thread, to put herself en rapport with her unhappy husband. Hence his sudden starting up in his bed, his apparent conversation with some invisible being, and his fragmentary disclosures, too broken, however, to be comprehended.

The question of apparitions has been so often discussed, that I feel no inclination to enter here upon the truth or fallacy of the ghostly theory. I myself believe in ghosts. Alice, my wife—for we are married, dear reader—believes in them firmly; and if it suited me to do so, I could overwhelm you with a scientific theory of my own on the subject, reconciling ghosts and natural phenomena. I will spare you, however, for I intend to deliver a lecture on the subject at Hope Chapel this winter, and if I disclosed my theory now, someone of our "gifted lecturers" would perhaps forestall me, and make "his arrangements for the season" on the strength of my ideas. Anyone, however, who wishes to investigate this subject, will find an opportunity by addressing a note to Mr. Harry Escott, care of the publishers of this magazine.

Aylmer Vance and the Vampire

Alice and Claude Askew

Aylmer Vance had rooms in Dover Street, Piccadilly, and now that I had decided to follow in his footsteps and to accept him as my instructor in matters psychic, I found it convenient to lodge in the same house. Aylmer and I quickly became close friends, and he showed me how to develop that faculty of clairvoyance which I had possessed without being aware of it. And I may say at once that this particular faculty of mine proved of service on several important occasions.

At the same time I made myself useful to Vance in other ways, not the least of which was that of acting as recorder of his many strange adventures. For himself, he never cared much about publicity, and it was some time before I could persuade him, in the interests of science, to allow me to give any detailed account of his experiences to the world.

The incidents which I will now narrate occurred very soon after we had taken up our residence together, and while I was still, so to speak, a novice.

It was about ten o'clock in the morning that a visitor was announced. He sent up a card which bore upon it the name of Paul Davenant.

The name was familiar to me, and I wondered if this could be the same Mr Davenant who was so well known for his polo playing and for his success as an amateur rider, especially over the hurdles? He was a young man of wealth and position, and I recollected that he had married, about a year ago, a girl who was reckoned the greatest beauty of the season. All the illustrated papers had given their portraits at the time, and I remember thinking what a remarkably handsome couple they made.

Mr Davenant was ushered in, and at first I was uncertain as to whether this could be the individual whom I had in mind, so wan and pale and ill did he appear. A finely-built, upstanding man at the time of his marriage, he had now acquired a languid droop of the shoulders and a shuffling gait, while his face, especially about the lips, was bloodless to an alarming degree.

And yet it was the same man, for behind all this I could recognise the shadow of the good looks that had once distinguished Paul Davenant.

He took the chair which Aylmer offered him—after the usual preliminary civilities had been exchanged—and then glanced doubtfully in my direction. 'I wish to consult you privately, Mr Vance,' he said. 'The matter is of considerable importance to myself, and, if I may say so, of a somewhat delicate nature.'

Of course I rose immediately to withdraw from the room, but Vance laid his hand upon my arm.

'If the matter is connected with research in my particular line, Mr Davenant,' he said, 'if there is any investigation you wish me to take up on your behalf, I shall be glad if you will include Mr Dexter in your confidence. Mr Dexter assists me in my work. But, of course——.'

'Oh, no,' interrupted the other, 'if that is the case, pray let Mr Dexter remain. I think,' he added, glancing at me with a friendly smile, 'that you are an Oxford man, are you not, Mr Dexter? It was before my time, but I have heard of your name in connection with the river. You rowed at Henley, unless I am very much mistaken.'

I admitted the fact, with a pleasurable sensation of pride. I was very keen upon rowing in those days, and a man's prowess at school and college always remain dear to his heart..After this we quickly became on friendly terms, and Paul Davenant proceeded to take Aylmer and myself into his confidence.

He began by calling attention to his personal appearance. 'You would hardly recognise me for the same man! was a year ago,' he said. 'I've been losing flesh steadily for the last six months. I came up from Scotland about a week ago, to consult a London doctor. I've seen two—in fact, they've held a sort of consultation over me—but the result, I may say, is far from satisfactory.

They don't seem to know what is really the matter with me.'

'Anaemia—heart' suggested Vance. He was scrutinising his visitor keenly, and yet without any particular appearance of doing so. 'I believe it not infrequently happens that you athletes overdo yourselves—put too much strain upon the heart—'

'My heart is quite sound,' responded Davenant. 'Physically it is in perfect condition. The trouble seems to be that it hasn't enough blood to pump into my veins. The doctors wanted to know if I had met with an accident involving a great loss of blood—but I haven't. I've had no accident at all, and as for anaemia, well, I don't seem to show the ordinary symptoms of it. The inexplicable thing is that I've lost blood without knowing it, and apparently this has been going on for some time, for I've been getting steadily worse. It was almost imperceptible at first—not a sudden collapse, you understand, but a gradual failure of health.'

'I wonder,' remarked Vance slowly, 'what induced you to consult me? For you know, of course, the direction in which I pursue my investigations. May I ask if you have reason to consider that your state of health is due to some cause which we may describe as super-physical?'

A slight colour came to Davenant's white cheeks.

'There are curious circumstances,' he said in a low and earnest tone of voice. 'I've been turning them over in my mind, trying to see light through them. I daresay it's all the sheerest folly—and I must tell you that I'm not in the least a superstitious sort of man. I don't mean to say that I'm absolutely incredulous, but I've never given thought to such things—I've led too active a life. But, as I have said, there are curious circumstances about my case, and that is why I decided upon consulting you.'

'Will you tell me everything without reserve?' said Vance. I could see that he was interested.

He was sitting up in his chair, his feet supported on a stool, his elbows on his knees, his chin in his hands—a favourite attitude of his. 'Have you,' he suggested, slowly, 'any mark upon your body, anything that you might associate, however remotely, with your present weakness and ill-health?'

'It's a curious thing that you should ask me that question,' returned Davenant, 'because I have got a curious mark, a sort of scar, that I can't account for. But I showed it to the doctors, and they assured me that it could have nothing whatever to do with my condition. In any case, if it had, it was something altogether outside their experience. I think they imagined it to be nothing more than a birthmark, a sort of mole, for they asked me if I'd had it all my life. But that I can swear I haven't. I only noticed it for the first time about six months ago, when my health began to fail. But you can see for yourself.'

He loosened his collar and bared his throat. Vance rose and made a careful scrutiny of the suspicious mark. It was situated a very little to the left of the central line, just above the clavicle, and, as Vance pointed out, directly over the big vessels of the throat. My friend called to me so that I might examine it, too. Whatever the opinion of the doctors may have been, Aylmer was obviously deeply interested..And yet there was very little to show. The skin was quite intact, and there was no sign of inflammation. There were two red marks, about an inch apart, each of which was inclined to be crescent in shape. They were more visible than they might otherwise have been owing to the peculiar whiteness of Davenant's skin.

'It can't be anything of importance,' said Davenant, with a slightly uneasy laugh. 'I'm inclined to think the marks are dying away.'

'Have you ever noticed them more inflamed than they are at present?' inquired Vance. 'If so, was it at any special time?'

Davenant reflected. 'Yes,' he replied slowly, 'there have been times, usually, I think perhaps invariably, when I wake up in the morning, that I've noticed them larger and more angry looking. And I've felt a slight sensation of pain—a tingling—oh, very slight, and I've never worried about it. Only now you suggest it to my mind, I believe that those same mornings I have felt particularly tired and done up—a sensation of lassitude absolutely unusual to me. And once, Mr Vance, I remember quite distinctly that there was a stain of blood close to the mark. I didn't think anything of it at the time, and just wiped it away.'

'I see.' Aylmer Vance resumed his seat and invited his visitor to do the same. 'And now,' he resumed, 'you said, Mr Davenant, that there are certain peculiar circumstances you wish to acquaint me with. Will you do so?'

And so Davenant readjusted his collar and proceeded to tell his story. I will tell it as far as I can, without any reference to the occasional interruptions of Vance and myself.

Paul Davenant, as I have said, was a man of wealth and position, and so, in every sense of the word, he was a suitable husband for Miss Jessica MacThane, the young lady who eventually became his wife. Before coming to the incidents attending his loss of health, he had a great deal to recount about Miss MacThane and her family history.

She was of Scottish descent, and although she had certain characteristic features of her race, she was not really Scotch in appearance. Hers was the beauty of the far South rather than that of the Highlands from which she had her origin. Names are not always suited to their owners, and Miss MacThane's was peculiarly inappropriate. She had, in fact, been christened Jessica in a sort of pathetic effort to counteract her obvious departure from normal type. There was a reason for this which we were soon to learn.

Miss MacThane was especially remarkable for her wonderful red hair, hair such as one hardly ever sees outside of Italy—not the Celtic red—and it was so long that it reached to her feet, and it had an extraordinary gloss upon it so that it seemed almost to have individual life of its own.

Then she had just the complexion that one would expect with such hair, the purest ivory white, and not in the least marred by freckles, as is so often the case with red-haired girls. Her beauty was derived from an ancestress who had been brought to Scotland from some foreign shore—no one knew exactly whence.

Davenant fell in love with her almost at once and he had every reason to believe, in spite of her many admirers, that his love was returned. At this time he knew very little about her personal history. He was aware only that she was very wealthy in her own right, an orphan, and the last representative of a race that had once been famous in the annals of history—or rather infamous, for the MacThanes had distinguished themselves more by cruelty and lust of blood than by deeds of chivalry. A clan of turbulent robbers in the past, they had helped to add many a bloodstained page to the history of their country.

Jessica had lived with her father, who owned a house in London, until his death when she was about fifteen years of age. Her mother had died in Scotland when Jessica was still a tiny child. Mr MacThane had been so affected by his wife's death that, with his little daughter, he had abandoned his Scotch estate altogether—or so it was believed—leaving it to the management of a bailiff—though, indeed, there was but little work for the bailiff to do, since there were practically no tenants left. Blackwick Castle had borne for many years a most unenviable reputation.

After the death of her father, Miss MacThane had gone to live with a certain Mrs Meredith, who was a connection of her mother's—on her father's side she had not a single relation left.

Jessica was absolutely the last of a clan once so extensive that intermarriage had been a tradition of the family, but for which the last two hundred years had been gradually dwindling to extinction.

Mrs Meredith took Jessica into Society—which would never have been her privilege had Mr MacThane lived, for he was a moody, self-absorbed man, and prematurely old—one who seemed worn down by the weight of a great grief.

Well, I have said that Paul Davenant quickly fell in love with Jessica, and it was not long before he proposed for her hand. To his great surprise, for he had good reason to believe that she cared for him, he met with a refusal; nor would she give any explanation, though she burst into a flood of pitiful tears.

Bewildered and bitterly disappointed, he consulted Mrs Meredith, with whom he happened to be on friendly terms, and from her he learnt that Jessica had already had several proposals, all from quite desirable men, but that one after another had been rejected.

Paul consoled himself with the reflection that perhaps Jessica did not love them, whereas he was quite sure that she cared for himself. Under these circumstances he determined to try again.

He did so, and with better result. Jessica admitted her love, but at the same time she repeated that she would not marry him. Love and marriage were not for her. Then, to his utter amazement, she declared that she had been born under a curse—a curse which, sooner or later was bound to show itself in her, and which, moreover, must react cruelly, perhaps fatally, upon anyone with whom she linked her life. How could she allow a man she loved to take such a risk? Above all, since the evil was hereditary, there was one point upon which she had quite made up her mind: no child should ever call her mother—she must be the last of her race indeed.

Of course, Davenant was amazed and inclined to think that Jessica had got some absurd idea into her head which a little reasoning on his part would dispel. There was only one other possible explanation. Was it lunacy she was afraid of? But Jessica shook her head, She did not know of any lunacy in her family. The ill was deeper, more subtle than that. And then she told him all that she knew.

The curse—she made us of that word for want of a better—was attached to the ancient race from which she had her origin. Her father had suffered from it, and his father and grandfather before him. All three had taken to themselves young wives who had died mysteriously, of some wasting disease, within a few years. Had they observed the ancient family tradition of intermarriage this might possibly not have happened, but in their case, since the family was so near extinction, this had not been possible.

For the curse—or whatever it was—did not kill those who bore the name of MacThane. It only rendered them a danger to others. It was as if they absorbed from the blood-soaked walls of their fatal castle a deadly taint which reacted terribly upon those with whom they were brought into contact, especially their nearest and dearest.

'Do you know what my father said we have it in us to become?' said Jessica with a shudder. 'He used the word vampires. Paul, think of it—vampires—preying upon the life blood of others.' And then, when Davenant was inclined to laugh, she checked him. 'No,' she cried out, 'it is not impossible. Think. We are a decadent race. From the earliest times our history has been marked by bloodshed and cruelty. The walls of Blackwick Castle are impregnated with evil—every stone could tell its tale, of violence, pain, lust, and murder. What can one expect of those who have spent their lifetime between its walls?'

'But you have not done so,' exclaimed Paul. 'You have been spared that, Jessica. You were taken away after your mother died, and you have no recollection of Blackwick Castle, none at all. And you need never set foot in it again.'

'I'm afraid the evil is in my blood,' she replied sadly, 'although I am unconscious of it now.

And as for not returning to Blackwick—I'm not sure I can help myself. At least, that is what my father warned me of. He said there is something there, some compelling force, that will call me to it in spite of myself. But, oh, I don't know—I don't know, and that is what makes it so difficult. If I could only believe that all this is nothing but an idle superstition, I might be happy again, for I have it in me to enjoy life, and I'm young, very young, but my father told me these things when he was on his death-bed.' She added the last words in a low, awe-stricken tone.

Paul pressed her to tell him all that she knew, and eventually she revealed another fragment of family history which seemed to have some bearing upon the case. It dealt with her own astonishing likeness to that ancestress of a couple of hundred years ago, whose existence seemed to have presaged the gradual downfall of the clan of the MacThanes.

A certain Robert MacThane, departing from the traditions of his family, which demanded that he should not marry outside his clan, brought home a wife from foreign shores, a woman of wonderful beauty, who was possessed of glowing masses of red hair and a complexion of ivory whiteness—such as had more or less distinguished since then every female of the race born in the direct line.

It was not long before this woman came to be regarded in the neighbourhood as a witch. Queer stories were circulated abroad as to her doings, and the reputation of Blackwick Castle became worse than ever before.

And then one day she disappeared. Robert MacThane had been absent upon some business for twenty-four hours, and it was upon his return that he found her gone. The neighbourhood was searched, but without avail, and then Robert, who was a violent man and who had adored his foreign wife, called together certain of his tenants whom he suspected, rightly or wrongly, of foul play, and had them murdered in cold blood. Murder was easy in those days, yet such an outcry was raised that Robert had to take to flight, leaving his two children in the care of their nurse, and for a long while Blackwick Castle was without a master.

But its evil reputation persisted. It was said that Zaida, the witch, though dead, still made her presence felt. Many children of the tenantry and young people of the neighbourhood sickened and died— possibly of quite natural causes; but this did not prevent a mantle of terror settling upon the countryside, for it was said that Zaida had been seen—a pale woman clad in white—flitting about the cottages at night, and where she passed sickness and death were sure to supervene.

And from that time the fortune of the family gradually declined. Heir succeeded heir, but no sooner was he installed at Blackwick Castle than his nature, whatever it may previously have been, seemed to undergo a change. It was as if he absorbed into himself all the weight of evil that had stained his family name—as if he did, indeed, become a vampire, bringing blight upon any not directly connected with his own house..And so, by degrees, Blackwick was deserted of its tenantry. The land around it was left uncultivated—the farms stood empty. This had persisted to the present day, for the superstitious peasantry still told their tales of the mysterious white woman who hovered about the neighbourhood, and whose appearance betokened death—and possibly worse than death.

And yet it seemed that the last representatives of the MacThanes could not desert their ancestral home. Riches they had, sufficient to live happily upon elsewhere, but, drawn by some power they could not contend against, they had preferred to spend their lives in the solitude of the now half-ruined castle, shunned by their neighbours, feared and execrated by the few tenants that still clung to their soil.

So it had been with Jessica's grandfather and great-grandfather.

Each of them had married a young wife, and in each case their love story had been all too brief. The vampire spirit was still abroad, expressing itself—or so it seemed—through the living representatives of bygone generations of evil, and young blood had been demanded as the sacrifice.

And to them had succeeded Jessica's father. He had not profited by their example, but had followed directly in their footsteps. And the same fate had befallen the wife whom he passionately adored. She had died of pernicious anaemia—so the doctors said—but he had regarded himself as her murderer.

But, unlike his predecessors, he had torn himself away from Blackwick—and this for the sake of his child. Unknown to her, however, he had returned year after year, for there were times when the passionate longing for the gloomy, mysterious halls and corridors of the old castle, for the wild stretches of moorland, and the dark pinewoods, would come upon him too strongly to be resisted. And so he knew that for his daughter, as for himself, there was no escape, and he warned her, when the relief of death was at last granted to him, of what her fate must be.

This was the tale that Jessica told the man who wished to make her his wife, and he made light of it, as such a man would, regarding it all as foolish superstition, the delusion of a mind overwrought. And at last—perhaps it was not very difficult, for she loved him with all her heart and soul—he succeeded in inducing Jessica to think as he did, to banish morbid ideas, as he called them from her brain, and to consent to marry him at an early date.

'I'll take any risk you like,' he declared. 'I'll even go and live at Blackwick if you should desire it. To think of you, my lovely Jessica, a vampire! Why, I never heard such nonsense in my life.'

'Father said I'm very like Zaida, the witch,' she protested, but he silenced her with a kiss.

And so they were married and spent their honeymoon abroad, and in the autumn Paul accepted an invitation to a house party in Scotland for the grouse shooting, a sport to which he was absolutely devoted, and Jessica agreed with him that there was no reason why he should forgo his pleasure.

Perhaps it was an unwise thing to do, to venture to Scotland, but by this time the young couple, more deeply in love with each other than ever, had got quite over their fears. Jessica was redolent with health and spirits, and more than once she declared that if they should be anywhere in the neighbourhood of Blackwick she would like to see the old castle out of curiosity, and just to show how absolutely she had got over the foolish terrors that used to assail her.

This seemed to Paul to be quite a wise plan, and so one day, since they were actually staying at no great distance, they motored over to Blackwick, and finding the bailiff, got him to show them over the castle.

It was a great castellated pile, grey with age, and in places falling into ruin. It stood on a steep hillside, with the rock of which it seemed to form part, and on one side of it there was a precipitous drop to a mountain stream a hundred feet below. The robber MacThanes of the old days could not have desired a better stronghold.

At the back, climbing up the mountainside were dark pinewoods, from which, here and there, rugged crags protruded, and these were fantastically shaped, some like gigantic and misshapen human forms, which stood up as if they mounted guard over the castle and the narrow gorge, by which alone it could be approached.

This gorge was always full of weird, uncanny sounds. It might have been a storehouse for the wind, which, even on calm days, rushed up and down as if seeking an escape, and it moaned among the pines and whistled in the crags and shouted derisive laughter as it was tossed from side to side of the rocky heights. It was like the plaint of lost souls—that is the expression Davenant made use of—the plaint of lost souls.

The road, little more than a track now, passed through this gorge, and then, after skirting a small but deep lake, which hardly knew the light of the sun so shut in was it by overhanging trees, climbed the hill to the castle.

And the castle! Davenant used but a few words to describe it, yet somehow I could see the gloomy edifice in my mind's eye, and something of the lurking horror that it contained communicated itself to my brain. Perhaps my clairvoyant sense assisted me, for when he spoke of them I seemed already acquainted with the great stone halls, the long corridors, gloomy and cold even on the brightest and warmest of days, the dark, oak-panelled rooms, and the broad central staircase up which one of the early MacThanes had once led a dozen men on horseback in pursuit of a stag which had taken refuge within the precincts of the castle. There was the keep, too, its walls so thick that the ravages of time had made no impression upon them, and beneath the keep were dungeons which could tell terrible tales of ancient wrong

32

and lingering pain.

Well, Mr and Mrs Davenant visited as much as the bailiff could show them of this ill-omened edifice, and Paul, for his part, thought pleasantly of his own Derbyshire home, the fine Georgian mansion, replete with every modern comfort, where he proposed to settle with his wife. And so he received something of a shock when, as they drove away, she slipped her hand into his and whispered:

'Paul, you promised, didn't you, that you would refuse me nothing?'

She had been strangely silent till she spoke those words. Paul, slightly apprehensive, assured her that she only had to ask—but the speech did not come from his heart, for he guessed vaguely what she desired.

She wanted to go and live at the castle—oh, only for a little while, for she was sure she would soon tire of it. But the bailiff had told her that there were papers, documents, which she ought to examine, since the property was now hers—and, besides, she was interested in this home of her ancestors, and wanted to explore it more thoroughly. Oh, no, she wasn't in the least influenced by the old superstition—that wasn't the attraction—she had quite got over those silly ideas. Paul had cured her, and since he himself was so convinced that they were without foundation he ought not to mind granting her her whim.

This was a plausible argument, not easy to controvert. In the end Paul yielded, though it was not without a struggle. He suggested amendments. Let him at least have the place done up for her—that would take time; or let them postpone their visit till next year—in the summer—not move in just as the winter was upon them.

But Jessica did not want to delay longer than she could help, and she hated the idea of redecoration. Why, it would spoil the illusion of the old place, and, besides, it would be a waste of money since she only wished to remain there for a week or two. The Derbyshire house was not quite ready yet; they must allow time for the paper to dry on the walls.

And so, a week later, when their stay with their friends was concluded, they went to Blackwick, the bailiff having engaged a few raw servants and generally made things as comfortable for them as possible. Paul was worried and apprehensive, but he could not admit this to his wife after having so loudly proclaimed his theories on the subject of superstition.

They had been married three months at this time—nine had

passed since then, and they had never left Blackwick for more than a few hours—till now Paul had come to London—alone.

'Over and over again,' he declared, 'my wife has begged me to go. With tears in her eyes, almost upon her knees, she has entreated me to leave her, but I have steadily refused unless she will accompany me. But that is the trouble, Mr Vance, she cannot; there is something, some mysterious horror, that holds her there as surely as if she were bound with fetters. It holds her more strongly even than it held her father— we found out that he used to spend six months at least of every year at Blackwick—months when he pretended that he was travelling abroad. You see the spell—or whatever the accursed thing may be—never really relaxed its grip of him.'

'Did you never attempt to take your wife away?' asked Vance.

'Yes, several times; but it was hopeless. She would become so ill as soon as we were beyond the limit of the estate that I invariably had to take her back. Once we got as far as Dorekirk—that is the nearest town, you know—and I thought I should be successful if only I could get through the night. But she escaped me; she climbed out of a window—she meant to go back on foot, at night, all those long miles. Then I have had doctors down; but it is I who wanted the doctors, not she. They have ordered me away, but I have refused to obey them till now.'

'Is your wife changed at all—physically?' interrupted Vance.

Davenant reflected. 'Changed,' he said, 'yes, but so subtly that I hardly know how to describe it. She is more beautiful than ever—and yet it isn't the same beauty, if you can understand me. I have spoken of her white complexion, well, one is more than ever conscious of it now, because her lips have become so red—they are almost like a splash of blood upon her face. And the upper one has a peculiar curve that I don't think it had before, and when she laughs she doesn't smile—

Do you know what I mean? Then her hair—it has lost its wonderful gloss. Of course, I know she is fretting about me; but that is so peculiar, too, for at times, as I have told you, she will implore me to go and leave her, and then perhaps only a few minutes later, she will wreathe her arms round my neck and say she cannot live without me. And I feel that there is a struggle going on within her, that she is only yielding slowly to the horrible influence—whatever it is—that she is herself when she begs me to go, but when she entreats me to stay—and it is then that her fascination is most intense—oh, I can't help remembering what she told me before we were married, and that

34

word'—he lowered his voice—'the word "vampire"—'

He passed his hand over his brow that was wet with perspiration. 'But that's absurd, ridiculous,' he muttered; 'these fantastic beliefs have been exploded years ago. We live in the twentieth century.'

A pause ensued, then Vance said quietly, 'Mr Davenant, since you have taken me into your confidence, since you have found doctors of no avail, will you let me try to help you? I think I may be of some use—if it is not already too late. Should you agree, Mr Dexter and I will accompany you, as you have suggested, to Blackwick Castle as early as possible—by tonight's mail North. Under ordinary circumstances I should tell you as you value your life, not to return—'. Davenant shook his head. 'That is advice which I should never take,' he declared. 'I had already decided, under any circumstances, to travel North tonight. I am glad that you both will accompany me.'

And so it was decided. We settled to meet at the station, and presently Paul Davenant took his departure. Any other details that remained to be told he would put us in possession of during the course of the journey.

'A curious and most interesting case,' remarked Vance when we were alone. 'What do you make of it, Dexter?'

'I suppose,' I replied cautiously, 'that there is such a thing as vampirism even in these days of advanced civilization? I can understand the evil influence that a very old person may have upon a young one if they happen to be in constant intercourse—the worn-out tissue sapping healthy vitality for their own support. And there are certain people—I could think of several myself—who seem to depress one and undermine one's energies, quite unconsciously, of course, but one feels somehow that vitality has passed from oneself to them. And in this case, when the force is centuries old, expressing itself, in some mysterious way, through Davenant's wife, is it not feasible to believe that he may be physically affected by it, even though the whole thing is sheerly mental?'

'You think, then,' demanded Vance, 'that it is sheerly mental? Tell me, if that is so, how do you account for the marks on Davenant's throat?'

This was a question to which I found no reply, and though I pressed him for his views, Vance would not commit himself further just then.

Of our long journey to Scotland I need say nothing. We did not reach Blackwick Castle till late in the afternoon of the following day. The place was just as I had conceived it—as I have already described it. And a sense of gloom settled upon me as our car jolted us over the rough road that led through the Gorge of the Winds—a gloom that deepened when we penetrated into the vast cold hall of the castle.

Mrs Davenant, who had been informed by telegram of our arrival, received us cordially. She knew nothing of our actual mission, regarding us merely as friends of her husband's. She was most solicitous on his behalf, but there was something strained about her tone, and it made me feel vaguely uneasy. The impression that I got was that the woman was impelled to everything that she said or did by some force outside herself—but, of course, this was a conclusion that the circumstances I was aware of might easily have conduced to. In every other aspect she was charming, and she had an extraordinary fascination of appearance and manner that made me readily understand the force of a remark made by Davenant during our journey.

'I want to live for Jessica's sake. Get her away from Blackwick, Vance, and I feel that all will be well. I'd go through hell to have her restored to me—as she was.'

And now that I had seen Mrs Davenant I realised what he meant by those last words. Her fascination was stronger than ever, but it was not a natural fascination—not that of a normal woman, such as she had been. It was the fascination of a Circe, of a witch, of an enchantress—and as such was irresistible.

We had a strong proof of the evil within her soon after our arrival. It was a test that Vance had quietly prepared. Davenant had mentioned that no flowers grew at Blackwick, and Vance declared that we must take some with us as a present for the lady of the house. He purchased a bouquet of pure white roses at the little town where we left the train, for the motorcar has been sent to meet us..Soon after our arrival he presented these to Mrs Davenant. She took them it seemed to me nervously, and hardly had her hand touched them before they fell to pieces, in a shower of crumpled petals, to the floor.

'We must act at once,' said Vance to me when we were descending to dinner that night. 'There must be no delay.'

'What are you afraid of?' I whispered.

'Davenant has been absent a week,' he replied grimly. 'He is stronger than when he went away, but not strong enough to survive the loss of more blood. He must be protected. There is danger tonight.'

'You mean from his wife?' I shuddered at the ghastliness of the suggestion.

'That is what time will show.' Vance turned to me and added a few words with intense earnestness. 'Mrs Davenant, Dexter, is at present hovering between two conditions. The evil thing has not yet completely mastered her—you remember what Davenant said, how she would beg him to go away and the next moment entreat him to stay? She has made a struggle, but she is gradually succumbing, and this last week, spent here alone, has strengthened the evil. And that is what I have got to fight, Dexter—it is to be a contest of will, a contest that will go on silently till one or the other obtains the mastery. If you watch, you may see. Should a change show itself in Mrs Davenant you will know that I have won.'

Thus I knew the direction in which my friend proposed to act. It was to be a war of his will against the mysterious power that had laid its curse upon the house of MacThane. Mrs Davenant must be released from the fatal charm that held her.

And I, knowing what was going on, was able to watch and understand. I realized that the silent contest had begun even while we ate dinner. Mrs Davenant ate practically nothing and seemed ill at ease; she fidgeted in her chair, talked a great deal, and laughed—it was the laugh without a smile, as Davenant had described it. And as soon as she was able to she withdrew.

Later, as we sat in the drawing-room, I could feel the clash of wills. The air in the room felt electric and heavy, charged with tremendous but invisible forces. And outside, round the castle, the wind whistled and shrieked and moaned—it was as if all the dead and gone MacThanes, a grim army, had collected to fight the battle of their race.

And all this while we four in the drawing-room were sitting and talking the ordinary commonplaces of after—dinner conversation! That was the extraordinary part of it—Paul Davenant suspected nothing, and I, who knew, had to play my part. But I hardly took my eyes from Jessica's face. When would the change come, or was it, indeed, too late!

At last Davenant rose and remarked that he was tired and would go to bed. There was no need for Jessica to hurry. We would sleep that night in his dressing-room and did not want to be disturbed.

And it was at that moment, as his lips met hers in a goodnight kiss, as she wreathed her enchantress arms about him, careless of our presence, her eyes gleaming hungrily, that the change came.

It came with a fierce and threatening shriek of wind, and a rattling of the casement, as if the horde of ghosts without was about to break in upon us. A long, quivering sigh escaped from Jessica's lips, her arms fell from her husband's shoulders, and she drew back, swaying a little from side to side.

'Paul,' she cried, and somehow the whole timbre of her voice was changed, 'what a wretch I've been to bring you back to Blackwick, ill as you are! But we'll go away, dear; yes, I'll go, too. Oh, will you take me away—take me away tomorrow?' She spoke with an intense earnestness—unconscious all the time of what had been happening to her. Long shudders were convulsing her frame. 'I don't know why I've wanted to stay here,' she kept repeating. 'I hate the place, really—it's evil—evil.'

Having heard these words I exulted, for surely Vance's success was assured. But I was to learn that the danger was not yet past.

Husband and wife separated, each going to their own room. I noticed the grateful, if mystified glance that Davenant threw at Vance, vaguely aware, as he must have been, that my friend was somehow responsible for what had happened. It was settled that plans for departure were to be discussed on the morrow.

'I have succeeded,' Vance said hurriedly, when we were alone, 'but the change may be a transitory. I must keep watch tonight. Go you to bed, Dexter, there is nothing that you can do.'

I obeyed—though I would sooner have kept watch, too—watch against a danger of which I had no understanding. I went to my room, a gloomy and sparsely furnished apartment, but I knew that it was quite impossible for me to think of sleeping. And so, dressed as I was, I went and sat by the open window, for now the wind that had raged round the castle had died down to a low moaning in the pinetrees—a whimpering of time-worn agony.

And it was as I sat thus that I became aware of a white figure that stole out from the castle by a door that I could not see, and, with hands clasped, ran swiftly across the terrace to the wood. I had but a momentary glance, but I felt convinced that the figure was that of Jessica Davenant.

And instinctively I knew that some great danger was imminent. It was, I think, the suggestion of despair conveyed by those clasped hands. At any rate, I did not hesitate. My window was some height from the ground, but the wall below was ivy-clad and afforded good foothold. The descent was quite easy. I achieved it, and was just in time to take up the pursuit in the right direction, which was into the thickness of the wood that clung to the slope of the hill.

I shall never forget that wild chase. There was just sufficient room to enable me to follow the rough path, which, luckily, since I had now lost sight of my quarry, was the only possible way that she could have taken; there were no intersecting tracks, and the wood was too thick on either side to permit of deviation.

And the wood seemed full of dreadful sounds—moaning and wailing and hideous laughter.

The wind, of course, and the screaming of night birds—once I felt the fluttering of wings in close proximity to my face. But I could not rid myself of the thought that I, in my turn, was being pursued, that the forces of hell were combined against me.

The path came to an abrupt end on the border of the sombre lake that I have already mentioned. And now I realized that I was indeed only just in time, for before me, plunging knee deep in the water, I recognized the white-clad figure of the woman I had been pursuing. Hearing my footsteps, she turned her head, and then threw up her arms and screamed. Her red hair fell in heavy masses about her shoulders, and her face, as I saw it in that moment, was hardly human for the agony of remorse that it depicted.

'Go!' she screamed. 'For God's sake let me die!'

But I was by her side almost as she spoke. She struggled with me—sought vainly to tear herself from my clasp—implored me, with panting breath, to let her drown.

'It's the only way to save him!' she gasped. 'Don't you understand that I am a thing accursed? For it is I—I—who have sapped his life blood! I know it now, the truth has been revealed to me tonight! I am a vampire, without hope in this world or the next, so for his sake—for the sake of his unborn child—let me die—let me die!'. Was ever so terrible an appeal made? Yet I—what could I do? Gently I overcame her resistance and drew her back to shore. By the time I reached it she was lying a dead weight upon my arm. I laid her down upon a mossy bank, and, kneeling by her side, gazed intently into her face.

And then I knew that I had done well. For the face I looked upon was not that of Jessica the vampire, as I had seen it that afternoon, it was the face of Jessica, the woman whom Paul Davenant had loved.

And later Aylmer Vance had his tale to tell.

'I waited', he said, 'until I knew that Davenant was asleep, and then I stole into his room to watch by his bedside. And presently she came, as I guessed she would, the vampire, the accursed thing that has preyed upon the souls of her kin, making them like to herself when they too have passed into Shadowland, and gathering sustenance for her horrid task from the blood of those who are alien to her race. Paul's body and Jessica's soul—it is for one and the other, Dexter, that we have fought.'

'You mean,' I hesitated, 'Zaida the witch?'

'Even so,' he agreed. 'Hers is the evil spirit that has fallen like a blight upon the house of MacThane. But now I think she may be exorcized for ever.'

'Tell me.'

'She came to Paul Davenant last night, as she must have done before, in the guise of his wife. You know that Jessica bears a strong resemblance to her ancestress. He opened his arms, but she was foiled of her prey, for I had taken my precautions; I had placed That upon Davenant's breast while he slept which robbed the vampire of her power of ill. She sped wailing from the room—a shadow—she who a minute before had looked at him with Jessica's eyes and spoken to him with Jessica's voice. Her red lips were Jessica's lips, and they were close to his when his eyes were opened and he saw her as she was—a hideous phantom of the corruption of the ages. And so the spell was removed, and she fled away to the place whence she had come—'

He paused. 'And now?' I inquired.

'Blackwick Castle must be razed to the ground,' he replied. 'That is the only way. Every stone of it, every brick, must be ground to powder and burnt with fire, for therein is the cause of all the evil. Davenant has consented.'

'And Mrs Davenant?'

'I think,' Vance answered cautiously, 'that all may be well with her. The curse will be removed with the destruction of the castle. She has not—thanks to you—perished under its influence. She was less guilty than she imagined—herself preyed upon rather than preying. But can't you understand her remorse when she realized, as she was bound to realise, the part she had played? And the knowledge of the child to come—its fatal inheritance—'

'I understand.' I muttered with a shudder. And then, under my breath, I whispered, 'Thank God!'

Carnacki, the Ghost Finder: The Gateway of the Monster

William Hope Hodgson

In response to Carnacki's usual card of invitation to have dinner and listen to a story, I arrived promptly at 427, Cheyne Walk, to find the three others who were always invited to these happy little times, there before me. Five minutes later, Carnacki, Arkright, Jessop, Taylor, and I were all engaged in the "pleasant occupation" of dining.

"You've not been long away, this time," I remarked, as I finished my soup; forgetting momentarily Carnacki's dislike of being asked even to skirt the borders of his story until such time as he was ready. Then he would not stint words.

"That's all," he replied, with brevity; and I changed the subject, remarking that I had been buying a new gun, to which piece of news he gave an intelligent nod, and a smile which I think showed a genuinely good-humoured appreciation of my intentional changing of the conversation.

Later, when dinner was finished, Carnacki snugged himself comfortably down in his big chair, along with his pipe, and began his story, with very little circumlocution:—

"As Dodgson was remarking just now, I've only been away a short time, and for a very good reason too—I've only been away a short distance. The exact locality I am afraid I must not tell you; but it is less than twenty miles from here; though, except for changing a name, that won't spoil the story. And it is a story too! One of the most extraordinary things ever I have run against.

"I received a letter a fortnight ago from a man I must call Anderson, asking for an appointment. I arranged a time, and when he came, I found that he wished me to investigate and see whether I could

41

not clear up a long-standing and well—too well—authenticated case of what he termed 'haunting.' He gave me very full particulars, and, finally, as the case seemed to present something unique, I decided to take it up.

"Two days later, I drove to the house late in the afternoon. I found it a very old place, standing quite alone in its own grounds. Anderson had left a letter with the butler, I found, pleading excuses for his absence, and leaving the whole house at my disposal for my investigations. The butler evidently knew the object of my visit, and I questioned him pretty thoroughly during dinner, which I had in rather lonely state. He is an old and privileged servant, and had the history of the Grey Room exact in detail. From him I learned more particulars regarding two things that Anderson had mentioned in but a casual manner. The first was that the door of the Grey Room would be heard in the dead of night to open, and slam heavily, and this even though the butler knew it was locked, and the key on the bunch in his pantry. The second was that the bedclothes would always be found torn off the bed, and hurled in a heap into a corner.

"But it was the door slamming that chiefly bothered the old butler. Many and many a time, he told me, had he lain awake and just got shivering with fright, listening; for sometimes the door would be slammed time after time—*thud! thud! thud!*—so that sleep was impossible.

"From Anderson, I knew already that the room had a history extending back over a hundred and fifty years. Three people had been strangled in it—an ancestor of his and his wife and child. This is authentic, as I had taken very great pains to discover; so that you can imagine it was with a feeling I had a striking case to investigate that I went upstairs after dinner to have a look at the Grey Room.

"Peter, the old butler, was in rather a state about my going, and assured me with much solemnity that in all the twenty years of his service, no one had ever entered that room after nightfall. He begged me, in quite a fatherly way, to wait till the morning, when there would be no danger, and then he could accompany me himself.

"Of course, I smiled a little at him, and told him not to bother. I explained that I should do no more than look 'round a bit, and, perhaps, affix a few seals. He need not fear; I was used to that sort of thing. But he shook his head when I said that.

"'There isn't many ghosts like ours, sir,' he assured me, with mournful pride. And, by Jove! he was right, as you will see.

"I took a couple of candles, and Peter followed with his bunch of keys. He unlocked the door; but would not come inside with me. He was evidently in a fright, and he renewed his request that I would put off my examination until daylight. Of course, I laughed at him again, and told him he could stand sentry at the door, and catch anything that came out.

"'It never comes outside, sir,' he said, in his funny, old, solemn manner. Somehow, he managed to make me feel as if I were going to have the 'creeps' right away. Anyway, it was one to him, you know.

"I left him there, and examined the room. It is a big apartment, and well furnished in the grand style, with a huge four-poster, which stands with its head to the end wall. There were two candles on the mantelpiece, and two on each of the three tables that were in the room. I lit the lot, and after that, the room felt a little less inhumanly dreary; though, mind you, it was quite fresh, and well kept in every way.

"After I had taken a good look 'round, I sealed lengths of baby ribbon across the windows, along the walls, over the pictures, and over the fireplace and the wall closets. All the time, as I worked, the butler stood just without the door, and I could not persuade him to enter; though I jested him a little, as I stretched the ribbons, and went here and there about my work. Every now and again, he would say:— 'You'll excuse me, I'm sure, sir; but I do wish you would come out, sir. I'm fair in a quake for you.'

"I told him he need not wait; but he was loyal enough in his way to what he considered his duty. He said he could not go away and leave me all alone there. He apologized; but made it very clear that I did not realise the danger of the room; and I could see, generally, that he was in a pretty frightened state. All the same, I had to make the room so that I should know if anything material entered it; so I asked him not to bother me, unless he really heard or saw something. He was beginning to get on my nerves, and the 'feel' of the room was bad enough, without making it any nastier.

"For a time further, I worked, stretching ribbons across the floor, and sealing them, so that the merest touch would have broken them, were anyone to venture into the room in the dark with the intention of playing the fool. All this had taken me far longer than I had anticipated; and, suddenly, I heard a clock strike eleven. I had taken off my coat soon after commencing work; now, however, as I had practically made an end of all that I intended to do, I walked across to the settee, and picked it up. I was in the act of getting into it, when the old butler's voice (he had not said a word for the last hour) came sharp and frightened:—'Come out, sir, quick! There's something going to happen!' Jove! but I jumped, and then, in the same moment, one of the candles on the table to the left went out. Now whether it was the wind, or what, I do not know; but, just for a moment, I was enough startled to make a run for the door; though I am glad to say that I pulled up, before I reached it. I simply could not bunk out, with the butler standing there, after having, as it were, read him a sort of lesson on 'bein' brave, y'know.' So I just turned right 'round, picked up the two candles off the mantelpiece, and walked across to the table near the bed. Well, I saw nothing. I blew out the candle that was still alight; then I went to those on the two tables, and blew them out. Then, outside of the door, the old man called again:—'Oh! sir, do be told! Do be told!'

"'All right, Peter,' I said, and by Jove, my voice was not as steady as I should have liked! I made for the door, and had a bit of work not to start running. I took some thundering long strides, as you can imagine. Near the door, I had a sudden feeling that there was a cold wind in the room. It was almost as if the window had been suddenly opened a little. I got to the door, and the old butler gave back a step, in a sort of instinctive way. 'Collar the candles, Peter!' I said, pretty sharply, and shoved them into his hands. I turned, and caught the handle, and slammed the door shut, with a crash. Somehow, do you know, as I did so, I thought I felt something pull back on it; but it must have been only fancy. I turned the key in the lock, and then again, double-locking the door. I felt easier then, and set-to and sealed the door. In addition, I put my card over the keyhole, and sealed it there; after which I pocketed the key, and went downstairs—with Peter; who was nervous and silent, leading the way. Poor old beggar! It had not struck me until that moment that he had been enduring a considerable strain during the last two or three hours.

"About midnight, I went to bed. My room lay at the end of the corridor upon which opens the door of the Grey Room. I counted the doors between it and mine, and found that five rooms lay between. And I am sure you can understand that I was not sorry. Then, just as I was beginning to undress, an idea came to me, and I took my candle and sealing wax, and sealed the doors of all five rooms. If any door slammed in the night, I should know just which one.

"I returned to my room, locked the door, and went to bed. I was waked suddenly from a deep sleep by a loud crash somewhere out in the passage. I sat up in bed, and listened, but heard nothing. Then I lit my candle. I was in the very act of lighting it when there came the bang of a door being violently slammed, along the corridor. I jumped out of bed, and got my revolver. I unlocked the door, and went out into the passage, holding my candle high, and keeping the pistol ready. Then a queer thing happened. I could not go a step toward the Grey Room. You all know I am not really a cowardly chap. I've gone into too many cases connected with ghostly things, to be accused of that; but I tell you I funked it; simply funked it, just like any blessed kid. There was something precious unholy in the air that night. I ran back into my bedroom, and shut and locked the door. Then I sat on the bed all night, and listened to the dismal thudding of a door up the corridor. The sound seemed to echo through all the house.

"Daylight came at last, and I washed and dressed. The door had not slammed for about an hour, and I was getting back my nerve again. I felt ashamed of myself; though, in some ways it was silly; for when you're meddling with that sort of thing, your nerve is bound to go, sometimes. And you just have to sit quiet and call yourself a coward until daylight. Sometimes it is more than just cowardice, I fancy. I believe at times it is something warning you, and fighting *for* you. But, all the same, I always feel mean and miserable, after a time like that.

"When the day came properly, I opened my door, and, keeping my revolver handy, went quietly along the passage. I had to pass the head of the stairs, along the way, and who should I see coming up, but the old butler, carrying a cup of coffee. He had merely tucked his nightshirt into his trousers, and he had an old pair of carpet slippers on.

"'Hullo, Peter!' I said, feeling suddenly cheerful; for I was as glad as any lost child to have a live human being close to me. 'Where are you off to with the refreshments?'

"The old man gave a start, and slopped some of the coffee. He stared up at me, and I could see that he looked white and done-up. He came on up the stairs, and held out the little tray to me. 'I'm very thankful indeed, sir, to see you safe and well,' he said. 'I feared, one time, you might risk going into the Grey Room, sir. I've lain awake all night, with the sound of the door. And when it came light, I thought I'd make you a cup of coffee. I knew you would want to look at the seals, and somehow it seems safer if there's two, sir.'

"'Peter,' I said, 'you're a brick. This is very thoughtful of you.' And I drank the coffee. 'Come along,' I told him, and handed him back the tray. 'I'm going to have a look at what the brutes have been up to. I simply hadn't the pluck to in the night.'

"'I'm very thankful, sir,' he replied. 'Flesh and blood can do nothing, sir, against devils; and that's what's in the Grey Room after dark.'

"I examined the seals on all the doors, as I went along, and found them right; but when I got to the Grey Room, the seal was broken; though the card, over the keyhole, was untouched. I ripped it off, and unlocked the door, and went in, rather cautiously, as you can imagine; but the whole room was empty of anything to frighten one, and there was heaps of light. I examined all my seals, and not a single one was disturbed. The old butler had followed me in, and, suddenly, he called out:—'The bedclothes, sir!'

"I ran up to the bed, and looked over; and, surely, they were lying in the corner to the left of the bed. Jove! you can imagine how queer I felt. Something *had* been in the room. I stared for a while, from the bed, to the clothes on the floor. I had a feeling that I did not want to touch either. Old Peter, though, did not seem to be affected that way. He went over to the bed coverings, and was going to pick them up, as, doubtless, he had done every day these twenty years back; but I stopped him. I wanted nothing touched, until I had finished my examination. This, I must have spent a full hour over, and then I let Peter straighten up the bed; after which we went out, and I locked the door; for the room was getting on my nerves.

"I had a short walk, and then breakfast; after which I felt more my own man, and so returned to the Grey Room, and, with Peter's help, and one of the maids, I had everything taken out of the room, except the bed—even the very pictures. I examined the walls, floor and ceiling then, with probe, hammer and magnifying glass; but found nothing suspicious. And I can assure you, I began to realise, in very truth, that some incredible thing had been loose in the room during the past night. I sealed up everything again, and went out, locking and sealing the door, as before.

"After dinner, Peter and I unpacked some of my stuff, and I fixed up my camera and flashlight opposite to the door of the Grey Room, with a string from the trigger of the flashlight to the door. Then, you see, if the door were really opened, the flashlight would blare out, and there would be, possibly, a very queer picture to examine in the morning. The last thing I did, before leaving, was to uncap the lens; and after that I went off to my bedroom, and to bed; for I intended to be up at midnight; and to ensure this, I set my little alarm to call me; also I left my candle burning.

"The clock woke me at twelve, and I got up and into my dressing gown and slippers. I shoved my revolver into my right side-pocket, and opened my door. Then, I lit my darkroom lamp, and withdrew the slide, so that it would give a clear light. I carried it up the corridor, about thirty feet, and put it down on the floor, with the open side away from me, so that it would show me anything that might approach along the dark passage. Then I went back, and sat in the doorway of my room, with my revolver handy, staring up the passage toward the place where I knew my camera stood outside the door of the Grey Room.

"I should think I had watched for about an hour and a half, when, suddenly, I heard a faint noise, away up the corridor. I was immediately conscious of a queer prickling sensation about the back of my head, and my hands began to sweat a little. The following instant, the whole end of the passage flicked into sight in the abrupt glare of the flash-light. There came the succeeding darkness, and I peered nervously up the corridor, listening tensely, and trying to find what lay beyond the faint glow of my dark-lamp, which now seemed ridiculously dim by contrast with the tremendous blaze of the flash-power. . . . And then, as I stooped forward, staring and listening, there came the crashing thud of the door of the Grey Room. The sound seemed to fill the whole of the large corridor, and go echoing hollowly through the house. I tell you, I felt horrible—as if my bones were water. Simply beastly. Jove! how I did stare, and how I listened.

"And then it came again—*thud, thud, thud,* and then a silence that was almost worse than the noise of the door; for I kept fancying that some awful thing was stealing upon me along the corridor. And then, suddenly, my lamp was put out, and I could not see a yard before me. I realised all at once that I was doing a very silly thing, sitting there, and I jumped up. Even as I did so, I *thought* I heard a sound in the passage, and quite *near* me. I made one backward spring into my room, and slammed and locked the door. I sat on my bed, and stared at the door. I had my revolver in my hand; but it seemed an abominably useless thing. I felt that there was something the other side of that door. For some unknown reason I *knew* it was pressed up against the door, and it was soft. That was just what I thought. Most extraordinary thing to think.

"Presently I got hold of myself a bit, and marked out a pentacle hurriedly with chalk on the polished floor; and there I sat in it almost until dawn. And all the time, away up the corridor, the door of the Grey Room thudded at solemn and horrid intervals. It was a miserable, brutal night.

"When the day began to break, the thudding of the door came gradually to an end, and, at last, I got hold of my courage, and went along the corridor in the half light to cap the lens of my camera. I can tell you, it took some doing; but if I had not done so my photograph would have been spoilt, and I was tremendously keen to save it. I got back to my room, and then set-to and rubbed out the five-pointed star in which I had been sitting.

"Half an hour later there was a tap at my door. It was Peter with my coffee. When I had drunk it, we both went along to the Grey Room. As we went, I had a look at the seals on the other doors; but they were untouched. The seal on the door of the Grey Room was broken, as also was the string from the trigger of the flashlight; but the card over the keyhole was still there. I ripped it off, and opened the door. Nothing unusual was to be seen until we came to the bed; then I saw that, as on the previous day, the bedclothes had been torn off, and hurled into the left-hand corner, exactly where I had seen them before. I felt very queer; but I did not forget to look at all the seals, only to find that not one had been broken.

"Then I turned and looked at old Peter, and he looked at me, nodding his head.

"'Let's get out of here!' I said. 'It's no place for any living human to enter, without proper protection.'

"We went out then, and I locked and sealed the door, again.

"After breakfast, I developed the negative; but it showed only the door of the Grey Room, half opened. Then I left the house, as I wanted to get certain matters and implements that might be necessary to life; perhaps to the spirit; for I intended to spend the coming night in the Grey Room.

"I go back in a cab, about half-past five, with my apparatus, and this, Peter and I carried up to the Grey Room, where I piled it carefully in the centre of the floor. When everything was in the room, including a cat which I had brought, I locked and sealed the door, and went toward the bedroom, telling Peter I should not be down for dinner. He said, 'Yes, sir,' and went downstairs, thinking that I was going to turn in, which was what I wanted him to believe, as I knew he would have worried both me and himself, if he had known what I intended.

"But I merely got my camera and flashlight from my bedroom, and hurried back to the Grey Room. I locked and sealed myself in, and set to work, for I had a lot to do before it got dark.

"First, I cleared away all the ribbons across the floor; then I carried the cat—still fastened in its basket—over toward the far wall, and left it. I returned then to the centre of the room, and measured out a space twenty-one feet in diameter, which I swept with a 'broom of hyssop.' About this, I drew a circle of chalk, taking care never to step over the circle. Beyond this I smudged, with a bunch of garlic, a broad belt right around the chalked circle, and when this was complete, I took from among my stores in the centre a small jar of a certain water. I broke away the parchment, and withdrew the stopper. Then, dipping my left forefinger in the little jar, I went 'round the circle again, making upon the floor, just within the line of chalk, the Second Sign of the *Saaamaaa* Ritual, and joining each sign most carefully with the left-handed crescent.

"I can tell you, I felt easier when this was done, and the 'water circle' complete. Then, I unpacked some more of the stuff that I had brought, and placed a lighted candle in the 'valley' of each Crescent. After that, I drew a Pentacle, so that each of the five points of the defensive star touched the chalk circle. In the five points of the star I placed five portions of the bread, each wrapped in linen, and in the five 'vales,' five opened jars of the water I had used to make the 'water circle.' And now I had my first protective barrier complete.

"Now, anyone, except you who know something of my methods of investigation, might consider all this a piece of useless and foolish superstition; but you all remember the Black Veil case, in which I believe my life was saved by a very similar form of protection, whilst Aster, who sneered at it, and would not come inside, died. I got the idea from the Sigsand MS., written, so far as I can make out, in the 14th century. At first, naturally, I imagined it was just an expression of the superstition of his time; and it was not until a year later that it occurred to me to test his 'Defence,' which I did, as I've just said, in that horrible Black Veil business. You know how *that* turned out. Later, I used it several times, and always I came through safe, until that Moving Fur case. It was only a partial 'Defence' therefore, and I nearly died in the pentacle. After that I came across Professor Garder's *Experiments with a Medium.*

"When they surrounded the medium with a current, in vacuum, he lost his power—almost as if it cut him off from the Immaterial. That made me think a lot; and that is how I came to make the Electric Pen-

tacle, which is a most marvellous 'Defence' against certain manifestations. I used the shape of the defensive star for this protection, because
I have, personally, no doubt at all but that there is some extraordinary
virtue in the old magic figure. Curious thing for a Twentieth Century
man to admit, is it not? But, then, as you all know, I never did, and
never will, allow myself to be blinded by the little cheap laughter. I ask
questions, and keep my eyes open.

"In this last case I had little doubt that I had run up against a supernatural monster, and I meant to take every possible care; for the
danger is abominable.

"I turned-to now to fit the Electric Pentacle, setting it so that each
of its 'points' and 'vales' coincided exactly with the 'points' and 'vales'
of the drawn pentagram upon the floor. Then I connected up the
battery, and the next instant the pale blue glare from the intertwining
vacuum tubes shone out.

"I glanced about me then, with something of a sigh of relief, and
realised suddenly that the dusk was upon me, for the window was grey
and unfriendly. Then 'round at the big, empty room, over the double
barrier of electric and candle light. I had an abrupt, extraordinary
sense of weirdness thrust upon me—in the air, you know; as it were,
a sense of something inhuman impending. The room was full of the
stench of bruised garlic, a smell I hate.

"I turned now to the camera, and saw that it and the flashlight
were in order. Then I tested my revolver, carefully, though I had little
thought that it would be needed. Yet, to what extent materialization
of an ab-natural creature is possible, given favourable conditions, no
one can say; and I had no idea what horrible thing I was going to see,
or feel the presence of. I might, in the end, have to fight with a mate-
rialized monster. I did not know, and could only be prepared. You see,
I never forgot that three other people had been strangled in the bed
close to me, and the fierce slamming of the door I had heard myself. I
had no doubt that I was investigating a dangerous and ugly case.

"By this time, the night had come; though the room was very light
with the burning candles; and I found myself glancing behind me,
constantly, and then all 'round the room. It was nervy work waiting for
that thing to come. Then, suddenly, I was aware of a little, cold wind
sweeping over me, coming from behind. I gave one great nerve-thrill,
and a prickly feeling went all over the back of my head. Then I hove
myself 'round with a sort of stiff jerk, and stared straight against that
queer wind. It seemed to come from the corner of the room to the

left of the bed—the place where both times I had found the heap of tossed bedclothes. Yet, I could see nothing unusual; no opening—nothing! . . .

"Abruptly, I was aware that the candles were all a-flicker in that unnatural wind. . . . I believe I just squatted there and stared in a horribly frightened, wooden way for some minutes. I shall never be able to let you know how disgustingly horrible it was sitting in that vile, cold wind! And then, *flick! flick! flick!* all the candles 'round the outer barrier went out; and there was I, locked and sealed in that room, and with no light beyond the weakish blue glare of the Electric Pentacle.

"A time of abominable tenseness passed, and still that wind blew upon me; and then, suddenly, I knew that something stirred in the corner to the left of the bed. I was made conscious of it, rather by some inward, unused sense than by either sight or sound; for the pale, short-radius glare of the Pentacle gave but a very poor light for seeing by. Yet, as I stared, something began slowly to grow upon my sight—a moving shadow, a little darker than the surrounding shadows.

"I lost the thing amid the vagueness, and for a moment or two I glanced swiftly from side to side, with a fresh, new sense of impending danger. Then my attention was directed to the bed. All the covering's were being drawn steadily off, with a hateful, stealthy sort of motion. I heard the slow, dragging slither of the clothes; but I could see nothing of the thing that pulled. I was aware in a funny, subconscious, introspective fashion that the 'creep' had come upon me; yet that I was cooler mentally than I had been for some minutes; sufficiently so to feel that my hands were sweating coldly, and to shift my revolver, half-consciously, whilst I rubbed my right hand dry upon my knee; though never, for an instant, taking my gaze or my attention from those moving clothes.

"The faint noises from the bed ceased once, and there was a most intense silence, with only the sound of the blood beating in my head. Yet, immediately afterward, I heard again the slurring of the bedclothes being dragged off the bed. In the midst of my nervous tension I remembered the camera, and reached 'round for it; but without looking away from the bed. And then, you know, all in a moment, the whole of the bed coverings were torn off with extraordinary violence, and I heard the flump they made as they were hurled into the corner.

"There was a time of absolute quietness then for perhaps a couple of minutes; and you can imagine how horrible I felt. The bedclothes had been thrown with such savageness! And, then again, the brutal unnaturalness of the thing that had just been done before me!

"Abruptly, over by the door, I heard a faint noise—a sort of crickling sound, and then a pitter or two upon the floor. A great nervous thrill swept over me, seeming to run up my spine and over the back of my head; for the seal that secured the door had just been broken. Something was there. I could not see the door; at least, I mean to say that it was impossible to say how much I actually saw, and how much my imagination supplied. I made it out, only as a continuation of the grey walls. . . . And then it seemed to me that something dark and indistinct moved and wavered there among the shadows.

"Abruptly, I was aware that the door was opening, and with an effort I reached again for my camera; but before I could aim it the door was slammed with a terrific crash that filled the whole room with a sort of hollow thunder. I jumped, like a frightened child. There seemed such a power behind the noise; as though a vast, wanton Force were 'out.' Can you understand?

"The door was not touched again; but, directly afterward, I heard the basket, in which the cat lay, creak. I tell you, I fairly pringled all along my back. I knew that I was going to learn definitely whether whatever was abroad was dangerous to life. From the cat there rose suddenly a hideous caterwaul, that ceased abruptly; and then—too late—I snapped off the flashlight. In the great glare, I saw that the basket had been overturned, and the lid was wrenched open, with the cat lying half in, and half out upon the floor. I saw nothing else, but I was full of the knowledge that I was in the presence of some being or thing that had power to destroy.

"During the next two or three minutes, there was an odd, noticeable quietness in the room, and you much remember I was half-blinded, for the time, because of the flashlight; so that the whole place seemed to be pitchy dark just beyond the shine of the Pentacle. I tell you it was most horrible. I just knelt there in the star, and whirled 'round, trying to see whether anything was coming at me.

"My power of sight came gradually, and I got a little hold of myself; and abruptly I saw the thing I was looking for, close to the 'water circle.' It was big and indistinct, and wavered curiously, as though the shadow of a vast spider hung suspended in the air, just beyond the barrier. It passed swiftly 'round the circle, and seemed to probe ever toward me; but only to draw back with extraordinary jerky movements, as might a living person if they touched the hot bar of a grate.

"'Round and 'round it moved, and 'round and 'round I turned.

Then, just opposite to one of the Vales' in the pentacles, it seemed to pause, as though preliminary to a tremendous effort. It retired almost beyond the glow of the vacuum light, and then came straight toward me, appearing to gather form and solidity as it came. There seemed a vast, malign determination behind the movement, that must succeed. I was on my knees, and I jerked back, falling on to my left hand, and hip, in a wild endeavour to get back from the advancing thing. With my right hand I was grabbing madly for my revolver, which I had let slip. The brutal thing came with one great sweep straight over the garlic and the 'water circle,' almost to the vale of the pentacle. I believe I yelled. Then, just as suddenly as it had swept over, it seemed to be hurled back by some mighty, invisible force.

"It must have been some moments before I realised that I was safe; and then I got myself together in the middle of the pentacles, feeling horribly gone and shaken, and glancing 'round and 'round the barrier; but the thing had vanished. Yet, I had learnt something, for I knew now that the Grey Room was haunted by a monstrous hand.

"Suddenly, as I crouched there, I saw what had so nearly given the monster an opening through the barrier. In my movements within the pentacle I must have touched one of the jars of water; for just where the thing had made its attack the jar that guarded the 'deep' of the 'vale' had been moved to one side, and this had left one of the 'five doorways' unguarded. I put it back, quickly, and felt almost safe again, for I had found the cause, and the 'Defence' was still good. And I began to hope again that I should see the morning come in. When I saw that thing so nearly succeed, I had an awful, weak, overwhelming feeling that the 'barriers' could never bring me safe through the night against such a Force. You can understand?

"For a long time I could not see the hand; but, presently, I thought I saw, once or twice, an odd wavering, over among the shadows near the door. A little later, as though in a sudden fit of malignant rage, the dead body of the cat was picked up, and beaten with dull, sickening blows against the solid floor. That made me feel rather queer.

"A minute afterward, the door was opened and slammed twice with tremendous force. The next instant the thing made one swift, vicious dart at me, from out of the shadows. Instinctively, I started sideways from it, and so plucked my hand from upon the Electric Pentacle, where—for a wickedly careless moment—I had placed it. The monster was hurled off from the neighbourhood of the pen-tacles; though—owing to my inconceivable foolishness—it had been enabled for a second time to pass the outer barriers. I can tell you, I shook for a time, with sheer funk. I moved right to the centre of the pentacles again, and knelt there, making myself as small and compact as possible.

"As I knelt, there came to me presently, a vague wonder at the two 'accidents' which had so nearly allowed the brute to get at me. Was I being *influenced* to unconscious voluntary actions that endangered me? The thought took hold of me, and I watched my every movement. Abruptly, I stretched a tired leg, and knocked over one of the jars of water. Some was spilled; but, because of my suspicious watchfulness, I had it upright and back within the vale while yet some of the water remained. Even as I did so, the vast, black, half-materialized hand beat up at me out of the shadows, and seemed to leap almost into my face; so nearly did it approach; but for the third time it was thrown back by some altogether enormous, overmastering force. Yet, apart from the dazed fright in which it left me, I had for a moment that feeling of spiritual sickness, as if some delicate, beautiful, inward grace had suffered, which is felt only upon the too near approach of the ab-human, and is more dreadful, in a strange way, than any physical pain that can be suffered. I knew by this more of the extent and closeness of the danger; and for a long time I was simply cowed by the butt-headed brutality of that Force upon my spirit. I can put it no other way.

"I knelt again in the centre of the pentacles, watching myself with more fear, almost, than the monster; for I knew now that, unless I guarded myself from every sudden impulse that came to me, I might simply work my own destruction. Do you see how horrible it all was?

"I spent the rest of the night in a haze of sick fright, and so tense that I could not make a single movement naturally. I was in such fear that any desire for action that came to me might be prompted by the Influence that I knew was at work on me. And outside of the barrier that ghastly thing went 'round and 'round, grabbing and grabbing in the air at me. Twice more was the body of the dead cat molested. The second time, I heard every bone in its body scrunch and crack. And all the time the horrible wind was blowing upon me from the corner of the room to the left of the bed.

"Then, just as the first touch of dawn came into the sky, that unnatural wind ceased, in a single moment; and I could see no sign of the hand. The dawn came slowly, and presently the wan light filled all the room, and made the pale glare of the Electric Pentacle look more unearthly. Yet, it was not until the day had fully come, that I made any attempt to leave the barrier, for I did not know but that there was some method abroad, in the sudden stopping of that wind, to entice me from the pentacles.

"At last, when the dawn was strong and bright, I took one last look 'round, and ran for the door. I got it unlocked, in a nervous and clumsy fashion, then locked it hurriedly, and went to my bedroom, where I lay on the bed, and tried to steady my nerves. Peter came, presently, with the coffee, and when I had drunk it, I told him I meant to have a sleep, as I had been up all night. He took the tray, and went out quietly, and after I had locked my door I turned in properly, and at last got to sleep.

"I woke about midday, and after some lunch, went up to the Grey Room. I switched off the current from the Pentacle, which I had left on in my hurry; also, I removed the body of the cat. You can under-stand I did not want anyone to see the poor brute. After that, I made a very careful search of the corner where the bedclothes had been thrown. I made several holes, and probed, and found nothing. Then it occurred to me to try with my instrument under the skirting. I did so, and heard my wire ring on metal. I turned the hook end that way, and fished for the thing. At the second go, I got it. It was a small object, and I took it to the window. I found it to be a curious ring, made of some greying material. The curious thing about it was that it was made in the form of a pentagon; that is, the same shape as the inside of the magic pentacle, but without the 'mounts,' which form the points of the defensive star. It was free from all chasing or engraving.

"You will understand that I was excited, when I tell you that I felt sure I held in my hand the famous Luck Ring of the Anderson family; which, indeed, was of all things the one most intimately connected with the history of the haunting. This ring was handed on from fa-ther to son through generations, and always—in obedience to some ancient family tradition—each son had to promise never to wear the ring. The ring, I may say, was brought home by one of the Crusaders, under very peculiar circumstances; but the story is too long to go into here.

"It appears that young Sir Hulbert, an ancestor of Anderson's, made a bet, in drink, you know, that he would wear the ring that night. He did so, and in the morning his wife and child were found strangled in the bed, in the very room in which I stood. Many people, it would seem, thought young Sir Hulbert was guilty of having done the thing in drunken anger; and he, in an attempt to prove his innocence, slept a second night in the room. He also was strangled. Since then, as you may imagine, no one has ever spent a night in the Grey Room, until I did so. The ring had been lost so long, that it had become almost a myth; and it was most extraordinary to stand there, with the actual thing in my hand, as you can understand.

"It was whilst I stood there, looking at the ring, that I got an idea. Supposing that it were, in a way, a doorway—You see what I mean? A sort of gap in the world-hedge. It was a queer idea, I know, and probably was not my own, but came to me from the Outside. You see, the wind had come from that part of the room where the ring lay. I thought a lot about it. Then the shape—the inside of a pentacle. It had no 'mounts,' and without mounts, as the Sigsand MS. has it:—

Thee mounts wych are thee Five Hills of safetie.
To lack is to gyve pow'r to thee daemon; and surelie to fayvor the Evill Thynge.

"You see, the very shape of the ring was significant; and I determined to test it.

"I unmade the pentacle, for it must be made afresh *and around* the one to be protected. Then I went out and locked the door; after which I left the house, to get certain matters, for neither '*yarbs nor fyre nor waier*' must be used a second time. I returned about seven thirty, and as soon as the things I had brought had been carried up to the Grey Room, I dismissed Peter for the night, just as I had done the evening before. When he had gone downstairs, I let myself into the room, and locked and sealed the door. I went to the place in the centre of the room where all the stuff had been packed, and set to work with all my speed to construct a barrier about me and the ring.

"I do not remember whether I explained it to you. But I had reasoned that, if the ring were in any way a 'medium of admission,' and it were enclosed with me in the electric pentacle, it would be, to express it loosely, insulated. Do you see? The Force, which had visible expression as a hand, would have to stay beyond the barrier which separates the ab from the normal; for the 'gateway' would be removed from accessibility.

"As I was saying, I worked with all my speed to get the barrier completed about me and the ring, for it was already later than I cared to be in that room 'unprotected.' Also, I had a feeling that there would be a vast effort made that night to regain the use of the ring. For I had the strongest conviction that the ring was a necessity to materialization. You will see whether I was right.

"I completed the barriers in about an hour, and you can imagine something of the relief I felt when I felt the pale glare of the electric pentacle once more all about me. From then, onward, for about two hours, I sat quietly, facing the corner from which the wind came. About eleven o'clock a queer knowledge came that something was near to me; yet nothing happened for a whole hour after that. Then, suddenly, I felt the cold, queer wind begin to blow upon me. To my astonishment, it seemed now to come from behind me, and I whipped 'round, with a hideous quake of fear. The wind met me in the face. It was blowing up from the floor close to me. I stared down, in a sickening maze of new frights. What on earth had I done now! The ring was there, close beside me, where I had put it.

"Suddenly, as I stared, bewildered, I was aware that there was something queer about the ring—funny shadowy movements and convolutions. I looked at them, stupidly. And then, abruptly, I knew that the wind was blowing up at me from the ring. A queer indistinct smoke became visible to me, seeming to pour upward through the ring, and mix with the moving shadows. Suddenly, I realised that I was in more than any mortal danger; for the convoluting shadows about the ring were taking shape, and the death-hand was forming *within* the Pentacle. My Goodness! do you realise it! I had brought the 'gateway' into the pentacles, and the brute was coming through—pouring into the material world, as gas might pour out from the mouth of a pipe.

"I should think that I knelt for a moment in a sort of stunned fright. Then, with a mad, awkward movement, I snatched at the ring, intending to hurl it out of the Pentacle. Yet it eluded me, as though some invisible, living thing jerked it hither and thither. At last, I gripped it; yet, in the same instant, it was torn from my grasp with incredible and brutal force. A great, black shadow covered it, and rose into the air, and came at me. I saw that it was the Hand, vast and nearly perfect in form. I gave one crazy yell, and jumped over the pentacle and the ring of burning candles, and ran despairingly for the door. I fumbled idiotically and ineffectually with the key, and all the time I stared, with a fear that was like insanity, toward the barriers. The hand was plunging toward me; yet, even as it had been unable to pass into the pentacle when the ring was without, so, now that the ring was within, it had no power to pass out. The monster was chained, as surely as any beast would be, were chains riveted upon it.

"Even then, I got a flash of this knowledge; but I was too utterly shaken with fright, to reason; and the instant I managed to get the key turned, I sprang into the passage, and slammed the door with a crash. I locked it, and got to my room somehow; for I was trembling so that I could hardly stand, as you can imagine. I locked myself in, and managed to get the candle lit; then I lay down on my bed, and kept quiet for an hour or two, and so I got steadied.

"I got a little sleep, later; but woke when Peter brought my coffee. When I had drunk it I felt altogether better, and took the old man along with me whilst I had a look into the Grey Room. I opened the door, and peeped in. The candles were still burning, wan against the daylight; and behind them was the pale, glowing star of the electric pentacle. And there, in the middle, was the ring . . . the gateway of the monster, lying demure and ordinary.

"Nothing in the room was touched, and I knew that the brute had never managed to cross the pentacles. Then I went out, and locked the door.

"After a sleep of some hours, I left the house. I returned in the afternoon in a cab. I had with me an oxy-hydrogen jet, and two cylinders, containing the gases. I carried the things into the Grey Room, and there, in the centre of the electric pentacle, I erected the little furnace. Five minutes later the Luck Ring, once the 'luck,' but now the 'bane,' of the Anderson family, was no more than a little solid splash of hot metal."

Carnacki felt in his pocket, and pulled out something wrapped in tissue paper. He passed it to me. I opened it, and found a small circle of greyish metal, something like lead, only harder and rather brighter.

"Well?" I asked, at length, after examining it and handing it 'round to the others. "Did that stop the haunting?"

Carnacki nodded. "Yes," he said. "I slept three nights in the Grey Room, before I left. Old Peter nearly fainted when he knew that I meant to; but by the third night he seemed to realise that the house was just safe and ordinary. And, you know, I believe, in his heart, he hardly approved."

Carnacki stood up and began to shake hands. "Out you go!" he said, genially. And presently we went, pondering, to our various homes.

Flaxman Low:
The Story of Baelbrow

E. and H. Heron

(pseud. for Katherine and Hesketh Prichard)

It is a matter for regret that so many of Mr. Flaxman Low's remi-
niscences should deal with the darker episodes of his career. Yet this
is almost unavoidable, as the more purely scientific and less strongly
marked cases would not, perhaps, contain the same elements of interest for the general public however valuable and instructive they might
be to the expert student. It has also been considered better to choose
the completer cases, those that ended in something like satisfactory
proof, rather than the many instances where the thread broke abruptly
amongst surmisings, which it was never possible to subject to con-
vincing tests.

North of a low-lying strip of promontory of Bael Ness thrusts
a blunt nose into the sea. On the ness, backed by pinewoods, stands
a square, comfortable stone mansion, known to the countryside as
Baelbrow. It has face the east winds for close upon three hundred
years, and during the whole period has been the home of the Swaffam
family, who were never in any wise put out of conceit of their ancestral dwelling by the fact that it had always been haunted. Indeed, the
Swaffams were proud of the Baelbrow Ghost, which enjoyed a wide
notoriety, and no one dreamt of complaining of its behaviour until
Professor Jungvort, of Nuremburg, laid information against it, and sent
an urgent appeal for help to Mr. Flaxman Low.

The professor, who was well acquainted with Mr. Low, detailed the
circumstances of his tenancy of Baelbrow, and the unpleasant events
that had followed thereupon.

It appeared that Mr. Swaffam, senior, who spent a large portion of his time abroad, had offered to lend his house to the professor for the summer season. When the Jungvorts arrived at Baelbrow, they were charmed with the place. The prospect, though not very varied, was at least extensive, and the air exhilarating. Also the Professor's daughter enjoyed frequent visits from her betrothed—Harold Swaffam—and the Professor was delightfully employed in overhauling the Swaffam library.

The Jungvorts had been duly told of the ghost, which lent distinction to the old house, but never in any way interfered with the comfort of the inmates. For some time they found this description to be strictly true, but with the beginning of October came a change. Up to this time and as far back as the Swaffam annals reached, the ghost had been a shadow, a rustle, a passing sigh—nothing definite or troublesome. But early in October strange things began to occur, and the terror culminated when a housemaid was found dead in a corridor three weeks later. Upon this the professor felt that it was time to send for Flaxman Low.

Mr. Low arrived upon a chilly evening when the house was already beginning to blur in the purple twilight, and the resinous scent of the pines came sweetly on the land breeze. Jungvort welcomed him in the spacious, firelit hall. He was a stout German with a quantity of white hair, round eyes emphasized by spectacles, and a kindly, dreamy face. His life-study was philology, and his two relaxations: chess and the smoking of a big Bismarck-bowled *meerschaum*.

"Now, Professor," said Mr. Low when they had settled themselves in the smoking room, "how did it all begin?"

"I will tell you," replied Jungvort, thrusting out his chin, and tapping his broad chest, and speaking as if an unwarrantable liberty had been taken with him. "First of all, it has shown itself to me!"

Mr. Flaxman Low smiled and assured him that nothing could be more satisfactory.

"But not at all satisfactory!" exclaimed the professor, "I was sitting here alone, it might have been midnight—when I hear something come creeping like a little dog with its nails, tick-tick, upon the oak flooring of the hall. I whistle, for I think it is the little 'Rags' of my daughter, and afterwards opened the door, and I saw"—he hesitated and looked hard at Low through his spectacles, "something that was just disappearing into the passage which connects the two wings of the house. It was a figure, not unlike the human figure, but narrow and straight. I fancied I saw a bunch of black hair, and a flutter of something detached, which may have been a handkerchief. I was overcome by a feeling of repulsion. I heard a few, clicking steps, then it stopped, as I thought, at the museum door. Come, I will show you the spot."

The professor conducted Mr. Low into the hall. The main staircase, dark and massive, yawned above them, and directly behind it ran the passage referred to by the professor. It was over twenty feet long, and about midway led past a deep arch containing a door reached by two steps. Jungvort explained that this door formed the entrance to a large room called the museum, in which Mr. Swaffam senior, who was something of a dilettante, stored the various curios he picked up during his excursions abroad. The professor went on to say that he immediately followed the figure, which he believed had gone into the museum, but he found nothing there except the cases containing Swaffam's treasures.

"I mentioned my experience to no one. I concluded that I had seen the ghost. But two days after, one of the female servants coming through the passage in the dark, declared that a man leapt out at her from the embrasure of the museum door, but she released herself and ran screaming into the servants' hall. We at once made a search but found nothing to substantiate her story.

"I took no notice of this, though it coincided pretty well my own experience. The week after, my daughter Lena came down late one night for a book. As she was about to cross the hall, something leapt upon her from behind. Women are of little use in serious investigations—she fainted! Since then she has been ill and the doctor says 'Run down.'" Here the professor spread out his hands. "So she leaves for a change tomorrow. Since then other members of the household have been attacked in much the same manner, with always the same result, they faint and are weak and useless when they recover.

"But, last Wednesday, the affair became a tragedy. By that time the servants had refused to come through the passage except in a crowd of three or four,—most of them preferring to go round by the terrace to reach this part of the house. But one maid, named Eliza Freeman, said she was not afraid of the Baelbrow Ghost, and undertook to put out the lights in the hall one night. When she had done, and was returning through the passage past the museum door, she appears to have been attacked, or at any rate frightened. In the grey of the morning they found her lying beside the steps dead. There was a little blood upon her sleeve but no mark upon her body except a small raised pustule under the ear. The doctor said the girl was extraordinarily anaemic, and that she probably died from fright, her heart being weak. I was surprised at this, for she had always seemed to be a particularly strong and active young woman."

"Can I see Miss Jungvort tomorrow before she goes?" asked Low, as the professor signified he had nothing more to tell.

The professor was rather unwilling that his daughter should be questioned, but he at last gave his permission, and next morning Low had a short talk with the girl before she left the house. He found her a very pretty girl, though listless and startlingly pale, and with a frightened stare in her light brown eyes. Mr. Low asked if she could describe her assailant.

"No," she answered, "I could not see him, for he was behind me. I only saw a dark, bony hand, with shining nails, and a bandaged arm pass just under my eyes before I fainted."

"Bandaged arm? I have heard nothing of this."

"Tut-tut, mere fancy!" put in the professor impatiently.

"I saw the bandages on the arm," repeated the girl, turning her head wearily away, "and I smelt the antiseptics it was dressed with."

"You have hurt your neck," remarked Mr. Low, who noticed a small circular patch of pink under her ear.

She flushed and paled, raising her hand to her neck with a nervous jerk, as she said in a low voice:

"It has almost killed me. Before he touched me, I knew he was there! I felt it!"

When they left her the professor apologised for the unreliability of her evidence, and pointed out the discrepancy between her statement and his own.

"She says she sees nothing but an arm, yet I tell you it had no arms! Preposterous! Conceive a wounded man entering this house to frighten the young women! I do not know what to make of it! Is it a man, or is it the Baelbrow Ghost?"

During the afternoon when Mr. Low and the professor returned from a stroll on the shore, they found a dark-browed young man with a bull neck, and strongly marked features, standing sullenly before the hall fire. The professor presented him to Mr. Low as Harold Swaffam. Swaffam seemed to be about thirty, but was already known as a far-seeing and successful member of the Stock Exchange.

"I am pleased to meet you, Mr. Low," he began, with a keen glance, "though you don't look sufficiently high-strung for one of your profession."

Mr. Low merely bowed.

"Come, you don't defend your craft against my insinuations?" went on Swaffam. "And so you have come to rout out our poor old ghost from Baelbrow? You forget that he is an heirloom, a family possession! What's this about his having turned rabid, eh, professor?" he ended, wheeling round upon Jungvort in his brusque way.

The Professor told the story over again. It was plain that he stood rather in awe of his prospective son-in-law.

"I heard much the same from Lena, whom I met at the station," said Swaffam. "It is my opinion that the women in this house are suffering from an epidemic of hysteria. You agree with me, Mr. Low?"

"Possibly. Though hysteria could hardly account for Freeman's death."

"I can't say as to that until I have looked further into the particulars. I have not been idle since I arrived. I have examined the museum. No one has entered it from the outside, and there is no other way of entrance except through the passage. The flooring is laid, I happen to know, on a thick layer of concrete. And there the case for the ghost stands at present." After a few moments of dogged reflection, he swung round on Mr. Low, in a manner that seemed peculiar to him when about to address any person. "What do you say to this plan, Mr. Low? I propose to drive the professor over to Ferryvale, to stop there for a day or two at the hotel, and I will also dispose of the servants who still remain in the house for, say, forty-eight hours. Meanwhile you and I can try to go further into the secret of the ghost's new pranks?"

Flaxman Low replied that this scheme exactly met his views. But the professor protested against being sent away. Harold Swaffam however was a man who liked to arrange things in his own fashion, and within forty-five minutes he and Jungvort departed in the dogcart.

The evening was lowering, and Baelbrow, like all houses built in exposed situations, was extremely susceptible to the changes of the weather. Therefore, before many hours were over, the place was full of creaking noises as the screaming gale battered at the shuttered windows, and the tree-branches tapped and groaned against walls.

Harold Swaffam, on his way back, was caught in the storm and drenched to the skin. It was, therefore, settled that after he had changed his clothes he should have a couple of hours' rest on the smoking-room sofa, while Mr. Low kept watch in the hall.

The early part of the night passed over uneventfully. A light burned faintly in the great wainscotted hall, but the passage was dark. There was nothing to be heard but the wild moan and whistle of the wind coming in from the sea, and the squalls of rain dashing against the windows. As the hours advanced, Mr. Low lit a lantern that lay at hand, and, carrying it along the passage, tried the museum door. It yielded, and the wind came muttering through to meet him. He looked round at the shutters and behind the big cases which held Mr. Swaffam's treasures, to make sure that the room contained no living occupant but himself.

Suddenly he fancied he heard a scraping noise behind him, and turned round, but discovered nothing to account for it. Finally, he laid the lantern on a bench so that its light should fall through the door into the passage, and returned again to the hall, where he put out the lamp, and then once more took up his station by the closed door of the smoking-room.

A long hour passed, during which the wind continued to roar down the wide hall chimney, and the old boards creaked as if furtive footsteps were gathering from every corner of the house. But Flaxman Low heeded none of these; he was waiting for a certain sound.

After a while, he heard it—the cautious scraping of wood on wood. He leant forward to watch the museum door. *Click, click* came the curious dog-like tread upon the tiled floor of the museum till the thing, whatever it was, paused and listened behind the open door. The wind lulled at the moment, and Low listened also, but no further sound was to be heard, only slowly across the broad ray of light falling through the door grew a stealthy shadow.

Again the wind rose, and blew in heavy gusts about the house, till even the flame in the lantern flickered, but when it steadied once more, Flaxman Low saw that the silent form had passed through the door, and was now on the steps outside. He could just make out a dim shadow in the dark angle of the embrasure.

Presently, from the shapeless shadow came a sound Mr. Low was not prepared to hear. The thing sniffed the air with the strong, audible inspiration of a bear, or some large animal. At the same moment, carried on the draughts of the hall, a faint, unfamiliar odour reached his nostrils. Lena Jungvort's words flashed back upon him—this, then, was the creature with the bandaged arm!

Again, as the storm shrieked and shook the windows, a darkness passed across the light. The thing had sprung out from the angle of the door, and Flaxman Low knew that it was making its way towards him through the illusive blackness of the hall. He hesitated for a second;

then he opened the smoking-room door.

Harold Swaffam sat up on the sofa, dazed with sleep.

"What has happened? Has it come?"

Low told him what he had just seen. Swaffam listened half-smilingly.

"What do you make of it now?" he said.

"I must ask you to defer that question for a little," replied Low.

"Then you mean me to suppose that you have a theory to fit all these incongruous items?"

"I have a theory, which may be modified by further knowledge," said Low. "Meantime, am I right in concluding from the name of this house that it was built on a barrow or burying-place"

"You are right, though that has nothing to do with the latest freaks of our ghost," returned Swaffam decidedly.

"I also gather that Mr. Swaffam has lately sent home one of the many cases now lying in the museum?" went on Mr. Low.

"He sent one, certainly, last September."

"And you have opened it," asserted Low.

"Yes; though I flattered myself I had left no trace of my handiwork."

"I have not examined the cases," said Low. "I inferred that you had done so from other facts."

"Now, one thing more," went on Swaffam, still smiling. "Do you imagine there is any danger—I mean to men like ourselves? Hysterical women cannot be taken into serious account."

"Certainly; the gravest danger to any person who moves about this part of the house alone after dark," replied Low.

Harold Swaffam leant back and crossed his legs.

"To go back to the beginning of our conversation, Mr. Low, may I remind you of the various conflicting particulars you will have to reconcile before you can present any decent theory to the world?"

"I am quite aware of that."

"First of all, our original ghost was a mere misty presence, rather guessed at from vague sounds and shadows—now we have something that is tangible, and that can, as we have proof, kill with fright. Next Jungvort declares the thing was a narrow, long and distinctly armless object, while Miss Jungvort has not only seen the arm and hand of a human being, but saw them clearly enough to tell us that the nails were gleaming and the arm bandaged. She also felt its strength. Jungvort, on the other hand, maintained that it clicked along like a dog—you bear out this description with the additional information that it sniffs like a wild beast. Now what can this thing be? It is capable of being seen, smelt, and felt, yet it hides itself successfully in a room where there is no cavity or space sufficient to afford covert to a cat! You still tell me that you believe that you can explain?"

"Most certainly," replied Flaxman Low with conviction.

"I have not the slightest intention or desire to be rude, but as a mere matter of common sense, I must express my opinion plainly. I believe the whole thing to be the result of excited imaginations, and I am about to prove it. Do you think there is any further danger to-night?"

"Very great danger tonight," replied Low.

"Very well as I said, I am going to prove it. I will ask you to allow, me to lock you up in one of the distant rooms, where I can get no help from you, and I will pass the remainder of the night walking about the passage and hall in the dark. That should give proof one way or the other."

"You can do so if you wish, but I must at least beg to be allowed to look on. I will leave the house and watch what goes on from the window in the passage, which I saw opposite the museum door. You cannot, in all fairness, refuse to let me be a witness."

"I cannot, of course," returned Swaffam. "Still, the night is too bad to turn a dog out into, and I warn you that I shall lock you out."

"That will not matter. Lend me a macintosh, and leave the lantern lit in the museum, where I placed it."

Swaffam agreed to this. Mr. Low gives a graphic account of what followed. He left the house and was duly locked out, and after groping his way round the house, found himself at length outside the window of the passage, which was almost opposite to the door of the museum. The door was still ajar and a thin band of light cut out into the gloom. Further down the hall gaped black and void. Low, sheltering himself as well as he could from the rain, waited for Swaffam's appearance. Was the terrible yellow watcher balancing itself upon its lean legs in the dim corner opposite, ready to spring out with its deadly strength upon the passer-by?

Presently Low heard a door bang inside the house, and the next moment Swaffam appeared with a candle in his hand, an isolated spread of weak rays against the vast darkness behind. He advanced steadily down the passage, his dark face grim and set, and as he came Mr. Low experienced that tingling sensation, which is so often the forerunner of some strange experience. Swaffam passed on towards the other end of the passage. There was a quick vibration of the museum door as a lean shape with a shrunken head leapt out into the passage after him. Then all together came a hoarse shout, the noise of a fall and utter darkness.

In an instant, Mr. Low had broken the glass, opened the window, and swung himself into the passage. There he lit a match and as it flared he saw by its dim light a picture painted for a second upon the obscurity beyond.

Swaffam's big figure lay with outstretched arms, face downwards, and as Low looked a crouching shape extricated itself from the fallen man, raising a narrow vicious head from his shoulder.

The match spluttered feebly and went out, and Low heard a flying step click on the boards, before he could find the candle Swaffam had dropped. Lighting it, he stooped over Swaffam and turned him on his back. The man's strong colour had gone, and the wax-white face looked whiter still against the blackness of hair and brows, and upon his neck under the ear, was a little raised pustule from which a thin line of blood was streaked up to the angle of his cheekbone.

Some instinctive feeling prompted Low to glance up at this moment. Half extended from the museum doorway were a face and bony neck—a high-nosed, dull-eyed, malignant face, the eye-sockets hollow, and the darkened teeth showing. Low plunged his hand into his pocket, and a shot rang out in the echoing passage-way and hall. The wind sighed through the broken panes, a ribbon of stuff fluttered along the polished flooring, and that was all, as Flaxman Low half dragged, half carried Swaffam into the smoking-room.

It was some time before Swaffam recovered consciousness. He listened to Low's story of how he had found him with a red angry gleam in his sombre eyes.

"The ghost has scored off me," he said with an odd, sullen laugh, "but now I fancy it's my turn! But before we adjourn to the museum to examine the place, I will ask you to let me hear your notion of things. You have been right in saying there was real danger. For myself I can only tell you that I felt something spring upon me, and I knew no more. Had this not happened I am afraid I should never have asked you a second time what your idea of the matter might be," he ended with a sort of sulky frankness.

"There are two main indications," replied Low. "This strip of yellow bandage, which I have just now picked up from the passage floor, and the mark on your neck."

"What's that you say?" Swaffam rose quickly and examined his neck in a small glass beside the mantelshelf.

"Connect those two, and I think I call leave you to work it out for yourself," said Low.

"Pray let us have your theory in full," requested Swaffam shortly.

"Very well," answered Low good-humouredly—he thought Swaffam's annoyance natural under the circumstances—"The long, narrow figure which seemed to the professor to be armless is developed on the next occasion. For Miss Jungvort sees a bandaged arm and a dark hand with gleaming—which means, of course, gilded—nails. The clicking sound of the footstep coincides with these particulars, for we know that sandals made of strips of leather are not uncommon in company with gilt nails and bandages. Old and dry leather would naturally click upon your polished floors."

"Bravo, Mr. Low! So you mean to say that this house is haunted by a mummy!"

"That is my idea, and all I have seen confirms me in my opinion"

"To do you justice, you held this theory before tonight—before, in fact, you had seen anything for yourself. You gathered that my father had sent home a mummy, and you went on to conclude that I had opened the case."

"Yes. I imagine you took off most of, or rather all, the outer bandages, thus leaving the limbs free, wrapped only in the inner bandages which were swathed round each separate limb. I fancy this mummy was preserved by the Theban method with aromatic spices which left the skin olive-coloured, dry and flexible, like tanned leather, the features remaining distinct, and the hair, teeth and eyebrows perfect."

"So far, good," said Swaffam. "But now, how about the intermittent vitality? The pustule on the neck of those whom it attacks? And where is our old Baelbrow ghost to come in?"

Swaffam tried to speak in a rallying tone, but his excitement and lowering temper were visible enough, in spite of the attempts he made to suppress them.

"To begin at the beginning," said Flaxman Low, "everybody who, in a rational and honest manner, investigates the phenomena of spiritism will, sooner or later, meet in them some perplexing element, which is not to be explained by any of the ordinary theories. For reasons into which I need not now enter, this present case appears to me to be one of these. I am led to believe that the ghost which has for so many years given dim and vague manifestations of its existence in this house is a vampire."

Swaffam threw back his head with an incredulous gesture.

"We no longer live in the middle ages, Mr. Low! And besides how could a vampire come here?" he said scoffingly.

"It is held by some authorities on these subjects that under certain conditions a vampire may be self-created. You tell me that this house is built upon an ancient barrow, in fact, on a spot where we might naturally expect to find such an elemental psychic germ. In those dead human systems were contained all the seeds for good and evil. The power which causes these psychic seeds or germs to grow is thought, and from being long dwelt on and indulged, a thought might finally gain a mysterious vitality, which could go increasing more and more by attracting to itself suitable and appropriate elements from its environment. For a long period this germ remained a helpless intelligence, awaiting the opportunity to assume some material form, by means of which to carry out its desires. The invisible is the real; the material only subserves its manifestation. The impalpable reality already existed, when you provided for it a physical medium for action by unwrapping the mummy's form. Now, we can only judge of the nature of the germ by its manifestation through matter. Here we have every indication of a vampire intelligence touching into life and energy the dead human frame. Hence the mark on the neck of its victims, and their bloodless and anaemic condition. For a vampire, as you know, sucks blood."

Swaffam rose, and took up the lamp.

"Now, for proof," he said bluntly. "Wait a second, Mr. Low. You say you fired at this appearance?" And he took up the pistol which Low had laid down on the table.

"Yes, I aimed at a small portion of its foot which I saw on the step."

Without more words, and with the pistol still in his hand, Swaffam led the way to the museum.

The wind howled round the house, and the darkness, which precedes the dawn, lay upon the world, when the two men looked upon one of the strangest sights it has ever been given to men to shudder at.

Half in and half out of an oblong wooden box in a corner of the great room, lay a lean shape in its rotten yellow bandages, the scraggy neck surmounted by a mop of frizzled hair. The toe strap of a sandal and a portion of the right foot had been shot away.

Swaffam, with a working face, gazed down at it, then seizing it by its tearing bandages, he flung it into the box, where if fell into life-like posture, its wide, moist-lipped mouth gaping up at them.

For a moment Swaffam stood over the thing; then with a curse he raised the revolver and shot into the grinning face again and again with a deliberate vindictiveness. Finally he rammed the thing down into the box, and clubbing the weapon, smashed the head into fragments with a vicious energy that coloured the whole horrible scene with a suggestion of murder done.

Then, turning to Low, he said:

"Help me to fasten the cover on it."

"Are you going to bury it?"

"No, we must rid the earth of it," he answered savagely. "I'll put it into the old canoe and burn it."

The rain had ceased when in the daybreak they carried the old canoe down to the shore. In it they placed the mummy case with its ghastly occupant, and piled faggots about it. The sail was raised and the pile lighted, and Low and Swaffam watched it creep out on the ebb-tide, at first a twinkling spark, then a flare of waving fire, until far out to sea the history of that dead thing ended 3000 years after the priests of Amen had laid it to rest in its appointed pyramid.

The Levitant

Gelett Burgess

Enoch F. Gerrish was a "prominent citizen." He had his name in large type in the directory and in the telephone book. He was often mentioned as "among those present" in the local columns of the dailies. He was a "solid business man," and could be seen any day on Montgomery Street, easily recognisable by his eyes, big as hard-boiled eggs, his paintbrush whiskers and his duck vest, which always had a button missing somewhere about it. He toed in slightly when he walked, but he could afford himself this and many other eccentricities, for he was rich. But he was most prominent as a member of the Society for Psychical Research, and to the reports of its proceedings he had contributed many bulky and remarkably uninteresting papers collated from the answers to thousands of postal-card catechisms sown recklessly abroad. He had tabulated, classified, and commented upon the replies to such questions as: "Have you ever seen a ghost?" "If not, why not?" "Has a ghost ever seen you?" etc., etc. His *Diagnosis of the Inter-Phantomic Relations of Sub-Spherical Spirits*" had given him prestige in the Society, and on the strength of fifteen thousand words anent "*Spectral and Pseudo-Spectral Anthropologia*" he had narrowly escaped the election to the Presidency of the body.

Yet, like so many of his fellow essayists on these ultra-scientific topics, Mr. Gerrish had never seen a ghost. He had talked with those who had, however, and he had an exhaustive lore ready at hand for recital, and when his audience was composed of women, he often made bold to broider the narrative with details of his own invention, and at these times did not hesitate to use the first person construction.

Mr. Gerrish was at this time engaged upon a new thesis; radical, even revolutionary. He was tired of his pose as an amateur ghost-seer, and the luminous idea of making capital out of his failures by using them to prove an original hypothesis swelled his vanity. Perhaps this would secure to him the president's chair, and he could have the delight of ringing the "ten minute bell" on verbose essayists. He had often been suppressed himself in this way, and he longed to be on the other side of the table.

"*Conditions of Levitation and Semi-Nudity in Dream*" was the title of his thesis.

He worked every night upon the development of his theory, keeping one eye open for spectral visitations, in case his new scheme should prove ineffective. He always kept on the table beside his bed a pistol, a non-explosive lamp (that wouldn't go out even if overthrown), a watch, a pencil and a pad of ruled paper upon which to take notes of supernatural occurrences. The top sheet of this pad was numbered (1), but it had remained otherwise blank for five months. He cut the "Death Notices" from the papers every day, and pinned them to the wall, near the head of his bed, in order to identify new-made ghosts.

The annual dinner of the S. P. R. was held on New Year's eve. Thirteen members were present.

The rest were celebrating less riotously.

Mr. Gerrish had allowed hints of his latest investigations to leak into the after-dinner personalities ; several of the speeches had made mention of the embarrassing situations due to "*Semi-Nudity in Dream.*" Reason demanded an explanation for the outrage so often put upon the sensibilities. Enoch F. Gerrish nearly burst with the efforts to restrain from exploiting his theories, but his policy and an enormous looped watchchain kept him from exploding. The time was not yet come. He drank like a camel to brace his nerve; he felt that a few leading questions would puncture his resolve and the secret would escape. He ate ravenously of the remnants of the dessert to cover his agitation. He felt that everyone was looking at him but only the president was. The president was wondering how a psychical researcher could eat so much—and live.

At the business meeting following, Enoch F. Gerrish was nominated for the Presidency for the ensuing year, but he did not realise it until three days later, when he was notified by the secretary in writing. He was now too busily engaged with a Welsh rabbit that the president had maliciously manufactured. The meeting came at last to an end, or at least it tapered off, the members waking up in turn and going home.

When Mr. Gerrish left, they were still reading papers. No one was listening. The president was drawing little circles on a sheet of paper with a soft pencil, and the secretary was making love to his watch.

Enoch found his way home with great difficulty and a large stick.

He felt as if he had been eating fireworks and they were going off inside of him.

The street was like the back of a whale that it was necessary to climb, and it seemed to be rolling on a long grounded swell. The houses circled about him like a merry-go-round. He tried to take his temperature with a little pocket-thermometer, but the mercury was all huddled into the top of the tube. Somehow things seemed to be going wrong with him; he knew that much, but very little more.

He did not remember his whole pilgrimage ; he believed finally that he had accomplished the stairs, because he found himself at the top. He could not remember whether he had gone through the door of his room, or climbed in a window, but he was inside, and was glad of it. He undressed himself carefully, and went to bed, thinking he should have done so earlier. He suddenly realised that it was New Year's day, and he at once decided to reform.

By this time it was two o'clock, and the Welsh rabbit, like a patriotic set-piece, still burned in his abdomen; he had almost given up hope, when he fell asleep, but his snoring was so terrible that it woke him up again. He arose unsteadily, and circumnavigated the room in search of cotton to plug his ears. He soon forgot what he was looking for, and returned in a bewildered condition to his bed, and began counting, wondering when it would be over. . . .

As he reached number thirteen, he opened his eyes. Something was rising out of the bed from between his feet. This did not seem at all right to him, and he was much hurt by the occurrence, until it became evident that it was a ghost. Now Mr. Gerrish was in no condition to entertain ghosts at this time, but he nerved himself for the interview and reached for his pistol and note-book, though he was uncertain which to use first. He tried to decide whether he was more afraid or surprised.

He remembered Bulwer-Lytton's distinction between fear and terror, and thought what rot it was.

Meanwhile, the phantom was emerging from the bed, or more properly through the bed. Mr. Gerrish rubbed his legs back and forth to see if he could feel the ghost, but he could not. Yet the apparition was sticking through the bed like a brochette. Mr. Gerrish thought this phenomenon interesting, and was about to make a note of it, when materialisation of the ghost set in so strongly as to absorb his whole attention.

He wondered where he had seen the ghost before, and decided that it was nowhere.

He remembered the circus of last year, and the athletes and tumblers at the Orpheum Theatre, and concluded that this was one of them. He did not know which. The spectre was dressed in trunks and tights ; he had longish hair, and was much more transparent than was becoming to a person of his size. His eyeballs were conspicuous, and ill placed, and as he hung over the bed like a huge interrogation point, waving his arms, Mr. Gerrish felt that something was about to happen. He felt, vaguely, that he should take the time; he was sure that none of the members would believe him, unless he told at what o'clock it happened. The reports of the Society generally gave the hour and minute, and sometimes it had been figured down to split seconds. He looked at his watch, but the hands seemed to be going backwards, and he gave up this detail with a sigh.

The horrible part of the affair was that the ghost did not speak. Mr. Gerrish was compelled to take the initiative ; six times he endeavoured to say something, but as he could think of nothing to say, little came of his attempts. At the seventh effort a volley of words burst from him, filling the room like the explosion of a barrel of firecrack-

ers. When it was over, there was a shocking silence, and he found he had exclaimed:

"Ghostly phantom, thing of evil, spectre, demon, spook, or devil, take thy legs from out my bedstead, take thy toes from off my floor!"

Somehow this seemed inadequate, and he began again. The ghost evidently expected something better of him, and still hung swaying over the counterpane, gibbering with gaunt grimaces. Mr. Gerrish at length began to regain his nerve; the rabbit within him grew more docile, and the spirit of the investigator awoke.

"Tell me," he began, "to what am I indebted for the honour?" etc., etc.

"Beware!" said the spectre. "No familiarities, please; I am sent to you to divulge the secrets of 'Levitation and Semi-Nudity in Dream.' This night shall illumine you! Come!" and seizing the psychical researcher by the shoulder, he dragged him to the window, and held him struggling like a kitten, outside the sash. The rays of a decrescent moon varnished the soles of the unfortunate victim's feet; an errant breeze slickered at his white nightrobe, and it was very cold. The spook shook him gently, as one might flap the crumbs from a table-cloth out of the window, and Mr. Gerrish grew green with fear. The pavement below seemed miles away. Mr. Gerrish felt rather than saw this. On the other hand, he saw rather than felt the ghost.

Suddenly all support was removed, and he fell!

He supposed about five years to have elapsed when he finally discovered that he was no longer falling.

It was like a long wait between the acts of a bad play, when one longs to have the suspense over, yet dreads the next sensation.

He knew from hearsay that if he reached the bottom he would die. That is, if it were a dream. The question then was, was it a dream? He could not decide.

At length he felt himself in the arms of the phantom giggling. This gave him, however, no clue as to whether he was awake or not.

"This is called the 'Sense of Falling,' to which you have already given five hundred words in your thesis," said the apparition.

"Oh!" said Mr. Gerrish, "but it is much easier imagined than described—as they say in the storybooks."

"My next act is levitation proper," said the ghost, and with the word he sprang into the air.

It was, at first, very terrible.

Mr. Gerrish waved his arms like a chicken that has been dropped

from the roof of a house. He could not realize that he was being carried, but he felt the responsibility of his own exertion, and he tried several kinds of swimming strokes, using his feet like a woman. He was high in the air before he realised that a mere effort of will was all that was necessary, and once assured, he began to like the sensation. "Do you often do this?" he asked the spirit. "All the world knows me," was the reply, "though few have seen me. They think they do it alone, and in the daylight they try to remember how it was done."

As he spoke, they passed the top of a steeple. Mr. Gerrish could not resist the temptation to lay hold of it. To his surprise it felt hard and real, and of a sudden, terror seized him. He perceived his immense distance from the street and became giddy. His normal senses returned to him, and he clung to the pinnacle, just below the vane.

Again the ghost left him.

He dared not look down again, but embraced the pyramid eagerly, as though he were afraid it might break away from his clutches.

He was alone in the sky.

He might have been an Arctic explorer at the actual North Pole, for any chance he had of relief. The spire seemed to bend in the wind, and recover its perpendicularity with much difficulty.

He felt like a damp shirt that had been hung out to dry, and had been forgotten.

He wished to yell for help, but hoped that no one below was looking at him.

Some time after the ghost reappeared, and hung in the air as if treading water to keep itself afloat. Mr. Gerrish wondered if it had been off to get a drink.

"If you have had enough of levitation," said the ghost, "we may continue our investigations." And Mr. Gerrish found himself at home in bed again. But he had by this time ceased to wonder at anything. He would have liked a programme, so as to know what to expect next, but he had lost a good deal of interest in the proceedings.

It was as if he were trying not to listen to a paper being read at a meeting of the researchers.

"We shall now proceed to the condition of *Semi-Nudity in Dream*," remarked the spectre.

"But I have had that," objected Enoch.

"I am afraid I have complicated things, but this will be a simple case. And first I'll show you what I can do at bed-tipping," and the spectre was as good as his word. The bed rocked like a steamer in the Channel. It soared like an aeroplane. It dived, ducked, danced dropped and doddered like an indecent *Pianchette*. Mr. Gerrish clung to the rail like the boatswain of a runaway whaleboat. Finally the ghost took the bed upon his head and walked out of the room with it, forthwith. Mr. Gerrish tried to be calm, but his head bumped against the ceiling.

He held his breath as they crowded through the front door.

Down the street they marched in a two-storey procession, ghost and man. No one was abroad, but the cocks were crowing in the distance.

It was like riding a camel, or swaying in a *palaquin* of a gouty elephant.

Mr. Gerrish felt that he could stand no more, but the worst was yet to come.

The ghost planted the bed in the middle of Market Street, and left him, this time for good.

Mr. Gerrish waited a long time, hiding under the sheets, hoping it was a dream. At length he peeped from under the covers, and saw, to his horror, that it had begun to get light. The milk wagons began to rumble in the side streets. Worst of all, he was over the slot of the car line, and of a sudden the cable began to rattle over the pulleys.

He did not want his bed to be pushed off the track by a Market Street car.

A policeman appeared in the vanishing point of the perspective of sidewalks, and walked steadily towards him. Mr. Gerrish decided to wait and see if it were a real policeman. The figure came nearer and nearer. The policeman left the sidewalk and approached the bed, rubbing his eyes. Mr. Gerrish was almost able to read the number on the helmet, when the policeman hesitated a moment in astonishment, then turned and ran like a hen up the middle of the street. He turned one block up, to the right, and disappeared.

A cable car with a red light appeared in the distance, and Mr. Gerrish saw the time had come for action. He left the bed on the track, and walked without dignity toward the northwest. He wondered why he did not run, but a thin fog seemed to blur his eyes, and he had great trouble in finding his way.

Every little while he walked off the kerbstone, and landed with a nasty jolt.

He had never known there were so many streets in San Francisco, and he wished them to remain straight, but they refused. Each street seemed to be tied into a bow knot with six ends. The sidewalks were set obliquely, the crossings led back to the same side of the way, so he could never get over. The houses were huddled into the middle of the pavement. The gutters ran vertically. He wondered why. He was in a labyrinth, clad immodestly. He tried to find a latch key, but he had no pocket.

He met wayfarers, but they did not seem to notice him.

He wondered if his bed would be returned. It was not marked, but he thought he might advertise for it.

Then there was a great blank, as if the whole world had been etherized; and then the void and chaos began to take form. Something looked familiar. Ten pink spots upon the horizon.

They were his toes, sticking through the covers of his bed, and he heard himself counting— "sixteen, seventeen, eighteen, nineteen, TWENTY."

The Ghost Detective
Mark Lemon

When I first came to London thirty years ago, I met a young man, James Loxley, who worked in the wine business. The company he worked for sold wine to pubs and restaurants, and just after I met him he got a new job in the company with more money. Because of this he was able to get married and I went to his wedding. His wife was a pretty girl with fair hair and blue eyes. It was clear to everyone that they loved each other.

They went to live in a new house outside London and I visited them often. Over the next three years, they had two beautiful children and they were a very happy family. They did not have much money and had only one servant, a rather stupid girl called Susan. One year they asked me to come to their home for Christmas dinner. We had a lovely meal and then sat in their sitting-room, laughing and talking. It was a small but comfortable room. In the corner was a Christmas tree and on the wall was a painting of Loxley's mother and father, who were both dead. Loxley loved this painting. He told me that it was just like his parents and he often felt that they were really in the room with him.

After Christmas Loxley came with me to visit my old uncle for a few days. He seemed very quiet during the trip and I thought perhaps he wanted to be with his wife and children. When the holiday was over, we travelled to London together early in the morning to go to work. He seemed worried during the journey but he did not say why. The next day I could not believe it when I heard that he was in prison for stealing money from his company. I immediately went to see him and on the way I remembered his quietness over the last few days. I also began to think about how expensive it was with two children and how Loxley probably needed money. But, no, it was impossible. I knew that he was an honest man.

At the prison I talked to him and this is the story he told me:

'On December the 24th, Christmas Eve, I went to one of my cus-
tomers, John Rogers, and asked him to pay his bill. He is often late
with payments and I wanted to get the money before the Christmas
holiday. He gave me a cheque and I immediately took it to the bank
and cashed it, because in the past this customer has written a cheque
and then stopped it before we could get the cash. It was too late to go
to the office, so I decided to keep the money until after the holiday. I
put it in my pocket and went home. On the day we left my house to
visit your uncle, I could not find the money and I became very worried. I looked all over the house, but it was nowhere. I was afraid to
go back to work. When I told my boss about it, he did not understand
why I didn't come to the office immediately when I couldn't find the
money. He did not believe my story and called me a thief.'

At that moment we heard someone crying and screaming outside
the door. It was Loxley's wife, Martha. She ran in, held her husband in
her arms and cried and cried. It was terrible to see. After some time
the prison guard told us to leave, and I took her home, still crying. She
became ill and her mother came to stay with her and the children. The
servant, Susan, was also there. She seemed to be a good girl and was
always ready to help, but she seemed very unhappy about the problem
and sometimes cried more than Martha. I visited the little house almost every day and, one day, I found Martha very excited.

'What's happened, Martha?' I asked.

'Well, you probably won't believe this,' she said, 'but last night I saw
my husband's ghost.'

'But James isn't dead,' I said, 'he's only in prison.'

'I know, I know,' she said, 'but listen to this. Last night at midnight
I was in the sitting-room — I couldn't sleep as usual. I was sitting
worrying about our problems. Suddenly I looked up and saw James
come into the room without a sound. He sat down over there in his
favourite chair and looked at the picture of his father for a few minutes without speaking. Then he stood up and looked at me with a face
full of love and walked out of the room.'

'Perhaps you were half asleep and dreamed it,' I said, but She was
sure about what happened and did not want to listen to me.

Susan, the servant girl, was in the room with us and was listening
to the conversation, looking very afraid. 'Did you speak to the ghost,
Mrs Loxley? Did it say anything to you?' she asked.

'No, Susan. I've told you everything that happened,' said Martha.

I left the house that day feeling very worried as Martha was looking so white and tired. I thought about calling a doctor, but I decided to wait and see what happened. The next day I visited them again and found Martha even more excited.

'He came again,' she almost shouted. 'This time he stood in front of the painting of his father and pointed at it. Then he turned to me and held out his arms. I ran towards him, but he disappeared and I crashed into the wall. I think he means there is something behind the picture. Please, will you help me to take it down and look?'

The painting was quite high on the wall and I needed a ladder to reach it. I called Susan and asked her to bring one.

'A ladder?' she asked. 'What for?'

When I explained about the painting I was surprised to see her face turn white. 'There isn't a ladder,' she said quickly.

'But I'm sure I saw one,' I said, 'just outside the kitchen door. Oh well, my mistake. Don't worry.'

Susan didn't leave the room but watched as I stood on a chair and began to take the picture of Loxley's father down. Suddenly she screamed, 'It was me, Mrs. Loxley. I know why the ghost came. The money's behind the picture. I hid it there.' She began to cry and cry, and it was some time before she could tell the story.

'It was on Christmas Eve,' she said. 'Mr. Loxley came home a bit late. I was behind him as he was walking upstairs, and he took his handkerchief out of his pocket. As he did so, the money fell out. He didn't notice, but I did and I picked it up. It was more money than I've seen in my life, Mrs. Loxley, I couldn't stop myself. Then I was frightened about someone finding it on me or in my room, so I hid it behind that picture. Oh, please Mrs. Loxley. Don't send me to prison.'

Well, as soon as Susan told her story to the police, James was a free man, and the family are now living happily in Australia.

Selecting a Ghost

A.k.a. *The Ghosts of Goresthorpe Grange*
Sir Arthur Conan Doyle

I am sure that Nature never intended me to be a self-made man. There are times when I can hardly bring myself to realise that twenty years of my life were spent behind the counter of a grocer's shop in the East End of London, and that it was through such an avenue that I reached a wealthy independence and the possession of Goresthorpe Grange. My habits are conservative, and my tastes refined and aristocratic. I have a soul which spurns the vulgar herd. Our family, the D'Odds, date back to a prehistoric era, as is to be inferred from the fact that their advent into British history is not commented on by any trustworthy historian. Some instinct tells me that the blood of a Crusader runs in my veins. Even now, after the lapse of so many years, such exclamations as "By'r Lady!" rise naturally to my lips, and I feel that, should circumstances require it, I am capable of rising in my stirrups and dealing an *infidel* a blow—say with a mace—which would considerably astonish him.

Goresthorpe Grange is a feudal mansion—or so it was termed in the advertisement which originally brought it under my notice. Its right to this adjective had a most remarkable effect upon its price, and the advantages gained may possibly be more sentimental than real. Still, it is soothing to me to know that I have slits in my staircase through which I can discharge arrows; and there is a sense of power in the fact of possessing a complicated apparatus by means of which I am enabled to pour molten lead upon the head of the casual visitor. These things chime in with my peculiar humour, and I do not grudge to pay for them. I am proud of my battlements and of the circular uncovered sewer which girds me round. I am proud of my portcullis and donjon and keep. There is but one thing wanting to round off the mediaevalism of my abode, and to render it symmetrically and completely antique. Goresthorpe Grange is not provided with a ghost.

Any man with old-fashioned tastes and ideas as to how such establishments should be conducted, would have been disappointed at the omission. In my case it was particularly unfortunate. From my childhood I had been an earnest student of the supernatural, and a firm believer in it. I have revelled in ghostly literature until there is hardly a tale bearing upon the subject which I have not perused. I learned the German language for the sole purpose of mastering a book upon demonology. When an infant I had secreted myself in dark rooms in the hope of seeing some of those bogies with which my nurse used to threaten me; and the same feeling is as strong in me now as then. It was a proud moment when I felt that a ghost was one of the luxuries which money might command.

It is true that there was no mention of an apparition in the advertisement. On reviewing the mildewed walls, however, and the shadowy corridors, I had taken it for granted that there was such a thing on the premises. As the presence of a kennel presupposes that of a dog, so I imagined that it was impossible that such desirable quarters should be untenanted by one or more restless shades. Good heavens, what can the noble family from whom I purchased it have been doing during these hundreds of years! Was there no member of it spirited enough to make away with his sweetheart, or take some other steps calculated to establish a hereditary spectre? Even now I can hardly write with patience upon the subject.

For a long time I hoped against hope. Never did rat squeak behind the wainscot, or rain drip upon the attic floor, without a wild thrill shooting through me as I thought that at last I had come upon traces of some unquiet soul. I felt no touch of fear upon these occasions. If it occurred in the night-time, I would send Mrs. D'Odd—who is a strong-minded woman—to investigate the matter, while I covered up my head with the bedclothes and indulged in an ecstacy of expectation. Alas, the result was always the same! The suspicious sound would be traced to some cause so absurdly natural and commonplace that the most fervid imagination could not clothe it with any of the glamour of romance.

I might have reconciled myself to this state of things, had it not been for Jorrocks of Havistock Farm. Jorrocks is a coarse, burly, matter-of-fact fellow, whom I only happened to know through the accidental circumstance of his fields adjoining my demesne. Yet this man, though utterly devoid of all appreciation of archaeological unities, is in possession of a well-authenticated and undeniable spectre. Its existence only dates back, I believe, to the reign of the Second George, when a young lady cut her throat upon hearing of the death of her lover at the battle of Dettingen. Still, even that gives the house an air of respectability, especially when coupled with blood stains upon the floor. Jorrocks is densely unconscious of his good fortune; and his language when he reverts to the apparition is painful to listen to. He little dreams how I covet every one of those moans and nocturnal wails which he describes with unnecessary objurgation. Things are indeed coming to a pretty pass when democratic spectres are allowed to desert the landed proprietors and annul every social distinction by taking refuge in the houses of the great unrecognised.

I have a large amount of perseverance. Nothing else could have raised me into my righful sphere, considering the uncongenial atmosphere in which I spent the earlier part of my life. I felt now that a ghost must be secured, but how to set about securing one was more than either Mrs. D'Odd or myself was able to determine. My reading taught me that such phenomena are usually the outcome of crime. What crime was to be done, then, and who was to do it? A wild idea entered my mind that Watkins, the house-steward, might be prevailed upon—for a consideration—to immolate himself or someone else in the interests of the establishment. I put the matter to him in a half-jesting manner; but it did not seem to strike him in a favourable light. The other servants sympathised with him in his opinion—at least, I cannot account in any other way for their having left the house in a body the same afternoon.

"My dear," Mrs. D'Odd remarked to me one day after dinner, as I sat moodily sipping a cup of sack—I love the good old names—"my dear, that odious ghost of Jorrocks' has been gibbering again."

"Let it gibber!" I answered, recklessly.

Mrs. D'Odd struck a few chords on her virginal and looked thoughtfully into the fire.

"I'll tell you what it is, Argentine," she said at last, using the pet name which we usually substituted for Silas, "we must have a ghost sent down from London."

"How can you be so idiotic, Matilda?" I remarked, severely. "Who could get us such a thing?"

"My cousin, Jack Brocket, could," she answered, confidently.

Now, this cousin of Matilda's was rather a sore subject between us.

He was a rakish, clever young fellow, who had tried his hand at many things, but wanted perseverance to succeed at any. He was, at that time, in chambers in London, professing to be a general agent, and really living, to a great extent, upon his wits. Matilda managed so that most of our business should pass through his hands, which certainly saved me a great deal of trouble; but I found that Jack's commission was generally considerably larger than all the other items of the bill put together. It was this fact which made me feel inclined to rebel against any further negotiations with the young gentleman.

"Oh yes, he could," insisted Mrs. D., seeing the look of disapprobation upon my face. "You remember how well he managed that business about the crest?"

"It was only a resuscitation of the old family coat-of-arms, my dear," I protested.

Matilda smiled in an irritating manner. "There was a resuscitation of the family portraits, too, dear," she remarked. "You must allow that Jack selected them very judiciously."

I thought of the long line of faces which adorned the walls of my banqueting-hall, from the burly Norman robber, through every gradation of casque, plume, and ruff, to the sombre Chesterfieldian individual who appears to have staggered against a pillar in his agony at the return of a maiden MS. which he grips convulsively in his right hand. I was fain to confess that in that instance he had done his work well, and that it was only fair to give him an order—with the usual commission—for a family spectre should such a thing be attainable.

It is one of my maxims to act promptly when once my mind is made up. Noon of the next day found me ascending the spiral stone staircase which leads to Mr. Brocket's chambers, and admiring the succession of arrows and fingers upon the whitewashed wall, all indicating the direction of that gentleman's sanctum. As it happened, artificial aids of the sort were entirely unnecessary, as an animated flap-dance overhead could proceed from no other quarter, though it was replaced by a deathly silence as I groped my way up the stair. The door was opened by a youth evidently astounded at the appearance of a client, and I was ushered into the presence of my young friend, who was writing furiously in a large ledger—upside down, as I afterwards discovered.

After the first greetings, I plunged into business at once. "Look here, Jack," I said, "I want you to get me a spirit, if you can."

"Spirits you mean!" shouted my wife's cousin, plunging his hand into the waste-paper basket and producing a bottle with the celerity of a conjuring trick. "Let's have a drink!"

I held up my hand as a mute appeal against such a proceeding so early in the day; but on lowering it again I found that I had almost involuntarily closed my fingers round the tumbler which my adviser had pressed upon me. I drank the contents hastily off, lest anyone should come in upon us and set me down as a toper. After all there was something very amusing about the young fellow's eccentricities.

"Not spirits," I explained, smilingly; "an apparition—a ghost. If such a thing is to be had, I should be very willing to negotiate."

"A ghost for Goresthorpe Grange?" inquired Mr. Brocket, with as much coolness as if I had asked for a drawing-room suite.

"Quite so," I answered.

"Easiest thing in the world," said my companion, filling up my glass again in spite of my remonstrance. "Let us see!" Here he took down a large red note-book, with all the letters of the alphabet in a fringe down the edge. "A ghost you said, didn't you? That's G. G— gems—gimlets—gas-pipes—gauntlets—guns—galleys. Ah, here we are. Ghosts. Volume nine, section six, page forty-one. Excuse me!" And Jack ran up a ladder and began rummaging among the pile of ledgers on a high shelf. I felt half inclined to empty my glass into the spittoon when his back was turned; but on second thoughts I disposed of it in a legitimate way.

"Here it is!" cried my London agent, jumping off the ladder with a crash, and depositing an enormous volume of manuscript upon the table. "I have all these things tabulated, so that I may lay my hands upon them in a moment. It's all right—it's quite weak" (here he filled our glasses again). "What were we looking up, again?"

"Ghosts," I suggested.

"Of course; page 41. Here we are. T.H. Fowler & Son, Dunkel Street, suppliers of mediums to the nobility and gentry; charms sold— love philtres—mummies—horoscopes cast.' Nothing in your line there, I suppose."

I shook my head despondently.

"'Frederick Tabb,'" continued my wife's cousin, "'sole channel of communication between the living and the dead. Proprietor of the spirits of Byron, Kirke White, Grimaldi, Tom Cribb, and Inigo Jones.' That's about the figure!"

"Nothing romantic enough there," I objected. "Good heavens! Fancy a ghost with a black eye and a handkerchief tied round its waist, or turning summersaults, and saying, 'How are you tomorrow?'" The very idea made me so warm that I emptied my glass and filled it again.

"Here is another," said my companion, "'Christopher McCarthy; bi-weekly seances—attended by all the eminent spirits of ancient and modern times. Nativities—charms—abracadabras, messages from the dead.' He might be able to help us. However, I shall have a hunt round myself tomorrow, and see some of these fellows. I know their haunts, and it's odd if I can't pick up something cheap. So there's an end of business," he concluded, hurling the ledger into the corner, "and now we'll have something to drink."

We had several things to drink—so many that my inventive faculties were dulled next morning, and I had some little difficulty in explaining to Mrs. D'Odd why it was that I hung my boots and spectacles upon a peg along with my other garments before retiring to rest. The new hopes excited by the confident manner in which my agent had undertaken the commission, caused me to rise superior to alcoholic reaction, and I paced about the rambling corridors and old-fashioned rooms, picturing to myself the appearance of my expected acquisition, and deciding what part of the building would harmonise best with its presence. After much consideration, I pitched upon the banqueting-hall as being, on the whole, most suitable for its reception. It was a long low room, hung round with valuable tapestry and interesting relics of the old family to whom it had belonged. Coats of mail and implements of war glimmered fitfully as the light of the fire played over them, and the wind crept under the door, moving the hangings to and fro with a ghastly rustling. At one end there was the raised dais, on which in ancient times the host and his guests used to spread their table, while a descent of a couple of steps led to the lower part of the hall, where the vassals and retainers held wassail. The floor was uncovered by any sort of carpet, but a layer of rushes had been scattered over it by my direction. In the whole room there was nothing to remind one of the nineteenth century; except, indeed, my own solid silver plate, stamped with the resuscitated family arms, which was laid out upon an oak table in the centre. This, I determined, should be the haunted room, supposing my wife's cousin to succeed in his negotiation with the spirit-mongers. There was nothing for it now but to wait patiently until I heard some news of the result of his inquiries.

A letter came in the course of a few days, which, if it was short, was at least encouraging. It was scribbled in pencil on the back of a playbill, and sealed apparently with a tobacco-stopper. "Am on the track," it said. "Nothing of the sort to be had from any professional spiritualist, but picked up a fellow in a pub yesterday who says he can manage it for you. Will send him down unless you wire to the contrary. Abrahams is his name, and he has done one or two of these jobs before." The letter wound up with some incoherent allusions to a cheque, and was signed by my affectionate cousin, John Brocket.

I need hardly say that I did not wire, but awaited the arrival of Mr. Abrahams with all impatience. In spite of my belief in the supernatural, I could scarcely credit the fact that any mortal could have such a command over the spirit-world as to deal in them and barter them against mere earthly gold. Still, I had Jack's word for it that such a trade existed; and here was a gentleman with a Judaical name ready to demonstrate it by proof positive. How vulgar and commonplace Jorrocks' eighteenth-century ghost would appear should I succeed in securing a real mediaeval apparition! I almost thought that one had been sent down in advance, for, as I walked round the moat that night before retiring to rest, I came upon a dark figure engaged in surveying the machinery of my portcullis and drawbridge. His start of surprise, however, and the manner in which he hurried off into the darkness, speedily convinced me of his earthly origin, and I put him down as some admirer of one of my female retainers mourning over the muddy Hellespont which divided him from his love. Whoever he may have been, he disappeared and did not return, though I loitered about for some time in the hope of catching a glimpse of him and exercising my feudal rights upon his person.

Jack Brocket was as good as his word. The shades of another evening were beginning to darken round Goresthorpe Grange, when a peal at the outer bell, and the sound of a fly pulling up, announced the arrival of Mr. Abrahams. I hurried down to meet him, half expecting to see a choice assortment of ghosts crowding in at his rear. Instead, however, of being the sallow-faced, melancholy-eyed man that I had pictured to myself, the ghost-dealer was a sturdy little podgy fellow, with a pair of wonderfully keen sparkling eyes and a mouth which was constantly stretched in a good-humoured, if somewhat artificial, grin. His sole stock-in-trade seemed to consist of a small leather bag jealously locked and strapped, which emitted a metallic chink upon being placed on the stone flags in the hall.

"And 'ow are you, sir?" he asked, wringing my hand with the utmost effusion. "And the missus, 'ow is she? And all the others—'ow's all their 'ealth?'"

I intimated that we were all as well as could reasonably be expected, but Mr. Abrahams happened to catch a glimpse of Mrs. D'Odd in the distance, and at once plunged at her with another string of inquiries as to her health, delivered so volubly and with such an intense earnestness, that I half expected to see him terminate his cross-examination by feeling her pulse and demanding a sight of her tongue. All this time his little eyes rolled round and round, shifting perpetually from the floor to the ceiling, and from the ceiling to the walls, taking in apparently every article of furniture in a single comprehensive glance.

Having satisfied himself that neither of us was in a pathological condition, Mr. Abrahams suffered me to lead him upstairs, where a repast had been laid out for him to which he did ample justice. The mysterious little bag he carried along with him, and deposited it under his chair during the meal. It was not until the table had been cleared and we were left together that he broached the matter on which he had come down.

"I hunderstand," he remarked, puffing at a trichinopoly, "that you want my 'elp in fitting up this 'ere 'ouse with a happarition."

I acknowledged the correctness of his surmise, while mentally wondering at those restless eyes of his, which still danced about the room as if he were making an inventory of the contents.

"And you won't find a better man for the job, though I says it as shouldn't," continued my companion. "Wot did I say to the young gent wot spoke to me in the bar of the Lame Dog? 'Can you do it?' says he. 'Try me,' says I, 'me and my bag. Just try me.' I couldn't say fairer than that."

My respect for Jack Brocket's business capacities began to go up very considerably. He certainly seemed to have managed the matter wonderfully well. "You don't mean to say that you carry ghosts about in bags?" I remarked, with diffidence.

Mr. Abrahams smiled a smile of superior knowledge. "You wait," he said; "give me the right place and the right hour, with a little of the essence of Lucoptolycus"—here he produced a small bottle from his waistcoat pocket—"and you won't find no ghost that I ain't up to. You'll see them yourself, and pick your own, and I can't say fairer than that."

As all Mr. Abrahams' protestations of fairness were accompanied by a cunning leer and a wink from one or other of his wicked little eyes, the impression of candour was somewhat weakened.

"When are you going to do it?" I asked, reverentially.

"Ten minutes to one in the morning," said Mr. Abrahams, with decision. "Some says midnight, but I says ten to one, when there ain't such a crowd, and you can pick your own ghost. And now," he continued, rising to his feet, "suppose you trot me round the premises, and let me see where you wants it; for there's some places as attracts 'em, and some as they won't hear of—not if there was no other place in the world."

Mr. Abrahams inspected our corridors and chambers with a most critical and observant eye, fingering the old tapestry with the air of a connoisseur, and remarking in an undertone that it would "match uncommon nice." It was not until he reached the banqueting-hall, however, which I had myself picked out, that his admiration reached the pitch of enthusiasm. "'Ere's the place!" he shouted, dancing, bag in hand, round the table on which my plate was lying, and looking not unlike some quaint little goblin himself. "'Ere's the place; we won't get nothin' to beat this! A fine room—noble, solid, none of your electroplate trash! That's the way as things ought to be done, sir. Plenty of room for 'em to glide here. Send up some brandy and the box of weeds; I'll sit here by the fire and do the preliminaries, which is more trouble than you'd think; for them ghosts carries on hawful at times, before they finds out who they've got to deal with. If you was in the room they'd tear you to pieces as like as not. You leave me alone to tackle them, and at half-past twelve come in, and I lay they'll be quiet enough by then."

Mr. Abrahams' request struck me as a reasonable one, so I left him with his feet upon the mantelpiece, and his chair in front of the fire, fortifying himself with stimulants against his refractory visitors. From the room beneath, in which I sat with Mrs. D'Odd, I could hear that, after sitting for some time, he rose up and paced about the hall with quick impatient steps. We then heard him try the lock of the door, and afterward drag some heavy article of furniture in the direction of the window, on which, apparently, he mounted, for I heard the creaking of the rusty hinges as the diamond-paned casement folded backward, and I knew it to be situated several feet above the little man's reach. Mrs. D'Odd says that she could distinguish his voice speaking in low and rapid whispers after this, but that may have been her imagination. I confess that I began to feel more impressed than I had deemed it possible to be. There was something awesome in the thought of the solitary mortal standing by the open window and summoning in from the gloom outside the spirits of the nether world. It was with a trepidation which I could hardly disguise from Matilda that I observed that the clock was pointing to half-past twelve, and that the time had come for me to share the vigil of my visitor.

He was sitting in his old position when I entered, and there were no signs of the mysterious movements which I had overheard, though his chubby face was flushed as with recent exertion.

"Are you succeeding all right?" I asked as I came in, putting on as careless an air as possible, but glancing involuntarily round the room to see if we were alone.

"Only your help is needed to complete the matter," said Mr. Abrahams, in a solemn voice. "You shall sit by me and partake of the essence of Lucoptolycus, which removes the scales from our earthly eyes. Whatever you may chance to see, speak not and make no movement, lest you break the spell." His manner was subdued, and his usual cockney vulgarity had entirely disappeared. I took the chair which he indicated, and awaited the result.

My companion cleared the rushes from the floor in our neighbourhood, and, going down upon his hands and knees, described a half-circle with chalk, which enclosed the fireplace and ourselves. Round the edge of this half-circle he drew several hieroglyphics, not unlike the signs of the zodiac. He then stood up and uttered a long invocation, delivered so rapidly that it sounded like a single gigantic word in some uncouth guttural language. Having finished this prayer, if prayer it was, he pulled out the small bottle which he had produced before, and poured a couple of teaspoonfuls of clear transparent fluid into a phial, which he handed to me with an intimation that I should drink it.

The liquid had a faintly sweet odour, not unlike the aroma of certain sorts of apples. I hesitated a moment before applying it to my lips, but an impatient gesture from my companion overcame my scruples, and I tossed it off. The taste was not unpleasant; and, as it gave rise to no immediate effects, I leaned back in my chair and composed myself for what was to come. Mr. Abrahams seated himself beside me, and I felt that he was watching my face from time to time, while repeating some more of the invocations in which he had indulged before.

A sense of delicious warmth and languor began gradually to steal over me, partly, perhaps, from the heat of the fire, and partly from some unexplained cause. An uncontrollable impulse to sleep weighed down my eyelids, while at the same time my brain worked actively, and a hundred beautiful and pleasing ideas flitted through it. So utterly lethargic did I feel that, though I was aware that my companion put his hand over the region of my heart, as if to feel how it were beating, I did not attempt to prevent him, nor did I even ask him for the reason of his action. Everything in the room appeared to be reeling slowly round in a drowsy dance, of which I was the centre. The great elk's head at the far end wagged solemnly backward and forward, while the massive salvers on the tables performed cotillons with the claret-cooler and the epergne. My head fell upon my breast from sheer heaviness, and I should have become unconscious had I not been recalled to myself by the opening of the door at the other end of the hall.

This door led on to the raised dais, which, as I have mentioned, the heads of the house used to reserve for their own use. As it swung slowly back upon its hinges, I sat up in my chair, clutching at the arms, and staring with a horrified glare at the dark passage outside. Something was coming down it—something unformed and intangible, but still a something. Dim and shadowy, I saw it flit across the threshold, while a blast of ice-cold air swept down the room, which seemed to blow through me, chilling my very heart. I was aware of the mysterious presence, and then I heard it speak in a voice like the sighing of an east wind among pine-trees on the banks of a desolate sea.

It said: "I am the invisible nonentity. I have affinities and am subtle. I am electric, magnetic, and spiritualistic. I am the great ethereal sigh-heaver. I kill dogs. Mortal, wilt thou choose me?"

I was about to speak, but the words seemed to be choked in my throat; and, before I could get them out, the shadow flitted across the hall and vanished in the darkness at the other side, while a long-drawn melancholy sigh quivered through the apartment.

I turned my eyes toward the door once more, and beheld, to my astonishment, a very small old woman, who hobbled along the corridor and into the hall. She passed backward and forward several times, and then, crouching down at the very edge of the circle upon the floor, she disclosed a face the horrible malignity of which shall never be banished from my recollection. Every foul passion appeared to have left its mark upon that hideous countenance.

"Ha! ha!" she screamed, holding out her wizened hands like the talons of an unclean bird. "You see what I am. I am the fiendish old woman. I wear snuff-coloured silks. My curse descends on people. Sir Walter was partial to me. Shall I be thine, mortal?"

I endeavoured to shake my head in horror; on which she aimed a blow at me with her crutch, and vanished with an eldritch scream.

By this time my eyes turned naturally toward the open door, and I was hardly surprised to see a man walk in of tall and noble stature. His face was deadly pale, but was surmounted by a fringe of dark hair which fell in ringlets down his back. A short pointed beard covered his chin. He was dressed in loose-fitting clothes, made apparently of yellow satin, and a large white ruff surrounded his neck. He paced across the room with slow and majestic strides. Then turning, he addressed me in a sweet, exquisitely modulated voice.

"I am the cavalier," he remarked. "I pierce and am pierced. Here is my rapier. I clink steel. This is a blood stain over my heart. I can emit hollow groans. I am patronised by many old Conservative families. I am the original manor-house apparition. I work alone, or in company with shrieking damsels."

He bent his head courteously, as though awaiting my reply, but the same choking sensation prevented me from speaking; and, with a deep bow, he disappeared.

He had hardly gone before a feeling of intense horror stole over me, and I was aware of the presence of a ghastly creature in the room, of dim outlines and uncertain proportions. One moment it seemed to pervade the entire apartment, while at another it would become invisible, but always leaving behind it a distinct consciousness of its presence. Its voice, when it spoke, was quavering and gusty. It said: "I am the leaver of footsteps and the spiller of gouts of blood. I tramp upon corridors. Charles Dickens has alluded to me. I make strange and disagreeable noises. I snatch letters and place invisible hands on people's wrists. I am cheerful. I burst into peals of hideous laughter. Shall I do one now?" I raised my hand in a deprecating way, but too late to prevent one discordant outbreak which echoed through the room. Before I could lower it the apparition was gone.

I turned my head toward the door in time to see a man come hastily and stealthily into the chamber. He was a sunburnt powerfully built fellow, with ear-rings in his ears and a Barcelona handkerchief tied loosely round his neck. His head was bent upon his chest, and his whole aspect was that of one afflicted by intolerable remorse. He paced rapidly backward and forward like a caged tiger, and I observed that a drawn knife glittered in one of his hands, while he grasped what appeared to be a piece of parchment in the other. His voice, when he spoke, was deep and sonorous. He said, "I am a murderer. I am a ruffian. I crouch when I walk. I step noiselessly. I know something of the Spanish Main. I can do the lost treasure business. I have charts. Am able-bodied and a good walker. Capable of haunting a large park." He looked toward me beseechingly, but before I could make a sign I was paralysed by the horrible sight which appeared at the door.

It was a very tall man, if, indeed, it might be called a man, for the gaunt bones were protruding through the corroding flesh, and the features were of a leaden hue. A winding-sheet was wrapped round the figure, and formed a hood over the head, from under the shadow of which two fiendish eyes, deep set in their grisly sockets, blazed and sparkled like red-hot coals. The lower jaw had fallen upon the breast, disclosing a withered, shrivelled tongue and two lines of black and jagged fangs. I shuddered and drew back as this fearful apparition advanced to the edge of the circle.

"I am the American blood-curdler," it said, in a voice which seemed to come in a hollow murmur from the earth beneath it. "None other is genuine. I am the embodiment of Edgar Allan Poe. I am circumstantial and horrible. I am a low-caste spirit-subduing spectre. Observe my blood and my bones. I am grisly and nauseous. No depending on artificial aid. Work with grave-clothes, a coffin-lid, and a galvanic battery. Turn hair white in a night." The creature stretched out its fleshless arms to me as if in entreaty, but I shook my head; and it vanished, leaving a low, sickening, repulsive odour behind it. I sank back in my chair, so overcome by terror and disgust that I would have very willingly resigned myself to dispensing with a ghost altogether, could I have been sure that this was the last of the hideous procession.

A faint sound of trailing garments warned me that it was not so. I looked up, and beheld a white figure emerging from the corridor into the light. As it stepped across the threshold I saw that it was that of a young and beautiful woman dressed in the fashion of a bygone day. Her hands were clasped in front of her, and her pale proud face bore traces of passion and of suffering. She crossed the hall with a gentle sound, like the rustling of autumn leaves, and then, turning her lovely and unutterably sad eyes upon me, she said. "I am the plaintive and sentimental, the beautiful and ill-used. I have been forsaken and betrayed. I shriek in the night-time and glide down passages. My antecedents are highly respectable and generally aristocratic. My tastes are aesthetic. Old oak furniture like this would do, with a few more coats of mail and plenty of tapestry. Will you not take me?"

Her voice died away in a beautiful cadence as she concluded, and she held out her hands as if in supplication. I am always sensitive to female influences. Besides, what would Jorrocks's ghost be to this? Could anything be in better taste? Would I not be exposing myself to the chance of injuring my nervous system by interviews with such creatures as my last visitor, unless I decided at once? She gave me a seraphic smile, as if she knew what was passing in my mind. That smile settled the matter. "She will do!" I cried; "I choose this one;" and as, in my enthusiasm, I took a step toward her I passed over the magic circle which had girdled me round.

"Argentine, we have been robbed!"

I had an indistinct consciousness of these words being spoken, or rather screamed, in my ear a great number of times without my being able to grasp their meaning. A violent throbbing in my head seemed to adapt itself to their rhythm, and I closed my eyes to the lullaby of "Robbed, robbed, robbed." A vigorous shake caused me to open them again, however, and the sight of Mrs. D'Odd in the scantiest of costumes and most furious of tempers was sufficiently impressive to recall all my scattered thoughts, and make me realise that I was lying on my back on the floor, with my head among the ashes which had fallen from last night's fire, and a small glass phial in my hand.

I staggered to my feet, but felt so weak and giddy that I was compelled to fall back into a chair. As my brain became clearer, stimulated by the exclamations of Matilda, I began gradually to recollect the events of the night. There was the door through which my supernatural visitors had filed. There was the circle of chalk with the hieroglyphics round the edge. There was the cigar-box and brandy-bottle which had been honoured by the attentions of Mr. Abrahams. But the seer himself—where was he? and what was this open window with a rope running out of it? And where, Oh where, was the pride of Goresthorpe Grange, the glorious plate which was to have been the delectation of generations of D'Odds? And why was Mrs. D. standing in the grey light of dawn, wringing her hands and repeating her monotonous refrain? It was only very gradually that my misty brain took these things in, and grasped the connection between them.

Reader, I have never seen Mr. Abrahams since; I have never seen the plate stamped with the resuscitated family crest; hardest of all, I have never caught a glimpse of the melancholy spectre with the trailing garments, nor do I expect that I ever shall. In fact my night's experiences have cured me of my mania for the supernatural, and quite reconciled me to inhabiting the humdrum nineteenth-century edifice on the outskirts of London which Mrs. D. has long had in her mind's eye.

As to the explanation of all that occurred—that is a matter which is open to several surmises. That Mr. Abrahams, the ghost-hunter, was identical with Jemmy Wilson, alias the Nottingham crackster, is considered more than probable at Scotland Yard, and certainly the description of that remarkable burglar tallied very well with the appearance of my visitor. The small bag which I have described was picked up in a neighbouring field next day, and found to contain a choice assortment of jemmies and centre-bits. Footmarks deeply imprinted in the mud on either side of the moat showed that an accomplice from below had received the sack of precious metals which had been let down through the open window. No doubt the pair of scoundrels, while looking round for a job, had overheard Jack Brocket's indiscreet inquiries, and promptly availed themselves of the tempting opening.

And now as to my less substantial visitors, and the curious grotesque vision which I had enjoyed—am I to lay it down to any real power over occult matters possessed by my Nottingham friend? For a long time I was doubtful upon the point, and eventually endeavoured to solve it by consulting a well-known analyst and medical man, sending him the few drops of the so-called essence of Lucoptolycus which remained in my phial. I append the letter which I received from him, only too happy to have the opportunity of winding up my little narrative by the weighty words of a man of learning:

Arundel Street

Dear Sir: Your very singular case has interested me extremely. The bottle which you sent contained a strong solution of chloral, and the quantity which you describe yourself as having swallowed must have amounted to at least eighty grains of the pure hydrate. This would of course have reduced you to a partial state of insensibility, gradually going on to complete coma. In this semi-unconscious state of chloralism it is not unusual for circumstantial and bizarre visions to present themselves—more especially to individuals unaccustomed to the use of the drug. You tell me in your note that your mind was saturated with ghostly literature, and that you had long taken a morbid interest in classifying and recalling the various forms in which apparitions have been said to appear.

You must also remember that you were expecting to see something of that very nature, and that your nervous system was worked up to an unnatural state of tension. Under the circumstances, I think that, far from the sequel being an astonishing one, it would have been very surprising indeed to any one versed in narcotics had you not experienced some such effects.—I remain, dear sir, sincerely yours,

T. E. Stube, M.D.

Argentine D'Odd, Esq.
The Elms, Brixton.

Green Tea

Sheridan Le Fanu

PROLOGUE
MARTIN HESSELIUS, THE GERMAN PHYSICIAN

Though carefully educated in medicine and surgery, I have never practised either. The study of each continues, nevertheless, to interest me profoundly. Neither idleness nor caprice caused my secession from the honourable calling which I had just entered. The cause was a very trifling scratch inflicted by a dissecting knife. This trifle cost me the loss of two fingers, amputated promptly, and the more painful loss of my health, for I have never been quite well since, and have seldom been twelve months together in the same place.

In my wanderings I became acquainted with Dr. Martin Hesselius, a wanderer like myself, like me a physician, and like me an enthusiast in his profession. Unlike me in this, that his wanderings were voluntary, and he a man, if not of fortune, as we estimate fortune in England, at least in what our forefathers used to term "easy circumstances." He was an old man when I first saw him; nearly five-and-thirty years my senior.

In Dr. Martin Hesselius, I found my master. His knowledge was immense, his grasp of a case was an intuition. He was the very man to inspire a young enthusiast, like me, with awe and delight. My admiration has stood the test of time and survived the separation of death. I am sure it was well-founded.

For nearly twenty years I acted as his medical secretary. His immense collection of papers he has left in my care, to be arranged, indexed and bound. His treatment of some of these cases is curious. He writes in two distinct characters. He describes what he saw and heard as an intelligent layman might, and when in this style of narrative he had seen the patient either through his own hall-door, to the light of day, or through the gates of darkness to the caverns of the dead, he returns upon the narrative, and in the terms of his art and with all the force and originality of genius, proceeds to the work of analysis, diagnosis and illustration.

Here and there a case strikes me as of a kind to amuse or horrify a lay reader with an interest quite different from the peculiar one which it may possess for an expert. With slight modifications, chiefly of language, and of course a change of names, I copy the following. The narrator is Dr. Martin Hesselius. I find it among the voluminous notes of cases which he made during a tour in England about sixty-four years ago.

It is related in series of letters to his friend Professor Van Loo of Leyden. The professor was not a physician, but a chemist, and a man who read history and metaphysics and medicine, and had, in his day, written a play.

The narrative is therefore, if somewhat less valuable as a medical record, necessarily written in a manner more likely to interest an unlearned reader.

These letters, from a memorandum attached, appear to have been returned on the death of the professor, in 1819, to Dr. Hesselius. They are written, some in English, some in French, but the greater part in German. I am a faithful, though I am conscious, by no means a graceful translator, and although here and there I omit some passages, and shorten others, and disguise names, I have interpolated nothing.

CHAPTER 1
DR. HESSELIUS RELATES HOW HE MET THE REV. MR. JENNINGS

The Rev. Mr. Jennings is tall and thin. He is middle-aged, and dresses with a natty, old-fashioned, high-church precision. He is naturally a little stately, but not at all stiff. His features, without being handsome, are well formed, and their expression extremely kind, but also shy.

I met him one evening at Lady Mary Heyduke's. The modesty and benevolence of his countenance are extremely prepossessing.

We were but a small party, and he joined agreeably enough in the conversation, He seems to enjoy listening very much more than contributing to the talk; but what he says is always to the purpose and well said. He is a great favourite of Lady Mary's, who it seems, consults him upon many things, and thinks him the most happy and blessed person on earth. Little knows she about him.

The Rev. Mr. Jennings is a bachelor, and has, they say sixty thousand pounds in the funds. He is a charitable man. He is most anxious to be actively employed in his sacred profession, and yet though always tolerably well elsewhere, when he goes down to his vicarage in Warwickshire, to engage in the actual duties of his sacred calling, his health soon fails him, and in a very strange way. So says Lady Mary.

There is no doubt that Mr. Jennings' health does break down in, generally, a sudden and mysterious way, sometimes in the very act of officiating in his old and pretty church at Kenlis. It may be his heart, it may be his brain. But so it has happened three or four times, or oftener, that after proceeding a certain way in the service, he has on a sudden stopped short, and after a silence, apparently quite unable to resume, he has fallen into solitary, inaudible prayer, his hands and his eyes uplifted, and then pale as death, and in the agitation of a strange shame and horror, descended trembling, and got into the vestry-room, leaving his congregation, without explanation, to themselves. This occurred when his curate was absent. When he goes down to Kenlis now, he always takes care to provide a clergyman to share his duty, and to supply his place on the instant should he become thus suddenly incapacitated.

When Mr. Jennings breaks down quite, and beats a retreat from the vicarage, and returns to London, where, in a dark street off Piccadilly, he inhabits a very narrow house, Lady Mary says that he is always perfectly well. I have my own opinion about that. There are degrees of course. We shall see.

Mr. Jennings is a perfectly gentlemanlike man. People, however, remark something odd. There is an impression a little ambiguous. One thing which certainly contributes to it, people I think don't remember; or, perhaps, distinctly remark. But I did, almost immediately. Mr. Jennings has a way of looking sidelong upon the carpet, as if his eye followed the movements of something there. This, of course, is not always. It occurs now and then. But often enough to give a certain oddity, as I have said, to his manner, and in this glance travelling along the floor there is something both shy and anxious.

A medical philosopher, as you are good enough to call me, elaborating theories by the aid of cases sought out by himself, and by him watched and scrutinised with more time at command, and consequently infinitely more minuteness than the ordinary practitioner can afford, falls insensibly into habits of observation, which accompany him everywhere, and are exercised, as some people would say, impertinently, upon every subject that presents itself with the least likelihood of rewarding inquiry.

There was a promise of this kind in the slight, timid, kindly, but reserved gentleman, whom I met for the first time at this agreeable little evening gathering. I observed, of course, more than I here set down; but I reserve all that borders on the technical for a strictly scientific paper.

I may remark, that when I here speak of medical science, I do so, as I hope someday to see it more generally understood, in a much more comprehensive sense than its generally material treatment would warrant. I believe the entire natural world is but the ultimate expression of that spiritual world from which, and in which alone, it has its life. I believe that the essential man is a spirit, that the spirit is an organised substance, but as different in point of material from what we ordinarily understand by matter, as light or electricity is; that the material body is, in the most literal sense, a vesture, and death consequently no interruption of the living man's existence, but simply his extrication from the natural body—a process which commences at the moment of what we term death, and the completion of which, at furthest a few days later, is the resurrection "in power."

The person who weighs the consequences of these positions will probably see their practical bearing upon medical science. This is, however, by no means the proper place for displaying the proofs and discussing the consequences of this too generally unrecognized state of facts.

In pursuance of my habit, I was covertly observing Mr. Jennings, with all my caution—I think he perceived it—and I saw plainly that he was as cautiously observing me. Lady Mary happening to address me by my name, as Dr. Hesselius, I saw that he glanced at me more sharply, and then became thoughtful for a few minutes.

After this, as I conversed with a gentleman at the other end of the room, I saw him look at me more steadily, and with an interest which I thought I understood. I then saw him take an opportunity of chatting with Lady Mary, and was, as one always is, perfectly aware of being the subject of a distant inquiry and answer.

This tall clergyman approached me by-and-by; and in a little time we had got into conversation. When two people, who like reading, and know books and places, having travelled, wish to discourse, it is very strange if they can't find topics. It was not accident that brought him near me, and led him into conversation. He knew German and had read my Essays on Metaphysical Medicine which suggest more than they actually say.

This courteous man, gentle, shy, plainly a man of thought and reading, who moving and talking among us, was not altogether of us, and whom I already suspected of leading a life whose transactions and alarms were carefully concealed, with an impenetrable reserve from, not only the world, but his best beloved friends—was cautiously weighing in his own mind the idea of taking a certain step with regard to me.

I penetrated his thoughts without his being aware of it, and was careful to say nothing which could betray to his sensitive vigilance my suspicions respecting his position, or my surmises about his plans respecting myself.

We chatted upon indifferent subjects for a time but at last he said:

"I was very much interested by some papers of yours, Dr. Hesselius, upon what you term Metaphysical Medicine—I read them in German, ten or twelve years ago—have they been translated?"

"No, I'm sure they have not—I should have heard. They would have asked my leave, I think."

"I asked the publishers here, a few months ago, to get the book for me in the original German; but they tell me it is out of print."

"So it is, and has been for some years; but it flatters me as an author to find that you have not forgotten my little book, although," I added, laughing, "ten or twelve years is a considerable time to have managed without it; but I suppose you have been turning the subject over again in your mind, or something has happened lately to revive your interest in it."

At this remark, accompanied by a glance of inquiry, a sudden embarrassment disturbed Mr. Jennings, analogous to that which makes a young lady blush and look foolish. He dropped his eyes, and folded his hands together uneasily, and looked oddly, and you would have said, guiltily, for a moment.

I helped him out of his awkwardness in the best way, by appearing not to observe it, and going straight on, I said: "Those revivals of interest in a subject happen to me often; one book suggests another, and often sends me back a wild-goose chase over an interval of twenty years. But if you still care to possess a copy, I shall be only too happy to provide you; I have still got two or three by me—and if you allow me to present one I shall be very much honoured."

"You are very good indeed," he said, quite at his ease again, in a moment: "I almost despaired—I don't know how to thank you."

"Pray don't say a word; the thing is really so little worth that I am only ashamed of having offered it, and if you thank me any more I shall throw it into the fire in a fit of modesty."

Mr. Jennings laughed. He inquired where I was staying in London, and after a little more conversation on a variety of subjects, he took his departure.

Chapter 2

The Doctor Questions Lady Mary, and She Answers

"I like your vicar so much, Lady Mary," said I, as soon as he was gone. "He has read, travelled, and thought, and having also suffered, he ought to be an accomplished companion."

"So he is, and, better still, he is a really good man," said she. "His advice is invaluable about my schools, and all my little undertakings at Dawlbridge, and he's so painstaking, he takes so much trouble—you have no idea—wherever he thinks he can be of use: he's so good-natured and so sensible."

"It is pleasant to hear so good an account of his neighbourly virtues. I can only testify to his being an agreeable and gentle companion, and in addition to what you have told me, I think I can tell you two or three things about him," said I.

"Really!"

"Yes, to begin with, he's unmarried."

"Yes, that's right—go on."

"He has been writing, that is he *was*, but for two or three years perhaps, he has not gone on with his work, and the book was upon some rather abstract subject—perhaps theology."

"Well, he was writing a book, as you say; I'm not quite sure what it was about, but only that it was nothing that I cared for; very likely you are right, and he certainly did stop—yes."

"And although he only drank a little coffee here tonight, he likes tea, at least, did like it extravagantly."

"Yes, that's *quite* true."

"He drank green tea, a good deal, didn't he?" I pursued.

"Well, that's very odd! Green tea was a subject on which we used almost to quarrel."

"But he has quite given that up," said I.

"So he has."

"And, now, one more fact. His mother or his father, did you know them?"

"Yes, both; his father is only ten years dead, and their place is near Dawlbridge. We knew them very well," she answered.

"Well, either his mother or his father—I should rather think his father, saw a ghost," said I.

"Well, you really are a conjurer, Dr. Hesselius."

"Conjurer or no, haven't I said right?" I answered merrily.

"You certainly have, and it *was* his father: he was a silent, whimsical man, and he used to bore my father about his dreams, and at last he told him a story about a ghost he had seen and talked with, and a very odd story it was. I remember it particularly, because I was so afraid of him. This story was long before he died—when I was quite a child—and his ways were so silent and moping, and he used to drop in sometimes, in the dusk, when I was alone in the drawing-room, and I used to fancy there were ghosts about him."

I smiled and nodded.

"And now, having established my character as a conjurer, I think I must say goodnight," said I.

"But how *did* you find it out?"

"By the planets, of course, as the gipsies do," I answered, and so, gaily we said goodnight.

Next morning I sent the little book he had been inquiring after, and a note to Mr. Jennings, and on returning late that evening, I found that he had called at my lodgings, and left his card. He asked whether I was at home, and asked at what hour he would be most likely to find me.

Does he intend opening his case, and consulting me "professionally," as they say? I hope so. I have already conceived a theory about him. It is supported by Lady Mary's answers to my parting questions. I should like much to ascertain from his own lips. But what can I do consistently with good breeding to invite a confession? Nothing. I rather think he meditates one. At all events, my dear Van L., I shan't make myself difficult of access; I mean to return his visit tomorrow. It will be only civil in return for his politeness, to ask to see him. Perhaps something may come of it. Whether much, little, or nothing, my dear Van L., you shall hear.

CHAPTER 3
DR. HESSELIUS PICKS UP SOMETHING IN LATIN BOOKS

Well, I have called at Bank Street.

On inquiring at the door, the servant told me that Mr. Jennings was engaged very particularly with a gentleman, a clergyman from Kenlis, his parish in the country. Intending to reserve my privilege, and to call again, I merely intimated that I should try another time, and had turned to go, when the servant begged my pardon, and asked me, looking at me a little more attentively than well-bred persons of his order usually do, whether I was Dr. Hesselius; and, on learning that I was, he said, "Perhaps then, sir, you would allow me to mention it to Mr. Jennings, for I am sure he wishes to see you."

The servant returned in a moment, with a message from Mr. Jennings, asking me to go into his study, which was in effect his back drawing-room, promising to be with me in a very few minutes.

This was really a study—almost a library. The room was lofty, with two tall slender windows, and rich dark curtains. It was much larger than I had expected, and stored with books on every side, from the floor to the ceiling. The upper carpet—for to my tread it felt that there were two or three—was a Turkey carpet. My steps fell noiselessly. The bookcases standing out, placed the windows, particularly narrow ones, in deep recesses. The effect of the room was, although extremely comfortable, and even luxurious, decidedly gloomy, and aided by the silence, almost oppressive. Perhaps, however, I ought to have allowed something for association. My mind had connected peculiar ideas with Mr. Jennings. I stepped into this perfectly silent room, of a very silent house, with a peculiar foreboding; and its darkness, and solemn clothing of books, for except where two narrow looking-glasses were set in the wall, they were everywhere, helped this sombre feeling.

While awaiting Mr. Jennings' arrival, I amused myself by looking into some of the books with which his shelves were laden. Not among these, but immediately under them, with their backs upward, on the floor, I lighted upon a complete set of Swedenborg's *Arcana Caelestia*, in the original Latin, a very fine folio set, bound in the natty livery which theology affects, pure vellum, namely, gold letters, and carmine edges. There were paper markers in several of these volumes, I raised and placed them, one after the other, upon the table, and opening where these papers were placed, I read in the solemn Latin phraseology, a series of sentences indicated by a pencilled line at the margin. Of these I copy here a few, translating them into English.

When man's interior sight is opened, which is that of his spirit, then there appear the things of another life, which cannot possibly be made visible to the bodily sight. . . .

By the internal sight it has been granted me to see the things that are in the other life, more clearly than I see those that are in the world. From these considerations, it is evident that external vision exists from interior vision, and this from a vision still more interior, and so on. . . .

There are with every man at least two evil spirits. . . .

With wicked *genii* there is also a fluent speech, but harsh and grating. There is also among them a speech which is not fluent, wherein the dissent of the thoughts is perceived as something secretly creeping along within it. . . .

The evil spirits associated with man are, indeed from the hells, but when with man they are not then in hell, but are taken out thence. The place where they then are, is in the midst between heaven and hell, and is called the world of spirits—when the evil spirits who are with man, are in that world, they are not in any infernal torment, but in every thought and affection of man, and so, in all that the man himself enjoys. But when they are remitted into their hell, they return to their former state. . .

If evil spirits could perceive that they were associated with man, and yet that they were spirits separate from him, and if they could flow in into the things of his body, they would attempt by a thousand means to destroy him; for they hate man with a deadly hatred. . . .

Knowing, therefore, that I was a man in the body, they were continually striving to destroy me, not as to the body only, but especially as to the soul; for to destroy any man or spirit is the very delight of the life of all who are in hell; but I have been continually protected by the Lord. Hence it appears how dangerous it is for man to be in a living consort with spirits, unless he be in the good of faith. . . .

Nothing is more carefully guarded from the knowledge of associate spirits than their being thus conjoint with a man, for if they knew it they would speak to him, with the intention to destroy him. . . .

The delight of hell is to do evil to man, and to hasten his eternal ruin. . . .

A long note, written with a very sharp and fine pencil, in Mr. Jennings' neat hand, at the foot of the page, caught my eye. Expecting his criticism upon the text, I read a word or two, and stopped, for it was something quite different, and began with these words, *Deus misereatur mei*—"May God compassionate me." Thus warned of its private nature, I averted my eyes, and shut the book, replacing all the volumes as I had found them, except one which interested me, and in which, as men studious and solitary in their habits will do, I grew so absorbed as to take no cognisance of the outer world, nor to remember where I was.

I was reading some pages which refer to "representatives" and "correspondents," in the technical language of Swedenborg, and had arrived at a passage, the substance of which is, that evil spirits, when seen by other eyes than those of their infernal associates, present themselves, by "correspondence," in the shape of the beast (*fera*) which represents their particular lust and life, in aspect direful and atrocious. This is a long passage, and particularises a number of those bestial forms.

CHAPTER 4
FOUR EYES WERE READING THE PASSAGE

I was running the head of my pencil-case along the line as I read it, and something caused me to raise my eyes.

Directly before me was one of the mirrors I have mentioned, in which I saw reflected the tall shape of my friend, Mr. Jennings, leaning over my shoulder, and reading the page at which I was busy, and with a face so dark and wild that I should hardly have known him.

I turned and rose. He stood erect also, and with an effort laughed a little, saying:

"I came in and asked you how you did, but without succeeding in awaking you from your book; so I could not restrain my curiosity, and very impertinently, I'm afraid, peeped over your shoulder. This is not your first time of looking into those pages. You have looked into Swedenborg, no doubt, long ago?"

"Oh dear, yes! I owe Swedenborg a great deal; you will discover traces of him in the little book on Metaphysical Medicine, which you were so good as to remember."

Although my friend affected a gaiety of manner, there was a slight flush in his face, and I could perceive that he was inwardly much perturbed.

"I'm scarcely yet qualified, I know so little of Swedenborg. I've only had them a fortnight," he answered, "and I think they are rather likely to make a solitary man nervous—that is, judging from the very little I have read—I don't say that they have made me so," he laughed; "and I'm so very much obliged for the book. I hope you got my note?"

I made all proper acknowledgments and modest disclaimers.

"I never read a book that I go with, so entirely, as that of yours," he continued. "I saw at once there is more in it than is quite unfolded. Do you know Dr. Harley?" he asked, rather abruptly.

In passing, the editor remarks that the physician here named was one of the most eminent who had ever practised in England.

I did, having had letters to him, and had experienced from him great courtesy and considerable assistance during my visit to England.

"I think that man one of the very greatest fools I ever met in my life," said Mr. Jennings.

This was the first time I had ever heard him say a sharp thing of anybody, and such a term applied to so high a name a little startled me.

"Really! and in what way?" I asked.

"In his profession," he answered.

I smiled.

"I mean this," he said: "he seems to me, one half, blind—I mean one half of all he looks at is dark—preternaturally bright and vivid all the rest; and the worst of it is, it seems *wilful*. I can't get him—I mean he won't—I've had some experience of him as a physician, but I look on him as, in that sense, no better than a paralytic mind, an intellect half dead. I'll tell you—I know I shall some time—all about it," he said, with a little agitation. "You stay some months longer in England. If I should be out of town during your stay for a little time, would you allow me to trouble you with a letter?"

"I should be only too happy," I assured him.

"Very good of you. I am so utterly dissatisfied with Harley."

"A little leaning to the materialistic school," I said.

"A *mere* materialist," he corrected me; "you can't think how that sort of thing worries one who knows better. You won't tell anyone—any of my friends you know—that I am hippish; now, for instance, no one knows—not even Lady Mary—that I have seen Dr. Harley, or any other doctor. So pray don't mention it; and, if I should have any threatening of an attack, you'll kindly let me write, or, should I be in town, have a little talk with you."

I was full of conjecture, and unconsciously I found I had fixed my eyes gravely on him, for he lowered his for a moment, and he said:

"I see you think I might as well tell you now, or else you are forming a conjecture; but you may as well give it up. If you were guessing all the rest of your life, you will never hit on it."

He shook his head smiling, and over that wintry sunshine a black cloud suddenly came down, and he drew his breath in, through his teeth as men do in pain.

"Sorry, of course, to learn that you apprehend occasion to consult any of us; but, command me when and how you like, and I need not assure you that your confidence is sacred."

He then talked of quite other things, and in a comparatively cheerful way and after a little time, I took my leave.

CHAPTER 5
DR. HESSELIUS IS SUMMONED TO RICHMOND

We parted cheerfully, but he was not cheerful, nor was I. There are certain expressions of that powerful organ of spirit–the human face— which, although I have seen them often, and possess a doctor's nerve, yet disturb me profoundly. One look of Mr. Jennings haunted me. It had seized my imagination with so dismal a power that I changed my plans for the evening, and went to the opera, feeling that I wanted a change of ideas.

I heard nothing of or from him for two or three days, when a note in his hand reached me. It was cheerful, and full of hope. He said that he had been for some little time so much better—quite well, in fact— that he was going to make a little experiment, and run down for a month or so to his parish, to try whether a little work might not quite set him up. There was in it a fervent religious expression of gratitude for his restoration, as he now almost hoped he might call it.

A day or two later I saw Lady Mary, who repeated what his note had announced, and told me that he was actually in Warwickshire, having resumed his clerical duties at Kenlis; and she added, "I begin to think that he is really perfectly well, and that there never was anything the matter, more than nerves and fancy; we are all nervous, but I fancy there is nothing like a little hard work for that kind of weakness, and he has made up his mind to try it. I should not be surprised if he did not come back for a year."

Notwithstanding all this confidence, only two days later I had this note, dated from his house off Piccadilly:

Dear Sir,—I have returned disappointed. If I should feel at all able to see you, I shall write to ask you kindly to call. At present, I am too low, and, in fact, simply unable to say all I wish to say. Pray don't mention my name to my friends. I can see no one. By-and-by, please God, you shall hear from me. I mean to take a run into Shropshire, where some of my people are. God bless you! May we, on my return, meet more happily than I can now write.

About a week after this I saw Lady Mary at her own house, the last person, she said, left in town, and just on the wing for Brighton, for the London season was quite over. She told me that she had heard from Mr. Jenning's niece, Martha, in Shropshire. There was nothing to be gathered from her letter, more than that he was low and nervous. In those words, of which healthy people think so lightly, what a world of suffering is sometimes hidden!

Nearly five weeks had passed without any further news of Mr. Jennings. At the end of that time I received a note from him. He wrote:

I have been in the country, and have had change of air, change of scene, change of faces, change of everything—and in everything—but *myself*. I have made up my mind, so far as the most irresolute creature on earth can do it, to tell my case fully to you. If your engagements will permit, pray come to me today, tomorrow, or the next day; but, pray defer as little as possible. You know not how much I need help.
I have a quiet house at Richmond, where I now am. Perhaps you can manage to come to dinner, or to luncheon, or even to tea. You shall have no trouble in finding me out. The servant at Blank Street, who takes this note, will have a carriage at your door at any hour you please; and I am always to be found. You will say that I ought not to be alone. I have tried everything. Come and see.

I called up the servant, and decided on going out the same evening, which accordingly I did.

He would have been much better in a lodging-house, or hotel, I thought, as I drove up through a short double row of sombre elms to a very old-fashioned brick house, darkened by the foliage of these trees, which overtopped, and nearly surrounded it. It was a perverse choice, for nothing could be imagined more triste and silent.

The house, I found, belonged to him. He had stayed for a day or two in town, and, finding it for some cause insupportable, had come out here, probably because being furnished and his own, he was relieved of the thought and delay of selection, by coming here.

The sun had already set, and the red reflected light of the western sky illuminated the scene with the peculiar effect with which we are all familiar. The hall seemed very dark, but, getting to the back drawing-room, whose windows command the west, I was again in the same dusky light.

I sat down, looking out upon the richly-wooded landscape that glowed in the grand and melancholy light which was every moment fading. The corners of the room were already dark; all was growing dim, and the gloom was insensibly toning my mind, already prepared for what was sinister. I was waiting alone for his arrival, which soon took place. The door communicating with the front room opened, and the tall figure of Mr. Jennings, faintly seen in the ruddy twilight, came, with quiet stealthy steps, into the room.

We shook hands, and, taking a chair to the window, where there was still light enough to enable us to see each other's faces, he sat down beside me, and, placing his hand upon my arm, with scarcely a word of preface began his narrative.

CHAPTER 6
How Mr. Jennings Met His Companion

The faint glow of the west, the pomp of the then lonely woods of Richmond, were before us, behind and about us the darkening room, and on the stony face of the sufferer—for the character of his face, though still gentle and sweet, was changed—rested that dim, odd glow which seems to descend and produce, where it touches, lights, sudden though faint, which are lost, almost without gradation, in darkness. The silence, too, was utter: not a distant wheel, or bark, or whistle from without; and within the depressing stillness of an invalid bachelor's house.

I guessed well the nature, though not even vaguely the particulars of the revelations I was about to receive, from that fixed face of suffering that so oddly flushed stood out, like a portrait of Schalken's, before its background of darkness.

"It began," he said, "on the 15th of October, three years and eleven weeks ago, and two days—I keep very accurate count, for every day is torment. If I leave anywhere a chasm in my narrative tell me.

"About four years ago I began a work, which had cost me very much thought and reading. It was upon the religious metaphysics of the ancients."

"I know," said I, "the actual religion of educated and thinking paganism, quite apart from symbolic worship? A wide and very interesting field."

"Yes, but not good for the mind—the Christian mind, I mean. Paganism is all bound together in essential unity, and, with evil sympathy, their religion involves their art, and both their manners, and the subject is a degrading fascination and the Nemesis sure. God forgive me!

"I wrote a great deal; I wrote late at night. I was always thinking on the subject, walking about, wherever I was, everywhere. It thoroughly infected me. You are to remember that all the material ideas connected with it were more or less of the beautiful, the subject itself delightfully interesting, and I, then, without a care."

He sighed heavily.

"I believe, that everyone who sets about writing in earnest does his work, as a friend of mine phrased it, *on* something—tea, or coffee, or tobacco. I suppose there is a material waste that must be hourly supplied in such occupations, or that we should grow too abstracted, and the mind, as it were, pass out of the body, unless it were reminded often enough of the connection by actual sensation. At all events, I felt the want, and I supplied it. Tea was my companion—at first the ordinary black tea, made in the usual way, not too strong: but I drank a good deal, and increased its strength as I went on. I never experienced an uncomfortable symptom from it. I began to take a little green tea. I found the effect pleasanter, it cleared and intensified the power of thought so, I had come to take it frequently, but not stronger than one might take it for pleasure.

"I wrote a great deal out here, it was so quiet, and in this room. I used to sit up very late, and it became a habit with me to sip my tea—green tea—every now and then as my work proceeded. I had a little kettle on my table, that swung over a lamp, and made tea two or three times between eleven o'clock and two or three in the morning, my hours of going to bed. I used to go into town every day. I was not a monk, and, although I spent an hour or two in a library, hunting up authorities and looking out lights upon my theme, I was in no morbid state as far as I can judge. I met my friends pretty much as usual and enjoyed their society, and, on the whole, existence had never been, I think, so pleasant before.

"I had met with a man who had some odd old books, German

editions in mediaeval Latin, and I was only too happy to be permitted access to them. This obliging person's books were in the City, a very out-of-the-way part of it. I had rather out-stayed my intended hour, and, on coming out, seeing no cab near, I was tempted to get into the omnibus which used to drive past this house. It was darker than this by the time the 'bus had reached an old house, you may have remarked, with four poplars at each side of the door, and there the last passenger but myself got out. We drove along rather faster. It was twilight now. I leaned back in my corner next the door ruminating pleasantly.

"The interior of the omnibus was nearly dark. I had observed in the corner opposite to me at the other side, and at the end next the horses, two small circular reflections, as it seemed to me of a reddish light. They were about two inches apart, and about the size of those small brass buttons that yachting men used to put upon their jackets. I began to speculate, as listless men will, upon this trifle, as it seemed. From what centre did that faint but deep red light come, and from what—glass beads, buttons, toy decorations—was it reflected? We were lumbering along gently, having nearly a mile still to go. I had not solved the puzzle, and it became in another minute more odd, for these two luminous points, with a sudden jerk, descended nearer and nearer the floor, keeping still their relative distance and horizontal position, and then, as suddenly, they rose to the level of the seat on which I was sitting and I saw them no more.

"My curiosity was now really excited, and, before I had time to think, I saw again these two dull lamps, again together near the floor; again they disappeared, and again in their old corner I saw them.

"So, keeping my eyes upon them, I edged quietly up my own side, towards the end at which I still saw these tiny discs of red.

"There was very little light in the 'bus. It was nearly dark. I leaned forward to aid my endeavour to discover what these little circles really were. They shifted position a little as I did so. I began now to perceive an outline of something black, and I soon saw, with tolerable distinctness, the outline of a small black monkey, pushing its face forward in mimicry to meet mine; those were its eyes, and I now dimly saw its teeth grinning at me.

"I drew back, not knowing whether it might not meditate a spring. I fancied that one of the passengers had forgot this ugly pet, and wishing to ascertain something of its temper, though not caring to trust my fingers to it, I poked my umbrella softly towards it. It remained immovable—up to it—*through* it. For through it, and back and forward it passed, without the slightest resistance.

"I can't, in the least, convey to you the kind of horror that I felt. When I had ascertained that the thing was an illusion, as I then supposed, there came a misgiving about myself and a terror that fascinated me in impotence to remove my gaze from the eyes of the brute for some moments. As I looked, it made a little skip back, quite into the corner, and I, in a panic, found myself at the door, having put my head out, drawing deep breaths of the outer air, and staring at the lights and tress we were passing, too glad to reassure myself of reality.

"I stopped the 'bus and got out. I perceived the man look oddly at me as I paid him. I dare say there was something unusual in my looks and manner, for I had never felt so strangely before."

CHAPTER 7
THE JOURNEY: FIRST STAGE

"When the omnibus drove on, and I was alone upon the road, I looked carefully round to ascertain whether the monkey had followed me. To my indescribable relief I saw it nowhere. I can't describe easily what a shock I had received, and my sense of genuine gratitude on finding myself, as I supposed, quite rid of it.

"I had got out a little before we reached this house, two or three hundred steps. A brick wall runs along the footpath, and inside the wall is a hedge of yew, or some dark evergreen of that kind, and within that again the row of fine trees which you may have remarked as you came.

"This brick wall is about as high as my shoulder, and happening to raise my eyes I saw the monkey, with that stooping gait, on all fours, walking or creeping, close beside me, on top of the wall. I stopped, looking at it with a feeling of loathing and horror. As I stopped so did it. It sat up on the wall with its long hands on its knees looking at me. There was not light enough to see it much more than in outline, nor was it dark enough to bring the peculiar light of its eyes into strong relief. I still saw, however, that red foggy light plainly enough. It did not show its teeth, nor exhibit any sign of irritation, but seemed jaded and sulky, and was observing me steadily.

"I drew back into the middle of the road. It was an unconscious recoil, and there I stood, still looking at it. It did not move.

"With an instinctive determination to try something—anything, I turned about and walked briskly towards town with askance look, all the time, watching the movements of the beast. It crept swiftly along the wall, at exactly my pace.

"Where the wall ends, near the turn of the road, it came down, and with a wiry spring or two brought itself close to my feet, and continued to keep up with me, as I quickened my pace. It was at my left side, so close to my leg that I felt every moment as if I should tread upon it.

"The road was quite deserted and silent, and it was darker every moment. I stopped dismayed and bewildered, turning as I did so, the other way—I mean, towards this house, away from which I had been walking. When I stood still, the monkey drew back to a distance of, I suppose, about five or six yards, and remained stationary, watching me.

"I had been more agitated than I have said. I had read, of course, as everyone has, something about 'spectral illusions,' as you physicians term the phenomena of such cases. I considered my situation, and looked my misfortune in the face.

"These affections, I had read, are sometimes transitory and sometimes obstinate. I had read of cases in which the appearance, at first harmless, had, step by step, degenerated into something direful and insupportable, and ended by wearing its victim out. Still as I stood there, but for my bestial companion, quite alone, I tried to comfort myself by repeating again and again the assurance, 'the thing is purely disease, a well-known physical affection, as distinctly as smallpox or neuralgia. Doctors are all agreed on that, philosophy demonstrates it. I must not be a fool. I've been sitting up too late, and I daresay my digestion is quite wrong, and, with God's help, I shall be all right, and this is but a symptom of nervous dyspepsia.' Did I believe all this? Not one word of it, no more than any other miserable being ever did who is once seized and riveted in this satanic captivity. Against my convictions, I might say my knowledge, I was simply bullying myself into a false courage.

"I now walked homeward. I had only a few hundred yards to go. I had forced myself into a sort of resignation, but I had not got over the sickening shock and the flurry of the first certainty of my misfortune.

"I made up my mind to pass the night at home. The brute moved close beside me, and I fancied there was the sort of anxious drawing toward the house, which one sees in tired horses or dogs, sometimes as they come toward home.

"I was afraid to go into town, I was afraid of any one's seeing and recognising me. I was conscious of an irrepressible agitation in my manner. Also, I was afraid of any violent change in my habits, such as going to a place of amusement, or walking from home in order to fatigue myself. At the hall door it waited till I mounted the steps, and when the door was opened entered with me.

"I drank no tea that night. I got cigars and some brandy and water. My idea was that I should act upon my material system, and by living for a while in sensation apart from thought, send myself forcibly, as it were, into a new groove. I came up here to this drawing-room. I sat just here. The monkey then got upon a small table that then stood *there*. It looked dazed and languid. An irrepressible uneasiness as to its movements kept my eyes always upon it. Its eyes were half closed, but I could see them glow. It was looking steadily at me. In all situations, at all hours, it is awake and looking at me. That never changes.

"I shall not continue in detail my narrative of this particular night. I shall describe, rather, the phenomena of the first year, which never varied, essentially. I shall describe the monkey as it appeared in daylight. In the dark, as you shall presently hear, there are peculiarities. It is a small monkey, perfectly black. It had only one peculiarity—a character of malignity—unfathomable malignity. During the first year it looked sullen and sick. But this character of intense malice and vigilance was always underlying that surly languor. During all that time it acted as if on a plan of giving me as little trouble as was consistent with watching me. Its eyes were never off me. I have never lost sight of it, except in my sleep, light or dark, day or night, since it came here, excepting when it withdraws for some weeks at a time, unaccountably.

"In total dark it is visible as in daylight. I do not mean merely its eyes. It is *all* visible distinctly in a halo that resembles a glow of red embers, and which accompanies it in all its movements.

"When it leaves me for a time, it is always at night, in the dark, and in the same way. It grows at first uneasy, and then furious, and then advances towards me, grinning and shaking, its paws clenched, and, at the same time, there comes the appearance of fire in the grate. I never have any fire. I can't sleep in the room where there is any, and it draws nearer and nearer to the chimney, quivering, it seems, with rage, and when its fury rises to the highest pitch, it springs into the grate, and up the chimney, and I see it no more.

"When first this happened, I thought I was released. I was now a new man. A day passed—a night—and no return, and a blessed week—a week—nother week. I was always on my knees, Dr. Hesselius, always, thanking God and praying. A whole month passed of liberty, but on a sudden, it was with me again."

CHAPTER 8
THE SECOND STAGE

"It was with me, and the malice which before was torpid under a sullen exterior, was now active. It was perfectly unchanged in every other respect. This new energy was apparent in its activity and its looks, and soon in other ways.

"For a time, you will understand, the change was shown only in an increased vivacity, and an air of menace, as if it were always brooding over some atrocious plan. Its eyes, as before, were never off me."

"Is it here now?" I asked.

"No," he replied, "it has been absent exactly a fortnight and a day—fifteen days. It has sometimes been away so long as nearly two months, once for three. Its absence always exceeds a fortnight, although it may be but by a single day. Fifteen days having past since I saw it last, it may return now at any moment."

"Is its return," I asked, "accompanied by any peculiar manifestation?"

"Nothing—no," he said. "It is simply with me again. On lifting my eyes from a book, or turning my head, I see it, as usual, looking at me, and then it remains, as before, for its appointed time. I have never told so much and so minutely before to anyone."

I perceived that he was agitated, and looking like death, and he repeatedly applied his handkerchief to his forehead; I suggested that he might be tired, and told him that I would call, with pleasure, in the morning, but he said:

"No, if you don't mind hearing it all now. I have got so far, and I should prefer making one effort of it. When I spoke to Dr. Harley, I had nothing like so much to tell. You are a philosophic physician. You give spirit its proper rank. If this thing is real—"

He paused looking at me with agitated inquiry.

"We can discuss it by-and-by, and very fully. I will give you all I think," I answered, after an interval.

"Well—very well. If it is anything real, I say, it is prevailing, little by little, and drawing me more interiorly into hell. Optic nerves, he talked of. Ah! well—there are other nerves of communication. May God Almighty help me! You shall hear.

"Its power of action, I tell you, had increased. Its malice became, in a way, aggressive. About two years ago, some questions that were pending between me and the bishop having been settled, I went down to my parish in Warwickshire, anxious to find occupation in my profession. I was not prepared for what happened, although I have since thought I might have apprehended something like it. The reason of my saying so is this—"

He was beginning to speak with a great deal more effort and reluctance, and sighed often, and seemed at times nearly overcome. But at this time his manner was not agitated. It was more like that of a sinking patient, who has given himself up.

"Yes, but I will first tell you about Kenlis, my parish.

"It was with me when I left this place for Dawlbridge. It was my silent travelling companion, and it remained with me at the vicarage. When I entered on the discharge of my duties, another change took place. The thing exhibited an atrocious determination to thwart me. It was with me in the church—in the reading-desk—in the pulpit—within the communion rails. At last, it reached this extremity, that while I was reading to the congregation, it would spring upon the book and squat there, so that I was unable to see the page. This happened more than once.

"I left Dawlbridge for a time. I placed myself in Dr. Harley's hands. I did everything he told me. He gave my case a great deal of thought. It interested him, I think. He seemed successful. For nearly three months I was perfectly free from a return. I began to think I was safe. With his full assent I returned to Dawlbridge.

"I travelled in a chaise. I was in good spirits. I was more—I was happy and grateful. I was returning, as I thought, delivered from a dreadful hallucination, to the scene of duties which I longed to enter upon. It was a beautiful sunny evening, everything looked serene and cheerful, and I was delighted. I remember looking out of the window to see the spire of my church at Kenlis among the trees, at the point where one has the earliest view of it. It is exactly where the little stream that bounds the parish passes under the road by a culvert, and where it emerges at the road-side, a stone with an old inscription is placed. As we passed this point, I drew my head in and sat down, and in the corner of the chaise was the monkey.

"For a moment I felt faint, and then quite wild with despair and horror. I called to the driver, and got out, and sat down at the road-side, and prayed to God silently for mercy. A despairing resignation supervened. My companion was with me as I re-entered the vicarage. The same persecution followed. After a short struggle I submitted, and soon I left the place.

"I told you," he said, "that the beast has before this become in certain ways aggressive. I will explain a little. It seemed to be actuated by intense and increasing fury, whenever I said my prayers, or even meditated prayer. It amounted at last to a dreadful interruption. You will ask, how could a silent immaterial phantom effect that? It was thus, whenever I meditated praying; It was always before me, and nearer and nearer.

"It used to spring on a table, on the back of a chair, on the chimney-piece, and slowly to swing itself from side to side, looking at me all the time. There is in its motion an indefinable power to dissipate thought, and to contract one's attention to that monotony, till the ideas shrink, as it were, to a point, and at last to nothing—and unless I had started up, and shook off the catalepsy I have felt as if my mind were on the point of losing itself. There are other ways," he sighed heavily; "thus, for instance, while I pray with my eyes closed, it comes closer and closer, and I see it. I know it is not to be accounted for physically, but I do actually see it, though my lids are dosed, and so it rocks my mind, as it were, and overpowers me, and I am obliged to rise from my knees. If you had ever yourself known this, you would be acquainted with desperation."

CHAPTER 9
THE THIRD STAGE

"I see, Dr. Hesselius, that you don't lose one word of my statement. I need not ask you to listen specially to what I am now going to tell you. They talk of the optic nerves, and of spectral illusions, as if the organ of sight was the only point assailable by the influences that have fastened upon me—I know better. For two years in my direful case that limitation prevailed. But as food is taken in softly at the lips, and then brought under the teeth, as the tip of the little finger caught in a mill crank will draw in the hand, and the arm, and the whole body, so the miserable mortal who has been once caught firmly by the end of the finest fibre of his nerve, is drawn in and in, by the enormous machinery of hell, until he is as I am. Yes, Doctor, as *I* am, for a while I talk to you, and implore relief, I feel that my prayer is for the impossible, and my pleading with the inexorable."

I endeavoured to calm his visibly increasing agitation, and told him that he must not despair.

While we talked the night had overtaken us. The filmy moonlight was wide over the scene which the window commanded, and I said:

"Perhaps you would prefer having candles. This light, you know, is odd. I should wish you, as much as possible, under your usual conditions while I make my diagnosis, shall I call it—otherwise I don't care."

"All lights are the same to me," he said; "except when I read or write, I care not if night were perpetual. I am going to tell you what happened about a year ago. The thing began to speak to me."

"Speak! How do you mean—speak as a man does, do you mean?"

"Yes; speak in words and consecutive sentences, with perfect coherence and articulation; but there is a peculiarity. It is not like the tone of a human voice. It is not by my ears it reaches me—it comes like a singing through my head.

"This faculty, the power of speaking to me, will be my undoing. It won't let me pray, it interrupts me with dreadful blasphemies. I dare not go on, I could not. Oh! Doctor, can the skill, and thought, and prayers of man avail me nothing!"

"You must promise me, my dear sir, not to trouble yourself with unnecessarily exciting thoughts; confine yourself strictly to the narrative of *facts*; and recollect, above all, that even if the thing that infests you be, you seem to suppose a reality with an actual independent life and will, yet it can have no power to hurt you, unless it be given from above: its access to your senses depends mainly upon your physical condition—this is, under God, your comfort and reliance: we are all alike environed. It is only that in your case, the *'paries,'* the veil of the flesh, the screen, is a little out of repair, and sights and sounds are transmitted. We must enter on a new course, sir,—be encouraged. I'll give tonight to the careful consideration of the whole case."

"You are very good, sir; you think it worth trying, you don't give me quite up; but, sir, you don't know, it is gaining such an influence over me: it orders me about, it is such a tyrant, and I'm growing so helpless. May God deliver me!"

"It orders you about—of course you mean by speech?"

"Yes, yes; it is always urging me to crimes, to injure others, or myself. You see, Doctor, the situation is urgent, it is indeed. When I was in Shropshire, a few weeks ago" (Mr. Jennings was speaking rapidly and trembling now, holding my arm with one hand, and looking in my face), "I went out one day with a party of friends for a walk: my persecutor, I tell you, was with me at the time. I lagged behind the rest:

the country near the Dee, you know, is beautiful.

"Our path happened to lie near a coal mine, and at the verge of the wood is a perpendicular shaft, they say, a hundred and fifty feet deep. My niece had remained behind with me—she knows, of course nothing of the nature of my sufferings. She knew, however, that I had been ill, and was low, and she remained to prevent my being quite alone.

"As we loitered slowly on together, the brute that accompanied me was urging me to throw myself down the shaft. I tell you now— oh, sir, think of it!—the one consideration that saved me from that hideous death was the fear lest the shock of witnessing the occurrence should be too much for the poor girl. I asked her to go on and walk with her friends, saying that I could go no further. She made excuses, and the more I urged her the firmer she became. She looked doubtful and frightened. I suppose there was something in my looks or manner that alarmed her; but she would not go, and that literally saved me. You had no idea, sir, that a living man could be made so abject a slave of Satan," he said, with a ghastly groan and a shudder.

There was a pause here, and I said, "You *were* preserved nevertheless. It was the act of God. You are in His hands and in the power of no other being: be therefore confident for the future."

Chapter 10

Home

I made him have candles lighted, and saw the room looking cheery and inhabited before I left him. I told him that he must regard his illness strictly as one dependent on physical, though *subtle* physical causes. I told him that he had evidence of God's care and love in the deliverance which he had just described, and that I had perceived with pain that he seemed to regard its peculiar features as indicating that he had been delivered over to spiritual reprobation. Than such a conclusion nothing could be, I insisted, less warranted; and not only so, but more contrary to facts, as disclosed in his mysterious deliverance from that murderous influence during his Shropshire excursion. First, his niece had been retained by his side without his intending to keep her near him; and, secondly, there had been infused into his mind an irresistible repugnance to execute the dreadful suggestion in her presence.

As I reasoned this point with him, Mr. Jennings wept. He seemed comforted. One promise I exacted, which was that should the monkey at any time return, I should be sent for immediately; and, repeating my assurance that I would give neither time nor thought to any other subject until I had thoroughly investigated his case, and that tomorrow he should hear the result, I took my leave.

Before getting into the carriage I told the servant that his master was far from well, and that he should make a point of frequently looking into his room. My own arrangements I made with a view to being quite secure from interruption.

I merely called at my lodgings, and with a travelling-desk and carpet-bag, set off in a hackney carriage for an inn about two miles out of town, called "The Horns," a very quiet and comfortable house, with good thick walls. And there I resolved, without the possibility of intrusion or distraction, to devote some hours of the night, in my comfortable sitting-room, to Mr. Jennings' case, and so much of the morning as it might require.

(There occurs here a careful note of Dr. Hesselius' opinion upon the case, and of the habits, dietary, and medicines which he prescribed. It is curious—some persons would say mystical. But, on the whole, I doubt whether it would sufficiently interest a reader of the kind I am likely to meet with, to warrant its being here reprinted. The whole letter was plainly written at the inn where he had hid himself for the occasion. The next letter is dated from his town lodgings.)

I left town for the inn where I slept last night at half-past nine, and did not arrive at my room in town until one o'clock this afternoon. I found a letter in Mr. Jennings' hand upon my table. It had not come by post, and, on inquiry, I learned that Mr. Jennings' servant had brought it, and on learning that I was not to return until today, and that no one could tell him my address, he seemed very uncomfortable, and said his orders from his master were that that he was not to return without an answer.

I opened the letter and read:

DEAR DR. HESSELIUS.—It is here. You had not been an hour gone when it returned. It is speaking. It knows all that has happened. It knows everything—it knows you, and is frantic and atrocious. It reviles. I send you this. It knows every word I have written—I write. This I promised, and I therefore write, but I fear very confused, very incoherently. I am so interrupted, disturbed.

Ever yours,
   sincerely yours,
    Robert Lynder Jennings.

"When did this come?" I asked.

"About eleven last night: the man was here again, and has been here three times today. The last time is about an hour since."

Thus answered, and with the notes I had made upon his case in my pocket, I was in a few minutes driving towards Richmond, to see Mr. Jennings.

I by no means, as you perceive, despaired of Mr. Jennings' case. He had himself remembered and applied, though quite in a mistaken way, the principle which I lay down in my Metaphysical Medicine, and which governs all such cases. I was about to apply it in earnest. I was profoundly interested, and very anxious to see and examine him while the "enemy" was actually present.

I drove up to the sombre house, and ran up the steps, and knocked. The door, in a little time, was opened by a tall woman in black silk. She looked ill, and as if she had been crying. She curtseyed, and heard my question, but she did not answer. She turned her face away, extending her hand towards two men who were coming down-stairs; and thus having, as it were, tacitly made me over to them, she passed through a side-door hastily and shut it.

The man who was nearest the hall, I at once accosted, but being now close to him, I was shocked to see that both his hands were covered with blood.

I drew back a little, and the man, passing downstairs, merely said in a low tone, "Here's the servant, sir."

The servant had stopped on the stairs, confounded and dumb at seeing me. He was rubbing his hands in a handkerchief, and it was steeped in blood.

"Jones, what is it? what has happened?" I asked, while a sickening suspicion overpowered me.

The man asked me to come up to the lobby. I was beside him in a moment, and, frowning and pallid, with contracted eyes, he told me the horror which I already half guessed.

His master had made away with himself.

I went upstairs with him to the room—what I saw there I won't tell you. He had cut his throat with his razor. It was a frightful gash. The two men had laid him on the bed, and composed his limbs. It had happened, as the immense pool of blood on the floor declared, at some distance between the bed and the window. There was carpet round his bed, and a carpet under his dressing-table, but none on the rest of the floor, for the man said he did not like a carpet on his bed-

124

room. In this sombre and now terrible room, one of the great elms that darkened the house was slowly moving the shadow of one of its great boughs upon this dreadful floor.

I beckoned to the servant, and we went downstairs together. I turned off the hall into an old-fashioned panelled room, and there standing, I heard all the servant had to tell. It was not a great deal.

"I concluded, sir, from your words, and looks, sir, as you left last night, that you thought my master was seriously ill. I thought it might be that you were afraid of a fit, or something. So I attended very close to your directions. He sat up late, till past three o'clock. He was not writing or reading. He was talking a great deal to himself, but that was nothing unusual. At about that hour I assisted him to undress, and left him in his slippers and dressing-gown. I went back softly in about half-an-hour. He was in his bed, quite undressed, and a pair of candles lighted on the table beside his bed. He was leaning on his elbow, and looking out at the other side of the bed when I came in. I asked him if he wanted anything, and he said No.

"I don't know whether it was what you said to me, sir, or something a little unusual about him, but I was uneasy, uncommon uneasy about him last night.

"In another half hour, or it might be a little more, I went up again. I did not hear him talking as before. I opened the door a little. The candles were both out, which was not usual. I had a bedroom candle, and I let the light in, a little bit, looking softly round. I saw him sitting in that chair beside the dressing-table with his clothes on again. He turned round and looked at me. I thought it strange he should get up and dress, and put out the candles to sit in the dark, that way. But I only asked him again if I could do anything for him. He said, No, rather sharp, I thought. I asked him if I might light the candles, and he said, 'Do as you like, Jones.' So I lighted them, and I lingered about the room, and he said, 'Tell me truth, Jones; why did you come again—you did not hear anyone cursing?' 'No, sir,' I said, wondering what he could mean.

"'No,' said he, after me, 'of course, no;' and I said to him, 'Wouldn't it be well, sir, you went to bed? It's just five o'clock;' and he said nothing, but, 'Very likely; goodnight, Jones.' So I went, sir, but in less than an hour I came again. The door was fast, and he heard me, and called as I thought from the bed to know what I wanted, and he desired me not to disturb him again. I lay down and slept for a little. It must have been between six and seven when I went up again. The door was still fast, and he made no answer, so I did not like to disturb him, and thinking he was asleep, I left him till nine. It was his custom to ring when he wished me to come, and I had no particular hour for calling him. I tapped very gently, and getting no answer, I stayed away a good while, supposing he was getting some rest then. It was not till eleven o'clock I grew really uncomfortable about him—for at the latest he was never, that I could remember, later than half-past ten. I got no answer. I knocked and called, and still no answer. So not being able to force the door, I called Thomas from the stables, and together we forced it, and found him in the shocking way you saw."

Jones had no more to tell. Poor Mr. Jennings was very gentle, and very kind. All his people were fond of him. I could see that the servant was very much moved.

So, dejected and agitated, I passed from that terrible house, and its dark canopy of elms, and I hope I shall never see it more. While I write to you I feel like a man who has but half waked from a frightful and monotonous dream. My memory rejects the picture with incredulity and horror. Yet I know it is true. It is the story of the process of a poison, a poison which excites the reciprocal action of spirit and nerve, and paralyses the tissue that separates those cognate functions of the senses, the external and the interior. Thus we find strange bed-fellows, and the mortal and immortal prematurely make acquaintance.

CONCLUSION
A WORD FOR THOSE WHO SUFFER

My dear Van L——, you have suffered from an affection similar to that which I have just described. You twice complained of a return of it.

Who, under God, cured you? Your humble servant, Martin Hesselius. Let me rather adopt the more emphasised piety of a certain good old French surgeon of three hundred years ago: "I treated, and God cured you."

Come, my friend, you are not to be hippish. Let me tell you a fact. I have met with, and treated, as my book shows, fifty-seven cases of this kind of vision, which I term indifferently "sublimated," "precocious," and "interior."

There is another class of affections which are truly termed—though commonly confounded with those which I describe—spectral illusions. These latter I look upon as being no less simply curable than a cold in the head or a trifling dyspepsia.

It is those which rank in the first category that test our promptitude of thought. Fifty-seven such cases have I encountered, neither more nor less. And in how many of these have I failed? In no one single instance.

There is no one affliction of mortality more easily and certainly reducible, with a little patience, and a rational confidence in the physician. With these simple conditions, I look upon the cure as absolutely certain.

You are to remember that I had not even commenced to treat Mr. Jennings' case. I have not any doubt that I should have cured him perfectly in eighteen months, or possibly it might have extended to two years. Some cases are very rapidly curable, others extremely tedious. Every intelligent physician who will give thought and diligence to the task, will effect a cure.

You know my tract on *The Cardinal Functions of the Brain*. I there, by the evidence of innumerable facts, prove, as I think, the high probability of a circulation arterial and venous in its mechanism, through the nerves. Of this system, thus considered, the brain is the heart. The fluid, which is propagated hence through one class of nerves, returns in an altered state through another, and the nature of that fluid is spiritual, though not immaterial, any more than, as I before remarked, light or electricity are so.

By various abuses, among which the habitual use of such agents as green tea is one, this fluid may be affected as to its quality, but it is more frequently disturbed as to equilibrium. This fluid being that which we have in common with spirits, a congestion found upon the masses of brain or nerve, connected with the interior sense, forms a surface unduly exposed, on which disembodied spirits may operate: communication is thus more or less effectually established.

Between this brain circulation and the heart circulation there is an intimate sympathy. The seat, or rather the instrument of exterior vision, is the eye. The seat of interior vision is the nervous tissue and brain, immediately about and above the eyebrow. You remember how effectually I dissipated your pictures by the simple application of iced *eau-de-cologne*. Few cases, however, can be treated exactly alike with anything like rapid success. Cold acts powerfully as a repellent of the nervous fluid. Long enough continued it will even produce that permanent insensibility which we call numbness, and a little longer, muscular as well as sensational paralysis.

I have not, I repeat, the slightest doubt that I should have first dimmed and ultimately sealed that inner eye which Mr. Jennings had inadvertently opened. The same senses are opened in delirium tremens, and entirely shut up again when the over-action of the cerebral heart, and the prodigious nervous congestions that attend it, are terminated by a decided change in the state of the body. It is by acting steadily upon the body, by a simple process, that this result is produced—and inevitably produced—I have never yet failed.

Poor Mr. Jennings made away with himself. But that catastrophe was the result of a totally different malady, which, as it were, projected itself upon the disease which was established. His case was in the distinctive manner a complication, and the complaint under which he really succumbed, was hereditary suicidal mania. Poor Mr. Jennings I cannot call a patient of mine, for I had not even begun to treat his case, and he had not yet given me, I am convinced, his full and unreserved confidence. If the patient do not array himself on the side of the disease, his cure is certain.

The Wood Devil Thing

Gordon McCreagh

A weird, hair-raising story of a terrible *Thing*, a strange presence that acted without leaving a trace—that came and went mysteriously, and showed a vicious vindictiveness that boded ill for the luckless victim who fell into it's power. A story redolent with the breath of Burmese jungles.

Sergeant McGrath, "Moro" McGrath, as he was called, of the Burma police, squatted chunkily on the ground cloth of a green waterproof E.P. tent and regarded with thin-lipped cynicism the uppermost of a sheaf of printed notices which the *dak* runner had just brought in.

Fresh from the government press, they announced, in English on one half and neat, round Burmese on the other, that five thousand *rupees* were offered for the capture, dead or alive, of one Boh Lu-Bain, convicted of *dacoity*, with murder, robbery under arms, arson, and an appalling list of subsidiary crimes.

The windproof acetylene camp lantern threw sharp, angular shadows across the hard-grain mahogany of the sergeant's face as it suddenly cracked into a grim smile.

"Huh! Looks like a pretty durn safe offer—seein' things is as they is," he grunted to himself aloud, after the manner of white men who spend much time in the far corners of the earth, with only natives to talk to. "Mister Boh is some slick conundrum."

His lips pressed slowly together again, and he caressed his wooden block of a chin in perplexed introspection. As he turned the case over in his mind and swore impatiently at the queerness of its attendant circumstances, another link was suddenly added to the chain of uncanniness. From out of the dense, black jungles that ringed the clearing there sounded a wild, quavering cry, so long-drawn and so pitiful that the subdued clamour from the other tents of the little camp stopped short as though cut off with a knife.

Before the long wail had ceased to vibrate through the still, hot air, in some miraculous manner a rifle had appeared in Sergeant Mc-Grath's hands and he stood outside of his tent, stepping with instinctive caution away from the thin shaft of light which cut far out across the blackness from the tent flap. He listened in the intense silence which had fallen. Then—

"*Hussein Jemadar!*" he called.

"*Huzoor!*"

A tall, uniformed figure appeared out of the darkness and saluted.

"Take two men and see what that cry was about."

The *jemadar* saluted again and disappeared; and McGrath stood peering like a nighthawk into the blacker shadows across the clearing. Presently an altercation was apparent among the men's tents. It waxed fiercer; and shortly the *jemadar* loomed up again.

"*Huzoor*, the men are mutinous. They insist that it is the *Nat* devil who shrieks as he rends some unfortunate, and their knees are limp with fear."

"Fathers of many fools!" barked the sergeant. "This is no time to make monkey-chatter. There is need of speed. I'll attend to the men later—when I come back. Make lights and double the sentry. Swift, now!"

For an instant he was a darker blot under the shadow of the trees, and then he merged into the blackness. The native *jemadar* had to marvel for the hundredth time at the speed and silence with which his superior melted into the undergrowth; and then he went to carry out his order and to acquaint the men who were afraid of *nats* of the greater hell which would presently occur to them when the *sahib* returned.

The sergeant glided swiftly on in the direction from which the cry had come; but, for all his unhesitating promptness, the chills kept racing up and down his spine. There was something mysterious about this case, something not altogether wholesome—to say nothing of plunging at night, and alone, into an inky tropical jungle where soft scufflings and padded footfalls sounded disquietingly from behind the tree trunks, how far or how close to be judged by ear alone. But if there had been light enough to distinguish details by, the sergeant's face would have shown the same alertness and relentless ferocity as the other night prowlers as he slipped in and out with hardly any more noise than they, and with all his muscles tensed to jump like a cat in any direction at any moment.

Presently he became aware of a gentle crackling of twigs before him. Instantly he pressed himself against a tree, motionless as the trunk itself, straining his eyes into the gloom, while pictures of all the things that might drop on him from above raced through his mind. The bushes swished again, and a dim shape crept out not twenty yards distant and crouched, a shadow among the shadows. Most men would have yelled and fired point-blank at the shape; but Moro McGrath never stirred, only his fingers tightened slowly over the stock of his rifle which hung easily at arm's length. He had graduated from that most efficient training school, the Philippines. Seven strenuous years had he put in as an independent scout before the high tides of his turbulent soul had drifted him just round the corner into Burma; and he rested secure in the knowledge that he could shoot from the shoulder or the hip or in midair with the speed of an electric spark.

The crouching shadow swayed up on all fours and came uncertainly forward; then it sank behind another bush, only ten yards away this time. The muzzle of the sergeant's rifle, still at arm's length, swung slowly and noiselessly round, and the thick forefinger curled round the trigger, just a fraction of an ounce below the necessary firing pull.

Then the thing groaned.

"God! An' I near drilled him!" exploded the sergeant. He sprang forward, all thoughts of things that might drop or jump out from behind trees banished from his mind, and lifted the broken thing in his arms. It only moaned.

"Pret-ty durn bad hit," he muttered. "Got some kind of a gun, too. Feels like—Curse this darkness!" He fumbled a while with the inert arms and legs, and then presently swung them easily over one wide shoulder and strode swiftly to the camp.

The clearing was a blaze of lights, and the sentry had contrived to collect three other supports round himself in the event of an attack by the expected *nat*. The *jemadar* and others came running. McGrath handed over his burden.

"Our uniform—what's left of it. Who's the man? Bring a light."

A man ran up with a petrol flare.

"*Allah*, have mercy!" burst from the *jemadar*. "*The man has no face!*"

The light flickered ghastly on a clotted smudge where the face should have been. Livid strips of twisted flesh were all that remained. Moro McGrath had seen what was left after the terrible sideswipe that

131

a bear may sometimes deliver; but this thing was just a horrid crimson mess. It was as if some malignant giant hand had deliberately blotted out all chance of recognition. The sergeant drew in his breath with a whistling sound.

"Take him to the doctor, *babu*, quick! An'—here, take also this remnant of a rifle. Prepare report. I follow."

He went to his own tent to wash up, for he was one of those men who somehow contrived to look neat and trim under the most impossible circumstances—a remnant of his soldier training. As he cleaned up, his eye fell again on the reward notices. The cynical look came back, tinged this time with something of awe.

"Five thou is a heap o' money; *but*—personal I don't want it bad enough to go scoutin' up *that* valley. Can't altogether blame my fellers for talkin' *nat*. Wonder what in thunder could 'a' done that to that poor devil." Thank Pete it's Brandon's district—"

He broke off and listened again, with his head cocked alert like a lynx. From out the jungle came another rending of undergrowth, heavy-footed and ponderous this time. The sergeant slipped out of the tent and once more became a motionless shadow at another point in the clearing. The crackling came nearer.

"Man!" muttered McGrath. "A big un. White, an' a city feller, I'll bet."

A tremendous figure broke out of the bushes not four feet from him, and plunged on past him, all unconscious. The man made straight for the lighted tent, and the watcher glided after him like a ghost. The big visitor strode into the shaft of light from the tent flap, and then wheeled like a bull *gaur* as the sergeant's voice broke on him from right at his heels:

"Durned if it ain't Dickie Travers! How'd you blow up here? Fired from the laboratory job in Rangoon?"

"Moro, old scout! Say, I'm dashed glad to see you! They told me back at the village that I'd find your camp on the Kindat Road. Tried to scare me at the same time by swearing that the woods here were full of devils, all red-hot and howling. But say, I want to see you awful bad; you're the only man in Burma who can help me out, and I had to risk the devils." The big man laughed and stretched his great shoulders.

'An', since you think you can lick your weight in devils any day, you jest came along, hey?" the sergeant grinned quizzically. "Well, there's more in heaven an' earth, son, an' particularly in the almighty jungle, than is dreamed of in Rangoon city. Cm'on in an' moisten up

132

an' unload your chest."

The younger man needed no more urging to break into a long and enthusiastic harangue, the coherence of which was considerably marred by continuous and unnecessary digressions devoted to glowing descriptions of a certain third party. The sergeant chewed on a pipe and grinned tolerantly at his friend's ardour, though, as the story progressed, his dark face took on an expression of concern. Finally he rose very deliberately and knocked out his pipe, carefully dropping the ash into an empty tobacco tin.

"Well," he announced, with conviction, "if you think the girl's worth this damfool scheme of yours, you got it good an' proper; worse 'n I ever gave you discredit for. Now lemme tell you somep'n about this *Boh* man. Listen careful, now.

"This Lu-Bain chief is the hardest proposition in *dacoits* since the famous Boh Da-Thone. An' he's no ignorant savage, lemme tell you. He's a Pali scholar an' a graduate of Rangoon College. Also he's a high-class gun artist, an' incidental the ugliest brute in Burma. Got a face like a gorilla; an' his actions are just about as inhuman."

"I don't care," persisted Travers doggedly, setting his lips with grim determination. "I've got to get that money."

Moro McGrath spun round on him from his short walk up and down the tent and shot out a sinewy forefinger at him.

"Wait a minute, son! Don't be so malice an' prepense against the man. The parade ain't commenced yet. Listen! This *Boh* party accrued a considerable gang an' waltzed around the country in the usual way, destroyin' the populace most prodigal, an'—Well, we had to get after him with two or three detachments, an' we hived most o' the bunch—there's some eighteen or twenty heads stuck up in the Taungyen market place for identification right now—but this *Boh* ideal is a slick number, an' he gets away clear. I chase him an' one or two other hard citizens into this valley of Hankow, which is the thickest, stinkiest, malariest jungle in all Chindwin, an' which, thank Pete, is out o' my district; an' here he lays up, bottled.

"So far, fine an' dandy, thank you. But now listen, son, careful. The Burmans an' my fool Punjabi constables say it's plumb impossible for any human bein' to live in that jungle 'count o' fever an' snakes an' beasts an' hell all else. Wherefore, with *pucca* native reasonin' most circumstantial an' proper, they prove that he's changed himself by means o' magic into a high-class wood demon, or not, all teeth an' claws an' smoke."

"Hold on!" interrupted Tracy eagerly. "How d'you know he's bottled? What proof have you that he's not gone out of the valley?"

"Proof an' to spare. Every now an' then some jungle man comes in scared stiff an' reports how he seen the famous yellow silk *gaungbaung* headdress an' the rifle with the solid-silver stock; an' once in a while friend *Boh* sends along a little proof, extra an' unsolicited, jest to show he's happy an' keepin' his end up. F'r instance, a jungle man comes in the other day with his hands tied behind him an' his ears hung around his neck on a string, an' he throws up a yarn about devils howlin' an' dancin' in the dark that'd paralyze you. An' not long after, a raft floats down the river with one o' my own men, crucified an' generally used up somethin' horrible." The sergeant grimaced and shuddered at the recollection. Then he continued with deliberate conviction: "Now all that's plain *dacoit* humour, an' don't raise my belief in devils any; but— Now, mark me, I maintains right here that the *Boh's* gone crazy with the heat or the hardship or the loneliness or somep'n; but the rest o' the story ain't normal; there's somep'n I can't figure out, somep'n outside human range. Listen:

"More recently these outbursts of enthusiasm has taken on a—a kinder unwholesome nature. Two jungle men come in in a canoe with a body whose arm is wrenched complete off. *Torn*, mind you, not hacked. Then comes another, crushed jest to pulp; every bone broken, like he'd fallen out a flyin' machine. The Burmans say right away it's a *nat*; the strength required to do those stunts ain't human. An', by God, it *ain't*"

Sergeant McGrath paused and looked darkly up through his eyebrows at his friend. Travers was visibly affected by the uncanny recital; his usual attitude of careless confidence had left him, but the determination showed relentlessly in his face.

"It's weird, Moro, old scout, and maybe dangerous; but you don't head me off yet," he maintained seriously. "I'm out after that reward, and I'm going to get it."

"Hm!" grunted the older man. "Sudden death or sudden matrimony; you lose either way. Well, there's another chapter been added to the story just before you come in. Maybe we can get some information at firsthand—if the poor devil can talk. Cm'on to the hospital tent."

The fussy little native doctor explained with much circumstance in the exaggerated whisper of his kind that his skill had so far revived the man that he was able to talk and anxious to make his report.

"Have you found out who it is?" asked McGrath in a responsive whisper, unconsciously affected by the technical jargon and calculated impressiveness of the "profession."

A mass of bandages heaved itself up onto an elbow on the cot and saluted.

"It is Misri-Khan, *sahib, nambar sebentin*," mumbled a muffled voice from out the wrappings, and then proceeded, weakly and with many relapses, to unfold an amazing story, the gist of which was: First, that he, Misri-Khan, was a brave man, and, therefore, ignoring the devil stories, had scouted up that dim valley where all others feared to go, looking for tracks of the *Boh*. Secondly, that the total absence of tracks convinced him that the *Boh* had indeed become a *Nat*—for *Nats*, of course, travelled over the ground without leaving trace. Nevertheless, did he continue on the trail for the honour of the service, and would the protector of the poor see that he received suitable reward therefore? And finally: On the second day, *sahib*, as I sought in the darkest part of the forest among great trees of *Padouk* and *Sal* many cubits high, it happened that I heard a great rending of wood, and—*Allah* is my witness, *sahib*—lifting my eyes, I beheld the father of all the *Nats* tear a great tree asunder and spring at me from the bowels thereof.

"The face was the face of the *Boh*, only more terrible, but the arms were of the thickness of a man's leg, and hairy as those of a spider. *Huzoor*, I have distinguished service medal; but at that sight my knees were turned to water, and I fell upon the ground; yet did I remember to fire my carbine. I am also second- class marksman, *sahib*, and at that distance could I assuredly not miss. Yet the ball went through the devil, and he leaped upon me, howling magic words which I knew not. That is all, *sahib*. He left me for dead; yet by the favour of *Allah* did I recover and crawl with much tribulation to the jungle's edge, where the *sahib*, may *Allah* reward him, found me. There is yet one more thing, *sahib*. The *Nat*, having smitten me, took my carbine and bent the barrel as a bow is bent. In witness whereof the gun is now in the hands of the *jemadar*. *Bus*, I have finished."

McGrath asked a few more questions, gave some directions for the man's comfort, and then, with significant and pointed silence, took his friend by the arm and led him out to examine the rifle. It was as the man had said. The steel barrel was bent into an arc. McGrath took it to the light and examined it with critical, narrowed eyes. The puzzled expression on his face increased to dark amazement.

"Now that's durn queer," he muttered. "I figured it might possibly have been hammered that way, or even bitten by some powerful animal; but lookut here, Dick, there's not a mark; the bluein' ain't got a scratch on it. An' a durn queer story; of course padded out a whole heap with the good old Oriental fairy stuff; but there's somep'n mighty unhealthy in this whole business, Dick, my son. D'ja still feel all het up to go *Boh* devil huntin'?"

The determined lines on Travers' face assumed an expression of dogged obstinacy.

"Queer it is, Moro," he admitted grudgingly.

"But this bogy talk is all hot air. Anyhow, if it was the devil himself, I'm not going to back out now. I've *got* to get that reward, and in a hurry, 'cause if I don't, her old dad's sending her home to God's country next month. But look here, Moro, old scout, you don't stand to gain anything out of this; you don't have to come. In fact, I'd hate to drag you into it; I can get a guide and go alone."

McGrath looked sourly up at him from under one raised eyebrow.

"You're in love," he snorted, "so I ain't takin' offense at anything you say. Sure I don't *have* to come. I ain't gettin' married; so I don't have to figure on a violent death as a cheerful alternative. But I know you when you look that way, an' if you're so durned desperate as all that, someone's got to take care of you. 'Tain't my district, an' I ain't hankerin' to prospect that valley, but—well, I got a feelin' that I'm the goat."

Travers shot forth a great paw and gripped his friend's hand with an enthusiasm which amounted almost to adoration in his frank, open eyes. The sergeant extricated himself hastily and hid his confusion under a gruff growl of:

"Aw, I need a holiday, anyway; an' I got a new gun to try out. 'Sides, don't you talk to me about a guide. You can't get any man to take you into that valley; an' I can't send any o' my fool Punjabis; they'd be worse'n useless. There's only one man I know who's got the guts, an' that's Moung Tha-Dun, an old Burman hunter; an' he won't go without me, you can lay to that. So it's got to be jest We, Us, and Company."

Moro McGrath was a man who knew men. His diagnosis of the morale of his police constables was unerring. His natural impulse was to drive them, as he well knew how; but he reflected that he could not very well force them to accompany him on a private venture outside of his district. He was also peculiarly accurate in his estimate of Tha-

Dun. The old tracker never hesitated. He came with direful warnings, it is true, and much misgiving; but his confidence in McGrath's experience and resourcefulness was infinite.

So it was that only three men stood the following evening shoulder deep in a patch of *kaing* grass at the lower end of the forbidding-looking valley. They looked microscopically insignificant in their giant surroundings. High overhead was a mat of huge, interlaced branches through which the discouraged sunlight filtered with difficulty. Below a dense tangle of undergrowth out of which giant trunks shot sixty feet clear from the moist earth and gleamed ghostly pale in the perpetual twilight.

McGrath surveyed the gloomy surroundings with deep disapproval.

"Travers, my boy," he growled, "we've got one helluva job in front of us. It's goin' to take days to crawl through this, huntin' for a trail. If we find one, an' spot the *Boh* an' his fellers first, well *an'* good. If Mr. *Boh* spots us first—well, he can handle that silver-plated gun of his like an expert. Meanwhiles, no noise, no campfires, no dry clothes, an' no fresh grub. I'm goin' to have *some* holiday. Whosit says, '*fools rush in where angels fear to tread*'?"

"Meaning how?" demanded Travers.

"Well, we're havin' all this picnic so you can commit matrimonial *hara-kiri*; an' I've read somewheres that in heaven they neither marry nor are given in marriage. I infers that angels fear to tread."

"And that I'm a fool," laughed Travers, with a perfect understanding of the deep strength and determination that lay beneath his friend's misogynistic grumbling. "You're a cold-blooded beast, Moro, and a wicked cynic; but you're a crafty hunter all the same, and I guess you're right about cutting out all betraying fires and being mighty cautious. Today's march wasn't so bad, but I suppose the real campaign begins tomorrow."

"No, sir!" the other dissented immediately. "It begins right here, tonight. This is Hankow Valley, son, an' we don't take no chances on Mister *Boh* bein' away visitin' friend *Nat* this evening."

Tracy, with the omniscience of youth, was rather inclined to be impatient at the old campaigner's caution; but he was reminded of the reality of their nearness to danger with startling unpleasantness. With the setting of the sun every insect sound hushed—birds there were none in that sombre tangle of trees. It was just that period of brooding mystery which falls in the tropic twilight between the sleeping of the day creatures and the waking of the beings of the night, when the period of real silence brings a surprised realisation of the undercurrent of sound which has all the time been constituting the voice of the jungle. As the little party gathered wearily round their cold, cheerless meal, the eerie silence was suddenly broken by a weird, wild, whooping noise far up the valley, beginning with a low wail and ending up in a *staccato*, coughing shriek.

Moung Tha-Dun fell on his face and began muttering invocations to his guardian spirits.

"*Ahai!*" he moaned. "The *Nat!* It is the *Nat* who calls *Thakins*; let us depart from this evil place."

Even the white men were affected. The chill dusk, the gloomy valley, and that uncanny sound, all combined with the fantastic stories which they had been hearing to build up a creepy sensation of unwholesome mystery.

"What is it, Moro?" whispered Travers, with blanched face and wide, staring eyes.

"Damned if I know," replied the other uneasily. "It sounds kinder vaguely familiar, but I can't place it. Gee, I got chills crawlin' all up an' down my back. Wish we dared risk a fire. Guess we'd better watch two at a time tonight."

But the night passed without mishap, though once again, before darkness closed down on them, the fearsome sound rose and swelled in the distance. However, with the daylight came renewed confidence and a feeling of self-conscious humiliation at their nervousness of the night before. They discussed their plan of campaign eagerly, and arranged to work carefully up the valley, abreast of each other, and search for tracks; they were to separate so as to cover as much ground as possible, but should always remain within calling distance, in the event of anyone being pounced upon by some unknown thing. However, even with the satisfying knowledge of the proximity of friends, it was no drawing-room party. The undergrowth was appallingly thick and thorny, and progress was black, as well as heartbreakingly slow. Tha-Dun's attitude, with his imminent fear of the supernatural, was positively heroic, and what lent weight to his gloomy theories and forebodings was the fact that for five whole days never a track was found, though regularly as the darkness closed in that ghastly cry filled the air.

"It gets me," swore McGrath. "Not a durned scratch of trail of a single live thing. Even the animals have been scared out. That poor devil of a constable without a face spoke truer'n we ever gave him credit for. There's been no rain for two weeks, an' if there was any living thing in this unholy place we'd have found tracks by now."

Moung Tha-Dun dismally assured him that this was but to be expected, for *Nats* left no footprints, and the only reason they had escaped so long was that it was waiting for a favourable combination of the stars to spring upon them and rend them.

But that day at last brought to light a trail which seemed only to lend weight to the Burman's forebodings. McGrath, who was working up the centre of the valley, gave the mewing otter call which had been agreed upon as a signal, and brought the others hastening to his side. They found him with set lips, and the corrugations of his hard forehead crowded together in disquieting thought, bending over a skeleton.

"Look at that!" he directed their attention in a low voice. "His ribs have been crushed in like eggshells. See, in two wide bands. Jes' 's if some giant had taken an' hugged him."

"Giant is right," agreed Travers, with a feeling of awe. "No human being could have done it. What do you think it can be?"

"Durned if I know," speculated McGrath, searching back in his mind for some parallel. "A big snake might do it, but then a snake that could do that would easily have swallowed him."

Both voices had unconsciously fallen to whispers as they stood in the presence of this mystery, and they cast uneasy glances over their shoulders, half-expecting to see some fantastic monster creeping on them.

Moung Tha-Dun had meanwhile been searching the surrounding bush. "*Thakin*" he called tremulously. "Of a surety the *Nat* has done this thing, for yonder lies his gun, and no *man* would have left such a prize behind. Moreover," he added impressively, "the *Thakin* knows that poor jungle people have no guns."

"Well, what of it?" queried McGrath, not catching the drift of his meaning.

"None but a follower of the *Boh* would carry such a gun, *Thakin*."

"God! I never thought of that. The *Boh* sure wouldn't go killing his own people; an', if it ain't him, then who's doin' all this mysterious murder?"

"The *Nat!*" insisted Tha-Dun darkly.

"*Nat* be hanged!" growled McGrath. "Anyhow, it's durned funny, whatever it is. Looks to me that it'd be healthier not to separate so promiscuous. It'll take longer to cover the ground, but it'll be a heap more comfortable to my spine."

As they began to approach the region from which the nightly howlings proceeded, they were able to distinguish the fearsome sound more clearly. "*Whoo-oo Wha-aa Aa-ee-ee!*" it would rise, with blood-chilling shrillness, trailing off into a high-pitched chuckle which had not been audible before. But familiarity, in this case, surely bred no contempt. Each time that the sound burst with startling suddenness upon the dank evening air the three would instinctively shrink to-gether, and then look at one another shamefacedly.

"Damn it all!" exploded McGrath in exasperation. "It ain't the in-fernal noise that gets us; we've all heard worse before. It's the time an' the place an' the bogy stories mixed in with it that makes us jump. We got to steady up our nerves for when we do come across the thing."

"Tell you what," interposed Travers, "it seems that the Thing—I don't know what else to call it—comes out only in the evening; if that's so, we have nothing to fear as long as daylight lasts, such as it is in this dismal hole in the ground."

The others immediately agreed with him, and the party accord-ingly proceeded with more confidence. All thought of danger at the hands of the *Boh* had left them. The total absence of tracks convinced them that any human beings who might have been in the valley had long since left it or were dead. But their assurance received a rude setback, and the whole mystery was forced into startling prominence a day later, when they came upon unmistakable tracks—human tracks.

Moung Tha-Dun, whose foreboding terror vanished at the sight of something that he could understand, was down on all fours in an in-stant, questing, nosing like a hound. He led them some little distance, cunningly examining the ground and the bushes on either side before he spoke.

"*Thakin*" he whispered, "the trail is that of a man running, fleeing from some great fear, for he has run blindly, cutting his feet on the stones. Yet—*there are no footsteps that follow.*"

Moro McGrath, who was no mean tracker himself, had observed the same phenomenon.

"Funny! Damn queer!" he kept repeating in *staccato* barks. "What the devil did he run from? Go ahead, Tha-Dun. Better load with buck-shot, Travers; your Paradox at close quarters is better than a rifle."

The trail led disappointingly to rocky ground, where it was speedily lost; but Moung Tha-Dun, who was in the lead, presently uttered an exclamation of delight and darted forward. He returned with a beaming face.

"Behold what I have found, *Thakin!*" he jubilated. In his hand he held a long strip of yellow silk.

"Well, what's there to be so blamed happy about?" demanded Mc-Grath impatiently, even his drawn, wire nerves all of a jangle with this dark enigma. "The gink has dropped his headdress in the scare, that's all."

"The *Boh's gaungbaung, Thakin*, was of yellow silk," grinned the other. "And if it be the *Boh* who fled, why, then, he is assuredly not become a *Nat*, and I have nothing further to fear."

Travers groaned. "Is that all? Damn it, that only deepens the mystery. What the deuce *did* he run from? The *Boh* wasn't a man to be easily frightened from what you all tell me. Then what was this awful thing that scared him so?"

McGrath leaned, frowning, on his rifle for many minutes before he spoke, as was his habit when thinking. "Boys," he stated at length, "I ain't beginnin' to guess what kind of a *banshee* this is, but one thing's clear. We ain't counted on the *Boh* any of late; an' if these tracks is his, we got to watch out for him as well as for the Thing. All we can do is be durned leery; an' I've a notion we're bound to find out somep'n soon; we're right in the middle of things here."

He was right, though he was far from guessing the horrible way in which enlightenment was to come.

That night as they sat in their camp, waiting with a sort of fearful fascination for the familiar sound, a terrible cry rose on the night air. A human cry of deadly terror.

"*Amma-lé!*" it shrieked. "Spare me! Let me go! Let—" The words were cut short by a scream of anguish. In the appalling stillness that followed the three thought they could distinguish the low, fiendish chuckle which usually terminated those awe-inspiring howlings. They sprang to their feet with blanched faces, snatching up their rifles as they did so. For a long time they stood motionless, peering apprehensively into the dark.

"It's no use, boys," said McGrath shakily at last. "We can't do a thing in the dark. We'll jest have to sit right here. An' I don't care what happens; we're goin' to have a fire tonight."

"I'm with you!" agreed Travers emphatically. "A damn big fire!"

None of the three slept a wink the whole of that interminable night, and with the first breath of dawn they started out to discover that grim tragedy of the dark. It did not take long. Signs were plentiful enough. They soon came upon the ashes of a campfire under a great tree. Alongside lay the body of a man, gaunt and emaciated with starvation. But it was not the pinched frame with the bones almost protruding through the skin, nor the expression of awful terror stamped on the brutal gorilloid face that made the white men turn aside with sudden nausea. Neither hunger nor fear had killed the man. He lay on his back in a welter of blood with *half his chest torn completely out.* From beneath his body protruded the butt end of a rifle, gleaming silver through the clotted red. Even Moung Tha-Dun was affected. Death was nothing to him, and he had looked on worse mutilations before, the work of *dacoits*; but the horror of the superhuman force that had been brought into play gripped his soul. He shook it off, however, as instinctive habit began to assert itself, and he commenced to search for tracks. Carefully he went over the ground, examining every blade, every leaf. At last: "*Thakin,*" he whispered, "*here also there are no tracks!*"

"Damn it, man, there must be!" cried McGrath. "This thing ain't a ghost. It can't vanish into smoke. If it's material enough to tear a man in half, it must leave solid tracks somewhere." Suddenly an idea struck him. "Travers," he barked, "d'you remember exactly how that other fellow lay?"

"Yes, he lay on his back, too. Why?"

"Hell, no, I don't mean that! He lay under jest such a low-spreading tree, didn't he?"

"By George, that's so! I never thought of that. You mean that the Thing swoops down from a tree?"

"Pree-cisely. An' I'm goin' to see." With the prospect of immediate action and probable danger the fierce leopard light glowed again in his eyes. "Now you watch out good an' careful above. I got to rely entirely on your shooting."

Without further hesitation he scrambled up the trunk into whatever the leaves might hide, and began working his way along a great overhanging bough which passed over the body some seven feet above. Travers waited apprehensively.

"Here it is!" suddenly came the excited voice from above. "Here's a smear of blood—an' here's another! An' here's—well, I'll be damned!" He was directly above the body now. His voice dropped. "Here's the bark rubbed off in *two wide bands!*"

He swung clear and dropped lightly to the ground. "Now what d'you think o' that?" he demanded.

"It's evident that the Thing comes from a tree," answered Travers in a frightened whisper. "But what are those two wide bands always? The coils of a snake?"

"A big snake gripping the branch for a stroke might leave jest such a mark; but—there ain't no snake in the world could do that awful thing. I'm beginnin' to have a idea, son. That there noise is strikin' back kinder familiar. 'Jest the beginnin's of a idea. But it's too horrible; too durned fantastic; I gotta see more before I can tell you. But there's one thing clear. We *got* to keep away from overhanging branches—an' we can build all the fires we want. The *Boh*, poor devil, has squared up with the bank. There ain't nothin' owin'. Travers, my son, we'll camp right here; an' I'll guarantee the big show for this very night."

He selected a place nearby, free from low trees, and the day was spent under his direction in clearing away the surrounding scrub to guard against surprise and leave plenty of room for action. Then, as dusk drew on, they built a roaring fire over the unfortunate *Boh's* camp, and, at his further suggestion, retired to their clearing to wait.

"D'ja get me?" chuckled the cunning hunter. "That'll bring the Thing into the light, while we remain hid."

They were still discussing possibilities and plans when Moung Tha-Dun raised his hand with a warning gesture. His quick ear had detected the approaching sound of swishing leaves. They lay silent, while the disturbance came nearer. From the snapping of twigs and the soft thuds among the high branches it was evident that some large body was making its way toward them. Finally it could be heard in the upper branches of the lit-up tree. The three watchers were keyed up to an intolerable pitch of half-apprehensive excitement. What would the next few seconds disclose? Their overstrung imaginations conjured up all sorts of ghostly forms. But some fiendish, intuition seemed to make the Thing suspicious. It made querulous noises and shuffled about behind the screen of leaves above in evident hesitation about descending.

Suddenly McGrath reached for Travers' gun and glided off into the darkness without a word. Even through his excitement the latter could not help admiring the snakelike skill of his friend. The situation now became intense. The unknown horror in the treetop, and Mc-Grath swallowed up in the silent dark! Travers had to keep a grip on himself to prevent himself from shouting aloud. Suddenly the Thing moved again. It shifted its position. Travers heard the quick click of a lifted hammer, followed by a flash and a report. There came a short, coughing roar, and a vast shape hurled itself full twenty feet to the next tree, and went crashing off into the darkness.

McGrath rushed up, falling over his words. "Did you see it? What was it like? What the hell have you got in this gun?" All in one breath.

"My God!" stammered Travers. "It looked like—like a devil."

Moung Tha-Dun was on his face. "*Amma-lé!*" he wailed. "The *Nat!* It is a *Nat*, indeed!"

Meanwhile, McGrath had snapped open the breech and torn out the empty shell. "Oh, fool! Fool that I am!" he groaned. "To take up a gun without looking at the load! Man, you've got No. 4, an' I told you buckshot! Course I only tickled him. Here, gimme my rifle, an' load up this toy with somep'n solid! Tha-Dun, father of an idiot, quit your howlin' an' get up an' hustle! We got to build a whole circle of fires now. It'll sure come back; an' there ain't no use in tryin' to hide now!"

They threw themselves fiercely into the work, collecting up all the brush which they had cut during the day, and frantically chopping more, halting every minute to listen for the malignant Thing's approach. Progress was cruelly slow.

"Moro," panted Travers, "we'll never do it; and don't forget we've got to keep our fires going. I guess if we make two more big blazes in a triangle they'll light up all lines of approach."

"Guess you're right, son," grunted McGrath. "Take one each. Tha-Dun, you pile s'm' more stuff on the first!"

They had barely got their defences lit, when a swoop and a crash in the trees announced the creature's return.

"D'ja get that?" snapped McGrath. "It comes from another direction. *It can think!*"

It almost seemed that he was right. With devilish cunning the Thing kept out of range of the firelight, coughing and whooping with rage as it circled round behind the high screen of leaves looking for an opening, while the three men slowly pivoted with it.

For an hour this deadly game continued.

One of the fires began to burn low. A malignant ill fortune seemed to direct that it should be just the most difficult one to tend. At this point the rushing stream cut a swath between deep clay banks, and the giant trees hung lower over the water than anywhere else. The men watched the sinking flame apprehensively.

With uncanny intelligence the Thing quickly noticed its advantage, and hung about at that point, growing bolder.

"We got to pile up that fire," muttered McGrath. "See here, fellers! I'm goin' out a ways an' draw it to one side, an' one o' you make a run for it."

He looked carefully to his rifle, and ostentatiously went off in the opposite direction, almost disappearing in the dark shadows. It was sheer heroism. The Thing began to circle round toward him. Moung Tha-Dun thought he saw his opportunity, and raced out to the dying fire. He piled on an armful of brushwood, when the creature saw the trick. With a howl of rage it swung itself back and downward.

"Look out, Tha-Dun!" yelled Travers.

But it was too late.

An enormous leap carried the Thing to the nearest tree. From there it dropped full thirty feet to the ground, and, with a bound, was on him. The wretched man had barely time to draw his heavy *dah* and slash at the hairy chest, when two long arms shot out and gripped him. There was a quick spurt of blood, a choking shriek, and a dark mass rolled together on the ground. Travers, pale with horror, dodged about, levelling his gun and dropping it again, afraid to fire in that light at the confused heap. Then Moro McGrath rushed past him, right up to the clawing, howling mass of venom and fight, and, thrusting his rifle close up against the thick, hairy neck, pulled both triggers at once.

The heavy charge almost tore the great head from its shoulders. A convulsive shudder tensed the huge frame, and it leaped back, clawing the air. It spun round, tottered a moment over the sheer bank, and then lurched forward into the swift black water beneath. At that moment the flames burst through the fresh pile of brushwood and lit up the ghastly scene. Moung Tha-Dun lay with his neck and back and limbs all twisted into the impossible contortions of a straw dummy. McGrath did not need to lift the broken form.

"Poor devil!" he muttered, turning away his head with his customary qualm. Travers leaned on his gun, white and shaken with horror.

"What was it?" he queried hoarsely.

McGrath looked darkly down the bank where the Thing had disappeared, shaking his head with tightly pressed lips.

"I wonder," he replied finally. "I had a sort o' suspicion; that noise, you know. I'd heard somep'n like it down in Borneo once." He sank into gloomy contemplation again. After a while he added: "An' those two wide bands always; they'd point unmistakable to the grip of some enormously powerful hands an' arms. I'd 'a' said it was a freak specimen of the *Mai-As* ape, or orang. They sometimes run to a size like that; but—"

"But good God, Moro, what made the thing so malignant? Why should it have become so malevolent?"

"Dunno," said McGrath shortly. Then he added suddenly: "Perhaps the *Nat*. There's more things in heaven—an' the jungles, son, than all you science sharps know about."

He sat a long while in gloomy introspection. At last he jumped up and shook himself as out of a dream.

"Cm'on, son!" he barked, with swift return of his customary energy. "We got a heap to do before we're through here. I want to get outa this unholy place with the daylight. I've had enough holiday to go on with for a long time; but—there's promotion for rounding up the last of the *Boh's* gang—an' I guess you'll be wishful to find a telegraph office in Kindat, an' send about ten dollars' worth o' message to Rangoon city in a hurry."

Carnacki, the Ghost Finder:
The House Among the Laurels
William Hope Hodgson

"This is a curious yarn that I am going to tell you," said Carnacki, as after a quiet little dinner we made ourselves comfortable in his cosy dining room.

"I have just got back from the West of Ireland," he continued. "Wentworth, a friend of mine, has lately had rather an unexpected legacy, in the shape of a large estate and manor, about a mile and a half outside of the village of Korunton. This place is named Gannington Manor, and has been empty a great number of years; as you will find is almost always the case with houses reputed to be haunted, as it is usually termed.

"It seems that when Wentworth went over to take possession, he found the place in very poor repair, and the estate totally uncared for, and, as I know, looking very desolate and lonesome generally. He went through the big house by himself, and he admitted to me that it had an uncomfortable feeling about it; but, of course, that might be nothing more than the natural dismalness of a big, empty house, which has been long uninhabited, and through which you are wandering alone.

"When he had finished his look 'round, he went down to the village, meaning to see the one-time agent of the estate, and arrange for someone to go in as caretaker. The agent, who proved by the way to be a Scotchman, was very willing to take up the management of the estate once more; but he assured Wentworth that they would get no one to go in as caretaker; and that his—the agent's—advice was to have the house pulled down, and a new one built.

"This, naturally, astonished my friend, and, as they went down to the village, he managed to get a sort of explanation from the man. It seems that there had been always curious stories told about the place, which in the early days was called Landru Castle, and that within the last seven years there had been two extraordinary deaths there. In each case they had been tramps, who were ignorant of the reputation of the house, and had probably thought the big empty place suitable for a night's free lodging. There had been absolutely no signs of violence to indicate the method by which death was caused, and on each occasion the body had been found in the great entrance hall.

"By this time they had reached the inn where Wentworth had put up, and he told the agent that he would prove that it was all rubbish about the haunting, by staying a night or two in the manor himself. The death of the tramps was certainly curious; but did not prove that any supernatural agency had been at work. They were but isolated accidents, spread over a large number of years by the memory of the villagers, which was natural enough in a little place like Korunton. Tramps had to die some time, and in some place, and it proved nothing that two, out of possibly hundreds who had slept in the empty house, had happened to take the opportunity to die under shelter.

"But the agent took his remark very seriously, and both he and Dennis the landlord of the inn, tried their best to persuade him not to go. For his 'sowl's sake,' Irish Dennis begged him to do no such thing; and because of his 'life's sake,' the Scotchman was equally in earnest.

"It was late afternoon at the time, and as Wentworth told me, it was warm and bright, and it seemed such utter rot to hear those two talking seriously about the impossible. He felt full of pluck, and he made up his mind he would smash the story of the haunting, at once by staying that very night, in the manor. He made this quite clear to them, and told them that it would be more to the point and to their credit, if they offered to come up along with him, and keep him company. But poor old Dennis was quite shocked, I believe, at the suggestion; and though Tabbit, the agent, took it more quietly, he was very solemn about it.

"It seems that Wentworth did go; and though, as he said to me, when the evening began to come on, it seemed a very different sort of thing to tackle.

"A whole crowd of the villagers assembled to see him off; for by this time they all knew of his intention. Wentworth had his gun with him, and a big packet of candles; and he made it clear to them all that it would not be wise for anyone to play any tricks; as he intended to shoot 'at sight.' And then, you know, he got a hint of how serious they considered the whole thing; for one of them came up to him, leading a great bullmastiff, and offered it to him, to take to keep him company. Wentworth patted his gun; but the old man who owned the dog shook his head and explained that the brute might warn him in sufficient time for him to get away from the castle. For it was obvious that he did not consider the gun would prove of any use.

"Wentworth took the dog, and thanked the man. He told me that, already, he was beginning to wish that he had not said definitely that he would go; but, as it was, he was simply forced to. He went through the crowd of men, and found suddenly that they had all turned in a body and were keeping him company. They stayed with him all the way to the manor, and then went right over the whole place with him.

"It was still daylight when this was finished; though turning to dusk; and, for a while, the men stood about, hesitating, as if they felt ashamed to go away and leave Wentworth there all alone. He told me that, by this time, he would gladly have given fifty pounds to be going back with them. And then, abruptly, an idea came to him. He suggested that they should stay with him, and keep him company through the night. For a time they refused, and tried to persuade him to go back with them; but finally he made a proposition that got home to them all. He planned that they should all go back to the inn, and there get a couple of dozen bottles of whisky, a donkey-load of turf and wood, and some more candles. Then they would come back, and make a great fire in the big fireplace, light all the candles, and put them 'round the place, open the whisky and make a night of it. And, by Jove! he got them to agree.

"They set off back, and were soon at the inn, and here, whilst the donkey was being loaded, and the candles and whisky distributed, Dennis was doing his best to keep Wentworth from going back; but he was a sensible man in his way, for when he found that it was no use, he stopped. You see, he did not want to frighten the others from accompanying Wentworth.

"'I tell ye, sorr,' he told him, ''tis of no use at all, thryin' ter reclaim ther castle. 'Tis curst with innocent blood, an' ye'll be betther pullin' it down, an' buildin' a fine new wan. But if ye be intendin' to shtay this night, kape the big dhoor open whide, an' watch for the bhlood-dhrip. If so much as a single dhrip falls, don't shtay though all the gold in the worrld was offered ye.'

"Wentworth asked him what he meant by the blood-drip.

"'Shure,' he said, "'tis the bhlood av thim as ould Black Mick 'way back in the ould days kilt in their shlape. 'Twas a feud as he pretendid to patch up, an' he invited thim—the O'Haras they was—siventy av thim. An' he fed thim, an' shpoke soft to thim, an' thim thrustin' him, sthayed to shlape with him. Thin, he an' thim with him, stharted in an' mhurdered thim was an' all as they slep'. 'Tis from me father's grand-father ye have the sthory. An' sence thin 'tis death to any, so they say, to pass the night in the castle whin the bhlood-dhrip comes. 'Twill put out candle an' fire, an' thin in the darkness the Virgin Herself would be powerless to protect ye.'

"Wentworth told me he laughed at this; chiefly because, as he put it:—'One always must laugh at that sort of yarn, however it makes you feel inside.' He asked old Dennis whether he expected him to believe it.

"'Yes, sorr,' said Dennis, 'I do mane ye to b'lieve it; an' please God, if ye'll b'lieve, ye may be back safe befor' mornin'.' The man's serious simplicity took hold of Wentworth, and he held out his hand. But, for all that, he went; and I must admire his pluck.

"There were now about forty men, and when they got back to the manor—or castle as the villagers always call it—they were not long in getting a big fire going, and lighted candles all 'round the great hall. They had all brought sticks; so that they would have been a pretty formidable lot to tackle by anything simply physical; and, of course, Wentworth had his gun. He kept the whisky in his own charge; for he intended to keep them sober; but he gave them a good strong tot all 'round first, so as to make things seem cheerful; and to get them yearning. If you once let a crowd of men like that grow silent, they begin to think, and then to fancy things.

"The big entrance door had been left wide open, by his orders; which shows that he had taken some notice of Dennis. It was a quiet night, so this did not matter, for the lights kept steady, and all went on in a jolly sort of fashion for about three hours. He had opened a sec-ond lot of bottles, and everyone was feeling cheerful; so much so that one of the men called out aloud to the ghosts to come out and show themselves. And then, you know a very extraordinary thing happened; for the ponderous main door swung quietly and steadily to, as though pushed by an invisible hand, and shut with a sharp click.

"Wentworth stared, feeling suddenly rather chilly. Then he remem-bered the men, and looked 'round at them. Several had ceased their talk, and were staring in a frightened way at the big door; but the great

150

number had never noticed, and were talking and yarning. He reached for his gun, and the following instant the great bullmastiff set up a tremendous barking, which drew the attention of the whole company.

"The hall I should tell you is oblong. The south wall is all windows; but the north and east have rows of doors, leading into the house, whilst the west wall is occupied by the great entrance. The rows of doors leading into the house were all closed, and it was toward one of these in the north wall that the big dog ran; yet he would not go very close; and suddenly the door began to move slowly open, until the blackness of the passage beyond was shown. The dog came back among the men, whimpering, and for a minute there was an absolute silence.

"Then Wentworth went out from the men a little, and aimed his gun at the doorway.

"'Whoever is there, come out, or I shall fire,' he shouted; but nothing came, and he blazed forth both barrels into the dark. As though the report had been a signal, all the doors along the north and east walls moved slowly open, and Wentworth and his men were staring, frightened into the black shapes of the empty doorways.

"Wentworth loaded his gun quickly, and called to the dog; but the brute was burrowing away in among the men; and this fear on the dog's part frightened Wentworth more, he told me, than anything. Then something else happened. Three of the candles over in the corner of the hall went out; and immediately about half a dozen in different parts of the place. More candles were put out, and the hall had become quite dark in the corners.

"The men were all standing now, holding their clubs, and crowded together. And no one said a word. Wentworth told me he felt positively ill with fright. I know the feeling. Then, suddenly, something splashed on to the back of his left hand. He lifted it, and looked. It was covered with a great splash of red that dripped from his fingers. An old Irishman near to him, saw it, and croaked out in a quavering voice:—'The bhlood-dhrip!' When the old man called out, they all looked, and in the same instant others felt it upon them. There were frightened cries of:—'The bhlood-dhrip! The bhlood-dhrip!' And then, about a dozen candles went out simultaneously, and the hall was suddenly dark. The dog let out a great, mournful howl, and there was a horrible little silence, with everyone standing rigid. Then the tension broke, and there was a mad rush for the main door. They wrenched it open, and tumbled out into the dark; but something slammed it with a crash after them, and shut the dog in; for Wentworth heard it howling as they raced down the drive. Yet no one had the pluck to go back to let it out, which does not surprise me.

"Wentworth sent for me the following day. He had heard of me in connection with that Steeple Monster Case. I arrived by the night mail, and put up with Wentworth at the inn. The next day we went up to the old manor, which certainly lies in rather a wilderness; though what struck me most was the extraordinary number of laurel bushes about the house. The place was smothered with them; so that the house seemed to be growing up out of a sea of green laurel. These, and the grim, ancient look of the old building, made the place look a bit dank and ghostly, even by daylight.

"The hall was a big place, and well lit by daylight; for which I was not sorry. You see, I had been rather wound-up by Wentworth's yarn. We found one rather funny thing, and that was the great bullmastiff, lying stiff with its neck broken. This made me feel very serious; for it showed that whether the cause was supernatural or not, there was present in the house some force exceedingly dangerous to life.

"Later, whilst Wentworth stood guard with his shotgun, I made an examination of the hall. The bottles and mugs from which the men had drunk their whisky were scattered about; and all over the place were the candles, stuck upright in their own grease. But in the somewhat brief and general search, I found nothing; and decided to begin my usual exact examination of every square foot of the place—not only of the hall, in this case, but of the whole interior of the castle.

"I spent three uncomfortable weeks, searching; but without result of any kind. And, you know, the care I take at this period is extreme; for I have solved hundreds of cases of so-called 'hauntings' at this early stage, simply by the most minute investigation, and the keeping of a perfectly open mind. But, as I have said, I found nothing. During the whole of the examination, I got Wentworth to stand guard with his loaded shotgun; and I was very particular that we were never caught there after dusk.

"I decided now to make the experiment of staying a night in the great hall, of course 'protected.' I spoke about it to Wentworth; but his own attempt had made him so nervous that he begged me to do no such thing. However, I thought it well worth the risk, and I managed in the end to persuade him to be present.

"With this in view, I went to the neighbouring town of Gaunt, and by an arrangement with the chief constable I obtained the services of six policemen with their rifles. The arrangement was unofficial, of course, and the men were allowed to volunteer, with a promise of payment.

"When the constables arrived early that evening at the inn, I gave them a good feed; and after that we all set out for the Manor. We had four donkeys with us, loaded with fuel and other matters; also two great boarhounds, which one of the police led. When we reached the house, I set the men to unload the donkeys; whilst Wentworth and I set-to and sealed all the doors, except the main entrance, with tape and wax; for if the doors were really opened, I was going to be sure of the fact. I was going to run no risk of being deceived by ghostly hallucination, or mesmeric influence.

"By the time that this was done, the policemen had unloaded the donkeys, and were waiting, looking about them, curiously. I set two of them to lay a fire in the big grate, and the others I used as I required them. I took one of the boarhounds to the end of the hall furthest from the entrance, and there I drove a staple into the floor, to which I tied the dog with a short tether. Then, 'round him, I drew upon the floor the figure of a Pentacle, in chalk. Outside of the Pentacle, I made a circle with garlic. I did exactly the same thing with the other hound; but over more in the northeast corner of the big hall, where the two rows of doors make the angle.

"When this was done, I cleared the whole centre of the hall, and put one of the policemen to sweep it; after which I had all my apparatus carried into the cleared space. Then I went over to the main door and hooked it open, so that the hook would have to be lifted out of the hasp, before the door could be closed. After that, I placed lighted candles before each of the sealed doors, and one in each corner of the big room; and then I lit the fire. When I saw that it was properly alight, I got all the men together, by the pile of things in the centre of the room, and took their pipes from them; for, as the Sigsand MS. has it:—

Theyre must noe lyght come from wythin the barryier.

"And I was going to make sure.

"I got my tape measure then, and measured out a circle thirty-three feet in diameter, and immediately chalked it out. The police and Wentworth were tremendously interested, and I took the opportunity to warn them that this was no piece of silly mumming on my part; but done with a definite intention of erecting a barrier between us and any ab-human thing that the night might show to us. I warned them that, as they valued their lives, and more than their lives it might be, no one must on any account whatsoever pass beyond the limits of the barrier that I was making.

"After I had drawn the circle, I took a bunch of the garlic, and smudged it right 'round the chalk circle, a little outside of it. When this was complete, I called for candles from my stock of material. I set the police to lighting them, and as they were lit, I took them, and sealed them down on the floor, just within the chalk circle, five inches apart. As each candle measured approximately one inch in diameter, it took sixty-six candles to complete the circle; and I need hardly say that every number and measurement has a significance.

"Then, from candle to candle I took a 'gayrd' of human hair, entwining it alternately to the left and to the right, until the circle was completed, and the ends of the hair shod with silver, and pressed into the wax of the sixty-sixth candle.

"It had now been dark some time, and I made haste to get the 'Defence' complete. To this end, I got the men well together, and began to fit the electric pentacle right around us, so that the five points of the defensive star came just within the hair circle. This did not take me long, and a minute later I had connected up the batteries, and the weak blue glare of the intertwining vacuum tubes shone all around us. I felt happier then; for this pentacle is, as you all know, a wonderful 'Defence.' I have told you before, how the idea came to me, after reading Professor Garder's *Experiments with a Medium*. He found that a current, of a certain number of vibrations, *in vacuo,* 'insulated' the medium. It is difficult to suggest an explanation non-technically, and if you are really interested you should read Carder's lecture on *Astral Vibrations Compared with Matero-involuted Vibrations below the Six–Billion Limit.*

"As I stood up from my work, I could hear outside in the night a constant drip from the laurels, which as I have said, come right up around the house, very thick. By the sound, I knew that a 'soft' rain had set in; and there was absolutely no wind, as I could tell by the steady flames of the candles.

"I stood a moment or two, listening, and then one of the men touched my arm, and asked me in a low voice, what they should do. By his tone, I could tell that he was feeling something of the strangeness of it all; and the other men, including Wentworth, were so quiet that I was afraid they were beginning to get shaky.

"I set-to, then, and arranged them with their backs to one common centre; so that they were sitting flat upon the floor, with their feet radiating outward. Then, by compass, I laid their legs to the eight chief points, and afterward I drew a circle with chalk around them; and opposite to their feet, I made the eight signs of the *Saaamaaa* Ritual. The eighth place was, of course, empty; but ready for me to occupy at any moment; for I had omitted to make the Sealing Sign to that point, until I had finished all my preparations, and could enter the Inner Star.

"I took a last look 'round the great hall, and saw that the two big hounds were lying quietly, with their noses between their paws. The fire was big and cheerful, and the candles before the two rows of doors, burnt steadily, as well as the solitary ones in the corners. Then I went 'round the little star of men, and warned them not to be frightened whatever happened; but to trust to the 'Defence'; and to let nothing tempt or drive them to cross the barriers. Also, I told them to watch their movements, and to keep their feet strictly to their places. For the rest, there was to be no shooting, unless I gave the word.

"And now at last, I went to my place, and, sitting down, made the eighth sign just beyond my feet. Then I arranged my camera and flash-light handy, and examined my revolver.

"Wentworth sat behind the first sign, and as the numbering went 'round reversed, that put him next to me on my left. I asked him, in a low voice, how he felt; and he told me, rather nervous; but that he felt confidence in my knowledge and was resolved to go through with the matter, whatever happened.

"We settled down to wait. There was no talking, except that, once or twice, the police bent toward one another, and whispered odd remarks concerning the hall, that appeared queerly audible in the intense silence. But in a while there was not even a whisper from anyone, and only the monotonous drip, drip of the quiet rain without the great entrance, and the low, dull sound of the fire in the big fireplace.

"It was a queer group that we made sitting there, back to back, with our legs starred outward; and all around us the strange blue glow of the pentacle, and beyond that the brilliant shining of the great ring of lighted candles. Outside of the glare of the candles, the large empty hall looked a little gloomy, by contrast, except where the lights shone before the sealed doors, and the blaze of the big fire made a good honest mass of flame. And the feeling of mystery! Can you picture it all?

"It might have been an hour later that it came to me suddenly that I was aware of an extraordinary sense of *dreeness*, as it were, come into

155

the air of the place. Not the nervous feeling of mystery that had been with us all the time; but a new feeling, as if there were something going to happen any moment.

"Abruptly, there came a slight noise from the east end of the hall, and I felt the star of men move suddenly. 'Steady! Keep steady!' I shouted, and they quietened. I looked up the hall, and saw that the dogs were upon their feet, and staring in an extraordinary fashion toward the great entrance. I turned and stared, also, and felt the men move as they craned their heads to look. Suddenly, the dogs set up a tremendous barking, and I glanced across to them, and found they were still 'pointing' for the big doorway. They ceased their noise just as quickly, and seemed to be listening. In the same instant, I heard a faint chink of metal to my left, that set me staring at the hook which held the great door wide. It moved, even as I looked. Some invisible thing was meddling with it. A queer, sickening thrill went through me, and I felt all the men about me, stiffen and go rigid with intensity. I had a certainty of something impending: as it might be the impression of an invisible, but overwhelming, presence. The hall was full of a queer silence, and not a sound came from the dogs. *Then I saw the hook slowly raised from out of its hasp, without any visible thing touching it.* Then a sudden power of movement came to me. I raised my camera, with the flashlight fixed, and snapped it at the door. There came the great blare of the flashlight, and a simultaneous roar of barking from the two dogs.

"The intensity of the flash made all the place seem dark for some moments, and in that time of darkness, I heard a jingle in the direction of the door, and strained to look. The effect of the bright light passed, and I could see clearly again. The great entrance door was being slowly closed. It shut with a sharp snick, and there followed a long silence, broken only by the whimpering of the dogs.

"I turned suddenly, and looked at Wentworth. He was looking at me.

"'Just as it did before,' he whispered.

"'Most extraordinary,' I said, and he nodded and looked 'round, nervously.

"The policemen were pretty quiet, and I judged that they were feeling rather worse than Wentworth; though, for that matter, you must not think that I was altogether natural; yet I have seen so much that is extraordinary, that I daresay I can keep my nerves steady longer than most people.

"I looked over my shoulder at the men, and cautioned them, in a low voice, not to move outside of the barriers, *whatever happened*; not even though the house should seem to be rocking and about to tumble on to them; for well I knew what some of the great forces are capable of doing. Yet, unless it should prove to be one of the cases of the more terrible *Saiitii* Manifestation, we were almost certain of safety, so long as we kept to our order within the pentacle.

"Perhaps an hour and a half passed, quietly, except when, once in a way, the dogs would whine distressfully. Presently, however, they ceased even from this, and I could see them lying on the floor with their paws over their noses, in a most peculiar fashion, and shivering visibly. The sight made me feel more serious, as you can understand.

"Suddenly, the candle in the corner furthest from the main door, went out. An instant later, Wentworth jerked my arm, and I saw that the candle before one of the sealed doors had been put out. I held my camera ready. Then, one after another, every candle about the hall was put out, and with such speed and irregularity, that I could never catch one in the actual act of being extinguished. Yet, for all that, I took a flashlight of the hall in general.

"There was a time in which I sat half-blinded by the great glare of the flash, and I blamed myself for not having remembered to bring a pair of smoked goggles, which I have sometimes used at these times. I had felt the men jump, at the sudden light, and I called out loud to them to sit quiet, and to keep their feet exactly to their proper places. My voice, as you can imagine, sounded rather horrid and frightening in the great room, and altogether it was a beastly moment.

"Then, I was able to see again, and I stared here and there about the hall; but there was nothing showing unusual; only, of course, it was dark now over in the corners.

"Suddenly, I saw that the great fire was blackening. It was going out visibly, as I looked. If I said that some monstrous, invisible, impossible creature sucked the life from it, I could best explain the way the light and flame went out of it. It was most extraordinary to watch. In the time that I watched it, every vestige of fire was gone from it, and there was no light outside of the ring of candles around the pentacle.

"The deliberateness of the thing troubled me more than I can make clear to you. It conveyed to me such a sense of a calm deliberate force present in the hall: The steadfast intention to 'make a darkness' was horrible. The extent of the power to affect the material was now the one constant, anxious questioning in my brain. You can understand?

"Behind me, I heard the policemen moving again, and I knew that they were getting thoroughly frightened. I turned half 'round, and told them, quietly but plainly, that they were safe only so long as they stayed within the pentacle, in the position in which I had put them. If they once broke, and went outside of the barrier, no knowledge of mine could state the full extent of the dreadfulness of the danger.

"I steadied them up, by this quiet, straight reminder; but if they had known, as I knew, that there is no certainty in any 'Protection,' they would have suffered a great deal more, and probably have broken the 'Defence,' and made a mad, foolish run for an impossible safety.

"Another hour passed, after this, in an absolute quietness. I had a sense of awful strain and oppression, as though I were a little spirit in the company of some invisible, brooding monster of the unseen world, who, as yet, was scarcely conscious of us. I leant across to Wentworth, and asked him in a whisper whether he had a feeling as if something were in the room. He looked very pale, and his eyes kept always on the move. He glanced just once at me, and nodded; then stared away 'round the hall again. And when I came to think, I was doing the same thing.

"Abruptly, as though a hundred unseen hands had snuffed them, every candle in the barrier went dead out, and we were left in a darkness that seemed, for a little, absolute; for the light from the pentacle was too weak and pale to penetrate far across the great hall.

"I tell you, for a moment, I just sat there as though I had been frozen solid. I felt the 'creep' go all over me, and seem to stop in my brain. I felt all at once to be given a power of hearing that was far beyond the normal. I could hear my own heart thudding most given a power of hearing that was far beyond the normal. I could hear my own heart thudding most extraordinarily loud. I began, however, to feel better, after a while; but I simply had not the pluck to move. You can understand?

"Presently, I began to get my courage back. I gripped at my camera and flashlight, and waited. My hands were simply soaked with sweat. I glanced once at Wentworth. I could see him only dimly. His shoulders were hunched a little, his head forward; but though it was motionless, I knew that his eyes were not. It is queer how one knows that sort of thing at times. The police were just as silent. And thus a while passed.

"A sudden sound broke across the silence. From two sides of the room there came faint noises. I recognized them at once, as the breaking of the sealing-wax. *The sealed doors were opening.* I raised the camera and flashlight, and it was a peculiar mixture of fear and courage that helped me to press the button. As the great flare of light lit up the hall I felt the men all about me jump. The darkness fell like a clap of thunder, if you can understand, and seemed tenfold. Yet, in the moment of brightness, I had seen that all the sealed doors were wide open.

"Suddenly, all around us, there sounded a drip, drip, drip, upon the floor of the great hall. I thrilled with a queer, realising emotion, and a sense of a very real and present danger—*imminent*. The 'blood-drip' had commenced. And the grim question was now whether the barriers could save us from whatever had come into the huge room.

"Through some awful minutes the 'blood-drip' continued to fall in an increasing rain; and presently some began to fall within the Barriers. I saw several great drops splash and star upon the pale glowing intertwining tubes of the electric pentacle; but, strangely enough, I could not trace that any fell among us. Beyond the strange horrible noise of the 'drip,' there was no other sound. And then, abruptly, from the boarhound over in the far corner, there came a terrible yelling howl of agony, followed instantly by a sickening, breaking noise, and an immediate silence. If you have ever, when out shooting, broken a rabbit's neck, you will know the sound—in miniature! Like lightning, the thought sprang into my brain:—*IT has crossed the pentacle.* For you will remember that I had made one about each of the dogs. I thought instantly, with a sick apprehension, of our own barriers.

"There was something in the hall with us that had passed the barrier of the pentacle about one of the dogs. In the awful succeeding silence, I positively quivered. And suddenly, one of the men behind me, gave out a scream, like any woman, and bolted for the door. He fumbled, and had it open in a moment. I yelled to the others not to move; but they followed like sheep, and I heard them kick the candles flying, in their panic. One of them stepped on the electric pentacle, and smashed it, and there was an utter darkness. In an instant, I realised that I was defenceless against the powers of the Unknown World, and with one savage leap I was out of the useless barriers, and instantly through the great doorway, and into the night. I believe I yelled with sheer funk.

"The men were a little ahead of me, and I never ceased running, and neither did they. Sometimes, I glanced back over my shoulder; and I kept glancing into the laurels which grew all along the drive. The beastly things kept rustling, rustling in a hollow sort of way, as though something were keeping parallel with me, among them. The rain had stopped, and a dismal little wind kept moaning through the grounds. It was disgusting.

"I caught Wentworth and the police at the lodge gate. We got outside, and ran all the way to the village. We found old Dennis up, waiting for us, and half the villagers to keep him company. He told us that he had known in his 'sowl' that we should come back, that is, if we came back at all; which is not a bad rendering of his remark.

"Fortunately, I had brought my camera away from the house— possibly because the strap had happened to be over my head. Yet, I did not go straight away to develop; but sat with the rest of the bar, where we talked for some hours, trying to be coherent about the whole horrible business.

"Later, however, I went up to my room, and proceeded with my photography. I was steadier now, and it was just possible, so I hoped, that the negatives might show something.

"On two of the plates, I found nothing unusual: but on the third, which was the first one that I snapped, I saw something that made me quite excited. I examined it very carefully with a magnifying glass; then I put it to wash, and slipped a pair of rubber overshoes over my boots.

"The negative had showed me something very extraordinary, and I had made up my mind to test the truth of what it seemed to indicate, without losing another moment. It was no use telling anything to Wentworth and the police, until I was certain; and, also, I believed that I stood a greater chance to succeed by myself; though, for that matter, I do not suppose anything would have taken them up to the manor again that night.

"I took my revolver, and went quietly downstairs, and into the dark. The rain had commenced again; but that did not bother me. I walked hard. When I came to the lodge gates, a sudden, queer instinct stopped me from going through, and I climbed the wall into the park. I kept away from the drive, and approached the building through the dismal, dripping laurels. You can imagine how beastly it was. Every time a leaf rustled, I jumped.

"I made my way 'round to the back of the big house, and got in through a little window which I had taken note of during my search; for, of course, I knew the whole place from roof to cellars. I went silently up the kitchen stairs, fairly quivering with funk; and at the top, I went to the left, and then into a long corridor that opened, through one of the doorways we had sealed, into the big hall. I looked up it, and saw a faint flicker of light away at the end; and I tiptoed silently toward it, holding my revolver ready. As I came near to the open door, I heard men's voices, and then a burst of laughing. I went on, until I could see into the hall. There were several men there, all in a group. They were well dressed, and one, at least, I saw was armed. They were examining my 'barriers' against the supernatural, with a good deal of unkind laughter. I never felt such a fool in my life.

"It was plain to me that they were a gang of men who had made use of the empty manor, perhaps for years, for some purpose of their own; and now that Wentworth was attempting to take possession, they were acting up the traditions of the place, with the view of driving him away, and keeping so useful a place still at their disposal. But what they were, I mean whether coiners, thieves, inventors, or what, I could not imagine.

"Presently, they left the pentacle, and gathered 'round the living boarhound, which seemed curiously quiet, as though it were half-drugged. There was some talk as to whether to let the poor brute live, or not; but finally they decided it would be good policy to kill it. I saw two of them force a twisted loop of rope into its mouth, and the two bights of the loop were brought together at the back of the hound's neck. Then a third man thrust a thick walking-stick through the two loops. The two men with the rope, stooped to hold the dog, so that I could not see what was done; but the poor beast gave a sudden awful howl, and immediately there was a repetition of the uncomfortable breaking sound, I had heard earlier in the night, as you will remember.

"The men stood up, and left the dog lying there, quiet enough now, as you may suppose. For my part, I fully appreciated the calculated remorselessness which had decided upon the animal's death, and the cold determination with which it had been afterward executed so neatly. I guessed that a man who might get into the 'light' of those particular men, would be likely to come to quite as uncomfortable an ending.

"A minute later, one of the men called out to the rest that they should shift the wires. One of the men came toward the doorway of the corridor in which I stood, and I ran quickly back into the darkness of the upper end. I saw the man reach up, and take something from the top of the door, and I heard the slight, ringing jangle of steel wire.

"When he had gone, I ran back again, and saw the men passing, one after another, through an opening in the stairs, formed by one of the marble steps being raised. When the last man had vanished, the slab that made the step was shut down, and there was not a sign of the secret door. It was the seventh step from the bottom, as I took care to count: and a splendid idea; for it was so solid that it did not ring hollow, even to a fairly heavy hammer, as I found later.

"There is little more to tell. I got out of the house as quickly and quietly as possible, and back to the inn. The police came without any coaxing, when they knew the 'ghosts' were normal flesh and blood. We entered the park and the manor in the same way that I had done. Yet, when we tried to open the step, we failed, and had finally to smash it. This must have warned the haunters; for when we descended to a secret room which we found at the end of a long and narrow passage in the thickness of the walls, we found no one.

"The police were horribly disgusted, as you can imagine; but for my part, I did not care either way. I had 'laid the ghost,' as you might say, and that was what I set out to do. I was not particularly afraid of being laughed at by the others; for they had all been thoroughly 'taken in'; and in the end, I had scored, without their help.

"We searched right through the secret ways, and found that there was an exit, at the end of a long tunnel, which opened in the side of a well, out in the grounds. The ceiling of the hall was hollow, and reached by a little secret stairway inside of the big staircase. The 'blood-drip' was merely coloured water, dropped through the minute crevices of the ornamented ceiling. How the candles and the fire were put out, I do not know; for the haunters certainly did not act quite up to tradition, which held that the lights were put out by the 'blood-drip.' Perhaps it was too difficult to direct the fluid, without positively squirting it, which might have given the whole thing away. The candles and the fire may possibly have been extinguished by the agency of carbonic acid gas; but how suspended, I have no idea.

"The secret hiding paces were, of course, ancient. There was also, did I tell you? a bell which they had rigged up to ring, when anyone entered the gates at the end of the drive. If I had not climbed the wall, I should have found nothing for my pains; for the bell would have warned them had I gone in through the gateway."

"What was on the negative?" I asked, with much curiosity.

"A picture of the fine wire with which they were grappling for the hook that held the entrance door open. They were doing it from one of the crevices in the ceiling. They had evidently made no preparations for lifting the hook. I suppose they never thought that anyone would make use of it, and so they had to improvise a grapple. The wire was too fine to be seen by the amount of light we had in the hall; but the flashlight 'picked it out.' Do you see?

"The opening of the inner doors was managed by wires, as you will have guessed, which they unshipped after use, or else I should soon have found them, when I made my search.

"I think I have now explained everything. The hound was killed, of course, by the men direct. You see, they made the place as dark as possible, first. Of course, if I had managed to take a flashlight just at that instant, the whole secret of the haunting would have been exposed. But Fate just ordered it the other way."

"And the tramps?" I asked.

"Oh, you mean the two tramps who were found dead in the manor," said Carnacki. "Well, of course it is impossible to be sure, one way or the other. Perhaps they happened to find out something, and were given a hypodermic. Or it is just as probable that they had come to the time of their dying, and just died naturally. It is conceivable that a great many tramps had slept in the old house, at one time or another."

Carnacki stood up, and knocked out his pipe. We rose also, and went for our coats and hats.

"Out you go!" said Carnacki, genially, using the recognized formula. And we went out on to the Embankment, and presently through the darkness to our various homes.

Flaxman Low:
The Story of Konnor Old House

E. and H. Heron

(pseud. for Katherine and Hesketh Prichard)

"I hold," Mr. Flaxman Low, the eminent psychologist, was saying, "that there are no other laws in what we term the realm of the supernatural but those which are the projections or extensions of natural laws."

"Very likely that's so," returned Naripse, with suspicious humility. "But, all the same, Konnor Old House presents problems that won't work in with any natural laws I'm acquainted with. I almost hesitate to give voice to them, they sound so impossible and—and absurd."

"Let's judge of them," said Low.

"It is said," said Naripse, standing up with his back to the fire, "it is said that a Shining Man haunts the place. Also a light is frequently seen in the library—I've watched it myself of a night from here—yet the dust there, which happens to lie very thick over the floor and the furniture, has afterwards shown no sign of disturbance."

"Have you satisfactory evidence of the presence of the Shining Man?"

"I think so," replied Naripse shortly. "I saw him myself the night before I wrote asking you to come up to see me. I went into the house after dusk, and was on the stairs when I saw him: the tall figure of a man, absolutely white and shining. His back was towards me, but the sullen, raised shoulders and sidelong head expressed a degree of sinister animosity that exceeded anything I've ever met with. So I left him in possession, for it's a fact that anyone who has tried to leave his card at Konnor Old House has left his wits with it."

"It certainly sounds rather absurd," said Mr. Low, "but I suppose we have not heard all about it yet?"

"No, there is a tragedy connected with the house, but it's quite a commonplace sort of story and in no way accounts for the Shining Man."

Naripse was a young man of means, who spent most of his time abroad, but the above conversation took place at the spot to which he always referred as home—a shooting-lodge connected with his big grouse-moor on the West Coast of Scotland. The lodge was a small new house built in a damp valley, with a trout-stream running just beyond the garden-hedge.

From the high ground above, where the moor stretched out towards the Solway Firth, it was possible on a fine day to see the dark cone of Ailsa Crag rising above the shimmering ripples. But Mr. Low happened to arrive in a spell of bad weather, when nothing was visible about the lodge but a few roods of sodden lowland, and a curve of the yellow tumbling little river, and beyond a murky outline of shouldering hills blurred by the ever-falling rain. It may have been eleven o'clock on a depressing, muggy night, when Naripse began to talk about Konnor Old House as he sat with his guests over a crackling flaming fire of pinewood.

"Konnor Old House stands on a spur of the ridge opposite-one of the finest sites possible, and it belongs to me. Yet I am obliged to live in this damp little boghole, for the man who would pass a night in Konnor is not to be met with in this county!"

Sullivan, the third man present, replied he was, perhaps—with a glance at Low—there were two, which stung Naripse, who turned his words into a deliberate challenge.

"Is it a bet?" asked Sullivan, rising. He was a tallish man, dark, and clean-shaven, whose features were well-known to the public in connection with the emerald green jersey of the Rugby International Football Team of Ireland. "If it is, it's a bet I'm going to win! Goodnight. In the morning, Naripse, I'll trouble you for the difference."

"The affair is much more in Low's line than in yours," said Naripse. "But you're not really going?"

"You may take it I am though!"

"Don't be a fool, Jack! Low, tell him not to go, tell him there are things no man ought to meddle with—" he broke off.

"There are things no man can meddle with," replied Sullivan, obstinately fixing his cap on his head, "and my backing out of this bet would stand in as one of them!"

Naripse was strangely urgent.

"Low, speak to him! You know——"

Flaxman Low saw that the big Irishman's one vanity had got upon its legs; he also saw that Naripse was very much in earnest.

"Sullivan's big enough to take care of himself:' he said laughing. "At the same time, if he doesn't object, we might as well hear the story before he starts."

Sullivan hesitated, then flung his cap into a corner.

"That's so," he said.

It was a warm night for the time of the year, and they could hear, through the open window, the splashing downpour of the rain.

"There's nothing so lonely as the drip of heavy rain!" began Naripse, "I always associate it with Konnor Old House. The place has stood empty for ten years or more, and this is the story they tell about it. It was last inhabited by a Sir James Mackian, who had been a merchant of sorts in Sierra Leone. When the baronetcy fell to him, he came to England and settled down in this place with a pretty daughter and a lot of servants, including a nigger, named Jake, whose life he was said to have saved in Africa. Everything went on well for nearly two years, when Sir James had occasion to go to Edinburgh for a few days. During his absence his daughter was found dead in her bed, having taken an overdose of some sleeping draught. The shock proved too great for her father. He tried travelling, but, on his return home, he fell into a settled melancholy, and died some months later a dumb imbecile at the asylum."

"Well, I shan't object to meeting the girl as she's so pretty," remarked Sullivan with a laugh. "But there's not much in the story."

"Of course," added Naripse, "countryside gossip adds a good deal of colour to the plain facts of the case. It is said that terrible details connected with Miss Mackian's death were suppressed at the inquest, and people recollected afterwards that for months the girl had worn an unhappy, frightened look. It seemed she disliked the negro, and had been heard to beg her father to send him away, but the old man would not listen to her."

"What became of the negro in the end?" asked Flaxman Low.

"In the end Sir James kicked him out after a violent scene, in the course of which he appears to have accused Jake of having some hand in causing the girl's death. The nigger swore he'd be revenged on him, but, as a matter of fact, he left the place almost immediately, and has never been heard of since—which disposes of the nigger. A short time after the old man went mad; he was found lying on a couch in the library—a hopeless imbecile." Saying this, Naripse went to the window, and looked out into the rainy darkness. "Konnor Old House stands on the ridge opposite, and a part of the building, including the library window, where the light is sometimes seen, is visible through the trees from here. There is no light there tonight, though."

Sullivan laughed his big, full laugh.

"How about your shining man? I hope we may have the luck to meet. I suspect some canny Scots tramp knows where to get a snug roost rent free."

"That may be so," replied Naripse, with a slow patience. "I can only say that after seeing the light of a night, I have more than once gone up in the morning to have a look at the library, and never found the thick dust in the least disturbed."

"Have you noticed if the light appears at regular intervals?" said Low.

"No; it's there on and off. I generally see it in rainy weather."

"What sort of people have gone crazy in Konnor Old House?" asked Sullivan.

"One was a tramp. He must have lived pleasantly in the kitchen for days. Then he took to the library, which didn't agree with him apparently. He was found in a dying state lying upon Sir James's couch, with horrible black patches on his face. He was too far gone to speak, so nothing was gleaned from him."

"He probably had a dirty face, and, having caught cold in the rain, went into Konnor Old House and died quietly there of pneumonia or something of the kind, just as you or I might have done, tucked up in our own little beds at home," commented Sullivan.

"The last man to try his luck with the ghosts," went on Naripse, without noticing this remark, "was a young fellow, called Bowie, a nephew of Sir James. He was a student at Edinburgh University and he wanted to clear up the mystery. I was not at home, but my factor allowed him to pass a night in the house. As he did not appear next day, they went to look for him. He was found lying on the couch— and he has not spoken a rational word since."

"Sheer—mere physical fright, acting on an overwrought brain!" Sullivan summed up the case scornfully. "And now I'm off. The rain has stopped, and I'll get up to the house before midnight. You may expect me at dawn to tell you what I've seen."

"What do you intend to do when you get there?" asked Flaxman

Low.

"I'll pass the night on the ghostly couch which I suppose I shall find in the library. Take my word for it, madness is in Sir James's family; father and daughter and nephew all gave proof of it in different ways. The tramp, who was perhaps in there for a couple of days, died a natural death. It only needs a healthy man to run the gauntlet and set all this foolish talk at rest."

Naripse was plainly much disturbed though he made no further objection, but when Sullivan was gone, he moved restlessly about the room looking out of the window from time to time. Suddenly he spoke:

"There it is! The light I mentioned to you."

Mr. Low went to the window. Away on the opposite ridge a faint light glimmered out through the thick gloom. Then he glanced at his watch.

"Rather over an hour since he started," he remarked. " Well, now, Naripse, if you will be so good as to hand me *Human Origins* from the shelf behind you, I think we may settle down to wait for dawn. Sullivan's just the man to give a good account of himself—under most circumstances."

"Heaven send there may be no black side to this business!" said Naripse. "Of course I was a fool to say what I did about the Old House, but nobody except an ass like Jack would think I meant it. I wish the night was well over! That light is due to go out in two hours anyway."

Even to Mr. Low the night seemed unbearably long; but at the first streak of dawn he tossed his book on to the sofa, stretched himself, and said: "We may as well be moving; let's go and see what Sullivan is doing."

The rain began to fall again, and was coming down in close straight lines as the two men drove up the avenue to Konnor Old House. As they ascended, the trees grew thicker on the banks of the cutting which led them in curves to the terrace on which stood the house. Although it was a modern red-brick building, rather picturesque with its gables and sharply-pitched overhanging roofs, it looked desolate and forbidding enough in the grey daybreak. To the left lay lawns and gardens, to the right the cliff fell away steeply to where the burn roared in spate some three hundred feet below. They drove round to the empty stables, and then hurried back to the house on foot by a path that debouched directly under the library window. Naripse stopped under it, and shouted: "Hullo! Jack, where are you?"

But no answer came, and they went on to the hall door. The gloom of the wet dawning and the heavy smell of stagnant air filled the big hall as they looked round at its dreary emptiness. The silence within the house itself was oppressive. Again Naripse shouted, and the noise echoed harshly through the passages, jarring on the stillness, then he led the way to the library at a run.

As they came in sight of the doorway a wave of some nauseating odour met them, and at the same moment they saw Sullivan lying just outside the threshold, his body twisted and rigid like a man in the extremity of pain, his contorted profile ivory-pale against the dark oak flooring, As they stooped to raise him, Mr. Low had just time to notice the big gloomy room beyond, with its heaped and trampled layers of accumulated dust. There was no time for more than a glance, for the indescribable, fetid odour almost overpowered them as they hastened to carry Sullivan into the open air.

"We must get him home as soon as we can," said Mr. Low, "for we have a very sick man on our hands."

This proved to be true. But in a few days, thanks to Mr. Low's treatment and untiring care, the severe physical symptoms became less urgent, and in due time Sullivan's mind cleared.

The following account is taken from the written statement of his experience in Konnor Old House:

"On reaching the house he entered as noiselessly as possible, and made for the library, finding his way by the help of a series of matches to Sir James's couch, upon which he lay down. He was conscious at once of an acrid taste in his mouth, which he accounted for by the clouds of dust he had raised in crossing the room.

"First he began to think about the approaching football match with Scotland, for which he was already in training. He was still in his mood of derisive incredulity. The house seemed vastly empty, and wrapped in an uneasy silence, a silence which made each of his comfortable movements an omen of significance. Presently the sense of a presence in the room was borne in upon him. He sat up, and spoke softly. He almost expected someone to answer him, and so strong did this feeling become that he called out: 'Who's there?' No reply came, and he sat on amidst the oppressive silence. He says the slightest noise would have been a relief. It was the listening in the silence that bred in him so intense a longing to grapple with some solid opponent.

"Fear! He, who had denied the very existence of cause for fear, found himself shivering with an untranslatable terror! This was fear! He realised it with an infinite recoil of anger.

"Presently he became aware that the darkness about him was clearing. A feeble light filtered slowly through it from above. Looking up at the ceiling, he perceived directly above his head an irregular patch of pale phosphorescent luminance, which grew gradually brighter. How long he sat with his head thrown back, staring at the light, he does not know. It seemed years. Then he spoke to himself plainly. With an immense effort, he forced his eyes away from the light and got upon his feet to drag his limbs round the room. The phosphorescence was of a greenish tint, and as strong as moonlight, but the dust rose like vapour at the slightest movement, and somewhat obscured its power. He moved about, but not for long. A clogging weight, such as one feels in nightmare, pressed upon him, and his exhaustion was intensified by the overpowering physical disgust bred in him by the repulsive odour which passed across his face as he staggered back to the couch.

"For a few moments he would not look up. He says he had an impression that someone was watching him through the radiance as through a window. The atmosphere about him was thickening and cloaking the walls with drowsy horror, while his senses revolted and choked at the growing odour. Then followed a state of semi-sleep, for he recollects no more until he found himself staring again at the luminous patch on the ceiling.

"By this time the brightness was beginning to dim; dark smears showed through it here and there, which ran slowly together till out of them grew and protruded a fat, black, evil face. A second later Sullivan was aware that the horrible face was sinking down nearer and nearer to his own, while all about it the light changed to black, dripping fluid, that formed great drops and fell.

"It seemed as if he could not save himself; he could not move! The fighting blood in him had died out; Then fear, mad fear and strong loathing gave him the strength to act. He saw his own hand working savagely, it passed through and through the impending face, yet he swears that he felt a slight impact and that he saw the fat, glazed skin quiver! Then, with a final struggle, he tore it himself from the couch, and, rushing to the door, he wrenched open, and plunged forward into a red vacancy, down—down—After that he remembered no more."

While Sullivan still lay ill and unable to give an account of himself or of what had happened at Konnor Old House, Mr. Flaxman Low expressed his intention of paying a visit to the asylum for the purpose of seeing young Bowie. But on arrival at the asylum, he found that Bowie had died during the previous night. A weary-eyed assistant doctor took Mr. Low to see the body. Bowie had evidently been of a gaunt, but powerful build. The features, though harsh, were noble, the face being somewhat disfigured by a rough, raised discoloration, which extended from the centre of the forehead to behind the right ear.

Mr. Low asked a question.

"Yes, it is a very obscure case," observed the assistant, "but it is the disease he died of. When he was brought here some months ago he had a small dark spot on his forehead, but it spread rapidly, and there are now similar large patches over the whole of his body. I take it to be of a cancerous character, likely to occur in a scrofulous subject after a shock and severe mental strain, such as Bowie chose to subject himself to by passing a night in Konnor Old House. The first result of the shock was the imbecility, an increasing lethargic condition of the body supervened and finally coma."

While the doctor was speaking, Mr. Low bent over the dead man and closely examined the mark upon the face.

"This mark appears to be the result of a fungoid growth, perhaps akin to the Indian disease known as *mycetoma*?" he said at length.

"It may be so. The case is very obscure, but the disease, whatever we may call it, appears to be in Bowie's family, for I believe his uncle, Sir James Mackian, had precisely similar symptoms during his last illness. He also died in this institution, but that was before my time," replied the assistant.

After a further examination of the body Mr. Low took his leave, and during the following day or two was busily engaged in a spare empty room placed at his disposal by Naripse. A deal table and chair were all he required, Mr. Low explained, and to these he added a microscope, an apparatus for producing a moist heat, and the coat worn by Sullivan on the night of his adventure. At the end of the third day, as Sullivan was already on the road to recovery, Mr. Low, accompanied by Naripse, paid a second visit to Konnor Old House, during which Low mentioned some of his conclusions about the strange events which had occurred there. It will be an easy task to compare Mr. Flaxman Low's theory with the experience detailed by Sullivan and with the one or two subsequent discoveries that added something like confirmation to his conclusions.

Mr. Low and his host drove up as on the previous occasion, and stabled the horse as before. The day was dry, but grey, and the time the early afternoon. As they ascended the path leading to the house, Mr. Low remarked, after gazing up for a few seconds at the library window:

"That room has the air of being occupied."

"Why?—What makes you think so?" asked Naripse nervously.

"It is hard to say, but it produces that impression." Naripse shook his head despondently.

"I've always noticed it myself," he returned, "I wish Sullivan were all right again and able to tell us what he saw in there. Whatever it was it has nearly cost him his life. I don't suppose we shall ever know anything more definite about the matter."

"I fancy I can tell you," replied Low, "but let us get on into the library, and see what it looks like before we enter into the subject any further. By the way, I should advise you to tie your handkerchief over your mouth and nose before we go into the room."

Naripse, upon whom the events of the last few days had had a very strong effect, was in a state of scarcely-controllable excitement.

"What do you mean, Low?—you can't have any idea—"

"Yes, I believe the dust in that house to be simply poisonous. Sullivan inhaled any amount of it—hence his condition."

The same suggestion of loneliness and stagnation hung about the house as they passed through the hall and entered the library. They halted at the door and looked in. The amount of greenish dust in the room was extraordinary; it lay in little drifts and mounds over the floor, but most abundantly just about the couch. Immediately above this spot, they perceived on the ceiling a long, discoloured stain. Naripse pointed to it.

"Do you see that? It is a bloodstain, and, I give you my word, it grows larger and larger every year!" He finished the sentence in a low voice, and shuddered.

"Ah, so I should have expected," observed Flaxman Low, who was looking at the stained ceiling with much interest. "That, of course, explains everything."

"Low, tell me what you mean? A bloodstain that grows year by year explains everything?" Naripse broke off and pointed to the couch. "Look there! a cat's been walking over that sofa."

Mr. Low put his hand on his friend's shoulder and smiled.

"My dear fellow! That stain on the ceiling is simply a patch of mould and fungi, Now come in carefully without raising the dust, and let us examine the cat's footsteps, as you call them."

Naripse advanced to the couch and considered the marks gravely.

"They are not the footmarks of any animal, they are something much more unaccountable. They are raindrops. And why should raindrops be here in this perfectly watertight room, and even then only in one small part of it? You can't very well explain that, and you certainly can't have expected it?"

"Look round and follow my points," replied Mr. Low. "When we came to fetch Sullivan, I noticed the dust which far exceeds the ordinary accumulation even in the most neglected places. You may also notice that it is of a greenish colour and of extreme fineness. This dust is of the same nature as the powder you find in a puff-ball, and is composed of minute sporuloid bodies. I found that Sullivan's coat was covered with this fine dust, and also about the collar and upper portion of the sleeve I found one or two gummy drops which correspond to these raindrops, as you call them. I naturally concluded from their position that they had fallen from above. From the dust, or rather spores, which I found on Sullivan's coat, I have since cultivated no fewer than four specimens of fungi, of which three belong to known African species; but the fourth, so far as I know, has never been described, but it approximates most closely to one of the *phalliodei.*"

"But how about the raindrops, or whatever they are? I believe they drop from that horrible stain."

"They are drops from the stain, and are caused by the unnamed fungus I have just alluded to. It matures very rapidly, and absolutely decays as it matures, liquefying into a sort of dark mucilage, full of spores, which drips down, and diffuses a most repulsive odour. In time the mucilage dries, leaving the dust of the spores."

"I don't know much about these things myself," replied Naripse dubiously, "and it strikes me you know more than enough. But look here; how about the light? You saw it last night yourself."

"It happens that the three species of African fungi possess well known phosphorescent properties, which are manifested not only during decomposition, but also during the period of growth. The light is only visible from time to time; probably climatic and atmospheric conditions only admit of occasional efflorescence."

"But," object Naripse, "supposing it to be a case of poisoning by fungi as you say, how is it that Sullivan, though exposed to precisely the same sources of danger as the others who have passed a night here, has escaped? He has been very ill, but his mind has already regained its balance, whereas, in the three other cases, the mind was wholly destroyed."

Mr. Low looked very grave.

"My dear fellow, you are such an excitable and superstitious person that I hesitate to put your nerves to any further test."

"Oh, go on!"

"I hesitate for two reasons. The one I have mentioned, and also because in my answer I must speak of curious and unpleasant things, some of which are proved facts, others only more or less well-founded assumptions. It is acknowledged that fungi exert an important influence in certain diseases, a few being directly attributable to fungi as a primary cause. Also it is an historical fact that poisonous fungi have more than once been used to alter the fate of nations. From the evidence before us and the condition of Bowie's body, I can but conclude that the unknown fungus I have alluded to is of a singularly malignant nature, and acts through the skin upon the brain with terrible rapidity afterwards gradually inter-penetrating all the tissues of the body, and eventually causing death. In Sullivan's case, luckily, the falling drops only touched his clothing, not his skin."

"But wait a minute, Low, how did these fungi come here? And how can we rid the house of them? Upon my word, it is enough to make a man go off his head to hear about it. What are you going to do now?"

"In the first place we will go upstairs and examine the flooring just above that stained patch of ceiling."

"You can't do that I'm afraid. The room above this happens to be divided into two portions by a hollow partition between 2ft. and 3ft. thick," said Naripse, "the interior of which may originally have been meant for a cupboard, but I don't think it has ever been used."

"Then let us examine the cupboard; there must be some way of getting into it."

Upon this Naripse led the way upstairs, but, as he gained the top, he leant back, and grasping Mr. Low by the arm thrust him violently forward.

"Look! the light—did you see the light?" he said.

For a second or two it seemed as if a light, like the elusive light thrown by a rotating reflector, quivered on the four walls of the landing, then disappeared almost before one could he certain of having seen it.

"Can you point me out the precise spot where you saw the shining figure you told us of?" asked Low.

Naripse pointed to a dark corner of the landing.

"Just there in front of that panel between the two doors. Now that I come to think of it, I fancy there is some means of opening the upper part of that panel. The idea was to ventilate the cupboard-like space I mentioned just now."

Naripse walked across the landing and felt round the panel, till he found a small metal knob. On turning this, the upper part of the panel fell back like a shutter, disclosing a narrow space of darkness beyond. Naripse thrust his head into the opening and peered into the gloom, but immediately started back with a gasp.

"The shining man!" he cried. "He's there!"

Mr. Flaxman Low, hardly knowing what to expect, looked over his shoulder; then, exerting his strength, pulled away some of the lower boarding. For within, at arm's length, stood a dimly shining figure! A tall man, with his back towards them, leaning against the left of the partition, and shrouded from head to foot in faintly luminous white mould.

The figure remained quite motionless while they stared at it in surprise; then Mr. Flaxman Low pulled on his glove, and, leaning forward, touched the man's head. A portion of the white mass came away in his fingers, the lower surface of which showed a bunch of frizzled negroid hair.

"Good Heavens, Low, what do you make of this?" asked Naripse. "It must be the body of Jake. But what is this shining stuff?"

Low stood under the wide skylight and examined what he held in his fingers.

"Fungus," he said at last. "And it appears to have some property allied to the mouldy fungus which attacks the common house-fly. Have you not seen them dead upon window-panes, stiffly fixed upon their legs, and covered with a white mould? Something of the same kind has taken place here."

"But what had Jake to do with the fungus? And how did he come here?"

"All that, of course, we can only surmise," replied Mr. Low. "There is little doubt that secrets of nature hidden from us are well known to the various African tribes. It is possible that the negro possessed some of these deadly spores, but how or why he made use of them are questions that can never be cleared up now."

"But what was he doing here?" asked Naripse.

"As I said before we can only guess the answer to that question, but I should suppose that the negro made use of this cupboard as a place where he could be free from interruption; that he here cultivated the spores is proved by the condition of his body and of the ceiling immediately below. Such an occupation is by no means free from danger, especially in an airless and enclosed space such as this. It is evident that either by design or accident he became infected by the fungus poison, which in time covered his whole body as you now see. The subject of *obeah*," Flaxman Low went on reflectively, "is one to the study of which I intend to devote myself at some future period. I have, indeed, already made some arrangements for an expedition in connection with the subject into the interior of Africa."

"And how is the horrible thing to be got rid of? Nothing short of burning the place down would be of any radical use," remarked Naripse.

Low, who by this time was deeply engrossed in considering the strange facts with which he had just become acquainted, answered abstractedly: "I suppose not."

Naripse said no more, and the words were only recalled to Mr. Low's mind a day or two later, when he received by post a copy of the *West Coast Advertiser*. It was addressed in the handwriting of Naripse, and the following extract was lightly scored:

Konnor Old House, the property of Thomas Naripse, Esquire, of Konnor Lodge, was, we regret to say, destroyed by fire last night. We are sorry to add that the loss to the owner will be considerable, as no insurance policy had been effected with regard to the property.

The Robbery on the "Stormy Petrel"
Richard Marsh

1

The case of the robbery on board the *Stormy Petrel* was notable for one thing if for no other—in it the Hon. Augustus Champnell received fees from three separate and, indeed, antagonistic individuals.

The Hon. Augustus had finished reading the morning papers, and was wondering—for business was slack—what the day might bring forth, when there came a tapping at the door, and there immediately entered two servants in livery, bearing between them an iron box, which they placed on a chair. One of them spoke—as if he had been an automaton.

"The Marquis of Bewlay's compliments to Mr. Champnell, and will Mr. Champnell drown the box in a cistern full of water, till the marquis arrives."

Mr. Champnell stared.

"And when will the marquis arrive?"

The marquis arrived almost as soon as the servants had gone. That ancient peer came hobbling into the room, leaning on two sticks, and as soon as he saw the box on the chair he seemed more than half disposed to back out again.

"Didn't the rascals tell you to drown the box in a cistern of water?"

"The rascals did. But the Marquis of Bewlay will permit me to observe that I always require a sufficient explanation before I act on instructions which I receive from strangers."

With Mr. Champnell's assistance the marquis took refuge in a chair.

"What's your fee?"

"My lowest fee is one hundred guineas."

177

"Too much."

"In the case of the Marquis of Bewlay my lowest fee will be one hundred and fifty guineas."

The marquis glanced up at him—and leered.

"You shall have it for your impudence—the Champnells always were an impudent lot. Find out who sent what is in that box, and you shall have your hundred and fifty. Here's the key, look inside—only mind, gently does it"

Unlocking the iron box with the key the marquis gave him, Mr. Champnell found that it contained other smaller wooden boxes, which were divided from each other by layers of cotton wool. Removing the covers of these wooden boxes he perceived that each contained what seemed to be some sort of oil can.

"Thirteen of them, aren't they?" On counting them Mr. Champnell discovered that the number was correct "Lucky number, and pretty playthings, every one of them. All infernal machines, or I'm a hatter. They've come raining in on me by every post—if you look at them you'll see that there is a different postmark on every one of them."

"Are you certain that they are infernal machines?"

"I'll lay you ten to one in anything you like to name that they are, and leave you to prove the contrary—that's the extent of my certainty, Mr. Champnell. Only if you take my advice you'll keep them immersed in water until the thing has been shown to demonstration, either one way or the other. I have no desire to be blown to pieces, if you have."

"Have you no sort of idea where they come from?"

"Once upon a time I was fool enough to enrol myself as a member of a certain secret society. I have broken since then pretty nearly every one of its rules, which I swore to observe, and I think it quite on the cards that these things may have come from some of the society's agents. I'll tell you what I'll do; instead of a hundred and fifty guineas, I'll give you two hundred, if you prove, beyond a shadow of doubt, that they don't I've come to you instead of going to the police, because I want the thing kept private, but at the same time I am particularly anxious to know if at last the beggars are beginning to try to do what they have threatened to do, times without number."

The marquis's story was a long one, and not a little involved; some of Mr. Champnell's questions he declined, point blank, to answer. When he had gone, Mr. Champnell still found himself in possession of very slight data to enable him to prosecute his researches. He summed the data up in his mind, telling himself, finally, that they really amounted to nothing at all, and had almost resolved to write to the marquis and decline the conduct of the case unless he furnished him with fuller information on certain points on which he had refused to give any information at all, when the servant came to announce that Mr. Golden, of the firm of Messrs. Ruby and Golden, was at the door and desirous of an interview.

A minute later Mr. Champnell found himself face to face with the junior partner of the famous firm of jewellers—a shrewd, sharp-looking man, who wasted no time in coming to the point

"I have been made the victim, Mr. Champnell, of an atrocious out-rage, and I come to you first, because the matter is one which requires delicate handling, and second, because the author of the outrage is a member of your own order. I may add that if you succeed in this mat-ter we may be able to place a good deal of business in your hands—business of a kind which requires the intervention of a diplomatist rather than of a policeman."

The Hon. Augustus bowed.

"You are acquainted with Lord Hardaway?" Another bow from Mr. Champnell "His lordship has been a customer of ours for some time, and is so largely in our debt that some months ago we felt bound to intimate that we could not allow him to add to the already large figure of his account

"We have recently received information, through side channels, that his Lordship was paying his addresses to Miss Bonnyer-Lees, the sole child and heiress of the eminent soap-boiler. And, ten days ago, we received a letter from his lordship himself, which was to the effect that he was about to start for a cruise in his yacht, the *Stormy Petrel*; that Miss Bonnyer-Lees was to accompany him, with other friends; that he had hopes of making Miss Bonnyer-Lees his wife; and he desired us to send him, at once, for his inspection and the lady's, a selection of the finest things we had in stock; in fact, he gave us to understand that matters had reached a stage in which he was anxious to make the lady a handsome present his Lordship went on to add that if he married Miss Bonnyer-Lees our account should receive an immediate settlement; while, on the other hand, if he did not marry her, it was quite possible that we should have to whistle—the word was his Lordship's own."

"Where was Lord Hardaway when he wrote this letter?"

"Staying at Miss Bonnyer-Lees' own residence in Kent But the day

179

after we received a telegram from him stating that they had decided to commence the cruise sooner than they had originally intended; that the day following they would be off Deal, on board the yacht, and that the goods were to be sent on board to be examined The telegram also contained what seemed to me, under the circumstances, to be a somewhat brutal intimation to the effect that if we did not telegraph a reply to say that the goods would be sent off at once the order would be placed elsewhere."

"Did you send the goods?"

"My impulse was to telegraph a refusal. In several little matters Lord Hardaway had not used us altogether well, and it seemed to me that in this matter he was not using us altogether well either; there was no necessity, for instance, for him to threaten us with the loss of his custom. My partner, however, Mr. Ruby, would not hear of a refusal He was naturally unwilling to lose the business which would be associated with what would, probably, be one of the weddings of the season. On one point I did stand firm. As I feared that, if he was the bearer of the goods, Mr. Ruby would quite probably allow himself to be wheedled out of them, without receiving any satisfactory promise of payment, I resolved to take the goods myself. Which I did do."

Mr. Golden paused. At this point of his narrative, which he had reached, a certain uneasiness seemed to possess him.

"It was about midday when I reached Deal. It was both blowing and raining, and what I should have called a regular gale was on. A sailor with the words *Stormy Petrel* on his cap came to me at the station, and, when I told him who I was, informed me that we must go off to the yacht at once, because his lordship had resolved to weigh anchor if I did not arrive by that train. I had never been to Deal in my life before, and I had some idea that the yacht might be anchored to the pier. But when I got down to the beach I found that there was no pier, and the sailor, pointing to what was merely a speck on the horizon, said, 'There's the *Stormy Petrel.*' When he said that, and I saw that the yacht was heaven knows how far from land, if I had not felt that the fellow was covertly grinning at me, and that I should never have heard the last of it from Ruby, I should have come straight back to town, which would have been a wiser thing than what I actually did do. I entrusted myself in a cranky boat to the mercy of the, literally, foaming billows."

Again Mr. Golden paused. It might have been imagination, but it seemed to the Hon. Augustus that, at the mere recollection of that experience of the horrors of the ocean, Mr. Golden became a little yellow.

"I am not ashamed, Mr. Champnell, to own that I am no sailor. I have felt qualms upon the Thames. What I suffered in that cockle-shell of a boat, tossed hither and thither amidst that seething mass of waters—I don't know if it was blowing or raining hardest—I will not now attempt to describe. When I reached the *Stormy Petrel* I was more dead than alive. Lord Hardaway received me on deck; he was, evidently, suffering no inconvenience from the weather. 'Hollo, Golden,' he said, 'you're looking queer.' 'If, my lord,' I answered, 'I am looking as queer as I feel I must be looking very queer indeed. I had no idea before I left town that such a storm was raging.' 'Storm!' he said, 'you don't call this a storm. It's only a capful of wind! Come below and have a peg?' I went downstairs and I had some brandy; then I must have had an-other attack of illness, because the next thing I can remember is Lord Hardaway clapping me on the shoulder and exclaiming, 'I say. Golden, where are those jewels of yours?'"

Once more there was a break in Mr. Golden's narrative—he seemed to be oppressed by the weight of his recollections.

"It will give you, Mr. Champnell, an adequate idea of my physical condition when I tell you that, until that moment, I had forgotten that I had the jewels on me, and when I add that I had taken with me from town jewels to the gross value of nearly £20,000 you will understand what that statement means. They were contained in a locked leather case, which was attached to a steel belt which was locked about my waist The keys both of the belt and of the case were in a secret pocket of my waistcoat—see here."

Unbuttoning his waistcoat, Mr. Golden disclosed a tiny pocket, which was ingeniously contrived in the lining.

"When his lordship spoke I put my hand to my waist and found that the belt and case had gone, and not only so, my waistcoat was unbuttoned and the keys had vanished.

"'My lord,' I cried, as I staggered to my feet, 'I've been robbed.'

"'By Jove,' he exclaimed, 'if I didn't think so. Come along. Golden, the thief has just gone overboard with the spoil—if you don't look alive he'll get clear away.' You will understand, Mr. Champnell, that I was disorganised both in mind and body—really incapable, in fact, of collecting my thoughts. I allowed his lordship to drag me up above. It seemed to me when I got into the open air that the storm was raging worse than ever; and taking me to the side of the deck, he pointed out a solitary individual who was rowing away from the ship in a little boat. 'There's the thief! I thought there was something suspicious about the way in which he came sneaking up from below. Before we knew what he was up to he had dropped into his boat and was off. If you look alive, Golden, you'll catch him yet, red-handed.' The boat in which I had come from shore was still alongside, and, before I had a chance to collect my scattered senses, his lordship had not only bundled me into it, but the boat itself was pushed off from the yacht.

"We chased that boat which contained the solitary rower, as it appeared to me, for hours. I will not dilate on what I still continued to suffer, but through all my agony I urged the rowers in pursuit. As soon as we were within hailing distance I shouted to the fellow, 'Stop!' Directly I did so, standing up in his boat, he dropped something into the sea. I distinctly saw that he dropped something, but what he was too far off for me to see. When we reached him he declared that he had merely thrown overboard some rubbish, but why he had chosen that singularly inopportune moment he did not condescend to explain. We took him in tow, he seeming not at all unwilling, and at last we reached the land. How thankful I was to do so no one but myself can have the faintest conception.

"Hardly had I set foot on *terra firma* than I became convinced that I had been duped from first to last The fellow we had chased turned out to be an honest, simple fisherman, who had been employed to take a telegram from the post office to the yacht, and who protested that he had never left his boat, and that he knew nothing of my belt or case. I believed, and I believe him. I have no doubt whatever that Lord Hardaway was himself the thief. I would have instituted a prosecution directly I returned to town only Ruby would not hear of it Mr. Ruby is always fearful of anything in the shape of a scandal. A week has passed. We have heard nothing of his lordship or of the jewels. That, at present, is how the matter stands."

"What is it you wish me to do?"

"To see that the jewels are returned to us."

"And in default?"

"We must either have the jewels or a guarantee of payment—a sufficient guarantee!—or we prosecute. Here is a list of the jewels that are missing, with the several values attached." Mr. Golden handed the Hon. Augustus a sheet of paper. "You perceive that it is a matter which requires delicate handling."

"Quite so. Where is Lord Hardaway now?"

"No one seems to have the least idea. As you are aware, the weather has been very boisterous during the last few days, and, for all anyone seems to know, he and the *Stormy Petrel* may be at the bottom of the sea together. Altogether, for us, it is a pleasant state of things!"

"Was Miss Bonnyer-Lees on board?"

"She was not. It appears only too probable that the whole business was a deliberately planned conspiracy. As I told you at the beginning, Mr. Champnell, I have been made the victim of an atrocious outrage."

2.

When, Mr. Golden having departed, the Hon. Augustus was left alone he laughed. The story of the jeweller's sufferings appealed to his sense of humour. He studied the list of the missing jewels.

"There appears to be some pretty baubles among them, and they appear to be marked at pretty prices. If Hardaway has got clean away with the spoil they ought to provide him with a pleasant little nest egg with which to start afresh."

He turned to the mantelpiece to get a light for his pipe. Just as he struck a match his ears were saluted by a curious sound which proceeded from behind his back.

"What's that?"

With the lighted match in his hand he turned to listen. The sound continued—it seemed to increase in volume. It was as if some rusty clockwork mechanism had suddenly been set in motion.

"It seems to come from the interior of the Marquis of Bewlay's precious iron case." The case in question still remained where it had originally been placed, upon a chair. Mr. Champnell went to it and raised the lid. "By George! it does! It strikes me that it comes from inside one of these pretty wooden boxes—from inside this one, unless I am mistaken."

He removed the cover from the box in question—the noise did seem to come from inside it No sooner had he done so than there was a sound as if a damp squib had been exploded, a quantity of what seemed like water was dashed into his face, and there drifted through the room a most unpleasant smoke. The Hon. Augustus was amazed.

"It occurs to me that the marquis was right, and that these ingenious contrivances are infernal machines. Unless I err, one of them has justified its existence by exploding. Considering that there are twelve more of them, I seem to be in a truly comfortable situation. It is a pity

Bewlay did not keep them in his possession a little longer, and allow them to explode on his own premises instead of on mine. What is this stuff on my face?" His head and face were covered with moisture. He allowed a drop to trickle into his mouth. "It tastes like sea-water. What is the meaning of this thing? I'll have a look at myself in the glass."

As he was moving towards a mirror something caught his eye which was lying on the floor.

"What the something's that?"

He might well ask—what seemed to be a circlet of scintillating light was lying almost at his feet He picked it up, staring at it, when he had it in his hand, with growing bewilderment.

"A bracelet!—of diamonds!—As I am a sinner!—How on earth did it get here?" An idea flashed into his brain. "Can it be—it can't be—I do believe it is one of Golden's."

He examined with eager eyes the list of the missing jewels.

"It is!—Here's the thing itself!—'A bracelet of twenty-four diamonds, in a plain gold setting, with pearl fastenings. When closed the fastening is heart-shaped. Five pearls in fastening.' It is Golden's. Hollo, another of the marquis's infernal machines seems to be evincing an inclination to go off."

The words were hardly out of his mouth when it did go off; indeed, the whole thirteen had gone off within ten minutes. They had evidently been ingeniously contrived to go off, as rapidly as possible, one after the other, so, as the schoolboys have it, to "keep the pot a-boiling." The room was full of suffocating smoke, Mr. Champnell was drenched with what seemed like sea-water, and he was in the possession of the whole of the missing jewels—they had been vomited forth by the infernal machines.

"Although this looks as if it were a fairy tale," he told himself, "I fancy it has a very simple explanation."

As, some half-hour after, he was driving down Bond Street in a cab, his attention was attracted to an individual who was advancing along the Piccadilly pavement.

"The man himself! So whatever may have become of the *Stormy Petrel*, milord himself is above water."

Stopping the cab, springing out of it, hastening towards the individual in question, Mr. Champnell accosted him—a tall, willowy man, with a dark, oval face, and big, wild, black eyes.

"I am glad to see, Hardaway, that you've not drowned, in spite of the boisterous weather which has recently prevailed in the Channel.

You have probably been kept alive in order to be arrested on a warrant emanating from Scotland Yard."

"Champnell, you don't mean it?"

"Don't I? When a man steals jewels to the value of twenty thousand pounds, puts them, with about two gallons of sea-water, into thirteen infernal machines; sends those infernal machines to the address of the Marquis of Bewlay; and they are brought to me, and explode, and nearly blow me up, and the whole place besides, it is generally supposed that that man has done something which necessitates the issue of a warrant"

"My dear fellow!—it was only a joke."

"For less pointed jokes men have been sent to penal servitude."

Lord Hardaway slipped his arm through Mr. Champnell's.

"I was so devilish wild, and Golden was so devilish sick, that I couldn't help but spoof him. As for Bewlay, I owe him one for a dozen different things; I was bound to be even with him some time. There was nothing in the tins but water and Golden's jewels."

"Then it doesn't occur to you that you have been guilty of felony, and also of what a hanging judge might construe as an attempt to murder?"

"I say, Champnell, spare my blushes! I hear, dear boy, you've turned detective; you might do me a good turn, and all in the way of business. The fact is, I'm engaged to be married—the Bonnyer-Lees." Lord Hardaway winked. "It will set me on my legs."

"I thought that Miss Bonnyer-Lees was not on board the *Stormy Petrel.*"

"She wasn't. That's what made me so devilish wild. She was to have gone, but when it began to blow she hoisted the white feather. I felt that I must have it out of somebody, so I had it out of Golden. But I saw her yesterday, and I made it all right, we're going to be married at once. I'm going to run straight—I swear I am! But if this tale got wind, it might spoil everything. I tell you what, old man, if, in the way of business, you'll make things square with Ruby and Golden, and with old Bewlay, I'll give you any sum in reason you like to name, say a couple of hundred guineas, cash down."

"A couple of hundred guineas, you say?" Mr. Champnell smiled; what at at the moment was not quite plain. "You don't seem conscious that it is a rather curious proposition which you are making me, especially as I happen to be already retained upon the other side, but I'll do the best for you I can."

185

When the Hon. Augustus reached Messrs. Ruby and Golden's establishment in Bond Street he was received by both the partners in a private room.

"Do I understand, gentlemen, if I return to you the missing jewels, exactly as they left Mr. Golden's hands, that, as they say in the advertisements, no questions will be asked?" Both partners were profuse in their protestations that he might so understand. "Then, in that case, gentlemen, here they are "He placed a leather case before them on the table. The partners stared. "If you will be so good as to examine them, at once, in my presence, you will perceive that they are intact You quite understand, that no questions are to be asked of anyone, and, in particular, nothing is to be said to Lord Hardaway. I may mention, by the way, that Lord Hardaway is to be married, almost immediately, to Miss Bonnyer-Lees."

Mr. Ruby rubbed his hands and smiled.

"We are delighted to hear it, Mr. Champnell—delighted! You may rely on us not to breathe a word to Lord Hardaway; we quite understand that it was only a little joke of his. His lordship is so full of humour."

Mr. Golden's tone—he was examining the jewels as he spoke— was not quite so effusive.

"If you had been in my place, and had suffered what I suffered, you might not have seen the joke quite so clearly, Ruby. There is such a thing as being almost too full of humour."

Mr. Champnell went straight from Bond Street to the Marquis of Bewlay's. He found the marquis in his smoking-room.

"You may make your mind easy on the subject of those infernal machines. Here they are." Mr. Champnell took thirteen empty tins from a bag which he was carrying. "They have all gone off, but as they were all filled with water it would seem as if somebody had been planning a practical joke at your expense. That sort of infernal machine hardly savours of a secret society."

"It certainly does not, and though you mayn't think it, Mr. Champnell, it's worth all of two hundred guineas to me to know it"

"I am very glad indeed to hear it"

And so the Hon. Augustus told himself again, when, having returned to his own quarters, he had propped up his feet against the mantelshelf and was lighting a cigar.

"I don't think that's a bad morning's stroke of business—five hundred guineas for doing nothing at all."

The House Surgeon
Rudyard Kipling

On an evening after Easter Day, I sat at a table in a homeward bound steamer's smoking-room, where half a dozen of us told ghost stories. As our party broke up a man, playing patience in the next alcove, said to me: "I didn't quite catch the end of that last story about the Curse on the family's first-born."

"It turned out to be drains," I explained. "As soon as new ones were put into the house the Curse was lifted, I believe. I never knew the people myself."

"Ah! I've had my drains up twice; I'm on gravel too."

"You don't mean to say you've a ghost in your house? Why didn't you join our party?"

"Any more orders, gentlemen, before the bar closes?" the steward interrupted.

"Sit down again, and have one with me," said the patience player. "No, it isn't a ghost. Our trouble is more depression than anything else."

"How interesting! Then it's nothing anyone can see?"

"It's—it's nothing worse than a little depression; And the odd part is that there hasn't been a death in the house since it was built—in 1863. The lawyer said so. That decided me—my good lady, rather—and he made me pay an extra thousand for it."

"How curious. Unusual, too!" I said.

"Yes; ain't it? It was built for three sisters—Moultrie was the name—three old maids. They all lived together; the eldest owned it. I bought it from her lawyer a few years ago, and if I've spent a pound on the place first and last, I must have spent five thousand. Electric light, new servants' wing, garden—all that sort of thing. A man and his family ought to be happy after so much expense, ain't it?" He looked at me through the bottom of his glass.

"Does it affect your family much?"

"My good lady—she's a Greek, by the way—and myself are middle-aged. We can bear up against depression; but it's hard on my little girl. I say little; but she's twenty. We send her visiting to escape it. She almost lived at hotels and hydros last year, but that isn't pleasant for her. She used to be a canary—a perfect canary—always singing. You ought to hear her. She doesn't sing now. That sort of thing's unwholesome for the young, ain't it?"

"Can't you get rid of the place?" I suggested.

"Not except at a sacrifice, and we are fond of it. Just suits us three. We'd love it if we were allowed."

"What do you mean by not being allowed?"

"I mean because of the depression. It spoils everything."

"What's it like exactly?"

"I couldn't very well explain. It must be seen to be appreciated, as the auctioneers say. Now, I was much impressed by the story you were telling just now."

"It wasn't true," I said.

"My tale is true. If you would do me the pleasure to come down and spend a night at my little place, you'd learn more than you would if I talked till morning. Very likely 'twouldn't touch your good self at all. You might be—immune, ain't it? On the other hand, if this influenza—influence *does* happen to affect you, why, I think it will be an experience."

While he talked he gave me his card, and I read his name was L. Maxwell M'Leod, Esq., of Holmescroft. A City address was tucked away in a corner.

"My business," he added, "used to be furs. If you are interested in furs—I've given thirty years of my life to 'em."

"You're very kind," I murmured.

"Far from it, I assure you. I can meet you next Saturday afternoon anywhere in London you choose to name, and I'll be only too happy to motor you down. It ought to be a delightful run at this time of year—the rhododendrons will be out. I mean it. You don't know how truly I mean it. Very probably—it won't affect you at all. And—I think I may say I have the finest collection of narwhal tusks in the world. All the best skins and horns have to go through London, and L. Maxwell M'Leod, he knows where they come from, and where they go to. That's his business."

For the rest of the voyage up-channel Mr. M'Leod talked to me of the assembling, preparation, and sale of the rarer furs; and told me things about the manufacture of fur-lined coats which quite shocked me. Somehow or other, when we landed on Wednesday, I found myself pledged to spend that weekend with him at Holmescroft.

On Saturday he met me with a well-groomed motor, and ran me out, in an hour and a half, to an exclusive residential district of dustless roads and elegantly designed country villas, each standing in from three to five acres of perfectly appointed land. He told me land was selling at eight hundred pounds the acre, and the new golf links, whose Queen Anne pavilion we passed, had cost nearly twenty-four thousand pounds to create.

Holmescroft was a large, two-storied, low, creeper-covered residence. A verandah at the south side gave on to a garden and two tennis courts, separated by a tasteful iron fence from a most park-like meadow of five or six acres, where two Jersey cows grazed. Tea was ready in the shade of a promising copper beech, and I could see groups on the lawn of young men and maidens appropriately clothed, playing lawn tennis in the sunshine.

"A pretty scene, ain't it?" said Mr. M'Leod. "My good lady's sitting under the tree, and that's my little girl in pink on the far court. But I'll take you to your room, and you can see 'em all later."

He led me through a wide parquet-floored hall furnished in pale lemon, with huge *Cloisonné* vases, an ebonized and gold grand piano, and banks of pot flowers in Benares brass bowls, up a pale oak staircase to a spacious landing, where there was a green velvet settee trimmed with silver. The blinds were down, and the light lay in parallel lines on the floors.

He showed me my room, saying cheerfully: "You may be a little tired. One often is without knowing it after a run through traffic. Don't come down till you feel quite restored. We shall all be in the garden."

My room was rather warm, and smelt of perfumed soap. I threw up the window at once, but it opened so close to the floor and worked so clumsily that I came within an ace of pitching out, where I should certainly have ruined a rather lop-sided laburnum below. As I set about washing off the journey's dust, I began to feel a little tired. But, I reflected, I had not come down here in this weather and among these new surroundings to be depressed; so I began to whistle.

And it was just then that I was aware of a little grey shadow, as it might have been a snowflake seen against the light, floating at an immense distance in the background of my brain. It annoyed me, and I shook my head to get rid of it. Then my brain telegraphed that it was the forerunner of a swift-striding gloom which there was yet time to escape if I would force my thoughts away from it, as a man leaping for life forces his body forward and away from the fall of a wall. But the gloom overtook me before I could take in the meaning of the message. I moved toward the bed, every nerve already aching with the foreknowledge of the pain that was to be dealt it, and sat down, while my amazed and angry soul dropped, gulf by gulf, into that horror of great darkness which is spoken of in the Bible, and which, as auctioneers say, must be experienced to be appreciated.

Despair upon despair, misery upon misery, fear after fear, each causing their distinct and separate woe, packed in upon me for an unrecorded length of time, until at last they blurred together, and I heard a click in my brain like the click in the ear when one descends in a diving bell, and I knew that the pressures were equalised within and without, and that, for the moment, the worst was at an end. But I knew also that at any moment the darkness might come down anew; and while I dwelt on this speculation precisely as a man torments a raging tooth with his tongue, it ebbed away into the little grey shadow on the brain of its first coming, and once more I heard my brain, which knew what would recur, telegraph to every quarter for help, release or diversion.

The door opened, and M'Leod reappeared. I thanked him politely, saying I was charmed with my room, anxious to meet Mrs. M'Leod, much refreshed with my wash, and so on and so forth. Beyond a little stickiness at the corners of my mouth, it seemed to me that I was managing my words admirably, the while that I myself cowered at the bottom of unclimbable pits. M'Leod laid his hand on my shoulder, and said: "You've got it now already, ain't it?"

"Yes," I answered. "It's making me sick!"

"It will pass off when you come outside. I give you my word it will then pass off. Come!"

I shambled out behind him, and wiped my forehead in the hall.

"You musn't mind," he said. "I expect the run tired you. My good lady is sitting there under the copper beech."

She was a fat woman in an apricot-coloured gown, with a heavily powdered face, against which her black long-lashed eyes showed like currants in dough. I was introduced to many fine ladies and gentlemen of those parts. Magnificently appointed landaus and covered motors swept in and out of the drive, and the air was gay with the merry outcries of the tennis players.

As twilight drew on they all went away, and I was left alone with Mr. and Mrs. M'Leod, while tall men-servants and maidservants took away the tennis and tea things. Miss M'Leod had walked a little down the drive with a light-haired young man, who apparently knew everything about every South American railway stock. He had told me at tea that these were the days of financial specialisation.

"I think it went off beautifully, my dear," said Mr. M'Leod to his wife; and to me : "You feel all right now, ain't it? Of course you do."

Mrs. M'Leod surged across the gravel. Her husband skipped nimbly before her into the south verandah, turned a switch, and all Holmes croft was flooded with light.

"You can do that from your room also," he said as they went in. "There is something in money, ain't it?"

Miss M'Leod came up behind me in the dusk. "We have not yet been introduced," she said, "but I suppose you are staying the night?"

"Your father was kind enough to ask me," I replied.

She nodded. "Yes, *I* know; and you know too, don't you? I saw your face when you came to shake hands with mamma. You felt the depression very soon. It is simply frightful in that bedroom sometimes. What do you think it is—bewitchment? In Greece, where I was a little girl, it might have been; but not in England, do you think? Or *do* you?"

"I don't know what to think," I replied. "I never felt anything like it. Does it happen often?"

"Yes, sometimes. It comes and goes."

"Pleasant!" I said, as we walked up and down the gravel at the lawn edge. "What has been your experience of it?"

"That is difficult to say, but—sometimes that—that depression is like as it were"—she gesticulated in most un-English fashion—"a light. Yes, like a light turned into a room—only a light of blackness, do you understand?—into a happy room. For sometimes we are so happy, all we three—so very happy. Then this blackness, it is turned on us just like—ah, I know what I mean now—like the head-lamp of a motor, and we are eclipsed. And there is another thing—"

The dressing-gong roared, and we entered the over-lighted hall. My dressing was a brisk athletic performance, varied with outbursts of song—careful attention paid to articulation and expression. But nothing happened. As I hurried downstairs, I thanked Heaven that nothing had happened.

Dinner was served breakfast fashion; the dishes were placed on the sideboard over heaters, and we helped ourselves.

"We always do this when we are alone, so we talk better," said Mr. M'Leod.

"And we are always alone," said the daughter.

"Cheer up, Thea. It will all come right," he insisted.

"No, papa." She shook her dark head. "Nothing is right while *it* comes."

"It is nothing that we ourselves have ever done in our lives—that I will swear to you," said Mrs. M'Leod suddenly. "And we have changed our servants several times. So we know it is not them."

"Never mind. Let us enjoy ourselves while we can," said Mr. M'Leod, opening the champagne.

But we did not enjoy ourselves. The talk failed. There were long silences.

"I beg your pardon," I said, for I thought someone at my elbow was about to speak.

"Ah! That is the other thing!" said Miss M'Leod. Her mother groaned.

We were silent again, and, in a few seconds it must have been, a live grief beyond words—not ghostly dread or horror, but aching, helpless grief—overwhelmed us, each, I felt, according to his or her nature, and held steady like the beam of a burning-glass. Behind that pain I was conscious there was a desire on somebody's part to explain something on which some tremendously important issue hung.

Meantime I rolled bread pills and remembered my sins; M'Leod considered his own reflection in a spoon; his wife seemed to be praying, and the girl fidgeted desperately with hands and feet, till the darkness passed on—as though the malignant rays of a burning-glass had been shifted from us."

"There," said Miss M'Leod, half rising. "Now you see what makes a happy home. Oh, sell it—sell it, father mine, and let us go away!"

"But I've spent thousands on it. You shall go to Harrogate next week, Thea dear."

"I'm only just back from hotels. I am *so* tired of packing."

"Cheer up, Thea. It is over. You know it does not often come here twice in the same night. I think we shall dare now to be comfortable."

He lifted a dish-cover, and helped his wife and daughter. His face was lined and fallen like an old man's after debauch, but his hand did not shake, and his voice was clear. As he worked to restore us by speech and action, he reminded me of a grey-muzzled collie herding demoralised sheep.

After dinner we sat round the dining-room fire—the drawing-room might have been under the Shadow for aught we knew—talking with the intimacy of gipsies by the, wayside, or of wounded comparing notes after a skirmish. By eleven o'clock the three between them had given me every name and detail they could recall that in any way bore on the house, and what they knew of its history.

We went to bed in a fortifying blaze of electric light. My one fear was that the blasting gust of depression would return—the surest way, of course, to bring it. I lay awake till dawn, breathing quickly and sweating lightly, beneath what De Quincey inadequately describes as *"the oppression of inexpiable guilt."* Now as soon as the lovely day was broken, I fell into the most terrible of all dreams—that joyous one in which all past evil has not only been wiped out of our lives, but has never been committed; and in the very bliss of our assured innocence, before our loves shriek and change countenance, we wake to the day we have earned.

It was a coolish morning, but we preferred to breakfast in the south verandah. The forenoon we spent in the garden, pretending to play games that come out of boxes, such as croquet and clock golf. But most of the time we drew together and talked. The young man who knew all about South American railways took Miss M'Leod for a walk in the afternoon, and at five M'Leod thoughtfully whirled us all up to dine in town.

"Now, don't say you will tell the Psychological Society, and that you will come again," said Miss M'Leod, as we parted. "Because I know you will not."

"You should not say that," said her mother. "You should say, 'Good-bye, Mr. Perseus. Come again.'"

"Not him!" the girl cried. "He has seen the Medusa's head!"

Looking at myself in the restaurant's mirrors, it seemed to me that I had not much benefited by my weekend. Next morning I wrote out all my Holmescroft notes at fullest length, in the hope that by so doing I could put it all behind me. But the experience worked on my mind, as they say certain imperfectly understood rays work on the body.

I am less calculated to make a Sherlock Holmes than any man I know, for I lack both method and patience, yet the idea of following up the trouble to its source fascinated me. I had no theory to go on, except a vague idea that I had come between two poles of a discharge, and had taken a shock meant for someone else. This was followed by a feeling of intense irritation. I waited cautiously on myself, expecting to be overtaken by horror of the supernatural, but myself persisted in being humanly indignant, exactly as though it had been the victim of a practical joke. It was in great pains and upheavals—that I felt in every fibre—but its dominant idea, to put it coarsely, was to get back a bit of its own. By this I knew that I might go forward if I could find the way.

After a few days it occurred to me to go to the office of Mr. J. M. M. Baxter—the solicitor who had sold Holmescroft to M'Leod. I explained I had some notion of buying the place. Would he act for me in the matter?

Mr. Baxter, a large, greyish, throaty-voiced man, showed no enthusiasm. "I sold it to Mr. M'Leod," he said. "It 'ud scarcely do for me to start on the running-down tack now. But I can recommend—"

"I know he's asking an awful price," I interrupted, "and atop of it he wants an extra thousand for what he calls your clean bill of health."

Mr. Baxter sat up in his chair. I had all his attention.

"Your guarantee with the house. Don't you remember it?"

"Yes, yes. That no death had taken place in the house since it was built. I remember perfectly."

He did not gulp as untrained men do when they lie, but his jaws moved stickily, and his eyes, turning towards the deed boxes on the wall, dulled. I counted seconds, one, two, three—one, two, three—up to ten. A man, I knew, can live through ages of mental depression in that time.

"I remember perfectly." His mouth opened a little as though it had tasted old bitterness.

"Of course *that* sort of thing doesn't appeal to me." I went on. "I don't expect to buy a house free from death."

"Certainly not. No one does. But it was Mr. M'Leod's fancy—his wife's rather, I believe; and since we could meet it—it was my duty to my clients—at whatever cost to my own feelings—to make him pay."

"That's really why I came to you. I understood from him you knew the place well."

"Oh, yes. Always did. It originally belonged to some connections of mine."

"The Misses Moultrie, I suppose. How interesting! They must have loved the place before the country round about was built up."

"They were very fond of it indeed."

"I don't wonder. So restful and sunny. I don't see how they could have brought themselves to part with it."

Now it is one of the most constant peculiarities of the English that in polite conversation—and I had striven to be polite—no one ever does or sells anything for mere money's sake.

"Miss Agnes—the youngest—fell ill" (he spaced his words a little), "and, as they were very much attached to each other, that broke up the home."

"Naturally. I fancied it must have been something of that kind. One doesn't associate the Staffordshire Moultries" (my Demon of Irresponsibility at that instant created 'em), "with—with being hard up."

"I don't know whether we're related to them," he answered importantly. "We may be, for our branch of the family comes from the Midlands."

I give this talk at length, because I am so proud of my first attempt at detective work. When I left him, twenty minutes later, with instructions to move against the owner of Holmescroft, with a view to purchase, I was more bewildered than any Doctor Watson at the opening of a story.

Why should a middle-aged solicitor turn plovers' egg colour and drop his jaw when reminded of so innocent and festal a matter as that no death had ever occurred in a house that he had sold? If I knew my English vocabulary at all, the tone in which he said the youngest sister "fell ill" meant that she had gone out of her mind. That might explain his change of countenance, and it was just possible that her demented influence still hung about Holmescroft; but the rest was beyond me.

I was relieved when I reached M'Leod's City office, and could tell him what I had done—not what I thought.

M'Leod was quite willing to enter into the game of the pretended purchase, but did not see how it would help if I knew Baxter.

"He's the only living soul I can get at who was connected with Holmescroft," I said.

"Ah! Living soul is good," said M'Leod. "At any rate our little girl will be pleased that you are still interested in us. Won't you come down some day this week?"

"How is it there now?" I asked.

He screwed up his face. "Simply frightful!" he said. "Thea is at Droitwich."

"I' should like it immensely, but I must cultivate Baxter for the present. You'll be sure and keep him busy your end, won't you?"

He looked at me with quiet contempt. "Do not be afraid. I shall be a good Jew. I shall be my own solicitor."

Before a fortnight was over, Baxter admitted ruefully that M'Leod was better than most firms in the business. We buyers were coy, argumentative, shocked at the price of Holmescroft, inquisitive, and cold by turns, but Mr. M'Leod the seller easily met and surpassed us; and Mr. Baxter entered every letter, telegram, and consultation at the proper rates in a cinematograph-film of a bill. At the end of a month he said it looked as though M'Leod, thanks to him, were really going to listen to reason. I was many pounds out of pocket, but I had learned something of Mr. Baxter on the human side. I deserved it. Never in my life have I worked to conciliate, amuse, and flatter a human being as I worked over my solicitor.

It appeared that he golfed. Therefore, I was an enthusiastic beginner, anxious to learn. Twice I invaded his office with a bag (M'Leod lent it) full of the spelicans needed in this detestable game, and a vocabulary to match. The third time the ice broke, and Mr. Baxter took me to his links, quite ten miles off, where in a maze of tramway lines, railroads, and nursery-maids, we skelped our divotted way round nine holes like barges plunging through head seas. He played vilely and had never expected to meet any one worse; but as he realised my form, I think he began to like me, for he took me in hand by the two hours together.

After a fortnight he could give me no more than a stroke a hole, and when, with this allowance, I once managed to beat him by one, he was honestly glad, and assured me that I should be a golfer if I stuck to it. I was sticking to it for my own ends, but now and again my conscience pricked me; for the man was a nice man. Between games he supplied me with odd pieces of evidence, such as that he had known the Moultries all his life, being their cousin, and that Miss Mary, the eldest, was an unforgiving woman who would never let bygones be. I naturally wondered what she might have against him; and somehow connected him unfavourably with mad Agnes.

"People ought to forgive and forget," he volunteered one day between rounds. "Specially where, in the nature of things, they can't be sure of their deductions. Don't you think so?"

"It all depends on the nature of the evidence on which one forms one's judgment," I answered.

"Nonsense!" he cried. "I'm lawyer enough to know that there's nothing in the world so misleading as circumstantial evidence. Never was."

"Why? Have you ever seen men hanged on it?"

"Hanged? People have been supposed to be eternally lost on it," his face turned grey again. "I don't know how it is with you, but my consolation is that God must know. He *must*! Things that seem on the face of 'em like murder, or say suicide, may appear different to God. Heh?"

"That's what the murderer and the suicide can always hope—I suppose."

"I have expressed myself clumsily as usual. The facts as God knows 'em—may *be* different—even after the most clinching evidence. I've always said that—both as a lawyer and a man, but some people won't—I don't want to judge 'em—we'll say they can't—believe it; whereas *I* say there's always a working chance—a certainty—that the worst hasn't happened." He stopped and cleared his throat. "Now, let's come on! This time next week. I shall be taking my holiday."

"What links?" I asked carelessly, while twins in a perambulator got out of our line of fire.

"A potty little nine-hole affair at a hydro in the Midlands. My cousins stay there. Always will. Not but what the fourth and the seventh holes take some doing. You could manage it, though," he said encouragingly. "You're doing much better. It's only your approach shots that are weak."

"You're right. I can't approach for nuts! I shall go to pieces while you're away—with no one to coach me," I said mournfully.

"I haven't taught you anything," he said, delighted with the compliment.

"I owe all I've learned to you, anyhow. When will you come back?"

"Look here," he began. "I don't know your engagements, but I've no one to play with at Burry Mills. Never have. Why couldn't you take a few days off and join me there? I warn you it will be rather dull. It's a throat and gout place—baths, massage, electricity, and so forth. But the fourth and the seventh holes really take some doing."

"I'm for the game," I answered valiantly; Heaven well knowing

197

that I hated every stroke and word of it.

"That's the proper spirit. As their lawyer I must ask you not to say anything to my cousins about Holmescroft. It upsets 'em. Always did. But speaking as man to man, it would be very pleasant for me if you could see your way to "

I saw it as soon as decency permitted, and thanked him sincerely. According to my now well-developed theory he had certainly misappropriated his aged cousins' monies under power of attorney, and had probably driven poor Agnes Moultrie out of her wits, but I wished that he was not so gentle, and good-tempered, and innocent-eyed.

Before I joined him at Burry Mills Hydro, I spent a night at Holmescroft. Miss M'Leod had returned from her Hydro, and first we made very merry on the open lawn in the sunshine over the manners and customs of the English resorting to such places. She knew dozens of hydros, and warned me how to behave in them, while Mr. and Mrs. M'Leod stood aside and adored her.

"Ah! That's the way she always comes back to us," he said. "Pity it wears off so soon, ain't it? You ought to hear her sing 'With mirth thou pretty bird.'"

We had the house to face through the evening, and there we neither laughed nor sung. The gloom fell on us as we entered, and did not shift till ten o'clock, when we crawled out, as it were, from beneath it.

"It has been bad this summer," said Mrs. M'Leod in a whisper after we realised that we were freed. "Sometimes I think the house will get up and cry out—it is so bad."

"How?"

"Have you forgotten what comes after the depression?"

So then we waited about the small fire, and the dead air in the room presently filled and pressed down upon us with the sensation (but words are useless here) as though some dumb and bound power were striving against gag and bond to deliver its soul of an articulate word. It passed in a few minutes, and I fell to thinking about Mr. Baxter's conscience and Agnes Moultrie, gone mad in the well-lit bedroom that waited me. These reflections secured me a night during which I rediscovered how, from purely mental causes, a man can be physically sick; but the sickness was bliss compared to my dreams when the birds waked. On my departure, M'Leod gave me a beautiful narwhal's horn, much as a nurse gives a child sweets for being brave at a dentist's.

"There's no duplicate of it in the world," he said, "else it would have come to old Max M'Leod," and he tucked it into the motor. Miss M'Leod on the far side of the car whispered, "Have you found out anything, Mr. Perseus?"

I shook my head.

"Then I shall be chained to my rock all my life," she went on. "Only don't tell papa."

I supposed she was thinking of the young gentleman who specialised in South American rails, for I noticed a ring on the third finger of her left hand.

I went straight from that house to Burry Mills Hydro, keen for the first time in my life on playing golf, which is guaranteed to occupy the mind. Baxter had taken me a room communicating with his own, and after lunch introduced me to a tall, horse-headed elderly lady of decided manners, whom a white-haired maid pushed along in a bath-chair through the park-like grounds of the Hydro. She was Miss Mary Moultrie, and she coughed and cleared her throat just like Baxter. She suffered—she told me it was a Moultrie caste-mark—from some obscure form of chronic bronchitis, complicated with spasm of the glottis; And, in a dead, flat voice, with a sunken eye that looked and saw not, told me what washes, gargles, pastilles, and inhalations she had proved most beneficial.

From her I was passed on to her younger sister, Miss Elizabeth, a small and withered thing with twitching lips, victim, she told me, to very much the same sort of throat, but secretly devoted to another set of medicines. When she went away with Baxter and the bath-chair, I fell across a major of the Indian army with gout in his glassy eyes, and a stomach which he had taken all round the Continent. He laid everything before me; and him I escaped only to be confided in by a matron with a tendency to follicular tonsilitis and eczema. Baxter waited hand and foot on his cousins till five o'clock, trying, as I saw, to atone for his treatment of the dead sister. Miss Mary ordered him about like a dog.

"I warned you it would be dull," he said when we met in the smoking-room.

"It's tremendously interesting," I said. "But how about a look round the links?"

"Unluckily damp always affects my eldest cousin. I've got to buy her a new bronchitis-kettle. Arthurs broke her old one yesterday."

We slipped out to the chemist's shop in the town, and he bought a large glittering tin thing whose workings he explained.

"I'm used to this sort of work. I come up here pretty often," he said. "I've the family throat too."

"You're a good man," I said. "A very good man."

He turned towards me in the evening light among the beeches, and his face was changed to what it might have been a generation before.

"You see," he said huskily, "there was the youngest—Agnes. Before she fell ill, you know. But she didn't like leaving her sisters. Never would." He hurried on with his odd-shaped load and left me among the ruins of my black theories. The man with that face had done Agnes Moultrie no wrong.

★★★★★★

We never played our game. I was waked between two and three in the morning from my hygienic bed by Baxter in an ulster over orange and white pyjamas, which I should never have suspected from his character.

"My cousin has had some sort of a seizure," he said. "Will you come? I don't want to wake the doctor. Don't want to make a scandal. Quick!"

So I came quickly, and led by the white-haired Arthurs in a jacket and petticoat, entered a double-bedded room reeking with steam and Friar's Balsam. The electrics were all on. Miss Mary—I knew her by her height—was at the open window, wrestling with Miss Elizabeth, who gripped her round the knees. Miss Mary's hand was at her own throat, which was streaked with blood.

"She's done it. She's done it too!" Miss Elizabeth panted. "Hold her! Help me!"

"Oh, I say! Women don't cut their throats," Baxter whispered.

"My God! Has she cut her throat?" the maid cried out, and with no warning rolled over in a faint. Baxter pushed her under the wash-basins, and leaped to hold the gaunt woman who crowed and whistled as she struggled toward the window. He took her by the shoulder, and she struck out wildly.

"All right! She's only cut her hand," he said. "Wet towel—quick!"

While I got that he pushed her backward. Her strength seemed almost as great as his. I swabbed at her throat when I could, and found no mark; then helped him to control her a little. Miss Elizabeth leaped back to bed, wailing like a child.

"Tie up her hand somehow," said Baxter. "Don't let it drip about

200

the place. She"—he stepped on broken glass in his slippers, "she must have smashed a pane."

Miss Mary lurched towards the open window again, dropped on her knees, her head on the sill, and lay quiet, surrendering the cut hand to me.

"What did she do?" Baxter turned towards Miss Elizabeth in the far bed.

"She was going to throw herself out of the window," was the answer. "I stopped her, and sent Arthurs for you. Oh, we can never hold up our heads again!"

Miss Mary writhed and fought for breath. Baxter found a shawl which he threw over her shoulders.

"Nonsense!" said he. "That isn't like Mary;" but his face worked when he said it.

"You wouldn't believe about Aggie, John. Perhaps you will now!" said Miss Elizabeth. "I saw her do it, and she's cut her throat too!"

"She hasn't," I said. "It's only her hand."

Miss Mary suddenly broke from us with an indescribable grunt, flew, rather than ran, to her sister's bed, and there shook her as one furious schoolgirl would shake another.

"No such thing," she croaked. "How dare you think so, you wicked little fool?"

"Get into bed, Mary," said Baxter. "You'll catch a chill."

She obeyed, but sat up with the grey shawl round her lean shoulders, glaring at her sister. "I'm better now," she panted. "Arthurs let me sit out too long. Where's Arthurs? The kettle."

"Never mind Arthurs," said Baxter. "*You* get the kettle." I hastened to bring it from the side table. "Now, Mary, as God sees you, tell me what you've done."

His lips were dry, and he could hot moisten them with his tongue.

Miss Mary applied herself to the mouth of the kettle, and between indraws of steam said: "The spasm came on just now, while I was asleep. I was nearly choking to death. So I went to the window. I've done it often before, without waking anyone. Bessie's such an old maid about draughts. I tell you I was choking to death. I couldn't manage the catch, and I nearly fell out. That window opens too low. I cut my hand trying to save myself. Who has tied it up in this filthy handkerchief? I wish you had had my throat, Bessie. I never was nearer dying!" She scowled on us all impartially, while her sister sobbed.

From the bottom of the bed we heard a quivering voice: "Is she dead? Have they took her away? Oh, I never could bear the sight o' blood!"

"Arthurs," said Miss Mary, "you are an hireling. Go away!"

It is my belief that Arthurs crawled out on all fours, but I was busy picking up broken glass from the carpet.

Then Baxter, seated by the side of the bed, began to cross-examine in a voice I scarcely recognised. No one could for an instant have doubted the genuine rage of Miss Mary against her sister, her cousin, or her maid; and that a doctor should have been called in—for she did me the honour of calling me doctor—was the last drop. She was choking with her throat; had rushed to the window for air; had near pitched out, and in catching at the window bars had cut her hand. Over and over she made this clear to the intent Baxter. Then she turned on her sister and tongue-lashed her savagely.

"You mustn't blame me," Miss Bessie faltered at last. "You know what we think of night and day."

"I'm coming to that," said Baxter. "Listen to me. What *you* did, Mary, misled four people into thinking you—you meant to do away with yourself."

"Isn't one suicide in the family enough? Oh God, help and pity us! You *couldn't* have believed that!" she cried.

"The evidence was complete. Now, don't you think," Baxter's finger wagged under her nose—"*can't* you think that poor Aggie did the same thing at Holmescroft when she fell out of the window?"

"She had the same throat," said Miss Elizabeth. "Exactly the same symptoms. Don't you remember, Mary?"

"Which was her bedroom?" I asked of Baxter in an undertone.

"Over the south verandah, looking on to the tennis lawn."

"I nearly fell out of that very window when I was at Holmescroft—opening it to get some air. The sill doesn't come much above your knees," I said.

"You hear that, Mary? Mary, do you hear what this gentleman says? Won't you believe that what nearly happened to you must have happened to poor Aggie that night? For God's sake—for her sake—Mary, *won't* you believe?"

There was a long silence while the steam kettle puffed.

"If I could have proof—if I could have proof," said she, and broke into most horrible tears.

Baxter motioned to me, and I crept away to my room, and lay

awake till morning, thinking more specially of the dumb Thing at Holmescroft which wished to explain itself. I hated Miss Mary as perfectly as though I had known her for twenty years, but I felt that, alive or dead, I should not like her to condemn me.

Yet at mid-day, when I saw Miss Mary in her bath-chair, Arthurs behind and Baxter and Miss Elizabeth on either side, in the park-like grounds of the Hydro, I found it difficult to arrange my words.

"Now that you know all about it," said Baxter aside, after the first strangeness of our meeting was over, "it's only fair to tell you that my poor cousin did not die in Holmescroft at all. She was dead when they found her under the window in the morning. Just dead."

"Under that laburnum outside the window?" I asked, for I suddenly remembered the crooked evil thing.

"Exactly. She broke the tree in falling. But no death has ever taken place *in* the house, so far as we were concerned. You can make yourself quite easy on that point. Mr. M'Leod's extra thousand for what you called the 'clean bill of health' was something toward my cousins' estate when we sold. It was my duty as their lawyer to get it for them— at any cost to my own feelings."

I know better than to argue when the English talk about their duty. So I agreed with my solicitor.

"Their sister's death must have been a great blow to your cousins," I went on. The bath-chair was behind me.

"Unspeakable," Baxter whispered. "They brooded on it day and night. No wonder. If their theory of poor Aggie making away with herself was correct, she was eternally lost!"

"Do you believe that she made away with herself?"

"No, thank God! Never have! And after what happened to Mary last night, I see perfectly what happened to poor Aggie. She had the family throat too. By the way, Mary thinks you are a doctor. Otherwise she wouldn't like your having been in her room."

"Very good. Is she convinced now about her sister's death?"

"She'd give anything to be able to believe it, but she's a hard woman, and brooding along certain lines makes one groovy. I have sometimes been afraid of her reason—on the religious side, don't you know. Elizabeth doesn't matter. Brain of a hen. Always had."

Here Arthurs summoned me to the bath-chair, and the ravaged face, beneath its knitted Shetland wool hood, of Miss Mary Moultrie.

"I need not remind you, I hope, of the seal of secrecy—absolute secrecy—in your profession," she began. "Thanks to my cousin's and my sister's stupidity, you have found out——" she blew her nose.

"Please don't excite her, sir," said Arthurs at the back.

"But, my dear Miss Moultrie, I only know what I've seen, of course, but it seems to me that what you thought was a tragedy in your sister's case, turns out, on your own evidence, so to speak, to have been an accident—a dreadfully sad one—but absolutely an accident."

"Do you believe that too?" she cried. "Or are you only saying it to comfort me?"

"I believe it from the bottom of my heart. Come down to Holmescroft for an hour—for half an hour—and satisfy yourself."

"Of what? You don't understand. I see the house every day—every night. I am always there in spirit—waking or sleeping. I couldn't face it in reality."

"But you must," I said. "If you go there in the spirit the greater need for you to go there in the flesh. Go to your sister's room once more, and see the window—I nearly fell out of it myself. It's—it's awfully low and dangerous. That would convince you," I pleaded.

"Yet Aggie had slept in that room for years," she interrupted.

"You've slept in your room here for a long time, haven't you? But you nearly fell out of the window when you were choking."

"That is true. That is one thing true," she nodded. "And I might have been killed as—perhaps—Aggie was killed."

"In that case your own sister and cousin and maid would have said you had committed suicide, Miss Moultrie. Come down to Holmescroft, and go over the place just once."

"You are lying," she said quite quietly. "You don't want me to come down to see a window. It is something else. I warn you we are Evangelicals. We don't believe in prayers for the dead. 'As the tree falls——'"

"Yes. I daresay. But you persist in thinking that your sister committed suicide——"

"No! No! I have always prayed that I might have misjudged her."

Arthurs at the bath-chair spoke up: "Oh, Miss Mary! you *would* 'ave it from the first that poor Miss Aggie 'ad made away with herself; an', of course, Miss Bessie took the notion from you. Only Master—Mister John stood out, and—and I'd 'ave taken my Bible oath you was making away with yourself last night."

Miss Mary leaned towards me, one finger on my sleeve.

"If going to Holmescroft kills me," she said, "you will have the murder of a fellow-creature on your conscience for all eternity."

"I'll risk it," I answered. Remembering what torment the mere reflection of her torments had cast on Holmescroft, and remembering, above all, the dumb Thing that filled the house with its desire to speak, I felt that there might be worse things.

Baxter was amazed at the proposed visit, but at a nod from that terrible woman went off to make arrangements. Then I sent a telegram to M'Leod bidding him and his vacate Holmescroft for that afternoon. Miss Mary should be alone with her dead, as I had been alone.

I expected untold trouble in transporting her, but to do her justice, the promise given for the journey, she underwent it without murmur, spasm, or unnecessary word. Miss Bessie, pressed in a corner by the window, wept behind her veil, and from time to time tried to take hold of her sister's hand. Baxter wrapped himself in his newly found happiness as selfishly as a bridegroom, for he sat still and smiled.

"So long as I know that Aggie didn't make away with herself," he explained, "I tell you frankly I don't care what happened. She's as hard as a rock—Mary. Always was. *She* won't die."

We led her out on to the platform like a blind woman, and so got her into the fly. The half-hour crawl to Holmescroft was the most racking experience of the day. M'Leod had obeyed my instructions. There was no one visible in the house or the gardens; and the front door stood open.

Miss Mary rose from beside her sister, stepped forth first, and entered the hall.

"Come, Bessie," she cried.

"I daren't. Oh, I daren't."

"Come!" Her voice had altered. I felt Baxter start. "There's nothing to be afraid of."

"Good heavens!" said Baxter. "She's running up the stairs. We'd better follow."

"Let's wait below. She's going to the room."

We heard the door of the bedroom I knew open and shut, and we waited in the lemon-coloured hall, heavy with the scent of flowers.

"I've never been into it since it was sold," Baxter sighed. "What a lovely, restful place it is! Poor Aggie used to arrange the flowers."

"Restful?" I began, but stopped of a sudden, for I felt all over my bruised soul that Baxter was speaking truth. It was a light, spacious, airy house, full of the sense of well-being and peace—above all things, of peace. I ventured into the dining-room where the thoughtful M'Leod's had left a small fire. There was no terror there, present or lurking; and in the drawing-room, which for good reasons we had never cared to enter, the sun and the peace and the scent of the flowers worked together as is fit in an inhabited house. When I returned to the hall, Baxter was sweetly asleep on a couch, looking most unlike a middle-aged solicitor who had spent a broken night with an exacting cousin.

There was ample time for me to review it all—to felicitate myself upon my magnificent acumen (barring some errors about Baxter as a thief and possibly a murderer), before the door above opened, and Baxter, evidently a light sleeper, sprang awake.

"I've had a heavenly little nap," he said, rubbing his eyes with the backs of his hands like a child. "Good Lord! That's not *their* step!"

But it was. I had never before been privileged to see the Shadow turned backward on the dial—the years ripped bodily off poor human shoulders—old sunken eyes filled and alight—harsh lips moistened and human.

"John," Miss Mary called, "I know now. Aggie didn't do it!" and "She didn't do it!" echoed Miss Bessie, and giggled.

"I did not think it wrong to say a prayer," Miss Mary continued. "Not for her soul, but for our peace. Then I was convinced."

"Then we got conviction," the younger sister piped.

"We've misjudged poor Aggie, John. But I feel she knows now. Wherever she is, she knows that we know she is guiltless."

"Yes, she knows. I felt it too," said Miss Elizabeth.

"I never doubted," said John Baxter, whose face was beautiful at that hour. "Not from the first. Never have!"

"You never offered me proof, John. Now, thank God, it will not be the same any more. I can think henceforward of Aggie without sorrow." She tripped, absolutely tripped, across the hall. "What ideas these Jews have of arranging furniture!" She spied me behind a big *Cloisonné* vase.

"I've seen the window," she said remotely. "You took a great risk in advising me to undertake such a journey. However, as it turns out . . . I forgive you, and I pray you may never know what mental anguish means! Bessie! Look at this peculiar piano! Do you suppose, doctor, these people would offer one tea? I miss mine."

"I will go and see," I said, and explored M'Leod's new-built servants' wing. It was in the servants' hall that I unearthed the M'Leod family, bursting with anxiety.

"Tea for three, quick," I said. "If you ask me any questions now, I

206

shall have a fit!" So Mrs. M'Leod got it, and I was butler, amid murmured apologies from Baxter, still smiling and self-absorbed, and the cold disapproval of Miss Mary, who thought the pattern of the china vulgar. However, she ate well, and even asked me whether I would not like a cup of tea for myself.

They went away in the twilight—the twilight that I had once feared. They were going to an hotel in London to rest after the fatigues of the day, and as their fly turned down the drive, I capered on the door step, with the all-darkened house behind me.

Then I heard the uncertain feet of the M'Leods and bade them not to turn on the lights, but to feel—to feel what I had done; for the Shadow was gone, with the dumb desire in the air. They drew short, but afterwards deeper, breaths, like bathers entering chill water, separated one from the other, moved about the hall, tiptoed upstairs, raced down, and then Miss M'Leod, and I believe her mother, though she denies this, embraced me. I know M'Leod did.

It was a disgraceful evening. To say we rioted through the house is to put it mildly. We played a sort of Blind Man's Buff along the darkest passages, in the unlighted drawing-room, and little dining-room, calling cheerily to each other after each exploration that here, and here, and here, the trouble had removed itself. We came up to *the* bedroom—mine for the night again—and sat, the women on the bed, and we men on chairs, drinking in blessed draughts of peace and comfort and cleanliness of soul, while I told them my tale in full, and received fresh praise, thanks, and blessings.

When the servants, returned from their day's outing, gave us a supper of cold fried fish, M'Leod had sense enough to open no wine. We had been practically drunk since nightfall, and grew incoherent on water and milk.

"I like that Baxter," said M'Leod. "He's a sharp man. The death wasn't in the house, but he ran it pretty close, ain't it?"

"And the joke of it is that he supposes I want to buy the place from you," I said. "Are you selling?"

"Not for twice what I paid for it—now," said M'Leod. "I'll keep you in furs all your life, but not our Holmescroft."

"No—never our Holmescroft," said Miss M'Leod. "We'll ask *him* here on Tuesday, mamma." They squeezed each other's hands.

"Now tell me," said Mrs. M'Leod—"that tall one I saw out of the scullery window—did *she* tell you she was always here in the spirit? I hate her. She made all this trouble. It was not her house after she had sold it. What do you think?"

"I suppose," I answered, "she brooded over what she believed was her sister's suicide night and day—she confessed she did—and her thoughts being concentrated on this place, they felt like a—like a burning glass."

"Burning glass is good," said M'Leod.

"I said it was like a light of blackness turned on us," cried the girl, twiddling her ring. "That must have been when the tall one thought worst about her sister and the house."

"Ah, the poor Aggie!" said Mrs. M'Leod. "The poor Aggie, trying to tell everyone it was not so! No wonder we felt Something wished to say Something. Thea, Max, do you remember that night—"

"We need not remember any more," M'Leod interrupted. "It is not our trouble. They have told each other now."

"Do you think, then," said Miss M'Leod, "that those two, the living ones, were actually told something—upstairs—in your—in the room?"

"I can't say. At any rate they were made happy, and they ate a big tea afterwards. As your father says, it is not our trouble any longer—thank God!"

"Amen!" said M'Leod. "Now, Thea, let us have some music after all these months. '*With mirth, thou pretty bird*,' ain't it? You ought to hear that."

And in the half-lighted hall, Thea sang an old English song that I had never heard before.

With mirth, thou pretty bird, rejoice
Thy Maker's praise enhanced;
Lift up thy shrill and pleasant voice,
Thy God is high advanced!
Thy food before He did provide,
And gives it in a fitting side,
Wherewith be thou sufficed!
Why shouldst thou now unpleasant be,
Thy wrath against God venting,
That He a little bird made thee,
Thy silly head tormenting,
Because He made thee not a man?
Oh, Peace! He hath well thought thereon,
Therewith be thou sufficed!

The Open Door

Mrs Riddell

Some people do not believe in ghosts. For that matter, some people do not believe in anything. There are persons who even affect incredulity concerning that open door at Ladlow Hall. They say it did not stand wide open—that they could have shut it; that the whole affair was a delusion; that they are sure it must have been a conspiracy; that they are doubtful whether there is such a place as Ladlow on the face of the earth; that the first time they are in Meadowshire they will look it up.

That is the manner in which this story, hitherto unpublished, has been greeted by my acquaintances. How it will be received by strangers is quite another matter. I am going to tell what happened to me exactly as it happened, and readers can credit or scoff at the tale as it pleases them. It is not necessary for me to find faith and comprehension in addition to a ghost story, for the world at large. If such were the case, I should lay down my pen.

Perhaps, before going further, I ought to premise there was a time when I did not believe in ghosts either. If you had asked me one summer's morning years ago when you met me on London Bridge if I held such appearances to be probable or possible, you would have received an emphatic 'No' for answer.

But, at this rate, the story of the Open Door will never be told; so we will, with your permission, plunge into it immediately.

★★★★★★

'Sandy!'

'What do you want?'

'Should you like to earn a sovereign?'

'Of course I should.'

A somewhat curt dialogue, but we were given to curtness in the office of Messrs Frimpton, Frampton and Fryer, auctioneers and estate agents, St Benet's Hill, City.

(My name is not Sandy or anything like it, but the other clerks so styled me because of a real or fancied likeness to some character, an ill-looking Scotchman, they had seen at the theatre. From this it may be inferred I was not handsome. Far from it. The only ugly specimen in my family, I knew I was very plain; and it chanced to be no secret to me either that I felt grievously discontented with my lot. I did not like the occupation of clerk in an auctioneer's office, and I did not like my employers. We are all of us inconsistent, I suppose, for it was a shock to me to find they entertained a most cordial antipathy to me.)

'Because,' went on Parton, a fellow, my senior by many years—a fellow who delighted in chaffing me, 'I can tell you how to lay hands on one.'

'How?' I asked, sulkily enough, for I felt he was having what he called his fun.

'You know that place we let to Carrison, the tea-dealer?'

Carrison was a merchant in the China trade, possessed of fleets of vessels and towns of warehouses; but I did not correct Parton's expression, I simply nodded.

'He took it on a long lease, and he can't live in it; and our governor said this morning he wouldn't mind giving anybody who could find out what the deuce is the matter, a couple of sovereigns and his travelling expenses.'

'Where is the place?' I asked, without turning my head; for the convenience of listening I had put my elbows on the desk and propped up my face with both hands.

'Away down in Meadowshire, in the heart of the grazing country.'

'And what is the matter?' I further enquired.

'A door that won't keep shut.'

'What?'

'A door that will keep open, if you prefer that way of putting it,' said Parton.

'You are jesting.'

'If I am, Carrison is not, or Fryer either. Carrison came here in a nice passion, and Fryer was in a fine rage; I could see he was, though he kept his temper outwardly. They have had an active correspondence it appears, and Carrison went away to talk to his lawyer. Won't make much by that move, I fancy.'

'But tell me,' I entreated, 'why the door won't keep shut?'

'They say the place is haunted.'

'What nonsense!' I exclaimed.

Then you are just the person to take the ghost in hand. I thought so while old Fryer was speaking.'

'If the door won't keep shut,' I remarked, pursuing my own train of thought, 'why can't they let it stay open?'

'I have not the slightest idea. I only know there are two sovereigns to be made, and that I give you a present of the information.'

And having thus spoken, Parton took down his hat and went out, either upon his own business or that of his employers.

There was one thing I can truly say about our office, we were never serious in it. I fancy that is the case in most offices nowadays; at all events, it was the case in ours. We were always chaffing each other, playing practical jokes, telling stupid stories, scamping our work, looking at the clock, counting the weeks to next St Lubbock's Day, counting the hours to Saturday.

For all that we were all very earnest in our desire to have our salaries raised, and unanimous in the opinion no fellows ever before received such wretched pay. I had twenty pounds a year, which I was aware did not half provide for what I ate at home. My mother and sisters left me in no doubt on the point, and when new clothes were wanted I always hated to mention the fact to my poor worried father.

We had been better off once, I believe, though I never remember the time. My father owned a small property in the country, but owing to the failure of some bank, I never could understand what bank, it had to be mortgaged; then the interest was not paid, and the mortgages foreclosed, and we had nothing left save the half-pay of a major, and about a hundred a year which my mother brought to the common fund.

We might have managed on our income, I think, if we had not been so painfully genteel; but we were always trying to do something quite beyond our means, and consequently debts accumulated, and creditors ruled us with rods of iron.

Before the final smash came, one of my sisters married the younger son of a distinguished family, and even if they had been disposed to live comfortably and sensibly she would have kept her sisters up to the mark. My only brother, too, was an officer, and of course the family thought it necessary he should see we preserved appearances.

It was all a great trial to my father, I think, who had to bear the brunt of the dunning and harass, and eternal shortness of money; and it would have driven me crazy if I had not found a happy refuge when matters were going wrong at home at my aunt's. She was my father's sister, and had married so 'dreadfully below her' that my mother refused to acknowledge the relationship at all.

For these reasons and others, Parton's careless words about the two sovereigns stayed in my memory.

I wanted money badly—I may say I never had sixpence in the world of my own—and I thought if I could earn two sovereigns I might buy some trifles I needed for myself, and present my father with a new umbrella. Fancy is a dangerous little jade to flirt with, as I soon discovered.

She led me on and on. First I thought of the two sovereigns; then I recalled the amount of the rent Mr Carrison agreed to pay for Ladlow Hall; then I decided he would gladly give more than two sovereigns if he could only have the ghost turned out of possession. I fancied I might get ten pounds—twenty pounds. I considered the matter all day, and I dreamed of it all night, and when I dressed myself next morning I was determined to speak to Mr Fryer on the subject.

I did so—I told that gentleman Parton had mentioned the matter to me, and that if Mr Fryer had no objection, I should like to try whether I could not solve the mystery. I told him I had been accustomed to lonely houses, and that I should not feel at all nervous; that I did not believe in ghosts, and as for burglars, I was not afraid of them.

'I don't mind your trying,' he said at last. 'Of course you understand it is no cure, no pay. Stay in the house for a week; if at the end of that time you can keep the door shut, locked, bolted, or nailed up, telegraph for me, and I will go down—if not, come back. If you like to take a companion there is no objection.'

I thanked him, but said I would rather not have a companion.

'There is only one thing, sir, I should like,' I ventured.

'And that—?' he interrupted.

'Is a little more money. If I lay the ghost, or find out the ghost, I think I ought to have more than two sovereigns.'

'How much more do you think you ought to have?' he asked.

His tone quite threw me off my guard, it was so civil and conciliatory, and I answered boldly:

'Well, if Mr Carrison cannot now live in the place perhaps he wouldn't mind giving me a ten-pound note.'

Mr Fryer turned, and opened one of the books lying on his desk.

He did not look at or refer to it in any way—I saw that.

'You have been with us how long, Edlyd?' he said.

'Eleven months tomorrow,' I replied.

'And our arrangement was, I think, quarterly payments, and one month's notice on either side?'

'Yes, sir.' I heard my voice tremble, though I could not have said what frightened me.

'Then you will please to take your notice now. Come in before you leave this evening, and I'll pay you three months' salary, and then we shall be quits.'

'I don't think I quite understand,' I was beginning, when he broke in:

'But I understand, and that's enough. I have had enough of you and your airs, and your indifference, and your insolence here. I never had a clerk I disliked as I do you. Coming and dictating terms, forsooth! No, you shan't go to Ladlow. Many a poor chap'—(he said 'devil')—'would have been glad to earn half a guinea, let alone two sovereigns; and perhaps you may be before you are much older.'

'Do you mean that you won't keep me here any longer, sir?' I asked in despair. I had no intention of offending you. I—'

'Now you need not say another word,' he interrupted, 'for I won't bandy words with you.

Since you have been in this place you have never known your position, and you don't seem able to realize it. When I was foolish enough to take you, I did it on the strength of your connections, but your connections have done nothing for me. I have never had a penny out of any one of your friends—if you have any. You'll not do any good in business for yourself or anybody else, and the sooner you go to Australia'—(here he was very emphatic)—'and get off these premises, the better I shall be pleased.'

I did not answer him—I could not. He had worked himself to a white heat by this time, and evidently intended I should leave his premises then and there. He counted five pounds out of his cash-box, and, writing a receipt, pushed it and the money across the table, and bade me sign and be off at once.

My hand trembled so I could scarcely hold the pen, but I had presence of mind enough left to return one pound ten in gold, and three shillings and fourpence I had, quite by the merest good fortune, in my waistcoat pocket.

'I can't take wages for work I haven't done,' I said, as well as sorrow

213

and passion would let me. 'Good-morning,' and I left his office and passed out among the clerks.

I took from my desk the few articles belonging to me, left the papers it contained in order, and then, locking it, asked Parton if he would be so good as to give the key to Mr Fryer.

'What's up?' he asked 'Are you going?'

I said, 'Yes, I am going'.

'Got the sack?'

'That is exactly what has happened.'

'Well, I'm——!' exclaimed Mr Parton.

I did not stop to hear any further commentary on the matter, but bidding my fellow-clerks goodbye, shook the dust of Frimpton's Estate and Agency Office from off my feet.

I did not like to go home and say I was discharged, so I walked about aimlessly, and at length found myself in Regent Street. There I met my father, looking more worried than usual.

'Do you think, Phil,' he said (my name is Theophilus), 'you could get two or three pounds from your employers?'

Maintaining a discreet silence regarding what had passed, I answered:

'No doubt I could.'

I shall be glad if you will then, my boy,' he went on, for we are badly in want of it.'

I did not ask him what was the special trouble. Where would have been the use? There was always something—gas, or water, or poor-rates, or the butcher, or the baker, or the bootmaker. Well, it did not much matter, for we were well accustomed to the life; but, I thought, 'if ever I marry, we will keep within our means'. And then there rose up before me a vision of Patty, my cousin—the blithest, prettiest, most useful, most sensible girl that ever made sunshine in poor man's house.

My father and I had parted by this time, and I was still walking aimlessly on, when all at once an idea occurred to me. Mr Fryer had not treated me well or fairly. I would hoist him on his own petard. I would go to headquarters, and try to make terms with Mr Carrison direct.

No sooner thought than done. I hailed a passing omnibus, and was ere long in the heart of the city. Like other great men, Mr Carrison was difficult of access—indeed, so difficult of access, that the clerk to whom I applied for an audience told me plainly I could not see him at all. I might send in my message if I liked, he was good enough to add, and no doubt it would be attended to. I said I should not send in a message, and was then asked what I would do. My answer was simple. I meant to wait till I did see him. I was told they could not have people waiting about the office in this way.

I said I supposed I might stay in the street. 'Carrison didn't own that,' I suggested.

The clerk advised me not to try that game, or I might get locked up.

I said I would take my chance of it.

After that we went on arguing the question at some length, and we were in the middle of a heated argument, in which several of Carrison's 'young gentlemen', as they called themselves, were good enough to join, when we were all suddenly silenced by a grave-looking individual, who authoritatively enquired:

'What is all this noise about?'

Before anyone could answer I spoke up:

'I want to see Mr Carrison, and they won't let me.'

'What do you want with Mr Carrison?'

'I will tell that to himself only.'

'Very well, say on—I am Mr Carrison.'

For a moment I felt abashed and almost ashamed of my persistency; next instant, however, what Mr Fryer would have called my 'native audacity' came to the rescue, and I said, drawing a step or two nearer to him, and taking off my hat:

'I wanted to speak to you about Ladlow Hall, if you please, sir.'

In an instant the fashion of his face changed, a look of irritation succeeded to that of immobility; an angry contraction of the eyebrows disfigured the expression of his countenance.

'Ladlow Hall!' he repeated; 'and what have you got to say about Ladlow Hall?'

'That is what I wanted to tell you, sir,' I answered, and a dead hush seemed to fall on the office as I spoke.

The silence seemed to attract his attention, for he looked sternly at the clerks, who were not using a pen or moving a finger.

'Come this way, then,' he said abruptly; and next minute I was in his private office.

'Now, what is it?' he asked, flinging himself into a chair, and addressing me, who stood hat in hand beside the great table in the middle of the room.

I began—I will say he was a patient listener—at the very beginning, and told my story straight through. I concealed nothing. I enlarged on nothing. A discharged clerk I stood before him, and in the capacity of a discharged clerk I said what I had to say. He heard me to the end, then he sat silent, thinking.

At last he spoke.

'You have heard a great deal of conversation about Ladlow, I suppose?' he remarked.

'No sir; I have heard nothing except what I have told you.'

'And why do you desire to strive to solve such a mystery?'

'If there is any money to be made, I should like to make it, sir.'

'How old are you?'

'Two-and-twenty last January.'

'And how much salary had you at Frimpton's?'

'Twenty pounds a year.'

'Humph! More than you are worth, I should say.'

'Mr Fryer seemed to imagine so, sir, at any rate,' I agreed, sorrowfully.

'But what do you think?' he asked, smiling in spite of himself.

'I think I did quite as much work as the other clerks,' I answered.

'That is not saying much, perhaps,' he observed. I was of his opinion, but I held my peace.

'You will never make much of a clerk, I am afraid,' Mr Carrison proceeded, fitting his disparaging remarks upon me as he might on a lay figure. 'You don't like desk work?'

'Not much, sir.'

'I should judge the best thing you could do would be to emigrate,' he went on, eyeing me critically.

'Mr Fryer said I had better go to Australia or—' I stopped, remembering the alternative that gentleman had presented.

'Or where?' asked Mr Carrison.

'The ——, sir' I explained, softly and apologetically.

He laughed—he lay back in his chair and laughed—and I laughed myself, though ruefully.

After all, twenty pounds was twenty pounds, though I had not thought much of the salary till I lost it.

We went on talking for a long time after that; he asked me all about my father and my early life, and how we lived, and where we lived, and the people we knew; and, in fact, put more questions than I can well remember.

216

'It seems a crazy thing to do,' he said at last; 'and yet I feel disposed to trust you. The house is standing perfectly empty. I can't live in it, and I can't get rid of it; all my own furniture I have removed, and there is nothing in the place except a few old-fashioned articles belonging to Lord Ladlow. The place is a loss to me. It is of no use trying to let it, and thus, in fact, matters are at a deadlock. You won't be able to find out anything, I know, because, of course, others have tried to solve the mystery ere now; still, if you like to try you may. I will make this bargain with you. If you like to go down, I will pay your reasonable expenses for a fortnight; and if you do any good for me, I will give you a ten-pound note for yourself. Of course I must be satisfied that what you have told me is true and that you are what you represent. Do you know anybody in the city who would speak for you?'

I could think of no one but my uncle. I hinted to Mr Carrison he was not grand enough or rich enough, perhaps, but I knew nobody else to whom I could refer him.

'What!' he said, 'Robert Dorland, of Cullum Street. He does business with us. If he will go bail for your good behaviour I shan't want any further guarantee. Come along.' And to my intense amazement, he rose, put on his hat, walked me across the outer office and along the pavements till we came to Cullum Street.

'Do you know this youth, Mr Dorland?' he said, standing in front of my uncle's desk, and laying a hand on my shoulder.

'Of course I do, Mr Carrison,' answered my uncle, a little apprehensively; for, as he told me afterwards, he could not imagine what mischief I had been up to. 'He is my nephew.'

'And what is your opinion of him—do you think he is a young fellow I may safely trust?'

My uncle smiled, and answered, 'That depends on what you wish to trust him with.'

'A long column of addition, for instance.'

'It would be safer to give that task to somebody else.'

'Oh, uncle!' I remonstrated; for I had really striven to conquer my natural antipathy to figures—worked hard, and every bit of it against the collar.

My uncle got off his stool, and said, standing with his back to the empty fire-grate. 'Tell me what you wish the boy to do, Mr Carrison, and I will tell you whether he will suit your purpose or not. I know him, I believe, better than he knows himself.'

In an easy, affable way, for so rich a man, Mr Carrison took possession of the vacant stool, and nursing his right leg over his left knee, answered:

'He wants to go and shut the open door at Ladlow for me. Do you think he can do that?'

My uncle looked steadily back at the speaker, and said, 'I thought, Mr Carrison, it was quite settled no one could shut it?'

Mr Carrison shifted a little uneasily on his scat, and replied: I did not set your nephew the task he fancies he would like to undertake.'

'Have nothing to do with it, Phil,' advised my uncle, shortly.

'You don't believe in ghosts, do you, Mr Dorland?' asked Mr Carrison, with a slight sneer.

'Don't you, Mr Carrison?' retorted my uncle.

There was a pause—an uncomfortable pause—during the course of which I felt the ten pounds, which, in imagination, I had really spent, trembling in the scale. I was not afraid. For ten pounds, or half the money, I would have faced all the inhabitants of spirit land. I longed to tell them so; but something in the way those two men looked at each other stayed my tongue.

'If you ask me the question here in the heart of the city, Mr Dorland,' said Mr Carrison, at length, slowly and carefully, 'I answer "No"; but it you were to put it to me on a dark night at Ladlow, I should beg time to consider. I do not believe in supernatural phenomena myself, and yet—the door at Ladlow is as much beyond my comprehension as the ebbing and flowing of the sea.'

And you can't live at Ladlow?' remarked my uncle.

'I can't live at Ladlow, and what is more, I can't get anyone else to live at Ladlow.'

'And you want to get rid of your lease?'

'I want so much to get rid of my lease that I told Fryer I would give him a handsome sum if he could induce anyone to solve the mystery. Is there any other information you desire, Mr Dorland? Because if here is, you have only to ask and have. I feel I am not here in a prosaic office in the city of London, but in the Palace of Truth.'

My uncle took no notice of the implied compliment. When wine is good it needs no bush. If a man is habitually honest in his speech and in his thoughts, he desires no recognition of the fact.

'I don't think so,' he answered; 'it is for the boy to say what he will do. If he be advised by me he will stick to his ordinary work in his employers' office, and leave ghost-hunting and spirit-laying alone.'

Mr Carrison shot a rapid glance in my direction, a glance which, implying a secret understanding, might have influenced my uncle could I have stooped to deceive my uncle.

'I can't stick to my work there any longer,' I said. 'I got my marching orders today.'

'What *had* you been doing, Phil?' asked my uncle.

'I wanted ten pounds to go and lay the ghost!' I answered, so dejectedly, that both Mr Carrison and my uncle broke out laughing.

'Ten pounds!' cried my uncle, almost between laughing and crying. 'Why, Phil boy, I had rather, poor man though I am, have given thee ten pounds than that thou should'st go ghost-hunting or ghostlaying.'

When he was very much in earnest my uncle went back to thee and thou of his native dialect. I liked the vulgarism, as my mother called it, and I knew my aunt loved to hear him use the caressing words to her. He had risen, not quite from the ranks it is true, but if ever a gentleman came ready born into the world it was Robert Dorland, upon whom at our home everyone seemed to look down.

'What will you do, Edlyd?' asked Mr Carrison; 'you hear what your uncle says, "Give up the enterprise", and what I say; I do not want either to bribe or force your inclinations.'

'I will go, sir,' I answered quite steadily. I am not afraid, and I should like to show you—' I stopped. I had been going to say, 'I should like to show you I am not such a fool as you all take me for,' but I felt such an address would be too familiar, and refrained.

Mr Carrison looked at me curiously. I think he supplied the end of the sentence for himself, but he only answered:

'I should like you to show me that door fast shut; at any rate, if you can stay in the place alone for a fortnight, you shall have your money.'

'I don't like it, Phil,' said my uncle: 'I don't like this freak at all.'

'I am sorry for that, uncle,' I answered, 'for I mean to go.'

'When?' asked Mr Carrison.

'Tomorrow morning,' I replied.

'Give him five pounds, Dorland, please, and I will send you my cheque. You will account to me for that sum, you understand,' added Mr Carrison, turning to where I stood.

'A sovereign will be quite enough,' I said.

'You will take five pounds, and account to me for it,' repeated Mr Carrison, firmly; 'also, you will write to me every day, to my private address, and if at any moment you feel the thing too much for you, throw it up. Good afternoon,' and without more formal leave-taking he departed.

'It is of no use talking to you, Phil, I suppose?' said my uncle.

'I don't think it is,' I replied; 'you won't say anything to them at home, will you?'

'I am not very likely to meet any of them, am I?' he answered, without a shade of bitterness—merely stating a fact.

'I suppose I shall not see you again before I start,' I said, 'so I will bid you goodbye now.

'Goodbye, my lad; I wish I could see you a bit wiser and steadier.'

I did not answer him; my heart was very full, and my eyes too. I had tried, but office-work was not in me, and I felt it was just as vain to ask me to sit on a stool and pore over writing and figures as to think a person born destitute of musical ability could compose an opera.

Of course I went straight to Patty; though we were not then married, though sometimes it seemed to me as if we never should be married, she was my better half then as she is my better half now.

She did not throw cold water on the project; she did not discourage me. What she said, with her dear face aglow with excitement, was, 'I only wish, Phil, I was going with you.' Heaven knows, so did I.

Next morning I was up before the milkman. I had told my people overnight I should be going out of town on business. Patty and I settled the whole plan in detail. I was to breakfast and dress there, for I meant to go down to Ladlow in my volunteer garments. That was a subject upon which my poor father and I never could agree; he called volunteering child's play, and other things equally hard to bear; whilst my brother, a very carpet warrior to my mind, was never weary of ridiculing the force, and chaffing me for imagining I was 'a soldier'.

Patty and I had talked matters over, and settled, as I have said, that I should dress at her father's.

A young fellow I knew had won a revolver at a raffle, and willingly lent it to me. With that and my rifle I felt I could conquer an army.

It was a lovely afternoon when I found myself walking through leafy lanes in the heart of Meadowshire. With every vein of my heart I loved the country, and the country was looking its best just then: grass ripe for the mower, grain forming in the ear, rippling streams, dreamy rivers, old orchards, quaint cottages.

'Oh that I had never to go back to London,' I thought, for I am one of the few people left on earth who love the country and hate cities. I walked on, I walked a long way, and being uncertain as to my road, asked a gentleman who was slowly riding a powerful roan horse under arching trees—a gentleman accompanied by a young lady mounted on a stiff white pony—my way to Ladlow Hall.

'That is Ladlow Hall,' he answered, pointing with his whip over the fence to my left hand. I thanked him and was going on, when he said:

'No one is living there now.'

'I am aware of that,' I answered.

He did not say anything more, only courteously bade me good-day, and rode off. The young lady inclined her head in acknowledgement of my uplifted cap, and smiled kindly. Altogether I felt pleased, little things always did please me. It was a good beginning—halfway to a good ending!

When I got to the Lodge I showed Mr Carrison's letter to the woman, and received the key.

'You are not going to stop up at the Hall alone, are you, sir?' she asked.

'Yes, I am,' I answered, uncompromisingly, so uncompromisingly that she said no more.

The avenue led straight to the house; it was uphill all the way, and bordered by rows of the most magnificent limes I ever beheld. A light iron fence divided the avenue from the park, and between the trunks of the trees I could see the deer browsing and cattle grazing. Ever and *anon* there came likewise to my ear the sound of a sheep-bell.

It was a long avenue, but at length I stood in front of the Hall—a square, solid-looking, old-fashioned house, three stories high, with no basement; a flight of steps up to the principal entrance; four windows to the right of the door, four windows to the left; the whole building flanked and backed with trees; all the blinds pulled down, a dead silence brooding over the place: the sun westering behind the great trees studding the park. I took all this in as I approached, and afterwards as I stood for a moment under the ample porch; then, remembering the business which had brought me so far, I fitted the great key in the lock, turned the handle, and entered Ladlow Hall.

For a minute—stepping out of the bright sunlight—the place looked to me so dark that I could scarcely distinguish the objects by which I was surrounded; but my eyes soon grew accustomed to the comparative darkness, and I found I was in an immense hall, lighted from the roof, a magnificent old oak staircase conducted to the upper rooms.

The floor was of black and white marble. There were two fireplaces, fitted with dogs for burning wood; around the walls hung pictures, antlers, and horns, and in odd niches and corners stood groups of statues, and the figures of men in complete suits of armour.

To look at the place outside, no one would have expected to find such a hall. I stood lost in amazement and admiration, and then I began to glance more particularly around.

Mr Carrison had not given me any instructions by which to identify the ghostly chamber— which I concluded would most probably be found on the first floor.

I knew nothing of the story connected with it—if there were a story. On that point I had left London as badly provided with mental as with actual luggage—worse provided, indeed, for a hamper, packed by Patty, and a small bag were coming over from the station; but regarding the mystery I was perfectly unencumbered. I had not the faintest idea in which apartment it resided.

Well, I should discover that, no doubt, for myself ere long.

I looked around me—doors—doors—doors I had never before seen so many doors together all at once. Two of them stood open— one wide, the other slightly ajar.

'I'll just shut them as a beginning,' I thought, 'before I go upstairs.'

The doors were of oak, heavy, well-fitting, furnished with good locks and sound handles. After I had closed I tried them. Yes, they were quite secure. I ascended the great staircase feeling curiously like an intruder, paced the corridors, entered the many bedchambers—some quite bare of furniture, others containing articles of an ancient fashion, and no doubt of considerable value—chairs, antique dressing-tables, curious wardrobes, and such like. For the most part the doors were closed, and I shut those that stood open before making my way into the attics.

I was greatly delighted with the attics. The windows lighting them did not, as a rule, overlook the front of the Hall, but commanded wide views over wood, and valley, and meadow. Leaning out of one, I could see, that to the right of the Hall the ground, thickly planted, shelved down to a stream, which came out into the daylight a little distance beyond the plantation, and meandered through the deer park. At the back of the Hall the windows looked out on nothing save a dense wood and a portion of the stable-yard, whilst on the side nearest the point from whence I had come there were spreading gardens surrounded by thick yew hedges, and kitchen-gardens protected by high walls; and further on a farmyard, where I could perceive cows and oxen, and, further still, luxuriant meadows, and fields glad with waving corn.

'What a beautiful place!' I said. 'Carrison must have been a duffer to leave it.' And then I thought what a great ramshackle house it was for anyone to be in all alone.

Getting heated with my long walk, I suppose, made me feel chilly, for I shivered as I drew my head in from the last dormer window, and prepared to go downstairs again.

In the attics, as in the other parts of the house I had as yet explored, I closed the doors, when there were keys locking them; when there were not, trying them, and in all cases, leaving them securely fastened.

When I reached the ground floor the evening was drawing on apace, and I felt that if I wanted to explore the whole house before dusk I must hurry my proceedings.

'I'll take the kitchens next,' I decided, and so made my way to a wilderness of domestic offices lying to the rear of the great hall. Stone passages, great kitchens, an immense servants'-hall, larders, pantries, coal-cellars, beer-cellars, laundries, brewhouses, housekeeper's room—it was not of any use lingering over these details. The mystery that troubled Mr Carrison could scarcely lodge amongst cinders and empty bottles, and there did not seem much else left in this part of the building.

I would go through the living-rooms, and then decide as to the apartments I should occupy myself.

The evening shadows were drawing on apace, so I hurried back into the hall, feeling it was a weird position to be there all alone with those ghostly hollow figures of men in armour, and the statues on which the moon's beams must fall so coldly. I would just look through the lower apartments and then kindle a fire. I had seen quantities of wood in a cupboard close at hand, and felt that beside a blazing hearth, and after a good cup of tea, I should not feel the solitary sensation which was oppressing me.

The sun had sunk below the horizon by this time, for to reach Ladlow I had been obliged to travel by cross lines of railway, and wait besides for such trains as condescended to carry third-class passengers; but there was still light enough in the hall to see all objects distinctly. With my own eyes I saw that one of the doors I had shut with my own hands was standing wide!

I turned to the door on the other side of the hall. It was as I had left it—closed. This, then, was the room—this with the open door For a second I stood appalled; I think I was fairly frightened.

That did not last long, however. There lay the work I had desired to undertake, the foe I had offered to fight; so without more ado I shut the door and tried it.

'Now I will walk to the end of the hall and see what happens,' I considered. I did so. I walked to the foot of the grand staircase and back again, and looked.

The door stood wide open.

I went into the room, after just a spasm of irresolution—went in and pulled up the blinds: a good-sized room, twenty by twenty (I knew, because I paced it afterwards), lighted by two long windows.

The floor, of polished oak, was partially covered with a Turkey carpet. There were two recesses beside the fireplace, one fitted up as a bookcase, the other with an old and elaborately caned cabinet. I was astonished also to find a bedstead in an apartment so little retired from the traffic of the house; and there were also some chairs of an obsolete make, covered, so far as I could make out, with faded tapestry. Beside the bedstead, which stood against the wall opposite to the door, I perceived another door. It was fast locked, the only locked door I had as yet met with in the interior of the house. It was a dreary, gloomy room: the dark panelled walls; the black, shining floor; the windows high from the ground; the antique furniture; the dull four-poster bedstead, with dingy velvet curtains; the gaping chimney; the silk counterpane that looked like a pall.

'Any crime might have been committed in such a room,' I thought pettishly; and then I looked at the door critically.

Someone had been at the trouble of fitting bolts upon it, for when I passed out I not merely shut the door securely, but bolted it as well.

'I will go and get some wood, and then look at it again,' I soliloquized. When I came back it stood wide open once more.

'Stay open, then!' I cried in a fury. 'I won't trouble myself any more with you tonight!'

Almost as I spoke the words, there came a ring at the front door. Echoing through the desolate house, the peal in the then state of my nerves startled me beyond expression.

It was only the man who had agreed to bring over my traps. I bade him lay them down in the hall, and, while looking out some small silver, asked where the nearest post-office was to be found. Not far from the park gates, he said; if I wanted any letter sent, he would drop it in the box for me; the mail-cart picked up the bag at ten o'clock.

I had nothing ready to post then, and told him so. Perhaps the money I gave was more than he expected, or perhaps the dreariness of my position impressed him as it had impressed me, for he paused with his hand on the lock, and asked:

'Are you going to stop here all alone, master?'

'All alone,' I answered, with such cheerfulness as was possible under the circumstances.

'That's the room, you know,' he said, nodding in the direction of the open door, and dropping his voice to a whisper.

'Yes, I know,' I replied.

'What you've been trying to shut it already, have you? Well, you are a game one!' And with this complementary if not very respectful comment he hastened out of the house. Evidently he had no intention of proffering his services towards the solution of the mystery.

I cast one glance at the door—it stood wide open. Through the windows I had left bare to the night, moonlight was beginning to stream cold and silvery. Before I did aught else I felt I must write to Mr Carrison and Patty, so straightway I hurried to one of the great tables in the hall, and lighting a candle my thoughtful link girl had provided, with many other things, sat down and dashed off the two epistles.

Then down the long avenue, with its mysterious lights and shades, with the moonbeams glinting here and there, playing at hide-and-seek round the boles of the trees and through the tracery of quivering leaf and stem, I walked as fast as if I were doing a match against time.

It was delicious, the scent of the summer odours, the smell of the earth; if it had not been for the door I should have felt too happy. As it was—

'Look here, Phil,' I said, all of a sudden; 'life's not child's play, as uncle truly remarks. That door is just the trouble you have now to face, and you must face it! But for that door you would never have been here. I hope you are not going to turn coward the very first night. Courage!—that is your enemy—conquer it.'

'I will try,' my other self answered back. 'I can but try. I can but fail.'

The post-office was at Ladlow Hollow, a little hamlet through which the stream I had remarked dawdling on its way across the park flowed swiftly, spanned by an ancient bridge.

As I stood by the door of the little shop, asking some questions of the postmistress, the same gentleman I had met in the afternoon mounted on his roan horse, passed on foot. He wished me goodnight as he went by, and nodded familiarly to my companion, who curtseyed her acknowledgements.

'His Lordship ages fast,' she remarked, following the retreating figure with her eyes.

'His Lordship,' I repeated. 'Of whom are you speaking?'

'Of Lord Ladlow,' she said.

'Oh! I have never seen him,' I answered, puzzled.

'Why, *that* was Lord Ladlow!' she exclaimed.

You may be sure I had something to think about as I walked back to the Hall—something beside the moonlight and the sweet nightscents, and the rustle of beast and bird and leaf, that make silence seem more eloquent than noise away down in the heart of the country.

Lord Ladlow! my word, I thought he was hundreds, thousands of miles away; and here I find him—he walking in the opposite direction from his own home—I an inmate of his desolate abode. Hi!—what was that? I heard a noise in a shrubbery close at hand, and in an instant I was in the thick of the underwood. Something shot out and darted into the cover of the further plantation. I followed, but I could catch never a glimpse of it. I did not know the lie of the ground sufficiently to course with success, and I had at length to give up the hunt—heated, baffled, and annoyed.

When I got into the house the moon's beams were streaming down upon the hall; I could see every statue, every square of marble, every piece of armour. For all the world it seemed to me like something in a dream; but I was tired and sleepy, and decided I would not trouble about fire or food, or the open door, till the next morning: I would go to sleep.

With this intention I picked up some of my traps and carried them to a room on the first floor I had selected as small and habitable. I went down for the rest, and this time chanced to lay my hand on my rifle.

It was wet. I touched the floor—it was wet likewise.

I never felt anything like the thrill of delight which shot through me. I had to deal with flesh and blood, and I would deal with it, heaven helping me.

The next morning broke clear and bright. I was up with the lark—had washed, dressed, breakfasted, explored the house before the postman came with my letters.

One from Mr Carrison, one from Patty, and one from my uncle: I gave the man half a crown, I was so delighted, and said I was afraid my being at the Hall would cause him some additional trouble.

'No, sir,' he answered, profuse in his expressions of gratitude; 'I pass here every morning on my way to her Ladyship's.'

'Who is her Ladyship?' I asked.

'The Dowager Lady Ladlow,' he answered—'the old lord's widow.'

'And where is her place?' I persisted.

'If you keep on through the shrubbery and across the waterfall, you come to the house about a quarter of a mile further up the stream.'

He departed, after telling me there was only one post a day; and I hurried back to the room in which I had breakfasted, carrying my letters with me.

I opened Mr Carrison's first. The gist of it was, 'Spare no expense; if you run short of money telegraph for it.'

I opened my uncle's next. He implored me to return; he had always thought me hair-brained, but he felt a deep interest in and affection for me, and thought he could get me a good berth if I would only try to settle down and promise to stick to my work. The last was from Patty. Oh Patty, God bless you! Such women, I fancy, the men who fight best in battle, who stick last to a sinking ship, who are firm in life's struggles, who are brave to resist temptation, must have known and loved. I can't tell you more about the letter, except that it gave me strength to go on to the end.

I spent the forenoon considering that door. I looked at it from within and from without. I eyed it critically. I tried whether there was any reason why it should fly open, and I found that so long as I remained on the threshold it remained closed; if I walked even so far away as the opposite side of the hall, it swung wide.

Do what I would, it burst from latch and bolt. I could not lock it because there was no key.

Well, before two o'clock I confess I was baffled.

At two there came a visitor—none other than Lord Ladlow himself. Sorely I wanted to take his horse round to the stables, but he would not hear of it.

'Walk beside me across the park, if you will be so kind,' he said; 'I want to speak to you.'

We went together across the park, and before we parted I felt I could have gone through fire and water for this simple-spoken nobleman.

'You must not stay here ignorant of the rumours which are afloat,'

227

he said. 'Of course, when I let the place to Mr Carrison I knew nothing of the open door.'

'Did you not, sir?—my lord, I mean,' I stammered.

He smiled. 'Do not trouble yourself about my title, which, indeed, carries a very empty state with it, but talk to me as you might to a friend. I had no idea there was any ghost story connected with the Hall, or I should have kept the place empty.'

I did not exactly know what to answer, so I remained silent.

'How did you chance to be sent here?' he asked, after a pause.

I told him. When the first shock was over, a lord did not seem very different from anybody else. If an emperor had taken a morning canter across the park, I might, supposing him equally affable, have spoken as familiarly to him as to Lord Ladlow. My mother always said I entirely lacked the bump of veneration!

Beginning at the beginning, I repeated the whole story, from Parton's remark about the sovereign to Mr Carrison's conversation with my uncle. When I had left London behind in the narrative, however, and arrived at the Hall, I became somewhat more reticent. After all, it was *his* Hall people could not live in—*his* door that would not keep shut; and it seemed to me these were facts he might dislike being forced upon his attention.

But he would have it. What had *I* seen? What did *I* think of the matter? Very honestly I told him I did not know what to say. The door certainly would not remain shut, and there seemed no human agency to account for its persistent opening; but then, on the other hand, ghosts generally did not tamper with firearms, and my rifle, though not loaded, had been tampered with—I was sure of that.

My companion listened attentively. 'You are not frightened, are you?' he enquired at length.

'Not now,' I answered. 'The door did give me a start last evening, but I am not afraid of that since I find someone else is afraid of a bullet.'

He did not answer for a minute; then he said:

'The theory people have set up about the open door is this: As in that room my uncle was murdered, they say the door will never remain shut till the murderer is discovered.'

'Murdered!' I did not like the word at all; it made me feel chill and uncomfortable.

'Yes—he was murdered sitting in his chair, and the assassin has never been discovered. At first many persons inclined to the belief that

I killed him; indeed, many are of that opinion still.'

'But you did not, sir—there is not a word of truth in that story, is there?'

He laid his hand on my shoulder as he said:

'No, my lad; not a word. I loved the old man tenderly. Even when he disinherited me for the sake of his young wife, I was sorry, but not angry; and when he sent for me and assured me he had resolved to repair that wrong, I tried to induce him to leave the lady a handsome sum in addition to her jointure. "If you do not, people may think she has not been the source of happiness you expected," I added.

"Thank you, Hal," he said. "You are a good fellow; we will talk further about this tomorrow."

And then he bade me goodnight.

'Before morning broke—it was in the summer two years ago— the household was aroused by a fearful scream. It was his death-cry. He had been stabbed from behind in the neck. He was seated in his chair writing—writing a letter to me. But for that I might have found it harder to clear myself than was in the case; for his solicitors came forward and said he had signed a will leaving all his personalty to me—he was very rich—unconditionally, only three days previously. That, of course, supplied the motive, as my lady's lawyer put it. She was very vindictive, spared no expense in trying to prove my guilt, and said openly she would never rest till she saw justice done, if it cost her the whole of her fortune.

The letter lying before the dead man, over which blood had spurt- ed, she declared must have been placed on his table by me; but the coroner saw there was an animus in this, for the few opening lines stated my uncle's desire to confide in me his reasons for changing his will—reasons, he said, that involved his honour, as they had destroyed his peace. "In the statement you will find sealed up with my will in—" At that point he was dealt his death-blow. The papers were never found, and the will was never proved. My lady put in the former will, leaving her everything. Ill as I could afford to go to law, I was obliged to dispute the matter, and the lawyers are at it still, and very likely will continue at it for years.

When I lost my good name, I lost my good health, and had to go abroad; and while I was away Mr Carrison took the Hall. Till I returned, I never heard a word about the open door. My solicitor said Mr Carrison was behaving badly; but I think now I must see them or him, and consider what can be done in the affair. As for yourself, it is of vital importance to me that this mystery should be cleared up, and if you are really not timid, stay on. I am too poor to make rash promises, but you won't find me ungrateful.'

'Oh, my lord!' I cried—the address slipped quite easily and naturally off my tongue—'I don't want any more money or anything, if I can only show Patty's father I am good for something—'

'Who is Patty?' he asked.

He read the answer in my face, for he said no more.

'Should you like to have a good dog for company?' he enquired after a pause.

I hesitated; then I said:

'No, thank you. I would rather watch and hunt for myself.'

And as I spoke, the remembrance of that 'something' in the shrubbery recurred to me, and I told him I thought there had been someone about the place the previous evening.

'Poachers,' he suggested; but I shook my head.

'A girl or a woman I imagine. However, I think a dog might hamper me.'

He went away, and I returned to the house. I never left it all day. I did not go into the garden, or the stable-yard, or the shrubbery, or anywhere; I devoted myself solely and exclusively to that door.

If I shut it once, I shut it a hundred times, and always with the same result. Do what I would, it swung wide. Never, however, when I was looking at it. So long as I could endure to remain, it stayed shut—the instant I turned my back, it stood open.

About four o'clock I had another visitor; no other than Lord Ladlow's daughter—the Honourable Beatrice, riding her funny little white pony.

She was a beautiful girl of fifteen or thereabouts, and she had the sweetest smile you ever saw.

'Papa sent me with this,' she said; 'he would not trust any other messenger,' and she put a piece of paper in my hand.

Keep your food under lock and key; buy what you require yourself. Get your water from the pump in the stable-yard. I am going from home; but if you want anything, go or send to my daughter.

'Any answer?' she asked, patting her pony's neck.

'Tell his lordship, if you please, I will "keep my powder dry"!' I replied.

'You have made papa look so happy,' she said, still patting that fortunate pony.

'If it is in my power, I will make him look happier still, Miss —' and I hesitated, not knowing how to address her.

'Call me Beatrice,' she said, with an enchanting grace; then added, slily, 'Papa promises me I shall be introduced to Patty ere long,' and before I could recover from my astonishment, she had tightened the bit and was turning across the park.

'One moment, please,' I cried. 'You can do something for me.'

'What is it?' and she came back, trotting over the great sweep in front of the house.

'Lend me your pony for a minute.'

She was off before I could even offer to help her alight—off, and gathering up her habit dexterously with one hand, led the docile old sheep forward with the other.

I took the bridle—when I was with horses I felt amongst my own kind—stroked the pony, pulled his ears, and let him thrust his nose into my hand.

Miss Beatrice is a countess now, and a happy wife and mother; but I sometimes see her, and the other night she took me carefully into a conservatory and asked:

'Do you remember Toddy, Mr Edlyd?'

'Remember him!' I exclaimed; 'I can never forget him!'

'He is dead!' she told me, and there were tears in her beautiful eyes as she spoke the words.

'Mr Edlyd, I *loved* Toddy!'

Well, I took Toddy up to the house, and under the third window to the right hand. He was a docile creature, and let me stand on the saddle while I looked into the only room in Ladlow Hall I had been unable to enter.

It was perfectly bare of furniture, there was not a thing in it— not a chair or table, not a picture on the walls, or ornament on the chimney-piece.

'That is where my grand-uncle's valet slept,' said Miss Beatrice. 'It was he who first ran in to help him the night he was murdered.'

'Where is the valet?' I asked.

'Dead,' she answered. 'The shock killed him. He loved his master more than he loved himself.'

I had seen all I wished, so I jumped off the saddle, which I had carefully dusted with a branch plucked from a lilac tree; between jest and earnest pressed the hem of Miss Beatrice's habit to my lips as I arranged its folds; saw her wave her hand as she went at a hand-gallop across the park; and then turned back once again into the lonely house, with the determination to solve the mystery attached to it or die in the attempt.

Why, I cannot explain, but before I went to bed that night I drove a gimlet I found in the stables hard into the floor, and said to the door: 'Now *I* am keeping you open.'

When I went down in the morning the door was close shut, and the handle of the gimlet, broken off short, lying in the hall.

I put my hand to wipe my forehead; it was dripping with perspiration. I did not know what to make of the place at all! I went out into the open air for a few minutes; when I returned the door again stood wide.

If I were to pursue in detail the days and nights that followed, I should weary my readers. I can only say they changed my life. The solitude, the solemnity, the mystery, produced an effect I do not profess to understand, but that I cannot regret.

I have hesitated about writing of the end, but it must come, so let me hasten to it.

Though feeling convinced that no human agency did or could keep the door open, I was certain that some living person had means of access to the house which I could not discover, This was made apparent in trifles which might well have escaped unnoticed had several, or even two people occupied the mansion, but that in my solitary position it was impossible to overlook. A chair would be misplaced, for instance; a path would be visible over a dusty floor; my papers I found were moved; my clothes touched—letters I carried about with me, and kept under my pillow at night; still, the fact remained that when I went to the post-office, and while I was asleep, someone did wander over the house.

On Lord Ladlow's return I meant to ask him for some further particulars of his uncle's death, and I was about to write to Mr Carrison and beg permission to have the door where the valet had slept broken open, when one morning, very early indeed, I spied a hairpin lying close beside it.

What an idiot I had been! If I wanted to solve the mystery of the open door, of course I must keep watch in the room itself. The door would not stay wide unless there was a reason for it, and most certainly a hairpin could not have got into the house without assistance.

I made up my mind what I should do—that I would go to the post early, and take up my position about the hour I had hitherto started for Ladlow Hollow. I felt on the eve of a discovery, and longed for the day to pass, that the night might come.

It was a lovely morning; the weather had been exquisite during the whole week, and I flung the hall-door wide to let in the sunshine and the breeze. As I did so, I saw there was a basket on the top step—a basket filled with rare and beautiful fruit and flowers.

Mr Carrison had let off the gardens attached to Ladlow Hall for the season—he thought he might as well save something out of the fire, he said, so my fare had not been varied with delicacies of that kind. I was very fond of fruit in those days, and seeing a card addressed to me, I instantly selected a tempting peach, and ate it a little greedily perhaps.

I might say I had barely swallowed the last morsel, when Lord Ladlow's caution recurred to me. The fruit had a curious flavour—there was a strange taste hanging about my palate. For a moment, sky, trees and park swam before my eyes; then I made up my mind what to do.

I smelt the fruit—it had all the same faint odour; then I put some in my pocket—took the basket and locked it away—walked round to the farmyard—asked for the loan of a horse that was generally driven in a light cart, and in less than half an hour was asking in Ladlow to be directed to a doctor.

Rather cross at being disturbed so early, he was at first inclined to pooh-pooh my idea; but I made him cut open a pear and satisfy himself the fruit had been tampered with.

'It is fortunate you stopped at the first peach,' he remarked, after giving me a draught, and some medicine to take back, and advising me to keep in the open air as much as possible. 'I should like to retain this fruit and see you again tomorrow.'

We did not think then on how many morrows we should see each other!

Riding across to Ladlow, the postman had given me three letters, but I did not read them till I was seated under a great tree in the park, with a basin of milk and a piece of bread beside me.

Hitherto, there had been nothing exciting in my correspondence. Patty's epistles were always delightful, but they could not be regarded as sensational; and about Mr Carrison's there was a monotony I had begun to find tedious. On this occasion, however, no fault could be found on that score. The contents of his letter greatly surprised me.

He said Lord Ladlow had released him from his bargain—that I could, therefore, leave the Hall at once. He enclosed me ten pounds, and said he would consider how he could best advance my interests; and that I had better call upon him at his private house when I returned to London.

'I do not think I shall leave Ladlow yet awhile,' I considered, as I replaced his letter in its envelope. 'Before I go I should like to make it hot for whoever sent me that fruit; so unless Lord Ladlow turns me out I'll stay a little longer.'

Lord Ladlow did not wish me to leave. The third letter was from him. He wrote:

I shall return home tomorrow night, and see you on Wednesday. I have arranged satisfactorily with Mr Carrison, and as the Hall is my own again, I mean to try to solve the mystery it contains myself. If you choose to stop and help me to do so, you would confer a favour, and I will try to make it worth your while.

'I will keep watch tonight, and see if I cannot give you some news tomorrow,' I thought. And then I opened Patty's letter—the best, dearest, sweetest letter any postman in all the world could have brought me.

If it had not been for what Lord Ladlow said about his sharing my undertaking, I should not have chosen that night for my vigil. I felt ill and languid—fancy, no doubt, to a great degree inducing these sensations. I had lost energy in a most unaccountable manner. The long, lonely days had told upon my spirits—the fidgety feeling which took me a hundred times in the twelve hours to look upon the open door, to close it, and to count how many steps I could take before it opened again, had tried my mental strength as a perpetual blister might have worn away my physical. In no sense was I fit for the task I had set myself, and yet I determined to go through with it. Why had I never before decided to watch in that mysterious chamber? Had I been at the bottom of my heart afraid? In the bravest of us there are depths of cowardice that lurk unsuspected till they engulf our courage.

The day wore on—the long, dreary day; evening approached—the night shadows closed over the Hall. The moon would not rise for a couple of hours more. Everything was still as death. The house had never before seemed to me so silent and so deserted.

I took a light, and went up to my accustomed room, moving about for a time as though preparing for bed; then I extinguished the candle, softly opened the door, turned the key, and put it in my pocket, slipped softly downstairs, across the hall, through the open door. Then I knew I had been afraid, for I felt a thrill of terror as in the dark I stepped over the threshold. I paused and listened—there was not a sound—the night was still and sultry, as though a storm were brewing.

Not a leaf seemed moving—the very mice remained in their holes! Noiselessly I made my way to the other side of the room. There was an old-fashioned easy-chair between the bookshelves and the bed; I sat down in it, shrouded by the heavy curtain.

The hours passed—were ever hours so long? The moon rose, came and looked in at the windows, and then sailed away to the west; but not a sound, no, not even the cry of a bird. I seemed to myself a mere collection of nerves. Every part of my body appeared twitching. It was agony to remain still; the desire to move became a form of torture. Ah! a streak in the sky; morning at last, Heaven be praised! Had ever anyone before so welcomed the dawn? A thrush began to sing—was there ever heard such delightful music? It was the morning twilight, soon the sun would rise; soon that awful vigil would be over, and yet I was no nearer the mystery than before. Hush! what was that? *It had come.* After the hours of watching and waiting; after the long night and the long suspense, it came in a moment.

The locked door opened—so suddenly, so silently, that I had barely time to draw back behind the curtain, before I saw a woman in the room. She went straight across to the other door and closed it, securing it as I saw with bolt and lock. Then just glancing around, she made her way to the cabinet, and with a key she produced shot back the wards. I did not stir, I scarcely breathed, and yet she seemed uneasy. Whatever she wanted to do she evidently was in haste to finish, for she took out the drawers one by one, and placed them on the floor; then, as the light grew better, I saw her first kneel on the floor, and peer into every aperture, and subsequently repeat the same process, standing on a chair she drew forward for the purpose. A slight, lithe woman, not a lady, clad all in black—not a bit of white about her. What on earth could she want? In a moment it flashed upon me—*The will and the letter! She is searching for them.*

I sprang from my concealment—I had her in my grasp; but she tore herself out of my hands, fighting like a wild-cat: she hit, scratched, kicked, shifting her body as though she had not a bone in it, and at last slipped herself free, and ran wildly towards the door by which she had entered.

If she reached it, she would escape me. I rushed across the room and just caught her dress as she was on the threshold. My blood was up, and I dragged her back: she had the strength of twenty devils, I think, and struggled as surely no woman ever did before.

'I do not want to kill you,' I managed to say in gasps, 'but I will if you do not keep quiet.'

'Bah!' she cried; and before I knew what she was doing she had the revolver out of my pocket and fired.

She missed: the ball just glanced off my sleeve. I fell upon her—I can use no other expression, for it had become a fight for life, and no man can tell the ferocity there is in him till he is placed as I was then—fell upon her, and seized the weapon. She would not let it go, but I held her so tight she could not use it. She bit my face; with her disengaged hand she tore my hair. She turned and twisted and slipped about like a snake, but I did not feel pain or anything except a deadly horror lest my strength should give out.

Could I hold out much longer? She made one desperate plunge, I felt the grasp with which I held her slackening; she felt it too, and seizing her advantage tore herself free, and at the same instant fired again blindly, and again missed.

Suddenly there came a look of horror into her eyes—a frozen expression of fear.

'See!' she cried; and flinging the revolver at me, fled.

I saw, as in a momentary flash, that the door I had beheld locked stood wide—that there stood beside the table an awful figure, with uplifted hand—and then I saw no more. I was struck at last; as she threw the revolver at me she must have pulled the trigger, for I felt something like red-hot iron enter my shoulder, and I could but rush from the room before I fell senseless on the marble pavement of the ball.

When the postman came that morning, finding no one stirring, he looked through one of the long windows that flanked the door; then he ran to the farmyard and called for help.

'There is something wrong inside,' he cried. 'That young gentleman is lying on the floor in a pool of blood.'

As they rushed round to the front of the house they saw Lord Ladlow riding up the avenue, and breathlessly told him what had happened.

'Smash in one of the windows,' he said; 'and go instantly for a doctor.'

They laid me on the bed in that terrible room, and telegraphed for my father. For long I hovered between life and death, but at length I recovered sufficiently to be removed to the house Lord Ladlow owned on the other side of the Hollow.

Before that time I had told him all I knew, and begged him to make instant search for the will.

'Break up the cabinet if necessary,' I entreated, 'I am sure the papers are there.'

And they were. His Lordship got his own, and as to the scandal and the crime, one was hushed up and the other remained unpunished. The dowager and her maid went abroad the very morning I lay on the marble pavement at Ladlow Hall—they never returned.

My lord made that one condition of his silence.

Not in Meadowshire, but in a fairer county still, I have a farm which I manage, and make both ends meet comfortably.

Patty is the best wife any man ever possessed—and I—well, I am just as happy if a trifle more serious than of old; but there are times when a great horror of darkness seems to fall upon me, and at such periods I cannot endure to be left alone.

The Spectre in the Cart
Thomas Nelson Page

I had not seen my friend Stokeman since we were at college to-gether, and now naturally we fell to talking of old times. I remembered him as a hard-headed man without a particle of superstition, if such a thing be possible in a land where we are brought up on superstition, from the bottle. He was at that time full of life and of enjoyment of whatever it brought. I found now that his wild and almost reckless spirits had been tempered by the years which had passed as I should not have believed possible, and that gravity had taken place of the gaiety for which he was then noted.

He used to maintain, I remember, that there was no apparition or supernatural manifestation, or series of circumstances pointing to such a manifestation, however strongly substantiated they appeared to be, that could not be explained on purely natural grounds.

During our stay at college a somewhat notable instance of what was by many supposed to be a supernatural manifestation occurred in a deserted house on a remote plantation in an adjoining county.

It baffled all investigation, and got into the newspapers, recalling the Cock Lane ghost, and many more less celebrated apparitions. Par-ties were organised to investigate it, but were baffled. Stokeman, on a bet of a box of cigars, volunteered to go out alone and explode the fraud; and did so, not only putting the restless spirit to flight, but cap-turing it and dragging it into town as the physical and indisputable witness both of the truth of his theory and of his personal courage. The exploit gave him immense notoriety in our little world.

I was, therefore, no little surprised to hear him say seriously now that he had come to understand how people saw apparitions.

"I have seen them myself," he added, gravely.

"You do not mean it!" I sat bolt upright in my chair in my astonishment. I had myself, largely through his influence, become a sceptic in matters relating to the supernatural.

"Yes, I have seen ghosts. They not only have appeared to me, but were as real to my ocular vision as any other external physical object which I saw with my eyes.

"Of course, it was an hallucination. Tell me; I can explain it."

"I explained it myself," he said, dryly. "But it left me with a little less conceit and a little more sympathy with the hallucinations of others not so gifted."

It was a fair hit.

"In the year ———," he went on, after a brief period of reflection, "I was the State's Attorney for my native county, to which office I had been elected a few years after I left college, and the year we emancipated ourselves from carpet-bag rule, and I so remained until I was appointed to the bench. I had a personal acquaintance, pleasant or otherwise, with every man in the county. The district was a close one, and I could almost have given the census of the population. I knew every man who was for me and almost every one who was against me. There were few neutrals. In those times much hung on the elections. There was no borderland. Men were either warmly for you or hotly against you.

"We thought we were getting into smooth water, where the sailing was clear, when the storm suddenly appeared about to rise again. In the canvass of that year the election was closer than ever and the contest hotter.

"Among those who went over when the lines were thus sharply drawn was an old darky named Joel Turnell, who had been a slave of one of my nearest neighbours, Mr. Eaton, and whom I had known all my life as an easygoing, palavering old fellow with not much principle, but with kindly manners and a likable way. He had always claimed to be a supporter of mine, being one of the two or three negroes in the county who professed to vote with the whites.

"He had a besetting vice of pilfering, and I had once or twice defended him for stealing and gotten him off, and he appeared to be grateful to me. I always doubted him a little; for I believed he did not have force of character enough to stand up against his people, and he was a chronic liar. Still, he was always friendly with me, and used to claim the emoluments and privileges of such a relation. Now, however, on a sudden, in this campaign he became one of my bitterest opponents. I attributed it to the influence of a son of his, named Absalom,

239

who had gone off from the county during the war when he was only a youth, and had stayed away for many years without anything being known of him, and had now returned unexpectedly. He threw himself into the fight. He claimed to have been in the army, and he appeared to have a deep-seated animosity against the whites, particularly against all those whom he had known in boyhood.

"He was a vicious-looking fellow, broad-shouldered and bow-legged, with a swagger in his gait. He had an ugly scar on the side of his throat, evidently made by a knife, though he told the negroes, I understood, that he had got it in the war, and was ready to fight again if he but got the chance. He had not been back long before he was in several rows, and as he was of brutal strength, he began to be much feared by the negroes. Whenever I heard of him it was in connection with some fight among his own people, or some effort to excite race animosity. When the canvass began he flung himself into it with fury, and I must say with marked effect.

"His hostility appeared to be particularly directed against myself, and I heard of him in all parts of the district declaiming against me. The negroes who, for one or two elections, had appeared to have quieted down and become indifferent as to politics were suddenly revivified. It looked as if the old scenes of the Reconstruction period, when the two sides were like hostile armies, might be witnessed again. Night meetings, or 'camp-fires,' were held all through the district, and from many of them came the report of Absalom Turnell's violent speeches stirring up the blacks and arraying them against the whites. Our side was equally aroused and the whole section was in a ferment. Our effort was to prevent any outbreak and tide over the crisis.

"Among my friends was a farmer named John Halloway, one of the best men in my county, and a neighbour and friend of mine from my boyhood. His farm, a snug little homestead of fifty or sixty acres, adjoined our plantation on one side; and on the other, that of the Eatons, to whom Joel Turnell and his son Absalom had belonged, and I remember that as a boy it was my greatest privilege and reward to go over on a Saturday and be allowed by John Halloway to help him plough, or cut his hay. He was a big, ruddy-faced, jolly boy, and even then used to tell me about being in love with Fanny Peel, who was the daughter of another farmer in the neighbourhood, and a Sunday-school scholar of my mother's. I thought him the greatest man in the world.

"He had a fight once with Absalom Turnell when they were both youngsters, and, though Turnell was rather older and much the heavier, whipped him completely. Halloway was a good soldier and a good son, and when he came back from the war and won his wife, who was a *belle* among the young farmers, and settled down with her on his little place, which he proceeded to make a bower of roses and fruit-trees, there was not a man in the neighbourhood who did not rejoice in his prosperity and wish him well. The Halloways had no children and, as is often the case in such instances, they appeared to be more to each other than are most husbands and wives. He always spoke of his wife as if the sun rose and set in her. No matter where he might be in the county, when night came he always rode home, saying that his wife would be expecting him. 'Don't keer whether she's asleep or not,' he used to say to those who bantered him, 'she knows I'm a–comin', and she always hears my click on the gate-latch, and is waitin' for me.'

"It came to be well understood throughout the county.

"'I believe you are henpecked,' said a man to him one night.

"'I believe I am, George,' laughed Halloway, 'and by Jings! I like it, too.'

"It was impossible to take offence at him, he was so good-natured. He would get out of his bed in the middle of the night, hitch up his horse and pull his bitterest enemy out of the mud. He had on an occasion ridden all night through a blizzard to get a doctor for the wife of a negro neighbour in a cabin near by who was suddenly taken ill. When someone expressed admiration for it, especially as it was known that the man had not long before been abusing Halloway to the provost-marshal, who at that time was in supreme command, he said:

"'Well, what's that got to do with it? Wa 'n 't the man's wife sick? I don't deserve no credit, though; if I had n't gone, my wife would n' 'a' let me come in her house.'

"He was an outspoken man, too, not afraid of the devil, and when he believed a thing he spoke it, no matter whom it hit. In this way John had been in trouble several times while we were under 'gun-rule'; and this, together with his personal character, had given him great influence in the county, and made him a power. He was one of my most ardent friends and supporters, and to him, perhaps, more than to any other two men in the county, I owed my position.

"Absalom Turnell's rancorous speeches had stirred all the county, and the apprehension of the outbreak his violence was in danger of bringing might have caused trouble but for John Halloway's coolness and level-headedness. John offered to go around and follow Absalom up at his meetings. He could spike his guns,' he said.

"Some of his friends wanted to go with him. 'You'd better not try that,' they argued. That fellow, Ab. Turnell's got it in for you.' But he said no. The only condition on which he would go was that he should go alone.

"'They ain't any of 'em going to trouble me. I know 'em all and I git along with 'em first rate. I don't know as I know this fellow Ab; he's sort o' grown out o' my recollection; but I want to see. He knows me, I know. I got my hand on him once when he was a boy—about my age, and he ain't forgot that, I know. He was a blusterer; but he didn't have real grit. He won't say nothin' to my face. But I must go alone. You all are too flighty.'

"So Halloway went alone and followed Ab. up at his 'camp-fires,' and if report was true his mere presence served to curb Ab's fury, and take the fire out of his harangues. Even the negroes got to laughing and talking about it 'Ab was jest like a dog when a man faced him,' they said; 'he could n' look him in the eye.'

"The night before the election there was a meeting at one of the worst places in the county, a country store at a point known as Burley's Fork, and Halloway went there, alone—and for the first time in the canvass thought it necessary to interfere. Absalom, stung by the taunts of some of his friends, and having stimulated himself with mean whiskey, launched out in a furious tirade against the whites generally, and me in particular; and called on the negroes to go to the polls next day prepared to 'wade in blood to their lips.' For himself, he said, he had 'drunk blood' before, both of white men and women, and he meant to drink it again. He whipped out and flourished a pistol in one hand and a knife in the other.

"His language exceeded belief, and the negroes, excited by his violence, were showing the effect on their emotions of his wild declamation, and were beginning to respond with shouts and cries when Halloway rose and walked forward. Absalom turned and started to meet him, yelling his fury and threats, and the audience were rising to their feet when they were stopped. It was described to me afterward.

"Halloway was in the midst of a powder magazine, absolutely alone, a single spark would have blown him to atoms and might have caused a catastrophe which would have brought untold evil. But he was as calm as a May morning. He walked through them, the man who told me said, as if he did not know there was a soul in a hundred miles of him, and as if Absalom were only something to be swept aside.

"'He wa' n't exac'ly laughin', or even smilin', said my informant, 'but he jest looked easy in his mine.'

"They were all waiting, he said, expecting Absalom to tear him to pieces on the spot; but as Halloway advanced, Absalom faltered and stopped. He could not stand his calm eye.

"'It was jest like a dog givin' way before a man who ain't afraid of him,' my man said. 'He breshed Absalom aside as if he had been a fly, and began to talk to us, and I never heard such a speech.'

"I got there just after it happened; for some report of what Absalom intended to do had reached me that night and I rode over hastily, fearing that I might arrive too late. When, however, I arrived at the place everything was quiet, Absalom had disappeared. Unable to face his downfall, he had gone off, taking old Joel with him. The tide of excitement had changed and the negroes, relieved at the relaxing of the tension, were laughing among themselves at their champion's defeat and disavowing any sympathy with his violence. They were all friendly with Halloway.

"'Dat man wa' n' nothin' but a' outside nigger, nohow,' they said. 'And he always was more mouth then anything else,' etc.

"'Good L—d! He say he want to drink blood!' declared one man to another, evidently for us to hear, as we mounted our horses.

"'Drink *whiskey!*' replied the other, dryly, and there was a laugh of derision.

"I rode home with Halloway.

"I shall never forget his serenity. As we passed along, the negroes were lining the roads on their way homeward, and were shouting and laughing among themselves; and the greetings they gave us as we passed were as civil and good-humoured as if no unpleasantness had ever existed. A little after we set out, one man, who had been walking very fast just ahead of us, and had been keeping in advance all the time, came close to Halloway's stirrup and said something to him in an undertone. All I caught was, layin' up something against him.'

"'That's all right, Dick; let him lay it up, and keep it laid up,' Halloway laughed.

"'Dat's a bad feller!' the negro insisted, uneasily, his voice kept in an undertone. 'You got to watch him. I'se knowed him from a boy.'

"He added something else in a whisper which I did not catch.

"'All right; certainly not! Much obliged to you, Dick. I'll keep my eyes open. Goodnight.'

"'Goodnight, gent'men'; and the negro fell back and began to talk with the nearest of his companions effusively.

"'Who is that?' I asked, for the man had kept his hat over his eyes.

"'That's Dick Winchester. You remember that old fellow 't used to belong to old Mr. Eaton—lived down in the pines back o' me, on the creek 't runs near my place. His wife died the year of the big snow.'

"It was not necessary for him to explain further. I remembered the negro for whom Halloway had ridden through the storm that night.

"I asked Halloway somewhat irrelevantly, if he carried a pistol. He said no, he had never done so.

"'Fact is, I'm afraid of killin' somebody. And I don't want to do that, I know. Never could bear to shoot my gun even durin' o' the war, though I shot her 'bout as often as any of 'em, I reckon—always used to shut my eyes right tight whenever I pulled the trigger. I reckon I was a mighty pore soldier,' he laughed. I had heard that he was one of the best in the army.

"'Besides, I always feel sort o' cowardly if I've got a pistol on. Looks like I was afraid of somebody—an' I ain't. I've noticed if two fellows have pistols on and git to fightin', mighty apt to one git hurt, maybe both. Sort o' like two dogs growling—long as don't but one of 'em growl it's all right. If don't but one have a pistol, t' other feller always has the advantage and sort o' comes out top, while the man with the pistol looks mean.'

"I remember how he looked in the dim moonlight as he drawled his quaint philosophy.

"'I'm a man o' peace, Mr. Johnny, and I learnt that from your mother—I learnt a heap o' things from her,' he added, presently, after a little period of reflection. 'She was the lady as used always to have a kind word for me when I was a boy. That's a heap to a boy. I used to think she was an angel. You think it's *you* I'm a fightin' for in this canvass? 'T ain't. I like you well enough, but I ain't never forgot your mother, and her kindness to my old people durin' the war when I was away. She give me this handkerchief for a weddin' present when I was married after the war—said 't was all she had to give, and my wife thinks the world and all of it; won't let me have it 'cept as a favour; but this mornin' she told me to take it—said 'twould bring me luck.' He took a big bandana out of his pocket and held it up in the moonlight. I remembered it as one of my father's.

"'She'll make me give it up tomorrow night when I git home,' he chuckled.

"We had turned into a road through the plantations, and had just come to the fork where Halloway's road turned off toward his place.

"'I lays a heap to your mother's door—purty much all this, I reckon.' His eye swept the moon-bathed scene before him. 'But for her I mightn't 'a got *her*. And ain't a' man in the world got a happier home, or as good a wife.' He waved his hand toward the little homestead that was sleeping in the moonlight on the slope the other side of the stream, a picture of peace.

"His path went down a little slope, and mine kept along the side of the hill until it entered the woods. A great sycamore tree grew right in the fork, with its long, hoary arms extending over both roads, making a broad mass of shadow in the white moonlight.

"The next day was the day of election. Halloway was at one poll and I was at another; so I did not see him that day. But he sent me word that evening that he had carried his poll, and I rode home knowing that we should have peace.

"I was awakened next morning by the news that both Halloway and his wife had been murdered the night before. I at once galloped over to his place, and was one of the first to get there. It was a horrible sight. Halloway had evidently been waylaid and killed by a blow of an axe just as he was entering his yard gate, and then the door of the house had been broken open and his wife had been killed, after which Halloway's body had been dragged into the house, and the house had been fired with the intention of making it appear that the house had burned by accident. But by one of those inscrutable fatalities, the fire, after burning half of two walls, had gone out.

"It was a terrible sight, and the room looked like a shambles. Halloway had plainly been caught unawares while leaning over his gate. The back of his head had been crushed in with the eye of an axe, and he had died instantly. The pleasant thought which was in his mind at the instant—perhaps, of the greeting that always awaited him on the click of his latch; perhaps, of his success that day; perhaps, of my mother's kindness to him when he was a boy—was yet on his face, stamped there indelibly by the blow that killed him. There he lay, face upward, as the murderer had thrown him after bringing him in, stretched out his full length on the floor, with his quiet face upturned! looking in that throng of excited, awe-stricken men, just what he had said he was: a man of peace. His wife, on the other hand, wore a terrified look on her face. There had been a terrible struggle. She had lived to taste the bitterness of death, before it took her."

Stokeman, with a little shiver, put his hand over his eyes as though to shut out the vision that recurred to him. After a long breath he began again.

"In a short time there was a great crowd there, white and black. The general mind flew at once to Absalom Turnell. The negroes present were as earnest in their denunciation as the whites; perhaps, more so, for the whites were past threatening. I knew from the grimness that trouble was brewing, and I felt that if Absalom were caught and any evidence were found on him, no power on earth could save him. A party rode off in search of him, and went to old Joel's house. Neither Absalom nor Joel were there; they had not been home since the election, one of the women said.

"As a law officer of the county I was to a certain extent in charge at Halloway's and in looking around for all the clews to be found, I came on a splinter of 'light-wood' not as large or as long as one's little finger, stuck in a crack in the floor near the bed: a piece of a stick of 'fat-pine,' such as negroes often carry about, and use as tapers. One end had been burned; but the other end was clean and was jagged just as it had been broken off. There was a small scorched place on the planks on either side, and it was evident that this was one of the splinters that had been used in firing the house. I called a couple of the coolest, most level-headed men present and quietly showed them the spot, and they took the splinter out and I put it in my pocket.

"By one of those fortuitous chances which so often happen in every lawyer's experience, and appear inexplicable, Old Joel Turnell walked up to the house just as we came out. He was as sympathetic as possible, appeared outraged at the crime, professed the highest regard for Halloway, and the deepest sorrow at his death. The sentiment of the crowd was rather one of sympathy with him, that he should have such a son as Absalom.

"I took the old man aside to have a talk with him, to find out where his son was and where he had been the night before. He was equally vehement in his declarations of his son's innocence, and of professions of regard for Halloway. And suddenly to my astonishment he declared that his son had spent the night with him and had gone away after sunrise.

"Then happened one of those fatuous things that have led to the detection of so many negroes and can almost be counted on in their prosecution. Joel took a handkerchief out of his pocket and wiped his face, and as he did so I recognized the very handkerchief Halloway had shown me the night before. With the handkerchief, Joel drew out several splinters of light-wood, one of which had been broken off from a longer piece. I picked it up and it fitted exactly into the piece that had been stuck in the crack in the floor. At first, I could scarcely believe my own senses. Of course, it became my duty to have Joel arrested immediately. But I was afraid to have it done there, the crowd was so deeply incensed. So I called the two men to whom I had shown the light-wood splinter, told them the story, and they promised to get him away and arrest him quietly and take him safely to jail, which they did.

"Even then we did not exactly believe that the old man had any active complicity in the crime, and I was blamed for arresting the innocent old father and letting the guilty son escape. The son, however, was arrested shortly afterward.

"The circumstances from which the crime arose gave the case something of a political aspect, and the prisoners had the best counsel to be procured, both at our local bar and in the capital. The evidence was almost entirely circumstantial, and when I came to work it up I found, as often occurs, that although the case was plain enough on the outside, there were many difficulties in the way of fitting all the circumstances to prove the guilt of the accused and to make out every link in the chain. Particularly was this so in the prosecution of the young man, who was supposed to be the chief criminal, and in whose case there was a strong effort to prove an alibi.

"As I worked, I found to my surprise that the guilt of the old man, though based wholly on circumstantial evidence, was established more clearly than that of his son—not indeed, as to the murders, but as to the arson, which served just as well to convict on. The handkerchief, which Joel had not been able to resist the temptation to steal, and the splinter of light-wood in his pocket, which fitted exactly into that found in the house, together with other circumstances, proved his guilt conclusively. But although there was an equal moral certainty of the guilt of the young man, it was not so easy to establish it by law.

"Old Dick Winchester was found dead one morning and the alibi was almost completely proved, and only failed by the incredibility of the witnesses for the defence. Old Joel persistently declared that Absalom was innocent, and but for a confession by Absalom of certain facts intended to shift the suspicion from himself to his father, I do not know how his case might have turned out.

"I believed him to be the instigator as well as the perpetrator of the crime.

"I threw myself into the contest, and prosecuted with all the vigour I was capable of. And I finally secured the conviction of both men. But it was after a hard fight. They were the only instances in which, representing the Commonwealth, I was ever conscious of strong personal feeling, and of a sense of personal triumph. The memory of my last ride with Halloway, and of the things he had said to me; the circumstances under which he and his wife were killed; the knowledge that in some sort it was on my account; and the bitter attacks made on me personally;(for in some quarters I was depicted as a bloodthirsty ruffian, and it was charged that I was for political reasons prosecuting men whom I personally knew to be innocent), all combined to spur me to my utmost effort. And when the verdicts were rendered, I was conscious of a sense of personal triumph so fierce as to shock me.

"Not that I did not absolutely believe in the guilt of both prisoners; for I considered that I had demonstrated it, and so did the jurors who tried them.

"The day of execution was set. An appeal was at once taken in both cases and a stay was granted, and I had to sustain the verdicts in the upper court. The fact that the evidence was entirely circumstantial had aroused great interest, and every lawyer in the State had his theory. The upper court affirmed in both cases and appeals were taken to the highest court, and again stay of execution was granted.

"The prisoners' counsel had moved to have the prisoners transferred to another county, which I opposed. I was sure that the people of my county would observe the law. They had resisted the first fierce impulse, and were now waiting patiently for justice to take its course. Months passed, and the stay of execution had to be renewed. The road to Halloway's grew up and I understood that the house had fallen in, though I never went that way again. Still the court hung fire as to its conclusion.

"The day set for the execution approached for the third time without the court having rendered its decision.

"On the day before that set for the execution, the court gave its decision. It refused to interfere in the case of old Joel, but reversed and set aside the verdict in that of the younger man. Of a series of over one hundred bills of exception taken by his counsel as a 'drag-net,' one held; and owing to the admission of a single question by a juror, the judgment was set aside in Absalom's case and a new trial was ordered.

"Being anxious lest the excitement might increase, I felt it my duty to stay at the county-seat that night, and as I could not sleep I spent the time going over the records of the two cases; which, like most causes, developed new points every time they were read.

"Everything was perfectly quiet all night, though the village was filling up with people from the country to see the execution, which at that time was still public. I determined next morning to go to my home in the country and get a good rest, of which I began to feel the need. I was detained, however, and it was well along in the forenoon before I mounted my horse and rode slowly out of town through a back street. The lane kept away from the main road except at one point just outside of town, where it crossed it at right angles.

"It was a beautiful spring day—a day in which it is a pleasure merely to live, and as I rode along through the quiet lane under the leafy trees I could not help my mind wandering and dwelling on the things that were happening. I am not sure, indeed, that I was not dozing; for I reached the highway without knowing just where I was.

"I was recalled to myself by a rush of boys up the street before me, with a crowd streaming along behind them. It was the head of the procession. The sheriff and his men were riding, with set faces, in front and on both sides of a slowly moving vehicle; a common horse-cart in which in the midst of his guards, and dressed in his Sunday clothes, with a clean white shirt on, seated on his pine coffin, was old Joel. I unconsciously gazed at him, and at the instant he looked up and saw me. Our eyes met as naturally as if he had expected to find me there, and he gave me as natural and as friendly a bow—not a particle reproachful; but a little timid, as though he did not quite know whether I would speak to him.

"It gave me a tremendous shock. I had a sudden sinking of the heart, and nearly fell from my horse.

"I turned and rode away; but I could not shake off the feeling. I tried to reassure myself with the reflection that he had committed a terrible crime. It did not compose me. What insisted on coming to my mind was the eagerness with which I had prosecuted him and the joy I had felt at my success.

"Of course, I know now it was simply that I was overworked and needed rest; but at that time the trouble was serious.

"It haunted me all day, and that night I could not sleep. For many days afterwards, it clung to me, and I found myself unable to forget it, or to sleep as I had been used to do.

"The new trial of Absalom came on in time, and the fight was had all over again. It was longer than before, as every man in our county

249

had an opinion, and a jury had to be brought from another county. But again the verdict was the same. And again an appeal was taken; was refused by the next higher court; and allowed by the highest; this time because a talesman had said he had expressed an opinion, but had not formed one. In time the appeal was heard once more, and after much delay, due to the number of cases on the docket and the immense labour of studying carefully so huge a record, it was decided. It was again reversed, on the technicality mentioned, and a new trial was ordered.

"That same day the court adjourned for the term.

"Having a bedroom adjoining my office, I spent that night in town. I did not go to sleep until late, and had not been asleep long when I was awakened by the continual repetition of a monotonous sound. At first I thought I was dreaming, but as I aroused it came to me distinctly: the sound of blows in the distance struck regularly. I awaked fully. The noise was in the direction of the jail. I dressed hastily and went down on the street. I stepped into the arms of a half-dozen masked men who quietly laid me on my back, blindfolded me and bound me so that I could not move. I threatened and struggled; but to no purpose, and finally gave it up and tried expostulation. They told me that they intended no harm to me; but that I was their prisoner and they meant to keep me. They had come for their man, they said, and they meant to have him. They were perfectly quiet and acted with the precision of old soldiers.

"All the time I could hear the blows at the jail as the mob pounded the iron door with sledges, and now and then a shout or cry from within.

"The blows were on the inner door, for the mob had quickly gained access to the outer corridor. They had come prepared and, stout as the door was, it could not resist long. Then one great roar went up and the blows ceased suddenly, and then one cry.

"In a little while I heard the regular tramp of men, and in a few minutes the column came up the street, marching like soldiers. There must have been five hundred of them. The prisoner was in the midst, bare-headed and walking between two mounted men, and was moaning and pleading and cursing by turns.

"I asked my captors if I might speak, and they gave me ten minutes. I stood up on the top step of the house, and for a few minutes I made what I consider to have been the best speech I ever made or shall make. I told them in closing that I should use all my powers to find out who they were, and if I could do so I should prosecute them, everyone, and try and have them hanged for murder.

"They heard me patiently, but without a word, and when I was through, one of the leaders made a short reply. They agreed with me about the law; but they felt that the way it was being used was such as to cause a failure of justice. They had waited patiently, and were apparently no nearer seeing justice executed than in the beginning. So they proposed to take the law into their own hands. The remedy was, to do away with all but proper defences and execute the law without unreasonable delay.

"It was the first mob I had ever seen, and I experienced a sensation of utter powerlessness and insignificance; just as in a storm at sea, a hurricane, or a conflagration. The individual disappeared before the irresistible force.

"An order was given and the column moved on silently.

"A question arose among my guards as to what should be done with me.

"They wished to pledge me to return to my rooms and take no steps until morning, but I would give no pledges. So they took me along with them.

"From the time they started there was not a word except the orders of the leader and his lieutenants and the occasional outcry of the prisoner, who prayed and cursed by turns.

"They passed out of the village and turned in at Halloway's place.

"Here the prisoner made his last struggle. The idea of being taken to Halloway's place appeared to terrify him to desperation. He might as well have struggled against the powers of the Infinite. He said he would confess everything if they would not take him there. They said they did not want his confession. He gave up, and from this time was quiet; and he soon began to croon a sort of hymn.

"The procession stopped at the big sycamore under which I had last parted from Halloway.

"I asked leave to speak again; but they said no. They asked the prisoner if he wanted to say anything. He said he wanted something to eat. The leader said he should have it; that it should never be said that any man—even he—had asked in vain for food in that county.

"Out of a haversack food was produced in plenty, and while the crowd waited, amidst profound silence the prisoner squatted down and ate up the entire plateful.

"Then the leader said he had just five minutes more to live and he had better pray.

"He began a sort of wild incoherent ramble; confessed that he had murdered Halloway and his wife, but laid the chief blame on his father, and begged them to tell his friends to meet him in heaven.

"I asked leave to go, and it was given me on condition that I would not return for twenty minutes. This I agreed to.

"I went to my home and aroused someone, and we returned. It was not much more than a half-hour since I had left, but the place was deserted. It was all as silent as the grave. There was no living creature there. Only under the great sycamore, from one of its long, pale branches that stretched across the road, hung that dead thing with the toes turned a little in, just out of our reach, turning and swaying a little in the night wind.

"We had to climb to the limb to cut the body down.

"The outside newspapers made a good deal of the affair. I was charged with indifference, with cowardice, with venality. Some journals even declared that I had instigated the lynching and participated in it, and said that I ought to be hanged.

"I did not mind this much. It buoyed me up, and I went on with my work without stopping for a rest, as I had intended to do.

"I kept my word and ransacked the county for evidence against the lynchers. Many knew nothing about the matter; others pleaded their privilege and refused to testify on the ground of self-crimination.

"The election came on again, and almost before I knew it I was in the midst of the canvass.

"I held that election would be an endorsement of me, and defeat would be a censure. After all, it is the endorsement of those about our own home that we desire.

"The night before the election I spoke to a crowd at Burley's Fork. The place had changed since Halloway checked Absalom Turnell there. A large crowd was in attendance. I paid Halloway my personal tribute that night, and it met with a deep response. I denounced the lynching. There was a dead silence. I was sure that in my audience were many of the men who had been in the mob that night.

"When I rode home quite a company started with me.

"The moon, which was on the wane, was, I remember, just rising as we set out It was a soft night, rather cloudy, but not dark, for the sad moon shone a little now and then, looking wasted and red. The other men dropped off from time to time as we came to the several roads that led to their homes and at last I was riding alone. I was dead tired and after I was left by my companions sat loungingly on my horse. My mind ran on the last canvass and the strange tragedy that had ended it, with its train of consequences. I was not aware when my horse turned off from the main road into the by-lane that led through the Halloway place to my own home. My horse was the same I had ridden that night. I awaked suddenly to a realization of where I was, and regretted for a second that I had come by that road. The next moment I put the thought away as a piece of cowardice and rode on, my mind perfectly easy. My horse presently broke into a canter and I took a train of thought distinctly pleasant.

"I mention this to account for my inability to explain what followed. I was thinking of old times and of a holiday I had once spent at Halloway's when old Joel came through on his way to his wife's house. It was the first time I remembered ever seeing Joel. I was suddenly conscious of something white moving on the road before me. At the same second my horse suddenly wheeled with such violence as to break my stirrup-leather and almost throw me over his neck. I pulled him up and turned him back, and there before me, coming along the unused road up the hill from Halloway's, was old Joel, sitting in a cart, looking at me, and bowing to me politely just as he had done that morning on his way to the gallows; while dangling from the white limb of the sycamore, swaying softly in the wind, hung the corpse of Absalom. At first I thought it was an illusion and I rubbed my eyes. But there they were. Then I thought it was a delusion; and I reined in my horse and reasoned about it. But it was not; for I saw both men as plainly as I saw my stirrup-leather lying there in the middle of the road, and in the same way. My horse saw them too, and was so terrified that I could not keep him headed to them.

"Again and again I pulled him around and looked at the men and tried to reason about them; but every time I looked there they were, and my horse snorted and wheeled in terror. I could see the clothes they wore: the clean, white shirt and neat Sunday suit old Joel had on, and the striped, hickory shirt, torn on the shoulders, and the gray trousers that the lynched man wore—I could see the white rope wrapped around the limb and hanging down, and the knot at his throat; I remembered them perfectly. I could not get near the cart, for the road down to Halloway's, on which it moved steadily without ever approaching, was stopped up. But I rode right under the limb on which the other man hung, and there he was just above my head. I reasoned with myself, but in vain. There he still hung silent and limp, swinging gently in the night wind and turning a little back and forth at the end of the white rope.

"In sheer determination to fight it through I got off my horse and picked up my stirrup. He was trembling like a leaf. I remounted and rode back to the spot and looked again, confident that the spectres would now have disappeared. But there they were, old Joel, sitting in his cart, bowing to me civilly with timid, sad, friendly eyes, as much alive as I was, and the dead man, with his limp head and arms and his toes turned in, hanging in midair.

"I rode up under the dangling body and cut at it with my switch. At the motion my horse bolted. He ran fully a mile before I could pursue him in.

"The next morning I went to my stable to get my horse to ride to the polls. The man a the stable said:

"'He ain't fit to take out, sir. You must 'a gi'n him a mighty hard ride last night—he won't tetch a moufful; he's been in a cold sweats all night.'

"Sure enough, he looked it.

"I took another horse and rode out by Halloway's to see the place by daylight.

"It was quiet enough now. The sycamore shaded the grass-grown track, and a branch, twisted and broken by some storm, hung by a strip of bark from the big bough that stretched across the road above my head, swaying, with limp leaves, a little in the wind; a dense dogwood bush in full bloom among the young pines, filled a fence-corner down the disused road where old Joel had bowed to me from his phantom cart the night before. But it was hard to believe that these were the things which had created such impressions on my mind—as hard to believe as that the quiet cottage peering out from amid the mass of peach-bloom on the other slope was one hour the home of such happiness, and the next the scene of such a tragedy." Once more he put his hand suddenly before his face as though to shut out something from his vision. "Yes, I have seen apparitions," he said, thoughtfully, "but I have seen what was worse."

The Deserted House

Ernest Theodor Amadeus Hoffmann

They were all agreed in the belief that the actual facts of life are often far more wonderful than the invention of even the liveliest imagination can be.

"It seems to me," spoke Lelio, "that history gives proof sufficient of this. And that is why the so-called historical romances seem so repulsive and tasteless to us, those stories wherein the author mingles the foolish fancies of his meagre brain with the deeds of the great powers of the universe."

Franz took the word. "It is the deep reality of the inscrutable secrets surrounding us that oppresses us with a might wherein we recognize the Spirit that rules, the Spirit out of which our being springs."

"Alas," said Lelio, "it is the most terrible result of the fall of man, that we have lost the power of recognizing the eternal verities."

"Many are called, but few are chosen," broke in Franz. "Do you not believe that an understanding of the wonders of our existence is given to some of us in the form of another sense? But if you would allow me to drag the conversation up from these dark regions where we are in danger of losing our path altogether up into the brightness of light-hearted merriment, I would like to make the scurrilous suggestion that those mortals to whom this gift of seeing the Unseen has been given remind me of bats. You know the learned anatomist Spallanzani has discovered a sixth sense in these little animals which can do not only the entire work of the other senses, but work of its own besides."

"Oho," laughed Edward, "according to that, the bats would be the only natural-born clairvoyants. But I know one who possesses that gift of insight, of which you were speaking, in a remarkable degree. Because of it he will often follow for days some unknown person who has happened to attract his attention by an oddity in manner, appearance, or garb; he will ponder to melancholy over some trifling incident, some lightly told story; he will combine the antipodes and raise up relationships in his imagination which are unknown to everyone else."

"Wait a bit," cried Lelio. "It is our Theodore of whom you are speaking now. And it looks to me as if he were having some weird vision at this very moment. See how strangely he gazes out into the distance."

Theodore had been sitting in silence up to this moment. Now he spoke: "If my glances are strange it is because they reflect the strange things that were called up before my mental vision by your conversation, the memories of a most remarkable adventure—"

"Oh, tell it to us," interrupted his friends.

"Gladly," continued Theodore. "But first, let me set right a slight confusion in your ideas on the subject of the mysterious. You appear to confound what is merely odd and unusual with what is really mysterious or marvellous, that which surpasses comprehension or belief. The odd and the unusual, it is true, spring often from the truly marvellous, and the twigs and flowers hide the parent stem from our eyes. Both the odd and the unusual and the truly marvellous are mingled in the adventure which I am about to narrate to you, mingled in a manner which is striking and even awesome." With these words Theodore drew from his pocket a notebook in which, as his friends knew, he had written down the impressions of his late journeyings. Refreshing his memory by a look at its pages now and then, he narrated the following story.

★★★★★★

You know already that I spent the greater part of last summer in X—. The many old friends and acquaintances I found there, the free, jovial life, the manifold artistic and intellectual interests—all these combined to keep me in that city. I was happy as never before, and found rich nourishment for my old fondness for wandering alone through the streets, stopping to enjoy every picture in the shop windows, every placard on the walls, or watching the passers-by and choosing some one or the other of them to cast his horoscope secretly to myself.

There is one broad avenue leading to the — Gate and lined with handsome buildings of all descriptions, which is the meeting place of the rich and fashionable world. The shops which occupy the ground floor of the tall palaces are devoted to the trade in articles of luxury, and the apartments above are the dwellings of people of wealth and position. The aristocratic hotels are to be found in this avenue, the palaces of the foreign ambassadors are there and you can easily imagine that such a street would be the centre of the city's life and gayety.

I had wandered through the avenue several times, when one day my attention was caught by a house which contrasted strangely with the others surrounding it. Picture to yourselves a low building but four windows broad, crowded in between two tall, handsome structures. Its one upper story was little higher than the tops of the ground-floor windows of its neighbours, its roof was dilapidated, its windows patched with paper, its discoloured walls spoke of years of neglect. You can imagine how strange such a house must have looked in this street of wealth and fashion. Looking at it more attentively I perceived that the windows of the upper story were tightly closed and curtained, and that a wall had been built to hide the windows of the ground floor.

The entrance gate, a little to one side, served also as a doorway for the building, but I could find no sign of latch, lock, or even a bell on this gate. I was convinced that the house must be unoccupied, for at whatever hour of the day I happened to be passing I had never seen the faintest signs of life about it. An unoccupied house in this avenue was indeed an odd sight. But I explained the phenomenon to myself by saying that the owner was doubtless absent upon a long journey, or living upon his country estates, and that he perhaps did not wish to sell or rent the property, preferring to keep it for his own use in the eventuality of a visit to the city.

You all, the good comrades of my youth, know that I have been prone to consider myself a sort of clairvoyant, claiming to have glimpses of a strange world of wonders, a world which you, with your hard common sense, would attempt to deny or laugh away. I confess that I have often lost myself in mysteries which after all turned out to be no mysteries at all. And it looked at first as if this was to happen to me in the matter of the deserted house, that strange house which drew my steps and my thoughts to itself with a power that surprised me. But the point of my story will prove to you that I am right in asserting that I know more than you do. Listen now to what I am about to tell you.

One day, at the hour in which the fashionable world is accustomed to promenade up and down the avenue, I stood as usual before the deserted house, lost in thought. Suddenly I felt, without looking up, that some one had stopped beside me, fixing his eyes on me. It was

Count P., whom I had found much in sympathy with many of my imaginings, and I knew that he also must have been deeply interested in the mystery of this house. It surprised me not a little, therefore, that he should smile ironically when I spoke of the strange impression that this deserted dwelling, here in the gay heart of the town, had made upon me. But I soon discovered the reason for his irony. Count P. had gone much farther than myself in his imaginings concerning the house. He had constructed for himself a complete history of the old building, a story weird enough to have been born in the fancy of a true poet. It would give me great pleasure to relate this story to you, but the events which happened to me in this connection are so interesting that I feel I must proceed with the narration of them at once.

When the count had completed his story to his own satisfaction, imagine his feelings on learning one day that the old house contained nothing more mysterious than a cake bakery belonging to the pastry cook whose handsome shop adjoined the old structure. The windows of the ground floor were walled up to give protection to the ovens, and the heavy curtains of the upper story were to keep the sunlight from the wares laid out there. When the count informed me of this I felt as if a bucket of cold water had been suddenly thrown over me. The demon who is the enemy of all poets caught the dreamer by the nose and tweaked him painfully.

And yet, in spite of this prosaic explanation, I could not resist stopping before the deserted house whenever I passed it, and gentle tremors rippled through my veins as vague visions arose of what might be hidden there. I could not believe in this story of the cake and candy factory. Through some strange freak of the imagination I felt as a child feels when some fairy tale has been told it to conceal the truth it suspects. I scolded myself for a silly fool; the house remained unaltered in its appearance, and the visions faded in my brain, until one day a chance incident woke them to life again.

I was wandering through the avenue as usual, and as I passed the deserted house I could not resist a hasty glance at its close-curtained upper windows. But as I looked at it, the curtain on the last window near the pastry shop began to move. A hand, an arm, came out from between its folds. I took my opera glass from my pocket and saw a beautifully formed woman's hand, on the little finger of which a large diamond sparkled in unusual brilliancy; a rich bracelet glittered on the white, rounded arm. The hand set a tall, oddly formed crystal bottle on the window ledge and disappeared again behind the curtain.

I stopped as if frozen to stone; a weirdly pleasurable sensation, mingled with awe, streamed through my being with the warmth of an electric current. I stared up at the mysterious window and a sigh of longing arose from the very depths of my heart. When I came to myself again, I was angered to find that I was surrounded by a crowd which stood gazing up at the window with curious faces. I stole away inconspicuously, and the demon of all things prosaic whispered to me that what I had just seen was the rich pastry cook's wife, in her Sunday adornment, placing an empty bottle, used for rose-water or the like, on the window sill. Nothing very weird about this.

Suddenly a most sensible thought came to me. I turned and entered the shining, mirror-walled shop of the pastry cook. Blowing the steaming foam from my cup of chocolate, I remarked: "You have a very useful addition to your establishment next door." The man leaned over his counter and looked at me with a questioning smile, as if he did not understand me. I repeated that in my opinion he had been very clever to set up his bakery in the neighbouring house, although the deserted appearance of the building was a strange sight in its contrasting surroundings. "Why, sir," began the pastry cook, "who told you that the house next door belongs to us? Unfortunately every attempt on our part to acquire it has been in vain, and I fancy it is all the better so, for there is something queer about the place."

You can imagine, dear friends, how interested I became upon hearing these words, and that I begged the man to tell me more about the house.

"I do not know anything very definite, sir," he said. "All that we know for a certainty is that the house belongs to the Countess S., who lives on her estates and has not been to the city for years. This house, so they tell me, stood in its present shape before any of the handsome buildings were raised which are now the pride of our avenue, and in all these years there has been nothing done to it except to keep it from actual decay. Two living creatures alone dwell there, an aged misanthrope of a steward and his melancholy dog, which occasionally howls at the moon from the back courtyard. According to the general story the deserted house is haunted. In very truth my brother, who is the owner of this shop, and myself have often, when our business kept us awake during the silence of the night, heard strange sounds from the other side of the wall. There was a rumbling and a scraping that frightened us both

"And not very long ago we heard one night a strange singing

which I could not describe to you. It was evidently the voice of an old woman, but the tones were so sharp and clear, and ran up to the top of the scale in cadences and long trills, the like of which I have never heard before, although I have heard many singers in many lands. It seemed to be a French song, but I am not quite sure of that, for I could not listen long to the mad, ghostly singing, it made the hair stand erect on my head. And at times, after the street noises are quiet, we can hear deep sighs, and sometimes a mad laugh, which seem to come out of the earth. But if you lay your ear to the wall in our back room, you can hear that the noises come from the house next door."

He led me into the back room and pointed through the window. "And do you see that iron chimney coming out of the wall there? It smokes so heavily sometimes, even in summer when there are no fires used that my brother has often quarrelled with the old steward about it, fearing danger. But the old man excuses himself by saying that he was cooking his food. Heaven knows what the queer creature may eat, for often, when the pipe is smoking heavily, a strange and queer smell can be smelled all over the house."

The glass doors of the shop creaked in opening. The pastry cook hurried into the front room, and when he had nodded to the figure now entering he threw a meaning glance at me. I understood him perfectly. Who else could this strange guest be, but the steward who had charge of the mysterious house! Imagine a thin little man with a face the colour of a mummy, with a sharp nose tight-set lips, green cat's eyes, and a crazy smile; his hair dressed in the old-fashioned style with a high toupee and a bag at the back, and heavily powdered. He wore a faded old brown coat which was carefully brushed, gray stockings, and broad, flat-toed shoes with buckles. And imagine further, that in spite of his meagreness this little person is robustly built, with huge fists and long, strong fingers, and that he walks to the shop counter with a strong, firm step, smiling his imbecile smile, and whining out: "A couple of candied oranges—a couple of macaroons—a couple of sugared chestnuts—" Picture all this to yourself and judge whether I had not sufficient cause to imagine a mystery here.

The pastry cook gathered up the wares the old man had demanded. "Weigh it out, weigh it out, honoured neighbour," moaned the strange man, as he drew out a little leathern bag and sought in it for his money. I noticed that he paid for his purchase in worn old coins, some of which were no longer in use. He seemed very unhappy and murmured: "Sweet—sweet—it must all be sweet! Well, let it be! The devil has pure honey for his bride—pure honey!"

The pastry cook smiled at me and then spoke to the old man. "You do not seem to be quite well. Yes, yes, old age, old age! It takes the strength from our limbs." The old man's expression did not change, but his voice went up: "Old age?—Old age?—Lose strength?—Grow weak?—Oho!" And with this he clapped his hands together until the joints cracked, and sprang high up into the air until the entire shop trembled and the glass vessels on the walls and counters rattled and shook. But in the same moment a hideous screaming was heard; the old man had stepped on his black dog, which, creeping in behind him, had laid itself at his feet on the floor. "Devilish beast—dog of hell!" groaned the old man in his former miserable tone, opening his bag and giving the dog a large macaroon.

The dog, which had burst out into a cry of distress that was truly human, was quiet at once, sat down on its haunches, and gnawed at the macaroon like a squirrel. When it had finished its tidbit, the old man had also finished the packing up and putting away of his purchases. "Goodnight, honoured neighbour," he spoke, taking the hand of the pastry cook and pressing it until the latter cried aloud in pain. "The weak old man wishes you a goodnight, most honourable Sir Neighbour," he repeated, and then walked from the shop, followed closely by his black dog. The old man did not seem to have noticed me at all. I was quite dumfoundered in my astonishment.

"There, you see," began the pastry cook. "This is the way he acts when he comes in here, two or three times a month, it is. But I can get nothing out of him except the fact that he was a former valet of Count S., that he is now in charge of this house here, and that every day—for many years now—he expects the arrival of his master's family. My brother spoke to him one day about the strange noises at night; but he answered calmly, 'Yes, people say the ghosts walk about in the house.' But do not believe it, for it is not true." The hour was now come when fashion demanded that the elegant world of the city should assemble in this attractive shop. The doors opened incessantly, the place was thronged, and I could ask no further questions.

This much I knew, that Count P.'s information about the ownership and the use of the house were not correct; also that the old steward, in spite of his denial, was not living alone there, and that some mystery was hidden behind its discoloured walls. How could I combine the story of the strange and gruesome singing with the appearance of the beautiful arm at the window? That arm could not be part of the wrinkled body of an old woman; the singing, according to the pastry cook's story, could not come from the throat of a blooming and youthful maiden. I decided in favour of the arm, as it was easy to explain to myself that some trick of acoustics had made the voice sound sharp and old, or that it had appeared so only in the pastry cook's fear-distorted imagination. Then I thought of the smoke, the strange odours, the oddly formed crystal bottle that I had seen, and soon the vision of a beautiful creature held enthralled by fatal magic stood as if alive before my mental vision.

The old man became a wizard who perhaps quite independently of the family he served, had set up his devil's kitchen in the deserted house. My imagination had begun to work, and in my dreams that night I saw clearly the hand with the sparkling diamond on its finger, the arm with the shining bracelet. From out thin, gray mists there appeared a sweet face with sadly imploring blue eyes, then the entire exquisite figure of a beautiful girl. And I saw that what I had thought was mist was the fine steam flowing out in circles from a crystal bottle held in the hands of the vision.

"Oh, fairest creature of my dreams," I cried in rapture. "Reveal to me where thou art, what it is that enthrals thee. Ah, I know it! It is black magic that holds thee captive—thou art the unhappy slave of that malicious devil who wanders about brown-clad and bewigged in pastry shops, scattering their wares with his unholy springing, and feeding his demon dog on macaroons, after they have howled out a Satanic measure in five-eight time. Oh, I know it all, thou fair and charming vision. The diamond is the reflection of the fire of thy heart. But that bracelet about thine arm is a link of the chain which the brown-clad one says is a magnetic chain. Do not believe it, O glorious one! See how it shines in the blue fire from the retort. One moment more and thou art free. And now, O maiden, open thy rosebud mouth and tell me—" In this moment a gnarled fist leaped over my shoulder and clutched at the crystal bottle, which sprang into a thousand pieces in the air. With a faint, sad moan, the charming vision faded into the blackness of the night.

When morning came to put an end to my dreaming I hurried to the avenue and placed myself before the deserted house. Heavy blinds were drawn before the upper windows. The street was still quite empty, and I stepped close to the windows of the ground floor and listened and listened; but I heard no sound. The house was as quiet as the grave. The business of the day began, the passers-by became more numerous, and I was obliged to go on. I will not weary you with the recital of how for many days I crept about the house at that hour, but without discovering anything of interest. None of my questionings could reveal anything to me, and the beautiful picture of my vision began finally to pale and fade away.

At last as I passed, late one evening, I saw that the door of the deserted house was half open and the brown-clad old man was peeping out. I stepped quickly to his side with a sudden idea. "Does not Councillor Binder live in this house?" Thus I asked the old man, pushing him before me as I entered the dimly lighted vestibule.

The guardian of the old house looked at me with his piercing eyes, and answered in gentle, slow tones: "No, he does not live here, he never has lived here, he never will live here, he does not live anywhere on this avenue. But people say the ghosts walk about in this house. Yet I can assure you that it is not true. It is a quiet, a pretty house, and tomorrow the gracious Countess S. will move into it. Goodnight, dear gentleman." With these words the old man manoeuvred me out of the house and locked the gate behind me. I heard his feet drag across the floor, I heard his coughing and the rattling of his bunch of keys, and I heard him descend some steps. Then all was silent. During the short time that I had been in the house I had noticed that the corridor was hung with old tapestries and furnished like a drawing-room with large, heavy chairs in red damask.

And now, as if called into life by my entrance into the mysterious house, my adventures began. The following day, as I walked through the avenue in the noon hour, and my eyes sought the deserted house as usual, I saw something glistening in the last window of the upper story. Coming nearer I noticed that the outer blind had been quite drawn up and the inner curtain slightly opened. The sparkle of a diamond met my eye. O kind Heaven! The face of my dream looked at me, gently imploring, from above the rounded arm on which her head was resting. But how was it possible to stand still in the moving crowd without attracting attention? Suddenly I caught sight of the benches placed in the gravel walk in the centre of the avenue, and I saw that one of them was directly opposite the house. I sprang over to it, and leaning over its back, I could stare up at the mysterious window undisturbed. Yes, it was she, the charming maiden of my dream! But her eye did not seem to seek me as I had at first thought; her glance was cold and unfocused, and had it not been for an occasional motion of the hand and arm, I might have thought that I was looking at a cleverly painted picture.

I was so lost in my adoration of the mysterious being in the window, so aroused and excited throughout all my nerve centres, that I did not hear the shrill voice of an Italian street hawker, who had been offering me his wares for some time. Finally he touched me on the arm, I turned hastily and commanded him to let me alone. But he did not cease his entreaties, asserting that he had earned nothing today, and begging me to buy some small trifle from him. Full of impatience to get rid of him I put my hand in my pocket. With the words: "I have more beautiful things here," he opened the under drawer of his box and held out to me a little, round pocket mirror. In it, as he held it up before my face, I could see the deserted house behind me, the window, and the sweet face of my vision there.

I bought the little mirror at once, for I saw that it would make it possible for me to sit comfortably and inconspicuously, and yet watch the window. The longer I looked at the reflection in the glass, the more I fell captive to a weird and quite indescribable sensation, which I might almost call a waking dream. It was as if a lethargy had lamed my eyes, holding them fastened on the glass beyond my power to loosen them. Through my mind there rushed the memory of an old nurse's tale of my earliest childhood. When my nurse was taking me off to bed, and I showed an inclination to stand peering into the great mirror in my father's room, she would tell me that when children looked into mirrors in the night time they would see a strange, hideous face there, and their eyes would be frozen so that they could not move them again. The thought struck awe to my soul, but I could not resist a peep at the mirror, I was so curious to see the strange face. Once I did believe that I saw two hideous glowing eyes shining out of the mirror. I screamed and fell down in a swoon.

All these foolish memories of my early childhood came trooping back to me. My blood ran cold through my veins. I would have thrown the mirror from me, but I could not. And now at last the beautiful eyes of the fair vision looked at me, her glance sought mine and shone deep down into my heart. The terror I had felt left me, giving way to the pleasurable pain of sweetest longing.

"You have a pretty little mirror there," said a voice beside me. I awoke from my dream, and was not a little confused when I saw smiling faces looking at me from either side. Several persons had sat down upon my bench, and it was quite certain that my staring into the window, and my probably strange expression, had afforded them great cause for amusement.

"You have a pretty little mirror there," repeated the man, as I did not answer him. His glance said more, and asked without words the reason of my staring so oddly into the little glass. He was an elderly man, neatly dressed, and his voice and eyes were so full of good nature that I could not refuse him my confidence. I told him that I had been looking in the mirror at the picture of a beautiful maiden who was sitting at a window of the deserted house. I went even farther; I asked the old man if he had not seen the fair face himself. "Over there? In the old house—in the last window?" He repeated my questions in a tone of surprise.

"Yes, yes," I exclaimed.

The old man smiled and answered: "Well, well, that was a strange delusion. My old eyes—thank Heaven for my old eyes! Yes, yes, sir. I saw a pretty face in the window there, with my own eyes; but it seemed to me to be an excellently well-painted oil portrait."

I turned quickly and looked toward the window; there was no one there, and the blind had been pulled down. "Yes," continued the old man, "yes, sir. Now it is too late to make sure of the matter, for just now the servant, who, as I know, lives there alone in the house of the Countess S., took the picture away from the window after he had dusted it, and let down the blinds."

"Was it, then, surely a picture?" I asked again, in bewilderment.

"You can trust my eyes," replied the old man. "The optical delusion was strengthened by your seeing only the reflection in the mirror. And when I was in your years it was easy enough for my fancy to call up the picture of a beautiful maiden."

"But the hand and arm moved," I exclaimed. "Oh, yes, they moved, indeed they moved," said the old man smiling, as he patted me on the shoulder. Then he arose to go, and bowing politely, closed his remarks with the words, "Beware of mirrors which can lie so vividly. Your obedient servant, sir."

You can imagine how I felt when I saw that he looked upon me as a foolish fantast. I began to be convinced that the old man was right, and that it was only my absurd imagination which insisted on raising up mysteries about the deserted house.

I hurried home full of anger and disgust, and promised myself that I would not think of the mysterious house, and would not even walk through the avenue for several days. I kept my vow, spending my days working at my desk, and my evenings in the company of jovial friends, leaving myself no time to think of the mysteries which so enthralled me. And yet, it was just in these days that I would start up out of my sleep as if awakened by a touch, only to find that all that had aroused me was merely the thought of that mysterious being whom I had seen in my vision and in the window of the deserted house. Even during my work, or in the midst of a lively conversation with my friends, I felt the same thought shoot through me like an electric current. I condemned the little mirror in which I had seen the charming picture to a prosaic daily use.

I placed it on my dressing-table that I might bind my cravat before it, and thus it happened one day, when I was about to utilise it for this important business, that its glass seemed dull, and that I took it up and breathed on it to rub it bright again. My heart seemed to stand still, every fibre in me trembled in delightful awe. Yes, that is all the name I can find for the feeling that came over me, when, as my breath clouded the little mirror, I saw the beautiful face of my dreams arise and smile at me through blue mists. You laugh at me? You look upon me as an incorrigible dreamer? Think what you will about it—the fair face looked at me from out of the mirror! But as soon as the clouding vanished, the face vanished in the brightened glass.

I will not weary you with a detailed recital of my sensations the next few days. I will only say that I repeated again the experiments with the mirror, sometimes with success, sometimes without. When I had not been able to call up the vision, I would run to the deserted house and stare up at the windows; but I saw no human being anywhere about the building. I lived only in thoughts of my vision; everything else seemed indifferent to me. I neglected my friends and my studies. The tortures in my soul passed over into, or rather mingled with, physical sensations which frightened me, and which at last made me fear for my reason. One day, after an unusually severe attack, I put my little mirror in my pocket and hurried to the home of Dr. K., who was noted for his treatment of those diseases of the mind out of which physical diseases so often grow.

I told him my story; I did not conceal the slightest incident from him, and I implored him to save me from the terrible fate which seemed to threaten me. He listened to me quietly, but I read astonishment in his glance. Then he said: "The danger is not as near as you believe, and I think that I may say that it can be easily prevented. You are undergoing an unusual psychical disturbance, beyond a doubt. But the fact that you understand that some evil principle seems to be trying to influence you, gives you a weapon by which you can combat it. Leave your little mirror here with me, and force yourself to take up with some work which will afford scope for all your mental energy. Do not go to the avenue; work all day, from early to late, then take a long walk, and spend your evenings in the company of your friends. Eat heartily, and drink heavy, nourishing wines. You see I am endeavouring to combat your fixed idea of the face in the window of the deserted house and in the mirror, by diverting your mind to other things, and by strengthening your body. You yourself must help me in this."

I was very reluctant to part with my mirror. The physician, who had already taken it, seemed to notice my hesitation. He breathed upon the glass and holding it up to me, he asked: "Do you see anything?"

"Nothing at all," I answered, for so it was.

"Now breathe on the glass yourself," said the physician, laying the mirror in my hands.

I did as he requested. There was the vision even more clearly than ever before.

"There she is!" I cried aloud.

The physician looked into the glass, and then said: "I cannot see anything. But I will confess to you that when I looked into this glass, a queer shiver overcame me, passing away almost at once. Now do it once more."

I breathed upon the glass again and the physician laid his hand upon the back of my neck. The face appeared again, and the physician, looking into the mirror over my shoulder, turned pale. Then he took the little glass from my hands, looked at it attentively, and locked it into his desk, returning to me after a few moments' silent thought.

"Follow my instructions strictly," he said. "I must confess to you that I do not yet understand those moments of your vision. But I hope to be able to tell you more about it very soon."

Difficult as it was to me, I forced myself to live absolutely according to the doctor's orders. I soon felt the benefit of the steady work and the nourishing diet, and yet I was not free from those terrible attacks, which would come either at noon, or, more intensely still, at midnight. Even in the midst of a merry company, in the enjoyment of wine and song, glowing daggers seemed to pierce my heart, and all the strength of my intellect was powerless to resist their might over me. I was obliged to retire, and could not return to my friends until I had recovered from my condition of lethargy. It was in one of these attacks, an unusually strong one, that such an irresistible, mad longing for the picture of my dreams came over me, that I hurried out into the street and ran toward the mysterious house. While still at a distance from it, I seemed to see lights shining out through the fast-closed blinds, but when I came nearer I saw that all was dark. Crazy with my desire I rushed to the door; it fell back before the pressure of my hand. I stood in the dimly lighted vestibule, enveloped in a heavy, close atmosphere. My heart beat in strange fear and impatience. Then suddenly a long, sharp tone, as from a woman's throat, shrilled through the house. I know not how it happened that I found myself suddenly in a great hall brilliantly lighted and furnished in old-fashioned magnificence of golden chairs and strange Japanese ornaments. Strongly perfumed incense arose in blue clouds about me.

"Welcome—welcome, sweet bridegroom! the hour has come, our bridal hour!" I heard these words in a woman's voice, and as little as I can tell, how I came into the room, just so little do I know how it happened that suddenly a tall, youthful figure, richly dressed, seemed to arise from the blue mists. With the repeated shrill cry: "Welcome, sweet bridegroom!" she came toward me with outstretched arms—and a yellow face, distorted with age and madness, stared into mine! I fell back in terror, but the fiery, piercing glance of her eyes, like the eves of a snake, seemed to hold me spellbound. I did not seem able to turn my eyes from this terrible old woman, I could not move another step. She came still nearer, and it seemed to me suddenly as if her hideous face were only a thin mask, beneath which I saw the features of the beautiful maiden of my vision. Already I felt the touch of her hands, when suddenly she fell at my feet with a loud scream, and a voice behind me cried:

"Oho, is the devil playing his tricks with your grace again? To bed, to bed, your grace. Else there will be blows, mighty blows! "

I turned quickly and saw the old steward in his night clothes, swinging a whip above his head. He was about to strike the screaming figure at my feet when I caught at his arm. But he shook me from him, exclaiming: "The devil, sir! That old Satan would have murdered you if I had not come to your aid. Get away from here at once!"

I rushed from the hall, and sought in vain in the darkness for the door of the house. Behind me I heard the hissing blows of the whip and the old woman's screams. I drew breath to call aloud for help, when suddenly the ground gave way under my feet; I fell down a short flight of stairs, bringing up with such force against a door at the bottom that it sprang open, and I measured my length on the floor of a small room. From the hastily vacated bed, and from the familiar brown coat hanging over a chair, I saw that I was in the bedchamber of the old steward. There was a trampling on the stair, and the old man himself entered hastily, throwing himself at my feet. "By all the saints, sir," he entreated with folded hands, "whoever you may be, and however her grace, that old Satan of a witch has managed to entice you to this house, do not speak to anyone of what has happened here. It will cost me my position. Her crazy Excellency has been punished, and is bound fast in her bed. Sleep well, good sir, sleep softly and sweetly. It is a warm and beautiful July night. There is no moon, but the stars shine brightly. A quiet goodnight to you."

While talking, the old man had taken up a lamp, had led me out of the basement, pushed me out of the house door, and locked it behind me. I hurried home quite bewildered, and you can imagine that I was too much confused by the gruesome secret to be able to form any explanation of it in my own mind for the first few days. Only this much was certain, that I was now free from the evil spell that had held me captive so long. All my longing for the magic vision in the mirror had disappeared, and the memory of the scene in the deserted house was like the recollection of an unexpected visit to a madhouse. It was evident beyond a doubt that the steward was the tyrannical guardian of a crazy woman of noble birth, whose condition was to be hidden from the world. But the mirror? and all the other magic? Listen, and I will tell you more about it.

Some few days later I came upon Count P. at an evening entertainment. He drew me to one side and said, with a smile, "Do you know that the secrets of our deserted house are beginning to be revealed?" I listened with interest; but before the count could say more the doors of the dining-room were thrown open, and the company proceeded to the table. Quite lost in thought at the words I had just heard, I had given a young lady my arm, and had taken my place mechanically in the ceremonious procession. I led my companion to the seats arranged for us, and then turned to look at her for the first time. The vision of my mirror stood before me, feature for feature, there was no deception possible! I trembled to my innermost heart, as you can imagine; but I discovered that there was not the slightest echo even, in my heart, of the mad desire which had ruled me so entirely when my breath drew out the magic picture from the glass. My astonishment, or rather my terror, must have been apparent in my eyes.

The girl looked at me in such surprise that I endeavoured to control myself sufficiently to remark that I must have met her somewhere before. Her short answer, to the effect that this could hardly be possible, as she had come to the city only yesterday for the first time in her life, bewildered me still more and threw me into an awkward silence. The sweet glance from her gentle eyes brought back my courage, and I began a tentative exploring of this new companion's mind. I found that I had before me a sweet and delicate being, suffering from some psychic trouble. At a particularly merry turn of the conversation, when I would throw in a daring word like a dash of pepper, she would smile, but her smile was pained, as if a wound had been touched. "You are not very merry tonight, countess. Was it the visit this morning?" An officer sitting near us had spoken these words to my companion, but before he could finish his remark his neighbour had grasped him by the arm and whispered something in his ear, while a lady at the other side of the table, with glowing cheeks and angry eyes, began to talk loudly of the opera she had heard last evening.

Tears came to the eyes of the girl sitting beside me. "Am I not foolish?" She turned to me. A few moments before she had complained of headache. "Merely the usual evidences of a nervous headache," I answered in an easy tone, "and there is nothing better for it than the merry spirit which bubbles in the foam of this poet's nectar." With these words I filled her champagne glass, and she sipped at it as she threw me a look of gratitude. Her mood brightened, and all would have been well had I not touched a glass before me with unexpected strength, arousing from it a shrill, high tone. My companion grew deadly pale, and I myself felt a sudden shiver, for the sound had exactly the tone of the mad woman's voice in the deserted house.

While we were drinking coffee I made an opportunity to get to the side of Count P. He understood the reason for my movement. "Do you know that your neighbour is Countess Edwina S.? And do you know also that it is her mother's sister who lives in the deserted house, incurably mad for many years? This morning both mother and daughter went to see the unfortunate woman. The old steward, the only person who is able to control the countess in her outbreaks, is seriously ill, and they say that the sister has finally revealed the secret to Dr. K. This eminent physician will endeavour to cure the patient, or if this is not possible, at least to prevent her terrible outbreaks of mania. This is all that I know yet."

Others joined us and we were obliged to change the subject. Dr. K.

was the physician to whom I had turned in my own anxiety, and you can well imagine that I hurried to him as soon as I was free, and told him all that had happened to me in the last days. I asked him to tell me as much as he could about the mad woman, for my own peace of mind; and this is what I learned from him under promise of secrecy.

"Angelica, Countess Z.," thus the doctor began," had already passed her thirtieth year, but was still in full possession of great beauty, when Count S., although much younger than she, became so fascinated by her charm that he wooed her with ardent devotion and followed her to her father's home to try his luck there. But scarcely had the count entered the house, scarcely had he caught sight of Angelica's younger sister, Gabrielle, when he awoke as from a dream. The elder sister appeared faded and colourless beside Gabrielle, whose beauty and charm so enthralled the count that he begged her hand of her father. Count Z. gave his consent easily, as there was no doubt of Gabrielle's feelings toward her suitor. Angelica did not show the slightest anger at her lover's faithlessness. 'He believes that he has forsaken me, the foolish boy! He does not perceive that he was but my toy, a toy of which I had tired.' Thus she spoke in proud scorn, and not a look or an action on her part belied her words. But after the ceremonious betrothal of Gabrielle to Count S., Angelica was seldom seen by the members of her family. She did not appear at the dinner table, and it was said that she spent most of her time walking alone in the neighbouring wood.

"A strange occurrence disturbed the monotonous quiet of life in the castle. The hunters of Count Z., assisted by peasants from the village, had captured a band of gypsies who were accused of several robberies and murders which had happened recently in the neighbourhood. The men were brought to the castle courtyard, fettered together on a long chain, while the women and children were packed on a cart. Noticeable among the last was a tall, haggard old woman of terrifying aspect, wrapped from head to foot in a red shawl. She stood upright in the cart, and in an imperious tone demanded that she should be allowed to descend. The guards were so awed by her manner and appearance that they obeyed her at once.

"Count Z. came down to the courtyard and commanded that the gang should be placed in the prisons under the castle. Suddenly Countess Angelica rushed out of the door, her hair all loose, fear and anxiety in her pale face Throwing herself on her knees, she cried in a piercing voice, 'Let these people go! Let these people go! They are innocent! Father, let these people go! If you shed one drop of their blood I will pierce my heart with this knife!' The countess swung a shining knife in the air and then sank swooning to the ground. 'Yes, my beautiful darling—my golden child—I knew you would not let them hurt us,' shrilled the old woman in red. She cowered beside the countess and pressed disgusting kisses to her face and breast, murmuring crazy words. She took from out the recesses of her shawl a little vial in which a tiny goldfish seemed to swim in some silver-clear liquid. She held the vial to the countess's heart. The latter regained consciousness immediately. When her eyes fell on the gypsy woman, she sprang up, clasped the old creature ardently in her arms, and hurried with her into the castle.

"Count Z., Gabrielle, and her lover, who had come out during this scene, watched it in astonished awe. The gypsies appeared quite indifferent. They were loosed from their chains and taken separately to the prisons. Next morning Count Z. called the villagers together. The gypsies were led before them and the count announced that he had found them to be innocent of the crimes of which they were accused, and that he would grant them free passage through his domains. To the astonishment of all present, their fetters were struck off and they were set at liberty. The red-shawled woman was not among them It was whispered that the gypsy captain, recognisable from the golden chain about his neck and the red feather in his high Spanish hat, had paid a secret visit to the count's room the night before. But it was discovered, a short time after the release of the gypsies, that they were indeed guiltless of the robberies and murders that had disturbed the district.

"The date set for Gabrielle's wedding approached. One day, to her great astonishment, she saw several large wagons in the courtyard being packed high with furniture, clothing, linen, with everything necessary for a complete household outfit. The wagons were driven away, and the following day Count Z. explained that, for many reasons, he had thought it best to grant Angelica's odd request that she be allowed to set up her own establishment in his house in X. He had given the house to her, and had promised her that no member of the family, not even he himself, should enter it without her express permission. He added also, that, at her urgent request, he had permitted his own valet to accompany her, to take charge of her household.

"When the wedding festivities were over, Count S. and his bride departed for their home, where they spent a year in cloudless happiness. Then the count's health failed mysteriously. It was as if some secret sorrow gnawed at his vitals, robbing him of joy and strength. All efforts of his young wife to discover the source of his trouble were fruitless. At last, when the constantly recurring fainting spells threatened to endanger his very life, he yielded to the entreaties of his physicians and left his home, ostensibly for Pisa. His young wife was prevented from accompanying him by the delicate condition of her own health.

"And now," said the doctor, "the information given me by Countess S. became, from this point on, so rhapsodical that a keen observer only could guess at the true coherence of the story. Her baby, a daughter, born during her husband's absence, was spirited away from the house, and all search for it was fruitless. Her grief at this loss deepened to despair, when she received a message from her father stating that her husband, whom all believed to be in Pisa, had been found dying of heart trouble in Angelica's home in X., and that Angelica herself had become a dangerous maniac. The old count added that all this horror had so shaken his own nerves that he feared he would not long survive it.

"As soon as Gabrielle was able to leave her bed, she hurried to her father's castle. One night, prevented from sleeping by visions of the loved ones she had lost, she seemed to hear a faint crying, like that of an infant, before the door of her chamber. Lighting her candle she opened the door. Great Heaven! there cowered the old gypsy woman, wrapped in her red shawl, staring up at her with eyes that seemed already glazing in death. In her arms she held a little child, whose crying had aroused the countess. Gabrielle's heart beat high with joy—it was her child—her lost daughter! She snatched the infant from the gypsy's arms, just as the woman fell at her feet lifeless. The countess's screams awoke the house, but the gypsy was quite dead and no effort to revive her met with success.

"The old count hurried to X. to endeavour to discover something that would throw light upon the mysterious disappearance and reappearance of the child. Angelica's madness had frightened away all her female servants; the valet alone remained with her. She appeared at first to have become quite calm and sensible. But when the count told her the story of Gabrielle's child she clapped her hands and laughed aloud, crying: 'Did the little darling arrive? You buried her, you say? How the feathers of the gold pheasant shine in the sun! Have you seen the green lion with the fiery blue eyes?' Horrified the count perceived that Angelica's mind was gone beyond a doubt, and he resolved to take her back with him to his estates, in spite of the warnings of his old valet. At the mere suggestion of removing her from the house Angelica's ravings increased to such an extent as to endanger her own life and that of the others.

"When a lucid interval came again Angelica entreated her father, with many tears, to let her live and die in the house she had chosen. Touched by her terrible trouble he granted her request, although he believed the confession which slipped from her lips during this scene to be a fantasy of her madness. She told him that Count S. had returned to her arms, and that the child which the gypsy had taken to her father's house was the fruit of their love. The rumour went abroad in the city that Count Z. had taken the unfortunate woman to his home; but the truth was that she remained hidden in the deserted house under the care of the valet. Count Z. died a short time ago, and Countess Gabrielle came here with her daughter Edwina to arrange some family affairs. It was not possible for her to avoid seeing her unfortunate sister. Strange things must have happened during this visit, but the countess has not confided anything to me, saying merely that she had found it necessary to take the mad woman away from the old valet. It had been discovered that he had controlled her outbreaks by means of force and physical cruelty; and that also, allured by Angelica's assertions that she could make gold, he had allowed himself to assist her in her weird operations.

"It would be quite unnecessary," thus the physician ended his story, "to say anything more to you about the deeper inward relationship of all these strange things. It is clear to my mind that it was you who brought about the catastrophe, a catastrophe which will mean recovery or speedy death for the sick woman. And now I will confess to you that I was not a little alarmed, horrified even, to discover that—when I had set myself in magnetic communication with you by placing my hand on your neck—I could see the picture in the mirror with my own eyes. We both know now that the reflection in the glass was the face of Countess Edwina."

I repeat Dr. K.'s words in saying that, to my mind also, there is no further comment that can be made on all these facts. I consider it equally unnecessary to discuss at any further length with you now the mysterious relationship between Angelica, Edwina, the old valet, and myself—a relationship which seemed the work of a malicious demon who was playing his tricks with us. I will add only that I left the city soon after all these events, driven from the place by an oppression I could not shake off. The uncanny sensation left me suddenly a month or so later, giving way to a feeling of intense relief that flowed through all my veins with the warmth of an electric current. I am convinced that this change within me came about in the moment when the mad woman died.

★★★★★★

Thus did Theodore end his narrative. His friends had much to say about his strange adventure, and they agreed with him that the odd and unusual, and the truly marvellous as well, were mingled in a strange and gruesome manner in his story. When they parted for the night, Franz shook Theodore's hand gently, as he said with a smile: "Goodnight, you Spallanzani bat, you."

ALSO FROM LEONAUR
AVAILABLE IN SOFTCOVER OR HARDCOVER WITH DUST JACKET

MR MUKERJI'S GHOSTS *by S. Mukerji*—Supernatural tales from the British Raj period by India's Ghost story collector.

KIPLINGS GHOSTS *by Rudyard Kipling*—Twelve stories of Ghosts, Hauntings, Curses, Werewolves & Magic.

THE COLLECTED SUPERNATURAL AND WEIRD FICTION OF WASHINGTON IRVING: VOLUME 1 *by Washington Irving*—Including one novel 'A History of New York', and nine short stories of the Strange and Unusual.

THE COLLECTED SUPERNATURAL AND WEIRD FICTION OF WASHINGTON IRVING: VOLUME 2 *by Washington Irving*—Including three novelettes 'The Legend of the Sleepy Hollow', 'Dolph Heyliger', 'The Adventure of the Black Fisherman' and thirty-two short stories of the Strange and Unusual.

THE COLLECTED SUPERNATURAL AND WEIRD FICTION OF JOHN KENDRICK BANGS: VOLUME 1 *by John Kendrick Bangs*—Including one novel 'Toppleton's Client or A Spirit in Exile', and ten short stories of the Strange and Unusual.

THE COLLECTED SUPERNATURAL AND WEIRD FICTION OF JOHN KENDRICK BANGS: VOLUME 2 *by John Kendrick Bangs*—Including four novellas 'A House-Boat on the Styx', 'The Pursuit of the House-Boat', 'The Enchanted Typewriter' and 'Mr. Munchausen' of the Strange and Unusual.

THE COLLECTED SUPERNATURAL AND WEIRD FICTION OF JOHN KENDRICK BANGS: VOLUME 3 *by John Kendrick Bangs*—Including twor novellas 'Olympian Nights', 'Roger Camerden: A Strange Story', and ten short stories of the Strange and Unusual.

THE COLLECTED SUPERNATURAL AND WEIRD FICTION OF MARY SHELLEY: VOLUME 1 *by Mary Shelley*—Including one novel 'Frankenstein or the Modern Prometheus', and fourteen short stories of the Strange and Unusual.

THE COLLECTED SUPERNATURAL AND WEIRD FICTION OF MARY SHELLEY: VOLUME 2 *by Mary Shelley*—Including one novel 'The Last Man', and three short stories of the Strange and Unusual.

THE COLLECTED SUPERNATURAL AND WEIRD FICTION OF AMELIA B. EDWARDS *by Amelia B. Edwards*—Contains two novelettes 'Monsieur Maurice', and 'The Discovery of the Treasure Isles', one ballad 'A Legend of Boisguilbert' and seventeen short stories to cill the blood.

AVAILABLE ONLINE AT **www.leonaur.com**
AND FROM ALL GOOD BOOK STORES
07/09

LEONAUR

ALSO FROM LEONAUR
AVAILABLE IN SOFTCOVER OR HARDCOVER WITH DUST JACKET

THE COLLECTED SCIENCE FICTION AND FANTASY OF STANLEY G. WEINBAUM 1—INTERPLANETARY ODYSSEYS *by Stanley G. Weinbaum*—Classic Tales of Interplanetary Adventure Including: A Martian Odyssey, its Sequel Valley of Dreams, the Complete 'Ham' Hammond Stories and Others.

THE COLLECTED SCIENCE FICTION AND FANTASY OF STANLEY G. WEINBAUM 2—OTHER EARTHS *by Stanley G. Weinbaum*—Classic Futuristic Tales Including: *Dawn of Flame* & its Sequel The Black Flame, plus The Revolution of 1960 & Others.

THE COLLECTED SCIENCE FICTION AND FANTASY OF STANLEY G. WEINBAUM 3—STRANGE GENIUS *by Stanley G. Weinbaum*—Classic Tales of the Human Mind at Work Including the Complete Novel The New Adam, the 'van Manderpootz' Stories and Others.

THE COLLECTED SCIENCE FICTION AND FANTASY OF STANLEY G. WEINBAUM 4—THE BLACK HEART *by Stanley G. Weinbaum*—Classic Strange Tales Including: the Complete Novel The Dark Other, Plus Proteus Island and Others.

THE COLLECTED SCIENCE FICTION & FANTASY OF JACK LONDON 1—BEFORE ADAM & OTHER STORIES *by Jack London*—included in this Volume Before Adam The Scarlet Plague A Relic of the Pliocene When the World Was Young The Red One Planchette A Thousand Deaths Goliah A Curious Fragment The Rejuvenation of Major Rathbone.

THE COLLECTED SCIENCE FICTION & FANTASY OF JACK LONDON 2—THE IRON HEEL & OTHER STORIES *by Jack London*—included in this Volume The Iron Heel The Enemy of All the World The Shadow and the Flash The Strength of the Strong The Unparalleled Invasion The Dream of Debs.

THE COLLECTED SCIENCE FICTION & FANTASY OF JACK LONDON 3—THE STAR ROVER & OTHER STORIES *by Jack London*—included in this Volume The Star Rover The Minions of Midas The Eternity of Forms The Man With the Gash.

THE CRETAN TEAT *by Brian Aldiss*—The Cretan Teat is a wry and comic novel that interweaves its own fiction with an inner fiction about the discovery of a Byzantine painting of the Mother of the Blessed Virgin Mary suckling the infant Jesus and a fake ikon that becomes an instrument of Nemesis.

LEONAUR

ALSO FROM LEONAUR
AVAILABLE IN SOFTCOVER OR HARDCOVER WITH DUST JACKET

THE FIRST BOOK OF AYESHA *by H. Rider Haggard*—Contains *She & Ayesha: the Return of She.*

THE SECOND BOOK OF AYESHA *by H. Rider Haggard*—Contains *She and Allan & Wisdom's Daughter.*

QUATERMAIN: THE COMPLETE ADVENTURES—1 *by H. Rider Haggard*—Contains *King Solomon's Mines & Allan Quatermain.*

QUATERMAIN: THE COMPLETE ADVENTURES—2 *by H. Rider Haggard*—Contains *Allan's Wife, Maiwa's Revenge & Marie.*

QUATERMAIN: THE COMPLETE ADVENTURES—3 *by H. Rider Haggard*—Contains *Child of Storm & Allan and the Holy Flower.*

QUATERMAIN: THE COMPLETE ADVENTURES—4 *by H. Rider Haggard*—Contains *Finished & The Ivory Child.*

QUATERMAIN: THE COMPLETE ADVENTURES—5 *by H. Rider Haggard*—Contains *The Ancient Allan & She and Allan.*

QUATERMAIN: THE COMPLETE ADVENTURES—6 *by H. Rider Haggard*—Contains *Heu-Heu or, the Monster & The Treasure of the Lake.*

QUATERMAIN: THE COMPLETE ADVENTURES—7 *by H. Rider Haggard*—Contains *Allan and the Ice Gods, Four Short Adventures & Nada the Lily.*

TROS OF SAMOTHRACE 1: WOLVES OF THE TIBER *by Talbot Mundy*—55 B.C.--an adventurer set during the Roman invasion of Britain.

TROS OF SAMOTHRACE 2: DRAGONS OF THE NORTH *by Talbot Mundy*—55 B.C. —Caesar plots, Britons war among themselves and the Vikings are coming.

TROS OF SAMOTHRACE 3: SERPENT OF THE WAVES *by Talbot Mundy*—55 B.C.--Caesar is poised to invade Britain—only a grand strategy can foil him!.

TROS OF SAMOTHRACE 4: CITY OF THE EAGLES *by Talbot Mundy*—54 B.C.—Rome—Tros treads in the streets of his sworn enemies!.

TROS OF SAMOTHRACE 5: CLEOPATRA *by Talbot Mundy*—Tros and the Roman Empire turn to the Egypt of the Pharaohs.

TROS OF SAMOTHRACE 6: THE PURPLE PIRATE *by Talbot Mundy*—The epic saga of the ancient world—Tros of Samothrace—draws to a conclusion in this sixth—and final—volume.